The Vesey Inheritance

I cannot tell you how pleasant Masham Square was that summer to a girl from the country, how splendid and elegant in a very London kind of way.

Errol Vesey is nineteen, the only child of a Suffolk rector, but she is neither unworldly nor gauche. Her mother was a famous beauty and her mother's family, the Maurices, have always been in the midst of things as soldiers, politicians and, particularly, courtiers.

So Errol comes to London and makes her debut, where she senses herself an object of more interest than her looks and social position would indicate. She even finds she has attracted the notice of the Court at Windsor and of Queen Victoria herself.

I was told the Queen thought me, 'Not as lovely as her mother, but a very nice girl, distinguished-looking, with a pretty figure'. Yet the great ladies of London society, all of whom thought me so romantic and interesting, and who loved Lady Geraldine too, were determined that I should not make a match of it with one of their sons.

There is a mystery in the Maurice family and at its centre is Errol's beautiful dead mother and her other child, Errol's unacknowledged half-brother. Errol's search for him leads her into danger in a very different world from that of Masham Square, the evil-smelling and murderous world of Jockey Fields Passage. She suspects her brother means to harm her but she does not know his name or what he looks like and the shock of recognition, when it finally comes, is a complete surprise, as is the revelation of the nature of her inheritance.

Romantic, mysterious and exciting, this is a marvellously enjoyable novel, a story of suspense and character set against a brilliantly observed landscape of Victorian England. *The Vesey Inheritance* is in the same tradition as Mrs Butler's much-praised *A Coffin for Pandora* and is certain to delight her many admirers.

THE
VESEY INHERITANCE

GWENDOLINE BUTLER

M

SBN 333 18628 1

First published in Great Britain 1976 by
MACMILLAN LONDON LIMITED
London and Basingstoke
Associated companies in New York Dublin
Melbourne Johannesburg and Delhi

Printed in Great Britain by
NORTHUMBERLAND PRESS LIMITED
Gateshead

'Against war, against capital punishment, against
flogging, demanding national education instead of
big guns, public libraries instead of warships ...
I rejoice that I played my part in educating England.'

ANNIE BESANT, 1893

CHAPTER ONE

I cannot tell you how pleasant Masham Square was that summer to a girl from the country, how splendid and elegant in a very London kind of way, with its gay window-boxes full of flowers, and its crisp awnings. The square was full of life, and noisy with the constant comings and goings of carriages, and errand boys arriving with interesting-looking parcels, whistling airs from *The Mikado*, which was all the go that May. The soldiers in their pillbox hats, the Guardsmen in scarlet as they strolled through Masham Square on their way back to barracks across the park delighted me too, although naturally I never told Lady Geraldine so. She disliked the Army and was, so she said, a woman of peace. There was a stirring foreign policy abroad that year which gave her constant occasion for saying so. We had the then Foreign Secretary living in the square (there was a policeman on duty outside his door, who saluted me delightfully) and I am sure he understood Lady Geraldine's views from the frigidity of her bow. Of course all this opinion of hers stemmed from the Palace, as why should it not?

It was all so marvellous and gay and interesting. In short, I was happy.

Joy and happiness and terror mingled in my life. Much was given to me, but much taken. I think of one man still. And know that one day we shall look at each other across a crowded ballroom and think of all that might have been between us, and all that was, and all that never could be.

When I say I, Errol Vesey, was a girl from the country, I was no country bumpkin. My father's rectory was dedicated to an austere, intellectual life, but we knew everything there. All the new ideas on politics and philosophy and science were discussed there. The foremost scholars in Europe visited my father and were his friends and mine. People said that my father would have been a bishop if he had not been so advanced in his views. I dare say it was true, but I myself think he had no taste for advancement and that all ambition fled from him at my mother's death. Secure in his social position as the son of a family established in East Anglia in the twelfth century, assured in his intellectual status as a man with a double first and a fellowship of his own college until his early marriage, he had no need to look for elevation outside. He had enough. Do I make him sound coldly self-assured? Although I loved him deeply I believe there was a little of this about him, and I used to think sometimes that the greatest impediment to his becoming a bishop was the impression he sometimes gave to lesser beings that he and God communicated on equal terms. He gave me an astringent intellectual training, but no softness. But then, there was no softness in his generation. You have to remember it was his contemporaries who went out and wrested an empire from a surprised world and presented it to a monarch who had little time for it. No, he gave me not much love, but had I been allowed to go into politics like a man I should have made an excellent debater. People who remember say he was different before my mother died. They had married young, but I was not born for some years after. I suppose my mother was almost too old for child-bearing by that time, and when I was born she died. So I remember nothing of my mother, and as a child possessed nothing except her work-box, which could not be locked because the key would not turn, and a little brooch with *Amor Vincit Omnia* set on it in brilliants. I am told that this cold and self-contained man threw off his coat and shovelled the earth on her coffin himself, spade by spade. Perhaps I couldn't expect love from him in the circumstances, but I emerged with sound powers of reasoning, a good education and a strong determination to do the best I could for myself in the world.

For I was my mother's daughter too, and surprisingly I could finger my inheritance from her. Oh no, not money, neither her illustrious family nor my father's made money or, if they married it, kept it. My inheritance was ambition. The Maurices have always been ambitious, but their saving grace has continually been a sense of humour. My father, I am sure, had humour, but it was of a strictly academic kind that needed a fellow-scholar to appreciate it to the full. I heard his dry little laugh often enough as he chuckled over his friends' writings. I learnt to know when he had detected an error, or a discrepancy, or a lack of judgement, and meant to correct it in a well-turned article of his own with a neat little pleasantry. Whereas what reduced the Maurices to desperate mirth was to see some poor fellow slip on an orange peel, or get a cup of soup in his lap. It was the sort of humour that made them very popular about Court (especially at Marlborough House, where the Waleses kept up a simple sense of humour), so perhaps in the end it was nothing but an example of their ambition in operation. At all events, they were courtiers, and followed the Court.

The house in Masham Square belonged to Lady Geraldine Maurice, my mother's younger sister. She was a widow who had married her cousin. There were so many Maurices and they were so gay and alert and attractive and suited each other so well, that it was almost impossible to stop them marrying each other. Which did not do much for their blood (all those fair-haired gals, as the Queen once said crossly, it weakens the stock) and even less for their bank balances, for they never had a penny to bless themselves with. Even the house in Masham Square was let whenever Lady Geraldine's agent could catch a rich American or one of the new South African millionaires from the goldfields.

This summer, however, she had it to herself. It was such a beautiful house, it was a deep pleasure to me to enter it. From the dark blue and white marble floor of the hall to the wide curve of the stair leading to the double drawing room where the ceiling was painted by Angelica Kauffmann, it was a place that charmed. You could believe, as I had been told, that Richard Brinsley Sheridan had walked up these stairs cracking jokes with a fellow Member of Parliament. For this had always been a political house. Situated as it was between Westminster and the Court, it was a handy posting place for men of both parties to drop in. As it had been, so it still was. Lady Geraldine's son was an M.P. He was still a young man with his reputation to make. He had great charm and knew everyone, and was always much quoted. 'Frank Maurice says' or 'Frank Maurice tells me' were phrases one heard all the time and on all sorts of subjects. I thought him elusive myself and never felt sure I had got to the bottom of him, but perhaps all politicians are like this. I know my father thought he had great kindness of heart and was thoroughly selfish at the same time, which is a combination all women find baffling.

I had arrived there one evening in early May. It was already hot and I was wearing my travelling clothes, which, although new and carefully chosen, had been made for me by a dressmaker in our county town; and, having observed a little of London life through the carriage window, already I felt provincial and missish and awkward. None of which pleased me. I had a theory that a lady could rise above any eccentricities of her dress, but I saw now that no one could surmount the cut of Mrs Taylor's flounces. This impression was reinforced by the quick glance I caught from Barlow, Lady Geraldine's own maid.

'M'Lady is out, Miss Errol, but I was to receive you and tell you she should be back before you dined.'

I nodded.

'You and M'Lady dine alone tonight, miss,' she added reassuringly, as if I was indeed a shy miss up from the country. But I didn't need the reassurance. I liked company.

'Those are all your bags, miss?'

I nodded again. I was standing there in the hall with my luggage around me. I had none of my own, so I had used old trunks of my father's. They had his name on them, Charles Vesey, and an old address, Magdalen College, Oxford, I made a movement towards them.

'No, leave them be, miss. Fletcher will move them.'

'Oh, is he still here?' I was delighted. I remembered Fletcher from my grandfather's time. But he had been old then, he must be about ninety now.

'This is *young* Fletcher,' said Barlow, and something in her tone told me that, for some reason or other, young Fletcher was not approved of.

'His grandson,' she explained. '*His* father, old Mr Fletcher's only son and a good deal older than the daughter, emigrated to Australia, leaving the boy behind. He died out there. Old Mr Fletcher is still alive but lives in retirement with his daughter. In Cheapside.'

'Oh, good,' I was mounting the stairs. 'He'd be happy there.'

'Indeed, he is, Miss Errol. His daughter, Mrs Bedower, makes him most comfortable. But she always was a most capable girl. She was in service with her ladyship for a while, you know, but she married a long time ago now.' Barlow was puffing as she mounted the stairs. It didn't stop her talking, though. 'She married very young. Such a lovely girl. One son. Here we are, Miss Errol.'

All this flow of information was delivered in a flat, unaccented tone, as if all information was of equal value. It was her way. I remembered Lady Geraldine: 'Barlow always knows everything, Errol, you'd better remember. And one half of what she says is quite worth listening to. Not that I listen myself, of course.' Not true, I remember thinking. Geraldine, like all her courtiers, liked to have her sources of information and Barlow was such a one. There were others. Very soon I was to be one myself, but I did not know that then. In accordance with this, Geraldine was a great letter-writer. She had a wide circle of correspondents, each of whom contributed her mite to the flow, and in turn was offered some scraps of comment and news for herself. I say herself, but the letter-writers were by no means only women, quite as many men were in the charmed circle. If asked, Lady Geraldine would have said that it was the first duty of a courtier to be well informed, and that she was only doing her job as a Woman of the Bedchamber.

I loved the room that my aunt had given me. Since I was a child it had spelt worldly elegance and charm to me, far removed from the spartan simplicities of my room in the rectory. There, I was obliged to shiver in the winter cold as I dressed; here, a warm fire had danced and leapt during so many Christmas holidays. At home, my father's taste had dictated plain, unadorned furniture,

12

most of it old stuff, made in the last century and out of fashion now. Here, all was flounces and muslin frills. My dressing-table was white damask, covered with muslin and looped with blue bows. I could almost hear the snort my father would have given at the sight of it, but to feminine eyes it had charm.

There was no fire today, instead the fireplace was filled with a bouquet of dried grass and lavender, scenting the air sweetly and reminding me of our lavender hedge in Suffolk. A tear came into my eye at the memory and was quickly blinked away, but Barlow saw. She was a kind old thing and no longer frightened me as she had done when I was a child.

'I'll tell Maria to bring you some tea.' It was the old servant's customary, almost automatic offer of comfort. I thought it told eloquently of the world from which they had sprung; the poor, overcrowded household where the cup of hot, fragrant Ceylon represented the one obtainable luxury in sorrow. I knew that Barlow had been a good and faithful servant to Lady Geraldine for years, but I also knew that she was still in touch with her aged parents and still kept up with her younger brothers and sisters. You see, she came from my part of the world. I knew her background as she knew mine. As my father's daughter I had been welcomed in many cottages.

'Thank you.' I smiled and was cheerful again.

'And it shall be in the Meissen china set you used to like so well.'

'The pot with a cherry on the lid?'

'The same,' she said with pleasure, 'and with the blossom in the cup.'

I had an idea that this set of porcelain was of extreme value, it had been part of a wedding present to Lady Geraldine's great grandmother from the Empress Maria Theresa, and would have been better in a museum. But nothing was reserved or put aside in Lady Geraldine's house; she would have thought it beneath her breeding to seem to hoard.

I was always surprised to see this set again, because they were great breakers in that house in Masham Square, but it came through, unchipped.

'There was a letter came for you, Miss Errol. Delivered by hand. Quite a rough fellow.' Her eyes were brightly watching me. 'It's on the work-table in the window.'

I looked towards the table and saw the envelope—'By Hand', and that a rough one. It was probably from my friend Jessie Falconet. I knew Jessie was in London, and she moved in strange circles. She was living at this moment in Holborn and might have many friends called 'rough' by Barlow.

I knew Barlow longed to know what was in it. Had I been a few years younger she would probably have asked. But she must wait. 'I'll open it later,' I said, and went to the window and looked out. The wind blew in, soft, sweet-smelling and hinting at rain.

And, immediately, my thoughts went back to that other rainy day, two months ago ...

Two months ago and a cold March day. March has daffodils and blue skies and sometimes pretends to be spring, but it is a winter month at heart.

In the country this March had been particularly wet and unpleasant. I remember the lane bottoms were so thick with mud that I could not walk in them and was restricted to daily dull walks in the shrubberies of the rectory. An earlier rector had laid out a winding gravel path, and on this I paced with my father when the weather allowed him out. It was hard on him to be as shut up in the house as he was. I knew he felt it much more than I did and really missed contact with the country world outside his study windows. He could detect the first spring birds, knew when the swallows came and where they nested and knew in which copse the wild daffodils showed first. 'You never look, Errol,' he said to me, but it wasn't true. I did look, but I didn't see.

Yet I think I noticed people more than he did, and I saw how frail and thin he was. Only the bright blue eyes and the tartness of his tongue showed the old vitality.

After the garden walk we sat together in the old-fashioned parlour and I read and worked and he wrote letters in his beautiful copperplate hand. The firelight shone on us both and I felt warm and dreamy. I remember my father sat at his desk and sealed the covers, after which he rang the bell for the maid and handed her the letters.

'See these are posted, please, Martha.'

'Yes, sir. I'll take them myself.'

So she would, I thought, and laugh with the young gardener pruning the willow trees on the river walk as she went.

'Good, willing girl,' said my father, who naturally knew nothing of the young gardener and the giggles and the stolen kiss. 'She is always willing to disturb her afternoon to go out for me.'

'Yes, father.' I was wistful, not condemning, I had no giggles and no kisses myself. Goodness knows I did not grudge Martha her George.

Later, much later, I wondered if my father did not perceive more than I guessed about Martha and her George, because after this speech he went to his desk and was thoughtful over papers for a long time. Then he came back and sat gazing into the fire without speaking. I think now he was remembering his youth, and my mother, and making up his mind to speak.

15

But the tea-tray had come and gone before he said anything. Then he surprised me. 'Errol, if you should ever consider marrying, and I am not here to advise you, I wish you to write at once to Mr Dalrymple.'

I put my sewing down in my lap and stared in surprise. Mr Dalrymple was our solicitor. I suppose my father saw my surprise and was touched, because he came over and stroked my hair.

'It is very difficult being young, is it not, Errol?'

'I don't know, father,' I said thoughtfully. I enjoyed being me, but I was shy of saying so. 'I'm not sure if I understand what you mean.'

'And yet you *are* young.'

How could I explain that what I meant was that my problem of managing to have good gloves and pretty evening slippers on my tiny dress-allowance was what constituted the difficulties of my life at present? I was adult enough and sufficiently sensitive to his expression to guess that this was not what he meant.

'More difficult in my generation than perhaps it is now,' he said, with a softer look on his face than I ever saw before.

'Why, father?' It was my turn to be puzzled.

'Yes. Oh, I mean you are more carefully watched over, standards are higher, lines more rigidly drawn ... We were a wilder lot ... We were not so far away from the old Regency days, remember ...'

His voice died away, he was lost to me. 'It was especially hard on the girls,' he said quietly to himself.

'Was it, father?'

He looked at me, but without seeing me. 'Girls have their strong emotions, too.' His voice trembled. 'We must never forget that, never judge ... I never did.'

I suppose I made a movement, because he looked at me and, this time, saw me. 'You, my dear, sheltered as you have been can have no idea ...' I continued to look at him. 'At public school, at Eton, I saw every variety of vice, as boys do. A bad thing, a bad thing. I would like to believe it is better ordered now ... And then again at university, at Oxford, there were temptations ... And yet, yet it meant one knew one's own nature and knew what to guard against ... Whereas a girl, thrown on to the world, a heedless mother, a stupid, idle fellow for a father ... no one to guard her, but her own loving, ignorant heart.'

I said nothing. I guessed he was trying to tell me something.

'Errol, my dear, there is something you ought to know.' I waited. Even so, it took several anxious turns about the room before he went on. 'My dear, you have a brother.'

I stared. It was the most unexpected news in the world. 'A brother?'

'A half-brother,' he corrected. 'A half-brother only.'

Still I stared. I started to put together his stumbling words, I was not a country girl for nothing. I understood what he must mean, sheltered upbringing or not. 'Father, did you, that is, have you ...?' I stopped. I found it hard to say to my parent: and do you have a bastard son, a little by-blow, a child under the blanket, or to use any of the other terms I had certainly heard about the kitchen and the stables but was not supposed to know about, much less use.

'No, my dear, not I.' And then he said the incredible words: 'Your mother.'

I remember turning my head slowly from him to look into the red heart of the fire, and then bringing my gaze slowly back.

'Do not judge, my dear,' he said swiftly. 'Do not presume to judge.

'No,' I shook my head. 'No, I do not.'

'You have never known. There has been no need for you to know ... Indeed I should not tell you now were it not ...' He paused again.

'But *you* knew, papa?' I said.

'Always. From the beginning,' he said proudly. 'I was told everything. By her, herself. Her whole heart was poured out to me.'

'And you didn't mind?'

'I understood. As you must, dear child. Think of her, so young and thrown so constantly into the company of that poor, wild young man, unprotected as she was by those who should have protected her. I have seen his face, the face of him she loved. It was a beautiful face, my dear, but I believe even then you could see death written on it. I have heard people speak of a fated face and thought it cant. Silly talk. But when I saw his portrait I knew what it meant.'

'How strange you should have seen his portrait.'

'Not strange at all. It hangs in ... well, better you should not know where it hangs. But he was not a young man of no family ...' He added sadly: 'Oh, I can understand so well how it happened. He was brought up to believe everything was his, at his will.'

'And he died?'

'No need to go into that. He does not concern us. Between them there could be no question of marriage. None at all. Whether he lived or died it would not matter. A child was born and it was a son. It was all most carefully hushed up. The child was taken away and no one knew. You should not know now if I did not think ...'

'Does Aunt Geraldine know?' I interrupted.

'Not a thing, not a thing. Your mother's sisters were younger than she and in the schoolroom. But your mother told me herself. Everything, without hesitation, freely, nobly, the day on which I asked her to be my wife. It made no difference.'

'So what happened to the child?'

'He was taken away, given another name, and adopted.' Then he said carefully: 'Although your mother never saw her son again, I thought it right to keep an eye on him as far as was possible ... I am afraid he has turned out a bad lot.' He sighed. 'A handsome fellow, I understand, and very clever, that was to be expected, of course.'

'Have you ever seen him then?' I was deeply curious about this half-brother.

'No, not seen exactly. Nor come into company with him. But from a distance ... I have been able to pick up scraps of information.' He sighed deeply, a huge gulping breath of air that made me look at him sharply.

'I tell you this now, Errol, because I am afraid he means you harm.'

I stared.

'Yes,' went on my father heavily. 'I think he would harm you if he could.'

'But why?' I began, then stopped. It did not need much imagination to know why a disowned and unhappy son might want to hurt this child who had been loved and cherished. 'Could he hurt me? Does he know me?' I supposed he did. It was a disquieting thought that there was someone who knew me and wished me ill and yet whose face and name were a mystery to me. 'Is he near to me, papa? What is his name?'

Again that heaviness about my father, as if he wished to communicate, but could not. He looked very tired. He got up. 'We will talk more tomorrow, Errol. But remember, if I am not here, Mr Dalrymple, the lawyer, will be your best friend. If you marry you know, Errol ...' he stopped. 'We will go on tomorrow. I am tired now.'

But that night his heart quietly stopped beating. When

his servant went to call him in the morning he was lying there, as if asleep, silent for ever.

I was too stunned and lost at first to think about my half-brother. It was not until I was beginning to sort out my father's papers, before I moved from the rectory for ever, that I remembered our conversation. And with the memory, a touch of fear came back.

It seemed only prudent I should know my half-brother's name and anything else my father might have noted down about him. So I searched through his books and letters and writings. There was only one thing that I thought related to the story he had told me. This was a pencilled sketch of a baby, wrapped still in its swaddling clothes and lying on a large pillow. It was amateur work, and I thought it must be the drawing done by my poor young mother of the child she had given away. On the back of the drawing was written: 'Florence, Italy, 1860'. But though I looked and looked I found nothing else. Whatever he had known, whatever he could have told me, had gone to the grave with my father.

I had brought this secret with me to London. In the excitement of the move it had receded into the background of my life, not quite forgotten, but not felt very sharply. I suppose, in a way, I had decided it was not a real problem.

I opened the letter casually. That it was not from Jessie I saw at a glance. Jessie always wrote on evil-looking paper, the cheapest and scruffiest she could find. As a woman of advanced views, it was almost a matter of principle with her. This was fine, elegant, white paper. The message inside was not elegant, however. It said: 'BLOOD IS THICKER THAN WATER'.

I read it once, and then again. I turned over the page, but there was nothing else, no enclosure, no signature.

I suppose I wouldn't have wanted one. I suppose I did not need one. I knew without being told that it was from my brother.

Barlow came bustling back in, followed by Maria and a young footman bearing a tea-tray. Maria carried a white linen napkin, lace-fringed. That made three of them, all to give one young female her tea. To someone who had lived in the austerity of the rectory it seemed excessive.

The tea-tray was on the round table by the window, Maria had spread the fine linen on my lap, Barlow had poured the tea and chivvied the footman out of the room before I let myself think about the letter.

I sipped the tea, and poured myself another cup and let it grow cold while I sat looking out of the window. I did not have to wonder how the unknown writer knew where to address his letter to me. Lady Geraldine had caused a paragraph about my arrival to live with her to be placed on the Court page of the London *Times*. So anyone and everyone could know where I was.

In Masham Square the sunlight shone on the lime trees lining the garden railings like soldiers. The strong light turned their leaves to gold and drew out the heavy scent of the yellow flowers. I never loved lime blossom so well again. It is associated for ever in my mind with that hot, happy, alarming summer when my life took shape.

A woman with a small boy holding her hand passed along the pavement on the other side of the square. They disappeared down the steps leading to the area of the house on the corner. A smart town brougham came clipping fast round the corner and bowled out of sight. A cab approached from the opposite direction. It reminded me that I was in London, that I had a small purse of money at my disposal and that I was free.

I would go to see Jessie. The decision made, I felt at once refreshed. Jessie was such a joy, and, if not exactly wise, very knowledgeable. She had been very well educated in the American fashion in both Germany and Italy. I emptied away the cold tea and poured myself some fresh, which had been kept hot in the pot by a little red teapot cover of quilted silk. I sipped the tea with pleasure: glad that Lady Geraldine was out, glad I was free to see Jessie, glad of everything.

The letter I put safely away in a drawer. I would not tell Jessie about it. There are some secrets too close even for one's closest friends.

I walked down the stairs, danced you might say, because my feet felt gay and light, and met no one except the footman standing in the hall ready to open the door. He looked a bit surprised at letting me out, having so recently let me in, but he was hardly in a position to refuse me. I knew, of course, that he would tell the butler and the butler would tell Barlow and she might or might not, according to the state of her temper and loyalties, tell my aunt. Young ladies did not go out on their own as I was going, but I had decided to ignore such trivial rules and do what I pleased. Start as you mean to go on is a very sound rule for young ladies intending to have their own way in life.

I had Jessie's address. 'I am living over a bookshop at Fifty-six High Holborn,' she had written. 'I have an excellent set of rooms where you will always be made welcome. My landlady is a thoroughly respectable woman.' I knew she had added that to reassure me in case I felt conventional or prudent. Jessie Falconet was ten years older than me, an American girl, whose father had lived in England for a while. Jessie was a free spirit and emancipated and worked for women's good. She had started a club for working women in Whitechapel.

At the end of the road leading out of the square I was tempted to hail a cab. I had never summoned one before

in my life, but I had seen my father do it often enough
and it looked easy. I could see a brougham idling at the
end of the road. But then an omnibus drew up. It came
from Victoria and had 'The Strand' and 'High Holborn'
printed in big black letters on a board in front. I jumped
on it with alacrity. Inside I saw several young ladies of
my own age who looked quite as respectable as I and
a good deal better dressed. I would *have* to get rid of Mrs
Taylor's flounces.

Soon we were bowling down Oxford Street, which I
recognised from visits to Waring and Gillow's with Lady
Geraldine on an earlier stay in London. The crowds on
the pavements seemed very well dressed and prosperous.
Good-humoured too, I thought. They crowded on to the
omnibus exchanging jokes with the conductor and repartee
with each other. No one bothered me except that the men
apologised politely as they jostled past. I decided I liked
my fellow Londoners. So we bumped on, the whole bus
load of us. My head began to ache slightly. Perhaps there
was something to be said for a private carriage, after all.

But we arrived in High Holborn and I stepped down
to the pavement in triumph. I was out of the omnibus
with a hop, skip and jump. 'You're a lively one, miss,'
said the conductor, as he pulled the bell.

I looked about me. I was in a busy main road, and,
judging by the numbers on the doors, about a few yards
yet from where Jessie lived. I walked along. I passed a
shop window full of sheet music, a milliner's, and a
German sausage shop. It seemed you could satisfy almost
every need in High Holborn. Then I saw the bookshop.
It had a most depressing appearance, but I knew enough
of Jessie not to expect gaiety in anywhere she lived.
'Truelove's Bookshop' ran the inscription above the door
in faded white letters. Later, I understood how little the
appearance of the shop mattered to his unworldly soul.

The contents were what counted and they filled the window, overflowed to boxes flanking the door, and were piled up on the counter to be seen through the glass door. Books, books and more books. Many pamphlets filled the gaps between the books and lined the window.

Some of the titles looked strange, and I was trying to make something of them. *A Treatise on Population: Maternal Welfare*; another book entitled *A Book For Parents*, and a third *Maternal Morality*. Behind me I heard the clip-clop of a cab horse. 'Medical matters,' I thought sagely, as I looked at the books, and stepped back into the arms of a stout matron just then passing. She drew her breath in with a little, hissing noise and moved away rapidly as if I had brought contagion with me. 'Shameful,' she said, in an angry voice. 'Come away, miss, before you disgrace yourself further.'

She must be mad, I thought, as I moved away with dignity. I had heard there were many mad women in London, my Aunt Geraldine often said so, but I hadn't understood she meant it so literally. Nevertheless there was a faint flush on my cheek and I regretted that Jessie should live in such a spot. After all, London was proving harder to understand than I had expected.

The staircase which led up to Jessie's rooms was neat and clean although the carpet was worn and very ugly. Jessie would never notice if anything was ugly or not, of course. I had been told to walk up by a tired-looking servant who had opened the door to me. Or I took her for a servant from her stiff white apron and her modest, slightly plaintive manner. She stood there below, watching me.

I knocked on the door. 'Come in,' sang out Jessie. She was standing in the middle of the room wearing a dark blue cotton dress, extremely tight and narrow in cut and beyond anything unbecoming.

24

'What a horrid dress,' I said frankly.

'Dress! It's not a dress, it's my uniform.'

'What, Jessie, have you joined the Army?' I threw up my hands.

Jessie laughed and kissed me. 'The same as ever, Errol. Do you never take anything seriously?'

'Everything, Jessie, everything. That's why I make jokes.'

She shook her head at me. 'This is my nurse's uniform. I am taking a course in nursing.'

Then I did stare at her. 'You mean you have given up all your other pursuits? You have ceased to be interested in politics? You no longer agitate that women should vote? You aren't an anarchist any longer?'

'I never was an anarchist,' said Jessie impatiently. 'That would be against my principles.'

'You took in that woman who tried to kill the Czar.'

'My dear, you know as well as I do that she never came anywhere near it ... She was sick, poor thing, and dying.'

Sickness, a dying look, or a rough handling from the servants of the Czar or the Emperor of Austria were sure passports to Jessie's heart.

'*Did* she die, Jessie?'

'Well, no, as it happens. She took up with a soldier and married him.' There was a slight huffiness in Jessie's tone and I knew her protégée was as good as dead in her eyes. I laughed.

'You can't blame her for choosing maintenance and a settled position. Security.'

'Is that how you think of marriage?'

I shrugged. 'It's part of it. I don't say it is why I would marry.'

Jessie looked at me, her lips pressed together, as if what she saw was grim. 'What a child you really are,

Errol, I forget how sheltered girls of your class are. How little you really know.'

I kept quiet and did not answer. I think Jessie had a somewhat romanticised view of me. I knew more of the world than she thought.

'You haven't explained your nursing,' I said, going back to an earlier point.

'Oh, I will. Sit down, my dear.' She cleared a chair of a heap of papers and a sleeping black kitten. 'But let me look at you, you pretty bird. How good it is to see you.' She studied my lavender and grey dress. 'In mourning, of course. But it suits you. Well, what are you doing here?'

'Visiting you, and you have hardly made me welcome. This is a very ugly house, Jessie, but the servant at the door has a most educated voice.'

'That was my landlady and not a servant,' said Jessie absently. 'She has suffered, poor thing. You are very welcome and you know it. But what do you do in London? Are you staying with your aunt, the Lady Geraldine?' That was ever Jessie's way. To ask a question and then to answer it herself. One of the more surprising things about Jessie was her quiet appreciation of Lady Geraldine, whose life and style embodied everything that you might suppose Jessie to be working against. But she said Lady Geraldine was 'a gem' and enjoyed her.

'Oh yes, I am to make my home there, but I shan't be idle, never fear. M'Lady has something in store for me to do. She mentioned it in a letter. "An interesting and worth-while task lies ahead of you," she said.'

'Indeed,' Jessie looked thoughtful. 'Can she have a marriage arranged for you?'

'No, I'm sure of it. In her own way Lady Geraldine agrees with you. Marriage is by no means the only career for a girl of aristocratic birth ... In fact, I believe she'd prefer us all to remain unmarried if we could. I suppose it comes from being so much at Court. The Queen hates the Princesses to marry. They all do, though.'

I looked about the room. I should have known it for Jessie's anywhere. It had her characteristic confusion of the valuable objects she had inherited, combined with the tawdry and cheap which she had bought for herself. She seemed to value them equally and to use them with equal carelessness. A beautiful little sofa was draped with a horrid plush shawl of a vile green. A delicate prie-dieu chair embroidered in petit-point was loaded with a blue tin bath, itself filled with a delicate porcelain toilet set. The pattern was repeated in her appearance. A valuable pearl necklace hung round her neck, banging against a string of jet. On her chest rested a pinchbeck watch the size and general shape of an onion. She saw me looking at it.

'I like a big watch,' she said, with contentment. 'You can see it easily. It's a help when nursing.'

I wondered what sort of a nurse she made. And once again I asked myself why she was doing it. I had learnt from experience that Jessie's motives were more complicated than one sometimes guessed.

'Everyone ought to know a little about nursing,' she said absently, as if answering me. Then she started to pace the room with short, rapid steps. 'Oh, Errol,' she said fiercely, 'you would not question, if you really knew. Ask women to care if they have a vote when the reality of their lives is bounded by one pregnancy after another. No, we must put first things first.'

I waited. I recognised the preliminary rumblings towards an explosion of energy. Not for nothing had many of Jessie's early years been spent in a country where the volcanoes were by no means extinct. Her father had studied in Naples and Florence; later, as a young diplomat, rich and of good Yankee stock, he had been attached to

27

the Court of St James's. Here he had met Lady Geraldine. They were old friends. Indeed, it was on the strength of her father's impeccable breeding that Jessie got away with as much as she did. And I always thought her casual possession of a pearl necklace once owned by Marie Antoinette added to her stature. People would forgive much in a girl who had such jewels and could treat them with such patrician disdain. It showed, you see, that she was all right at heart.

'Shall I tell you what sort of nurse I am, Errol? I am a midwife.'

I felt a pang of sympathy for those poor women who came up against Jessie and her rough energy at such a crisis in their lives, but then I recalled how gentle she could be and how tender and full of real understanding and was ashamed of my inner flash of mirth. I was a bit surprised, though. 'Isn't it hard work, Jess, and very difficult?'

'No, Nature does most of the work,' she said with grim amusement. 'It takes you out all hours, of course, but I've never minded that sort of thing, you know, and I go everywhere on foot. I am getting known in the district, and so everyone is most kind and helpful.'

'You're only a sort of apprentice, I suppose, Jessie?' I suggested doubtfully.

'Yes, yes. But I'm learning fast. And I find I'm quite good at it. I have the touch. And then, think what a chance it offers me to talk to all sorts of poor women when they are at a time to listen.'

When they are at your mercy and can't get away, I am afraid I thought unkindly at this.

I suppose Jessie saw the sceptical look appear on my face, because she said: 'I don't bully them, Errol. I only tell them what they want to hear.'

'What's that?'

28

'Never mind for now,' she said evasively. 'But I find I can help them. And I shall set up a sort of clinic for them and their babies that shall be a model of its kind.' She was off again, pacing the room.

'The money, Jessie?' I murmured. 'Where will you get the money?'

'I shall probably sell my grandmother's pearls.' She squinted down at them, and when I exclaimed in dismay (they were very beautiful), said impatiently: 'What matter? I have a better row in a bank in Boston that I never see.' So then I was quiet. I always had to remember the remarkable material possessions that Jessie had at her command if she chose: more than any English girl would have owned. 'Picture the lives of some of these poor women. One of them said to me only today: "Here I am, nurse, with one child at my breast and pushing down another".' Her eyes flashed. 'And I see the same all about me, wherever I go. How can I talk of women's rights to them? No, no, we must begin at the beginning.' There was a sort of menace in her voice.

'Nature ...' I began.

'Nature, rubbish,' said Jessie.

'And after you have dealt with Nature,' I said gently, 'then you will begin on politics and women's labour?'

'Exactly. So you see I have plenty to occupy myself with, without bothering whether the Czar or the Emperor of Austria should be assassinated. However,' she added with satisfaction, 'I believe the police watch me.'

'Jessie!'

'Yes. I observed a man I know to be a police constable walking up and down outside the house a good deal yesterday and at least once I think he may have wanted to speak to me. But it *may* have been on account of his wife—I believe she might be coming my way ...'

'Jessie,' I said, coming to the reason which had brought

me there. I drew out the pencilled drawing of the baby and showed it to her. 'Have you ever seen this? Does it mean anything to you?'

She picked it up and studied it. 'Nice little thing. Under a month, I'd guess. Babies lose that new-born look between a month and six weeks. That's something I've learned. Who drew it?'

'The mother, I think,' I said sadly.

She pointed with her finger. 'Funny effect she gets there. Almost like a shadow on the child.'

'I think it's because she couldn't draw very well.' There *was* a shadow on the child, but I did not want to go into that with her.

Jessie turned it over and saw what was written on the back. 'Yes, my father was in Florence in 1860. It was before Rome became the capital city of all Italy, of course. But this isn't me. I was a naughty little girl wearing a pinafore in my grandmother's house in New York about then.' She handed it back.

'Where did you get it?'

'I found it among my father's papers.'

'I don't think Dad knew your father. Oh, they may have met, but no more than that.'

'But between my mother's family and your family there was a great friendship, was there not?'

'Oh, yes.' She nodded confidently. 'The Falconets have always been very worldly, travelled people, and so have the Maurices, I guess. There's been a long friendship between them.'

I thought I knew now where my mother had been taken, whose house had sheltered her and who had arranged the fostering out of the child. But I was no nearer finding a name for him or a home, or even a country. I wondered how much my Aunt Geraldine knew. I did not share my father's trust in her ignorance. I might ask her.

The front door bell rang loudly in response to a long pull, and then rang again. Someone was urgent. 'That's for me, I expect,' said Jessie, getting up.

Sure enough, in a minute there was a tap on the door and her landlady's voice said, 'You're wanted, Miss Falconet.'

'Coming at once.' Jessie had put on a dark cloak and was slinging herself about with various objects. I saw an umbrella, a roll of blanket, what looked like another tin bath, a black bag. 'Have to go provided,' she said.

We went down the stairs, Jessie staggering slightly. Her landlady was waiting in the hall, her face pale and wan as if she had thought too much and struggled too hard against an adversary too strong for her. She handed Jessie a slip of paper. 'Balfour Place,' she said.

Jessie nodded and consulted the message. 'Mrs Addison? She's always in a hurry. Good-bye, Mrs B. See you later.'

Her landlady smiled, revealing a look of great sweetness. She was nursing the kitten or its twin. When she smiled I saw that there was more strength and vitality in her face than I had guessed.

On the step Jessie said to me: 'I walk a few yards on your way. We can get you a cab back to Belgravia. There's usually one hanging about on the corner here.'

A cab was turning the corner at that moment and I hailed it. The cabby looked down at me from his perch as if surprised to be hailed by a young and unaccompanied lady. I was stepping into the brougham when Jessie spoke.

'About that child whose picture you showed me.'

'Yes, Jessie?'

'Something wrong there, some little abnormality that the artist saw but did not wish to depict. I'm convinced of it.' She sounded troubled.

31

I sat down on the faded green upholstery of the cab and let my feet rest in the straw on the floor. I leaned back and watched Jessie from the cab window as I drove away. She was standing at the kerb, weighed down by all she carried, but with that keen, eager look on her face I knew so well. A darkly-dressed man standing by Jessie seemed like a shadow looming over her. Behind him stood a burly man with a large nose that looked as if it had been broken once. I felt a momentary fear, but Jessie knew how to look after herself, and even as I looked she moved away.

My feet scuffed around in the straw at the bottom of the cab and felt something, a hard object of some sort. I reached down and picked it up.

It was a pistol.

I sat with it in my lap and looked at it. I thought it looked ugly and sinister and its weight was considerable. I weighed it in my hands. Heavier than you would guess by looking at it. Too heavy for a woman. But I had never before held such a masculine object in my hands, so how could I know what it weighed or how a man's hold differed from a woman's? The dark metallic sheen of it had an elegance all its own, and I remember thinking: 'So that's what gunmetal looks like.' I had a silk dress of gunmetal moiré once. It was thought too dark for a girl, and people wondered at my father letting me wear it, although the truth was he had no control over me in matters of dress, no control at all. But the silk hadn't looked in the least like this.

The cab bowled on fast, we were just turning down into Piccadilly. There was St James's Church in all its Wren beauty. Another turn and then another and we were hurrying into Masham Square. I must give the gun to the cabby, although it could hardly be his, I thought.

We drew up with a flourish outside the house, Number Forty Masham Square.

I stepped out and paid the cab man. Then I produced the pistol and told him where I had found it. 'It was on the floor of your cab, partly hidden by the straw. An earlier passenger of yours must have lost it.'

He gave the pistol a quick, incredulous look and then hurriedly gathered up the reins in his hands. He was a dark-visaged, thin-faced man with gaunt bones, not a reassuring cast of countenance.

'I don't want nothing of it. Don't give it here, because I won't touch it. Not for nothing. Not on your life. I don't see, and I don't want to look. It's nothing to me. I know the police and their tricks. If I lay hands on it, never mind what I says, I'll be a done man.'

'But I'll explain,' I started to say.

'I'm off,' and so saying, he whipped up the horse and was away.

I stood there, incredulous and dismayed, the pistol still in my hand. Fortunately there was no one passing near me in the square. I pulled myself together, tucked the pistol beneath my mantle where it could not be seen and walked up the steps to pull the door bell.

It would have taken a stronger spirit than mine to walk into the hall at Masham Square and face Lady Geraldine carrying a pistol.

In fact, for once there was no one about, except the man who let me into the house, and his was a face I did not know, although he clearly knew me. The lack of the usual vigilant staff in the hall convinced me that there was a crisis brewing somewhere in Number Forty Masham Square. I knew the ways of the house and when danger flags were flying. If I was not mistaken they were flying now. It might be on my account, of course, because of my temporary departure, but I thought not. I associated alarms and crisis with my cousin Frank Maurice, Member of Parliament for a London constituency, art connoisseur and man of the world. I knew he was this last, because my father always said so. 'Frank's a man of the world,' he said more than once. 'With all his faults, he's a man of the world.' I used to long to know what his faults were, although I thought I could guess. Had I not once seen my cousin with a lovely lady riding in the park? A lady so striking that my aunt had turned her head away with a frozen look and muttered something about 'that dreadful Skittles'. Nicknames were a great thing in my cousin's world; even quite respectable, solid gentlemen from the Shires had nicknames like Boxer and Bluey, so I thought nothing of Skittles, although I judged her very beautiful. I knew what to make of my aunt's expression, however, and thought that Skittles would never be received at Court. Skittles, therefore, certainly represented a fault, and probably also, I guessed, part of the paraphernalia of being a man of the world as well. Another part of it was money, or in Frank's case, lack of it. He certainly spent great quantities of a commodity of which none of the Maurices had much, but I am told he did it with such style it was a pleasure to watch him. However, reckoning days come even for men such as Frank (although less often than you might think), so I had learnt to associate him with days of anxiety and tension. Once even Lady Geraldine had wept. But the Maurices are a resilient lot, and within days her smile was as radiant and her brilliant laugh as loud as ever.

I sped up the stairs, grateful if Frank was causing an alarm that would keep attention from me. A grey hat and pair of gloves and a stick flung carelessly down on a priceless Boulle table outside the drawing room door confirmed my imaginings. I hurried past.

Inside my room I paused to look at the pistol. For the

34

first time I noticed an engraving on the side of the butt above the maker's name. The name was Austrian, and the pistol had been made in Vienna. I was about to examine it more closely when the little French clock on the table struck eight strokes in a clear voice. I was late and must change my clothes to meet my aunt at dinner. I put the gun away in a drawer of the writing-table, locked it and took the key.

It would be necessary to do something about it and I might ask Cousin Frank. A man of the world should know what to do about a gun.

One look round the room showed me that my possessions had been unpacked and everything made ready for me to change my clothes from those I had travelled in to something suitable to meet my aunt in at dinner.

I was used to dressing myself and began in haste. I had little choice. I was in mourning and the dresses I could wear for evening were three in number: two black and one white. On such a warm evening I would prefer the white, but it was my newest and best and ought to be reserved for an occasion when under Lady Geraldine's eagle eye I must look well turned out. There was nothing for it but the black padua silk. It was a dress which had started life as pale yellow, been dyed to a blue as it aged, and was now dyed again to a deep black. Unluckily for me the ghosts of its yellow and its blue incarnations seemed to hang about it and I always startled myself when I caught sight of myself in the mirror and saw a girl in black.

I looked at myself now. In the gilt mirror over my dressing-table I saw a tall, slender girl with the deep blue eyes and the blonde hair that all the Maurices have. The height came from my father: the Maurices are not tall people.

Far below me I heard voices raised: my aunt and

Cousin Frank. I had once heard my aunt pass judgement on a young woman with a particularly carrying voice as 'an ill-bred gal'. It apparently troubled her not at all that her own voice was clear and resonant, not to say loud. Frank had a particularly well-modulated voice that was audible, always gentle, always listened to.

I walked down the stairs and put my arm round her waist and kissed her cheek. Grand lady or not, I stood on no ceremony with Lady Geraldine. 'Good evening, aunt, how are you?'

'Very well indeed, Errol, considering the untimely heat for May. Tidy your hair, my dear, it is coming down on the left. Who did your hair? No, don't answer. You did it yourself, of course. We must get you a maid. So you've been out already?'

She knew everything then, as usual.

'Hardly gadding, aunt,' I said mildly. 'Just to see a friend who might have been busy some other time.' I gave her a smile. I knew from experience that good-natured opposition disarmed her. She had to smile back, being a good-humoured woman herself, and so could no longer be cross.

'Got a kiss for me, cousin?' said Frank, coming forward.

'Oh yes, spare the legislator one,' said Lady Geraldine sardonically. 'No, no, go away, Frank, and don't be silly. Oh, how tiresome a grown man can be when he chooses.' Frank *was* out of favour. 'You are very welcome, Errol.'

She was wearing a black ottoman silk dress trimmed with bugles of jet. Not in mourning for my father, as you might think, but official Court mourning for the death of a remote German prince, kinsman of the Queen. They were in more or less perpetual mourning at Windsor. Lady Geraldine had just come out of waiting, and her clothes were still matched to the Court's mood. But in any case, as she said herself, she had little in her wardrobe but black, white, and lilac, as she really could not go to the expense of a set of bright clothes for the very few days in a year when the Court was out of mourning for one or other of the Queen's huge and mortal clan of relations. 'Court mourning is the greatest hypocrisy ever invented,' said Lady Geraldine with a yawn. 'And I am sure it's the greatest bore as well. All the Princesses detest it, and no wonder too, with their looks ... and poor Princess Louie's dyed her hair the colour of a canary.'

You got a different view of Court life through the sometimes racy lips of Lady Geraldine than through the Court page of the *Morning Post*, I reflected. Yet paradoxically I believed it was this raciness that endeared her to the Queen. It always had to be remembered that the Queen was a Hanoverian through and through, even though she kept that side of her heritage well under cover.

Frank laughed, a great explosive Maurice laugh, and Lady Geraldine remembered where she was and who she was and that she was seriously out of temper with him, and sat up straight and said: 'That's enough, Frank.'

Frank passed a hand over his face and was at once straight-faced, mirth wiped out as by a sponge. 'I won't be laughing this time tomorrow. Nor the day after, nor for the next few weeks as far as I can see.'

'Travel broadens the mind,' said Lady Geraldine serenely.

'A German provincial capital never broadened anyone's mind,' said Frank with great gloom.

'You'll hardly be there but you'll be back.'

'Stuttgart,' said Frank, in tones of lead.

So now I knew what he was to do, even if I did not know what he had done. He was to go on a journey for Lady Geraldine to Germany and he did not wish in the least to go. In fact, from his tone and hers I guessed it

37

was a sort of punishment for him.

Geraldine smiled at me radiantly as she led the way forward into the dining room. 'Frank is going to do a little errand for me and you see how he likes to help his mother. Errol, take care to drink the claret at dinner. You look too pale.'

The claret was good and the food delicious. After the austere table kept by my father, as a matter of principle as well as personal indifference to the taste of anything, I enjoyed it to the full.

The wine was served by a quiet figure I guessed to be 'young Fletcher'. He was young, too young for his position in such a house, and a noticeable change after the ancient dignity of his grandfather. He looked athletic and energetic as he moved about his duties, his face composed and expressionless. Except occasionally, when his eye caught Frank's and a look seemed to pass between them.

At the end of the meal, when my aunt and I were leaving while Frank dumbly faced the shining board of mahogany, the fruit, the decanter of port and his own thoughts, Fletcher spoke to my aunt in a low voice. 'You will be glad to know, my lady, that the young boy that came with Mr Frank has been satisfactorily accommodated for the night.'

The voice was low, but Lady Geraldine heard, Frank heard and I heard. I think perhaps Fletcher meant that all three should hear in concert. My eyes opened in surprise.

'Couldn't leave the poor little blighter,' muttered Frank, not meeting anyone's gaze. 'Decent little beggar. Mother just walked out and left him. Couldn't do the same myself.'

Lady Geraldine contented herself with looking grim. We left Frank sitting depressed in front of his full glass

and his unlit cigar. A pair of sad eyes followed us. Now
I knew what he had done.

Once in the drawing room I could contain myself no
longer. 'Is the child Frank's? Is it Frank's own son?'

'*No*. No, there at least I do believe him. But that he
should be on visiting terms with such a woman, a
notorious woman, a woman of ...' Lady Geraldine took
such a deep breath that the jet blossom on her bosom
shook. I felt sorry for her, torn as she was between what
she longed to say and what she felt she must hold back
in deference to my youth. She gulped and went on: 'He
visited her, quite innocently so he says, only today, went
in and found the boy there quite alone. Had been for some
days. Very little food and no money. No provision made
for his care at all and the mother quite gone off, no one
knows where. So Frank brought the child away. It was
quite proper he should, quite proper.' She was almost
tearful. 'But I'm sure I wish it had not been Frank that
found the boy.' She burst out, 'And I wish he had not
brought him here.'

I thought Frank had behaved with great niceness. Or
great laziness. It was hard to tell which. But he had cared
for the child.

'And what am I to tell the Queen?' said his mother.

'She will never know,' I said.

'She knows everything.'

'But if she is told you will know who has told her.
Circumscribed as she is, you must know. Indeed, I expect
you could guess now who would tell her. And such knowledge, well, that's power of a sort, isn't it, put into your
hands.'

Lady Geraldine gave me a long look. 'I can see you
will make a courtier, Errol.'

I was silent, not understanding quite what she meant.
Distantly, through the window opened to the evening

warmth, I could hear the sound of music. I did not tell her that I knew what I did about power and its working because my father had made me read the letters of Madame, the wife of Monsieur, brother to Louis XIV. 'That's music,' I said aloud. 'Music to dance to.'

'Oh, a ball,' said Lady Geraldine with a yawn. 'Lady Beauregard. She gives two a year. And with those gals to marry off well she may, poor thing. Luckily Beauregard is as rich as Croesus.'

'How many Beauregard girls are there?'

'Seven and then, finally, a boy,' said Lady Geraldine, still yawning. 'And only a new title, too, hardly worth bothering.'

Her own family patent of nobility went back to the first Elizabethan settlement of Ireland, and they had always been fecund of sons. Too many, some had said, seeing Maurice younger sons popping up everywhere, all full of charm. 'I had hopes of one of the girls for Frank, but there it is, he never even talks to a woman unless she's at least thirty and married.'

She lay back on a low chair and stretched out a hand to the dish of chocolates and sweetmeats placed on a round table at her elbow. Carefully she selected a macaroon and popped it in her mouth. A handsome woman still, she was just verging on plumpness. It was not unpleasing, however, and her hair was still shining and silver gilt and her eyes of a dark, deep blue. One delicate tapering hand with a triple row of jet bracelets round the dimpled wrist hung by her side.

From outside the sound of music swelled and became ever more beguiling: a waltz. My feet moved underneath my stiff gown. I loved to waltz. I suppose I looked wistfully, because my aunt spoke.

'We were asked, of course, but our mourning, you know, precludes it.'

Frank came in, took a cup of coffee from his mother, and sat heavily down in a chair by the window without saying a word. He sipped the coffee slowly.

'Frank could go,' said his mother. 'Lady Letty Little will be there. Such a nice girl. Twenty thousand a year at least.'

Frank sat there, his feet as heavy as lead, as if they would never dance again.

'And completely unencumbered,' persevered Lady Geraldine, pushed on by that terrible, perverse impulse we all have of going on and on when we know we should stop.

'She won't want to be encumbered by me, then,' said Frank, getting up. He still carried an unlighted cigar. 'Good night, mother. I'm off.'

She looked her question.

'To the House,' he said. 'There is a debate at which the Whips demand my attendance.'

'What is the subject?' I was interested.

'Need you ask? Ireland.'

'Ireland or money,' murmured Lady Geraldine. 'What else?' Surprisingly she rose too. 'Come, Errol. We must change. We are expected at an evening reception of Lady Bartholomew.'

'I may go?' I asked, enraptured.

'Oh yes, my dear, there you will only walk and talk and be offered a little champagne. No dancing.'

'You have my express permission to go and be bored,' said Frank, giving me a cousinly peck on the cheek and laughing his great laugh from the door. No one laughed more joyously than Frank at his own jokes. Indeed, all the Maurices did. Probably I did so myself. It was something to be watched.

Lady Geraldine heaved herself up, relinquished the soft chair and the dish of chocolates with obvious regret and departed to put on another black dress with a lower neck-line and rather more jet. After a pause I followed.

On the stairs I met Fletcher. 'Where is the boy?' I asked curiously.

'He's sleeping with the younger footman in the top attic.' He spoke with politeness, but with ease and no special deference. He was not subservient.

'And is he all right?'

'Perfectly all right. Very happy. The footman is sulking and ready to cry. It's the first time he ever had a bed to himself. He has eight brothers at home.' Not everyone can win, his expression said.

The evening seemed to be growing better as we drove away from Masham Square. The sound of music was billowing out in gusts from a house three doors away. I fancied I could hear voices and laughter. As we passed a woman and a man came down the steps of the house. The woman was in white satin and a glitter of diamonds. A carriage drew up and deposited another couple. More satin, more diamonds. My aunt leaned forward for a better look, then sat back, drawing in a satisfied breath.

'No one I know. I thought there wouldn't be. She never knows whom to invite.'

The coachman whipped up his horses and we started to move faster. It was already after eleven in the evening, but on every side was light and life and movement. In my country home I should have been in bed by now. Here in London I was going to a party. True, Frank said I should be bored, but I didn't believe him. Instead I was pleasantly excited. Piccadilly was crowded with carriages and people strolling on the pavement, although the hour seemed to me so late. The bright street lighting made it seem like day; but a day in which the shadows were sharp and dark and the unlighted alleys and passages like the entrances to another world. I sensed other people moving in these black pits, men and women of the night, whose world was not my world. Sometimes I caught a glimpse of a pale face at an alley mouth or saw movement down a side street. Lady Geraldine did not seem to see or notice, but I felt the presence of this other world very strongly.

St James's Church in Piccadilly stood out boldly. Two great lamps by the main gate were alight, and within I could see more lights. It seemed late for an evening service, and I said as much to Lady Geraldine.

'Oh no, there is some great wedding there tomorrow, I believe, and they will be getting the church ready. Miss Jessel and Mr Berry. A banking marriage. Every display, and at nine o'clock in the morning. Oh, how hot it is,' and she fanned herself. 'Mrs Bartlett was in love with the former organist there, so I'm told.'

'Mrs Bartlett?' The name meant nothing to me.

'Tried for poisoning two years ago,' she said briefly. 'Did it with liquid chloroform. Acquitted. But they wanted to ask her how she did it!'

'Why, Aunt Geraldine, I didn't know you took an interest in criminal cases.'

'Oh no, I don't really. Not on my own account.' She yawned. 'It's the Queen. *She* takes a passionate interest in such cases. One must always be well informed. Up to date with the latest details. She likes the details. *All* the details.'

'How strange.' I really wondered.

'No.' Lady Geraldine smiled. 'She is as curious as a child. In many ways she is childlike.'

But what a child, I thought, a child who had already been a Queen for fifty years and a widow for as long as I had been alive. A child who owned several palaces, many castles and the largest diamond in the world which, in spite of her perpetual mourning, my cousin Frank

43

assured me she wore. Queens can mourn in diamonds.

Something of this must have appeared in my face.

'Remember how little she really knows of how we poor mortals live,' said Geraldine tolerantly. 'She is thirsty to know. And through us she finds out. We are the books the Queen reads, the paper on which she writes, a mere means of communication. This is how I think of myself. I am simply a pair of eyes for the Queen to see through.'

We drew up before a large new house. It was built in brick and I saw at once I was entering a sort of modern palace, built not for a sovereign but a merchant prince. So the Medici might have lived. Soft pink marble clothed the hall and big double staircase. I swear I saw lapis lazuli on the walls. The footmen wore powdered hair and livery. It was a world away from Masham Square, and a whole universe removed from the rectory. A few words from Lady Geraldine had told me, in case I did not know, that my host's peerage was of respectable antiquity, but the opulence came from his wife, who was a Rothschild. But even I, a country mouse, knew of them. Their name was a byword for magnificence.

'Of course, it was right you should come,' murmured my aunt. 'We all come here. One meets everyone.' Unlike poor Lady Beauregard's, I thought, where one met nobody.

We followed a stream of people up the staircase, our names announced at every stage. 'Everyone' knew Lady Geraldine, of course, just as she 'knew' everyone. She lived in a small society, but one that was several hundred families bigger than it had been when she was a girl. Society was changing. It was by no means as exclusive as it once had been.

No one knew me, my clothes were undistinguished to the point of dowdiness, but I was happy to be in these perfect rooms. I looked at my hostess with pleasure. She was a plain woman, whom the taste of the times suited perfectly. The stiff, ornate line, the heavy brocade of her dress gave her a formal, imperial dignity like an Empress of old Cathay. Impossible to imagine her unbuttoned and *en négligée*.

As we walked through the rooms, with my aunt greeting people, talking to them for a while and then moving on, I began to notice something that at first seemed to me so absurd I dismissed it. I lowered my eyes and moved forward through the throng with Lady Geraldine.

But I could not be mistaken. I hoped I was not stupidly self-conscious, gauche, ill-bred, all the things I do not wish to be, but as I passed down the big salon I felt myself to be the object of much attention. On every side I was being observed and watched. I knew it. I felt it. A path seemed to open up down the centre of the room, through which we walked as if in a royal progress. Eyes watched me, behind me tongues whispered. Small groups seemed to form and nod together. It was all done smoothly and quietly, but I could not fail to be aware of it.

After a little while I became convinced that beneath her calm manner Lady Geraldine was aware of it too and did not like it any more than I did. We reached the head of the last drawing room, where supper was being served at many small round tables and where an orchestra played on a balcony. An elderly kinsman of Lady Geraldine came forward and sat us down at one with his wife and himself. He introduced himself to me as if I must know him and all about him. 'I'm your cousin Becky, m'dear, and this is my wife, Peebles.' It didn't seem a likely Christian name but she acknowledged it with a gentle smile.

'Lady Beckhampton and Lord Beckhampton,' murmured my aunt. 'Always called Becky,' he said. 'Becky for short, Becky for luck.' He had the Maurice laugh, all right. 'I've always been a lucky devil.' He too was looking at me with interested eyes, only his wife remained aloof and gentle and apparently uninterested.

The table was trimmed with pink and white flowers. Among the flowers were gardenias and roses, so that the mingled smell was sweet and strong. Never afterwards could I smell gardenias without remembering that room, and the hot May evening and the music floating out into the still air.

We drank champagne and ate salmon mousse and ice-cream *pralinée*.

'Food's always good here,' said Becky, tucking into the supper with gusto.

'I hope you won't be bored here in London, my dear,' said his wife, leaning across and giving my hand a gentle pressure.

'Oh no, I won't be bored.' I had been in the city only a few hours but already I had received an anonymous letter, found a pistol and been quietly inspected by a roomful of strangers. No, I would not find London boring.

The warm voluptuous air of the ballroom enveloped me. I was suddenly very happy. I was meant to live in this world.

We had finished supper and were moving through the house, now emptying, when I saw a man standing at the head of the stairs. He was just under the great Van Dyck painting of the young Duke of Richmond which hangs there. I was looking at the picture first and then my eyes travelled down and I looked at him. He was wearing a plain, dark suit and even at this distance appeared a spare, elegant figure. He was poised there, giving an impression of youthful energy momentarily at rest.

'Aunt, who is that man in black standing there, underneath the picture?'

She turned her head to look. 'Oh, just someone's

servant,' she said, her tone indifferent, her gaze unimpressed. 'Only a servant, my dear.'

Servant, I thought, my God, servant, what a servant. And marvelled that my aunt could not see the force and power that radiated from him. It was all masked from her by the fact that she could call him servant. But seen out of context, seen just as a man, what a man he was! Our eyes met: his, dark blue in a pale face. I felt as if I knew him, as if I had always known him, and as if I always should. A strange sensation reached down into the very pit of me. Then my aunt spoke to me and I had to turn away. When I looked again, he was gone.

In the carriage, on the dreamy drive home, I was thoughtful. It seemed to me that it would be easy to become like my aunt and fail to see certain people clearly because they were labelled servants. It wouldn't do for me. I promised myself a hard, clear look at young Fletcher. I spoke to my aunt, half-asleep in the corner.

'Why did everyone look at me so? It seemed to me they *studied* me.'

She opened her eyes, awaking languidly from a light doze.

'Oh, you are your mother's daughter, you see, I suppose they wanted to see your face.'

'And what does that signify?'

'She was a great beauty before ...' She stopped dead.

'Before what?'

She came to full consciousness with a little jerk. 'Before she married, my dear.'

'And I am not like her,' I said, not with any intention of attracting a compliment, but as one who spoke a fact. I knew I was not like my lovely mother; I had seen her portrait.

'Not in features, perhaps.' She hesitated, and then said with a little air of decision, 'But you have her expression.

47

Oh my dear, you have such a look of her.'

We drove on into a night grown strangely quiet, so that the sound of the horses seemed over loud.

As we went in I gave Fletcher a hard look, I can tell you, and it seemed to me I saw a man who knew his own mind and would take his own path when he chose to.

My aunt kissed me on the cheek and, yawning, went off to her bed.

I lay in bed but my body still spun with the motion of a dance I had not danced. Or was it that my spirit had gone dancing off?

I got up from my bed and in the moonlight went across to the bureau and drew out the pistol I had hidden there. In the pale light I could see an image engraved on the side. I traced it with my finger. A double-headed eagle.

The pistol was marked with the Imperial Austrian eagle. I was frightened then, I don't know why, but something cold seemed to reach out and touch me.

CHAPTER TWO

When I woke in the morning I knew already that my life was going to be more complex and puzzling than I had expected. I was not just an unknown young girl from the country. In some mysterious way I had been watched for, waited for, expected. The conviction had grown on me in the night, and now it seemed something perfectly comprehended and not yet fully understood. I had stepped into the great world like an actor arriving exactly on cue, but not quite sure of the play to be performed. I had an instinct I would learn. It was strange I should think in theatrical terms. I had been to the theatre so little in my life, and yet the image sprang immediately to my mind, as if what was in front of me was not natural and spontaneous, but somehow contrived.

Although I have been so little to the theatre, still, in the county town near to our rectory stood the Theatre Royal, where travelling companies used to visit. It was such an old theatre and so rustic that a family of birds had taken up lodgings in the roof and used to be seen and heard fluttering round as one took one's place and sat there waiting for the play to begin. But when the curtain went up the birds flew away. Sometimes they disappeared seconds before it rose, as if they had received a secret signal. Well, I had the feeling now that the birds had flown away and I was waiting for the curtain to go up.

Barlow arrived when I was fastening my jacket. I was wearing a tight-fitting silk bodice over a poplin skirt and over that a little loose jacket in the Empire style. At least, Mrs Taylor had called it the Empire style, but now I had it on, and was standing wearing it under Barlow's eyes, I wondered which Empire she could have had in mind. The sleeves fastened with countless small buttons and had large cuffs which fell over my hands. 'Perhaps it was Babylonian,' I said aloud absently, pondering my jacket's Imperial past.

'What's that, miss?'

'Just wondering about my jacket. It's said to be Empire style, I was wondering what Empire, and if it could be Babylonian. I saw such a pretty picture by Lord Leighton ...'

'Empire in dress means the Empress Josephine,' said Barlow, wooden-faced. 'Her ladyship wondered whether you would come to her while she was dressing.'

'Oh, I see,' I nodded. 'Napoleon and not Babylon.'

'It means high-waisted, miss,' snapped Barlow. She seemed cross this morning. 'Shall I tell her ladyship you'll come?'

I gathered my skirts in one hand. 'I'll come now,' I said meekly. I followed Barlow without another word.

In her large sunlit dressing room, Lady Geraldine was sitting in front of a mirror deftly piling her long hair up in rolls. She had a mouth full of hairpins, but she spoke through them without difficulty. She gave me a quick glance and condemned me. 'How badly she's cut your jacket, my dear. The cuffs are so ugly. We'll have to get you a good dressmaker. And your boots, dear, a little heavy, aren't they? Fortunately you have pretty hair and can dress it yourself.' She was continuing with her own hairdressing all the time, never once giving a look in the glass. 'Just as well, as the Queen is so particular.'

I wondered what the Queen had to do with it, but did not say so. No doubt the Queen loomed so largely in my aunt's mind that her judgements were heeded everywhere. But she needn't mind about my hair. I dressed it to suit myself not her.

'The black poult-de-soie jacket, please Barlow.' Lady Geraldine held out a hand. Now she did look at herself in the dressing-table mirror and I suppose she saw what I saw: a pink-cheeked, plumply pretty lady, wearing a satin corset cover trimmed with white roses and a muslin camisole tucked in pink. 'How pretty you look,' I said spontaneously.

She turned to me with the radiant Maurice smile. 'I'm always at my best in the mornings, my dear. Mornings and then the late evenings. All the Maurices are the same. It's the way we are built. You will find the same yourself.'

'I'm not all Maurice,' I said. I came and stood behind her, so that our faces were reflected together.

'No.' In the mirror I saw her look at my own image. 'You have more intellect. That comes from the Veseys. Sometimes, I think that makes you just a little bit of a stranger to me.' Her hand reached out and took mine. I felt her warm, firm grasp.

Now was the moment to ask her about my brother, but the moment drew out and lengthened and was gone. She took her hand away.

'You have a very pretty handwriting,' she said thoughtfully. The subject had been changed with a vengeance. 'Bold and clear.'

'Yes, my father set great store by that, and of course I wrote a lot for him. You know towards the end of his life I kept nearly all his correspondence, because his eyes ...'

'And your voice is very pretty too,' mused Lady Geraldine.

I stopped short. 'Is that bold and clear as well?' I asked.
'There's nothing to be done about your height, of course.'

'I should think not, indeed,' I said indignantly.

'Yes, it is very hard that women should have to match like horses,' said Lady Geraldine with a sigh. She was nicely into her morning gown, by now, settling and smoothing the band about her waist, while Barlow adjusted the folds at the back. 'Just a little more to the right, Barlow. Yes, thank you, exactly right.' She stretched out her hand for a pocket handkerchief to be put into it, which it was by the knowledgeable Barlow, who seemed to know exactly what her mistress wanted without being told. She sprinkled a little *Eau de Jasmin* on it, before she handed it forward. The delicate scent floated towards me, then disappeared, killed by the warm breeze from the window. 'And you speak, read and write German and French, do you not, Errol?'

'You engaged my German governess yourself, aunt,' I said dryly. 'And obliged me to write to you once a week in alternate French and German.'

'So I did.' She sounded surprised.

'I *thought* you never read them.'

She laughed easily. 'Oh, I am sure I read them, Errol dear, but the Maurices have shocking memories, and *backfisch* German, you know... Now, let me see, you can play the piano and read easily from sight? Yes,' she answered her own question, 'I know you can. And you ride, of course.'

'I had to in Suffolk. It was often the only way to go about, but I don't call myself a horsewoman.'

'No need, no need,' said my aunt from the depths of her thoughts. 'And then the best thing is that you are not engaged, or likely to get married.'

'Thank you, aunt,' I said with dignity.

'I mean, not in the near future,' said my aunt, looking at me, but not, I felt, really seeing me. 'And you are almost twenty? In November, I recall. A very good age.'

I wanted desperately to tell my aunt that I had a secret lover in Ireland who would soon be riding over to sweep me off, or that I was engaged to a sailor or a soldier, or even a tinker or a tailor, but alas, it was not true. Except for the Bishop of Ely's chaplain who had asked me to marry him one snowy Easter, exhausted and overcome, poor fellow, by the rigours of Holy Week and therefore looking for a helpmeet, I had received no serious proposals. Two or three unserious ones, perhaps. Of course, my aunt knew this, it was just the sort of feminine detail she would know. I thought she needed a shock, though, and I proceeded to administer one.

'I shan't marry, aunt,' I said calmly. 'I have decided to refuse all offers. I am going to be a free woman and support myself.'

She had finished dressing, had tucked a little posy of moss roses into her waist band and stood there poised and delicious-looking. 'Oh, my dearest,' she said, 'that is *just* what I am about to offer you. A career every girl would be proud of.' She studied her appearance in the mirror. 'I wish I could rouge,' she said. 'I need a touch of colour, but in my position it would never do.' She hummed a little tune. 'The Princess of Wales paints to perfection, of course. We could all take lessons from her. Mind, since her last illness she needs it.'

I stared at her suspiciously. Experience had taught me to distrust all of the Maurice family when they were in this cheerful, confident frame of mind. They could sweep you off your feet. I knew how I was myself in these brilliant moods, when the Maurice blood in me warred with the more cautious Vesey heritage. Sometimes I used to feel I could fly to the moon. I was all Maurice then. We could be dangerous, I thought.

'What is this position you have fashioned me for, aunt?'

She put a finger on her lips. 'Soon, soon, my dear. Meanwhile, discretion.'

She put her hand on my arm and let me lead her, in a regal fashion, which, it struck me, she had picked up from her illustrious mistress, down to breakfast in a small, square room of dull aspect on the mezzanine floor. My cousin Frank was there before us, idly turning over the pages of the *Illustrated London News* and smoking. He was wearing travelling clothes. He looked up when we came in and put out his cigarette. 'Well, I'm off.'

From overhead there came a series of tremendous thumps and bangs.

'Your trunks?' said Lady Geraldine, seating herself calmly behind the tea-tray at the breakfast table. 'Taking about twenty, as usual?'

'Fellow must be well turned out,' muttered Frank.

'You won't find this a dressy occasion,' observed his mother. 'Tea, Errol?' I shook my head. I preferred to drink coffee. The coffee urn stood on the sideboard. 'Pour me some coffee, Frank.' He brought the cup over and, encouraged by my example, drank some himself and cut a slice from the cold ham standing near the coffee. After this, he seemed to feel more cheerful and could even talk with good spirits about his journey, which he seemed to regard as a form of Siberian exile. 'Beastly bother, this travelling. Terrible food and never a decent bed to be had. To my mind there is no finer place than London and I prefer to stay in it. Except Paris. In Paris a fellow feels at home. But these Germans . . .' He shuddered.

'You'll be in good company,' said his mother serenely. 'Meeting the Duchess at Liverpool Street?'

54

'On the boat. She ain't coming by train ... Bringing her own carriage. And that'll be a song and dance, that will ...'

'She has her reasons.'

Frank got up. 'A little devilled kidney, Errol?'

'No thank you, Frank.'

'Quite right, Errol. Very bad for the complexion, all that highly spiced food. I always breakfast off a little fried bacon and toast.' Lady Geraldine was eating this now with a good appetite.

'Hasn't hurt my complexion,' said Frank.

'Errol hasn't got a beard and whiskers,' observed his mother.

'No, indeed, by Jove,' and Frank ran his hand over his own handsome silky beard. Their eyes met and they laughed their pealing, silvery laugh. Everything with them in the end was dissolved in good humour. 'You wait, Errol. Your turn is coming ... My word.'

'No doubt, but I'm not in a position to know about it yet.'

Frank opened his eyes wide. 'What, haven't you told her?'

Lady Geraldine held up her hands in deprecation at her son who gave a short whistle. 'You are a caution, mother.' He stood up, finished his devilled kidneys and collected his gloves from a chair. 'Here goes. Look after my little stranger for me till I get back.'

'You don't give me much chance not to,' she grumbled. 'What is his name?'

'Lord knows, I don't. Ask him. I expect he'll answer to something.'

'My dear, he's not a dog,' said his exasperated mother.

I was waiting for Frank to depart so that I could force Aunt Geraldine to tell me exactly what future life she was planning for me. Supposing she was planning to send me to the Colonies, or out to India? The riding being necessary suggested that. Her imagination could stretch so far. And it certainly sounded as though I was to be given an onerous and yet illustrious task. But no, it could not be India or the Colonies, or why should I need German and French and be able to play the piano?

We were interrupted by the appearance of Fletcher, bearing a telegram on a silver salver. Lady Geraldine picked it up with delicate finger tips. It was an art in itself, the way she took what the servants offered her on dish or salver. She read it silently, then handed it to Frank. 'Sent on from Windsor,' she said.

He took it, walked to the window, read it, then turned round and faced his mother. 'So be it,' he said. 'If the Duchess is ill and can't come I shall go on my own. Be better off without her. She's an old tattle bag.'

'Thank you, Frank,' said his mother gratefully.

'Once having set my hand to the plough, and all that. She's not ill, you know. She wants nothing of it, nothing.'

They became aware of my interested gaze and stopped. Without more ado Frank made his farewells to his mother and me. I noticed he limped a little as he went towards the door and reached out for his rosewood walking stick. The Maurices often suffered these small disabilities. Frank occasionally limped, Lady Geraldine had a stiff, sore wrist. I had observed it. It was as if Nature wanted to remind them that, for all their brilliance, there was human frailty underneath. Frank's mother noticed the limp, too, and sped after him, making suggestions of salt baths, massage, and Gregory's powder. I heard a final cry of 'Baden Baden' from the turn of the stairs, and the faint answering cry 'Abroad's bloody'.

I left them still at it and walked slowly up to my room. At the head of the stairs was the drawing room used by Lady Geraldine. To the right were a pair of double doors, always closed. I usually passed these doors without a second glance. Today, moved by what curiosity I hardly knew, I opened one of the doors and walked in.

I was in the ballroom, small as such rooms went, more suited to the decorous dances of a century ago than the modern waltz and polka, but an elegant, well-proportioned salon.

It was that still, nothing could destroy the harmony of its proportions, but otherwise it was an abandoned wreck, given up to dust and cobwebs, utterly neglected. One gilt chair with a broken leg lay on its side by the fireplace; a spotted mirror gleamed at me darkly from a further wall, a side table supported a dusty figure of Psyche. It was cold, cold with a chill that survived even this summer heat.

I stood on the threshold and stared. Then slowly I went in, closing the door behind me. I moved into the centre of the room. Above me the great chandelier hung in a canvas bag. It looked sinister, like a shrouded head. My entrance had disturbed the dead air so that cobwebs swayed on the ceiling. A mouse ran across one corner of the room and disappeared into the wainscoting. I pursed my lips and let a little surprised whistle escape, an un-ladylike trick I had learnt from the groom in the stables of the rectory. I wasn't scared of mice either, and I had learnt that in the stables too. Some things remain frightening, however, and the desolation of this room was sad and struck me to the heart. It was hard to believe it was part of the house in Masham Square. It looked more as if it had come out of the sleeping princess's castle.

The door opened behind me. I turned round to see Fletcher standing there.

'How neglected this ballroom is,' I said.

'It's not much used now, Miss Vesey.'

'Not at all, I should imagine.'

57

'In fact, it's usually kept locked up.' He produced a key.
'But the housekeeper thinks the mice are making a home
here.' He looked around him. 'The fact is, her ladyship
can't bear to cast eyes on it.'

I followed him back to the doors. Plainly he meant I
should follow him.

'Oh, why?'

'General Maurice died in here,' he said, after a moment's
hesitation.

I watched as he locked the doors and attached the keys
to a great bunch. Yes, I accepted his reason for the neglect
of the ballroom. It was nearly twelve years since General
Maurice had died. From the delayed result of a fever
caught on campaign, I had been told. The aversion to the
ballroom seemed understandable. My aunt shared the attitude to death, half-reverent, half-superstitious, of her royal
mistress.

Fletcher stood aside to let me go up the stairs. He had
a way of silently suggesting what you should do and
where you should go which was unassuming, yet commanding. I wondered, in fact, how much he dominated
the household with this quiet restraint. The Maurices
looked and acted all powerful, but no one knew better
than I their hidden weakness. They could be flattered.

I caught Fletcher's eyes, and was bound to admit that
the cool, measured gaze was no look of a flatterer. On the
contrary, I wondered if he even liked me, and I turned
away more lowered in spirits than I liked to admit. As if
it mattered: and yet I seemed to care.

On happenings like this, other events turn. Because
I felt cross and a little at odds with myself when I went
up to my room, instead of settling to my letters or my
work, I went to the drawer and drew out the letter I
had received yesterday.

I took it to the window and examined it. The message

itself still offered the same ambiguous threat: 'BLOOD IS THICKER THAN WATER'. So it was, I reflected, but it ran as readily. I had no real idea what the letter meant, but there was no denying that the introduction of the word 'blood' in a sentence is usually meant to alarm. Yes, and it succeeds in alarming, I thought.

There was only one person who wanted to hurt me, as far as I knew, and he was the person my father had warned me against, my half-brother. He wished me harm, it came back to that. He knew me, and yet I did not know him. I was exposed and vulnerable, while he was secret and hidden.

The sunlight came through the window and warmed me and gave me confidence. I lifted the letter up to the light. The paper was crisp and fresh. I should get no help there. The envelope had suffered more, and was grubby and stained as if it had rested in a dirty pocket. I held it up to my nose and sniffed the stain. I knew the smell, and once again my education had come through the stables. It was the smell of beer. The envelope of my letter was beer-stained.

As I stood there considering this fact, and wondering if anything could be made of it, the sunlight fell at an angle on the envelope and picked out the indentations of some writing. The envelope must have been underneath another sheet of paper upon which someone had written with such pressure that the letters came through. With excitement I realised that I could make it out.

A letter or two was obscure but the rest were clear enough. Besides, I had helped my father often enough with inscriptions on Greek and Roman coins to know a trick or two. I went over to my writing desk, took out a soft pencil and lightly shaded over the whole area of the indentation. The letters now stood out as pale ghosts on a darker background. I read: 'Jock y Fi lds Pass'.

It looked like an address. To the eye of faith it did, and I had plenty of faith in myself and in my luck. That was the old Maurice streak coming out on top, triumphing over the Vesey caution.

'It looks like an address,' I said aloud. 'And an easily recognisable one, at that.' I stood a moment longer in thought, and then I knew what I was going to do. I put on a hat and took my purse in my hand. Then I stepped briskly down the stairs, through the front door and was once again out in the world and about my own business. I felt triumphant and energetic. Only one day in London and already I was managing my own affairs. I *did* know the prediction about pride going before a fall, although you might not believe it.

Masham Square had its morning face on. A groom was trotting round the corner, leading away his mistress's horse, after her early ride in the park. The horse was a very pretty chestnut, a woman's horse if ever I saw one. A black-dressed, tightly-corseted woman was stepping out of a carriage carrying a tower of pale violet hat-boxes: a milliner arriving to show her latest inventions, I deduced. Hats were big this year. Outside the Foreign Secretary's house a carriage waited. On its door some august coat of arms was emblazoned. Without willing it, I found my feet taking me in that direction. A policeman was standing there, looking very upright as to bearing, and very friendly as to face. His eyes twinkled at me. He was quite young, and although a social gap yawned between us, my youth and his could leap the chasm. A smile passed between us. He saw me look at the coat of arms.

'That's the Shah of Persia's carriage, that is. *What* a potentate! This is just a private visit, 'course. If he'd come official, he'd have had to come with a dragoon of guards.'

The door behind him opened and a soberly dressed man

60

stood on the threshold. The policeman straightened his face and stood erect.

I sped on. Once on the main road I looked around for a cab. One soon bowled along and stopped near me at the kerb. His elderly woman passenger got out, grumbling as she handed over some coins. 'Nearly shook the teeth out of me, you did, cabby. What a gallop.'

'Go on, ma,' he said, with good humour. 'This old 'orse of mine can't gallop, bless him.'

I held up my hand.

He saw me and moved the equipage, a hansom, a few feet to let me step in. The horse turned his head to look at me, and I thought there was a nasty roll to the eye. I could believe in the gallop. He looked a wild one.

I got in, seated myself and announced serenely: 'Jockey Fields Passage'.

The cab gave a jerk forward so that I had to hold on to my seat.

'Good God Almighty, ma'am,' the driver said piously. 'Are you sure?'

'Jockey Fields Passage,' I repeated.

'Off we go, then.' He cracked his whip and with a lurch we rolled away.

It was an exciting ride in its way. I thought I had never been so close to death as when we drove straight at a heavy dray laden with barrels, avoiding it by inches and with much swearing on both sides. We nipped smartly between two omnibuses, clearing their wheels with a delicate precision that I wished I could believe was judgement more than luck. We turned off High Holborn not far from where Jessie now lived, and turned again. Suddenly my demon driver stopped.

'Can't take you no further, ma'am. The Passage is too narrow to allow me to get the 'orse down.' He pointed with his whip. 'You'll have to walk. That's your way.' I saw the entrance to a dark alley straight in front of me. A thin dog was sniffing at the corner.

'What's wrong with Jockey Fields Passage?' I asked as I paid the cabby.

He shrugged. 'It's not a place of very prime reputation. They had a bloody murder there last month. Never caught the man that did it. Never will. One of these poor unfortunates got it in the gizzard. Wouldn't let a daughter of mine go down the Passage. Still, young ladies like you know their own mind, I dare say.'

'Indeed I do.' He had succeeded in daunting me somewhat. On the other hand, it was daylight, and a sunny warm day at that, and murders take place at night and in the dark, don't they?

The dog was so thin and starved-looking that any fears I had of him changed to pity. He was nothing but skin and bones and hungry yellow teeth. There was a cookshop selling meat and sausages and pies, all hot and greasy-looking, a few yards away. I went and bought him a pie and crumbled it on the pavement before him. I could have left it whole, for in one great gulp it was all gone.

Jockey Fields Passage was entered by a narrow archway, but once through this it opened out into a wider thoroughfare than at first appeared. The ground was flagged with cracked and aged paving stones that looked as if they had been put down before the Great Fire of London in 1666. Down the centre of the passage ran a cobbled gutter, filled with decaying food and other rubbish that I turned my eyes from. On either side were houses crowded together. All doors and windows were open on this hot day and through them I could see shabby, dishevelled men and women, lounging and gossiping, and in more than one case sleeping. There were plenty of children, too, playing up and down the alley as cheerfully as if they were in the meadows of my rural home.

I soon noticed one thing: that although it was raffish enough, the Passage was neither starving nor desperately poor. It had an air of prospering secretly, as if it knew how to grow fat if it wanted. I know poverty and the face of true privation. The countryside knows what hunger can be. I have seen the look of those who are close to sinking. I did not see that look here.

Holding my skirts high above my ankles, I stepped carefully through the muck which lay everywhere. If I use a farmyard word it is because there was a farmyard smell of manure and ammonia. I was watched on every side and knew it. Still, I kept my head up and walked forward confidently. I didn't know where I was going, but why show it? I caught the eye of a woman standing at her front door with a child in her arms. She stared at me hard, though without hostility. But totally without friendliness, either. It was much the gaze of the cat as it studies the mouse it is about to eat, alert, intelligent anticipation. I began to see what the cabby had meant.

Halfway down the street was a public house called The Jockey. It was still sleepy in the morning sun, with shutters across the windows on the upper floors. A rusty-looking black cat slept in a patch of sunlight by the door.

A man came out of the door of The Jockey as I approached, and leaned against the wall smoking a pipe. He was frowsy and unwashed. From his striped apron and his shirt sleeves I judged he was the potman of the house.

The smell of beer got stronger as I came near. There was beer on my letter. I remembered that vividly. I had the envelope in my pocket and meant to make some use of it.

My friend in the stable had taught me how to look a man in the eye and size him up. 'Horse or man,' he said, 'look 'em straight in the eye and see how they strikes you.

That first look tells. Not the second or the third, don't trust to that, take the first.'

As I came up close I looked into this man's eyes as best I could, and behind the fatigue and the beer I saw a native shrewdness. Not a nice man, I thought, but not a man who would go too far wrong, because he would always know which side his bread was buttered. There are horses like that, too.

He continued to smoke calmly, not taking much apparent notice of me, beyond a glance. But I observed that his feet shuffled a few steps and the cat got up and moved away. I took the envelope from my pocket and held it out to him.

'Can you read?' I said. In my experience it was a necessary question with such as him.

'Happen,' he said, which I took to mean that he could read when it suited him.

'And write?'

'I can scrawl my monniker. What's it to you?'

'Did you write the name on this envelope? Do you know who did? Have you seen it before?' I let him see there was a coin in the other hand.

I had confused him with my rush of questions. He was not a quick thinker, and hard living and drink had slowed him even further. Still, he knew the chink of money with the best, and his gaze fell upon it, thoughtfully. I held out the envelope again. 'I think it smells of your beer,' I said.

'Tain't my beer,' he said slowly. ' 'Tis the Governor's, and all beer smells same.'

I waited, letting my money speak for itself. I thought he had seen the envelope before, and now remembered it. He was not quick enough to mask the look of recognition that had come into his eyes. A fat woman appeared at the door behind him and took up a pose.

'What you doing idling here, Jem, when there's pots wanting washing?'

Jem didn't answer at first, but took a puff or two of his pipe. Then he said, 'Lady here asking about this here written envelope.'

'Oh, is she, now?' She looked at me suspiciously. I was perfectly certain she had been listening all the time and had, indeed, watched me approach. She had appeared because there was a profit to be made. 'What is it to you, miss? And even more, what is it to us?'

'Well, not much, certainly,' I said, 'but something.' I smiled at her, the smile not meant to convey pleasure at the sight of her, but to let her know I had her measure. She smiled back. We understood each other thoroughly. 'I can't go home to my mistress without some information.' I told the lie deliberately and watched her face relax a little.

'Did I see old Rotten Potatoes carrying an envelope like that the other day? And didn't he slop his beer on it?'

'Something like it,' said Jem.

The woman turned to me, and held out her hand. 'There you are, then. Rotten Potatoes had it.'

I held on to my money. 'And who's Rotten Potatoes? And what a name! Why is he called that?'

'Eats 'em,' said Jem laconically. 'They comes cheaper that way.' He bared his teeth in a yellow smile. 'They needs to come very cheap indeed for Rotten Potatoes.'

'He's a poor man,' agreed the woman. 'Same as we all are.' She made it sound aggressive.

'He had money for beer,' I said.

'I dare say he was doing a little errand delivering a letter and that's how he earned the money for the beer. Indeed, I believe he mentioned as much. He can read, can Rotten Potatoes, and that's been worth a lot in money to him on and off.'

'Such a scholar like him,' sneered Jem. 'Can read, and write left-handed.'

I put my coin into her hand, which closed about it neatly and strongly. I drew my fingers away. She had seemed to cling on to them too, as if we might stick together for ever. 'Where is Rotten Potatoes now?' I asked.

'I couldn't tell you that, dear. Sleeps where he can, lives where he can, that's his way. Has to be. Ain't got the ready for no other life.'

'I shouldn't go looking for Rotty, if I was you,' Jem said. 'He ain't safe, he ain't.'

'Nevertheless, I'd like to see him.' I said firmly. 'Tell me where he can be found.'

They exchanged looks which I could read well enough; how much more money will she give us? I kept a tight hold on my purse. Once, in the country, a woman on the tramp tried to snatch my purse from me and I found then that my strength was quite equal to hers and my determination harder.

'Get back inside to your pots, Jem,' said the woman. 'We've wasted long enough with missy here.' Jem did not move, that is, his feet made a sort of token shuffle in the direction of the door, but he stayed where he was. The alley dog came prowling up and growled at Jem from a safe distance. I let another silver coin appear in my hand. 'He spent last night at the Casual Ward, I dessay.' She took the sixpence. 'He won't be there now, though. He usually starts to toddle this way when they turns 'em out of the Ward. Now that's the truth, more than that I can't say. He's pretty regular in his habits, give or take a day or two.'

'A day or two?' I questioned.

'A man ain't a machine, he ain't a clock or railway engine that must keep to a time, miss,' said Jem, with unconscious poetry.

I looked down Jockey Fields Passage. Even on this bright day it was gloomy. The children still played in the gutter and a woman carrying a box on her back approached from the distance. I could hear a baby crying. From a house nearby a man's voice rang out in anger and immediately a woman ran out into the Passage, her apron over her face, wailing. From an open window an old pair of boots was flung after her. She responded with a shower of curses. No one took any notice, least of all the dog, on whom one of the boots fell.

One hand still gripped my purse. I put up the other to brush a strand of hair from my face. For the first time the woman saw my hands clearly. She seized my wrist. 'Here, let me look.' She turned my hand over roughly and studied the palm. 'That's not the hand of a servant. You're no lady's maid. You're gentry.'

'Let me go.' I tried to draw my wrist away, but instead of releasing me, she seized the other and drew me closer to her. I was held to her breast so that I could see my own reflection in her eyes and smell her breath. She had a good grip on me, struggle as I might. Perhaps I was not as good at defending myself as I had thought.

'I'll have that purse off you first. That's fair payment. I don't owe nothing to one like you. Coming round here asking questions and lying.'

She put one hand on my purse. Then I reflected that, although large, she was flabby, and I put my elbows against her chest and pushed myself away.

'Bitch.' But her breath came in gusts, and she let go. I had all but winded her. A knife suddenly appeared in her hand.

I stepped back sharply. Jem had disappeared into the doorway. The children had stopped playing and had formed a hostile cluster across the Passage. The woman

67

carrying the box had put it down on the flagstones and stood watching expectantly.

I could scream, but no one would come. The Passage was indifferent and the world outside would find nothing to alarm it in a scream coming out of the alley.

I did not scream. I swung round, got my back firmly planted against the wall and confronted my attacker. I had seen a rat do this in the stables at the rectory and did not disdain to imitate. I clutched my purse in my right hand. It had a silver frame and would make a sharp weapon. 'There's no money in it,' I said to her. 'Do you think I would bring money down here? You've had all you will get.'

She was still out of breath. The cheeks of her fat face had gone a mottled red. 'Jem,' she called. He appeared silently in the door. But I had been right in thinking him a cautious man. He kept his distance. And I did not doubt that, if the matter should ever come under question, he would have seen nothing and heard nothing. I noticed that the ring of children had edged closer. I wondered if their part was entirely that of innocent spectators. They were quite silent. Then the woman with the box gave a laugh. It was the signal for action.

My enemy moved her hand up and I saw the knife glitter and then she rushed forward. At the same moment I moved myself, kicking at her shins with my stout country boots. Thank goodness for that provincial shoe-maker who put sturdy soles and stout toecaps before elegance. She staggered back with a yelp of pain. I almost felt sorry for her as I heard the crack of leather against bone.

She stood immobilised for a second, breathing deeply. I had hurt her twice now, and she was furiously angry. 'Jem,' she called, 'come here and hold her for me while I teach her a lesson.'

68

Jem shuffled forward, none to keen, as I could see. She had moved slightly to one side and in so doing had opened up a channel of escape for me. I saw that if I moved fast I could get behind her and be off. Ignominious, perhaps, but flight seemed a good idea. She saw the gap as soon as I did. 'Hurry up, Jem,' she said impatiently.

I moved, and she reached out a hand to grab me. But even as she did so, a rangy, snarling form leapt through the air, snapping and growling. The dog had joined in the fight. Her arm fell away. I darted round her, and was off up the Passage towards the street and escape.

No one followed or tried to stop me. I heard the dog barking loudly, then that too ceased. Near the road I paused for a moment to look back.

A man's figure was walking slowly down the Passage from the farther end. His face I was too far away to see, but something about his clothes, his walk and above all his bearing, made me stand there for a moment in surprise.

This was the man I had seen last night across the crowded room. A servant, my aunt had called him. He hadn't looked like a servant then, he did not look like one now. He strolled down the alley with the air of a master. I could see the oval of his face now, but not the expression in his eyes. He was hatless, which I suppose was the only thing that told of the servant. He seemed to be sightseeing, looking about him as he walked with a leisurely air. However, by his appearance he had halted the attack on me. In front of him, violence melted away.

I told myself I owed him a thanks. I might have escaped injury just now as much by his appearance as by the intervention of the dog. He looked an unusual saviour, I thought. There came a tug at my skirt. I looked down to see the dog pulling at my hem. I bent down to fondle his head. I was in a hurry but I could not ignore his plea. The smell of beef dripping and hot meat reminded me of what I could do. I went into the cooked-meat shop, where I bought him another meat pie. It seemed a small recompense for what he might have saved me from. I patted his rough head once again, and then jumped on an omnibus that had stopped to take on passengers. 'Good-bye, old boy,' I said.

We went extremely slowly. We lingered for a period at every stop where people were to be picked up, and then we pottered on. Sometimes we seemed to stop for no reason whatever that I could see. The driver explained the delay by saying that his horse was off his feed. It seemed to me the slowest journey there ever was. I began to dislike the slow horse, that might be hungry, or might just be lazy. If anyone could invent an alternative to the horse it would be very welcome.

I used the lull of the bus ride to tidy my appearance, which a quick glance in a mirror in the cook-shop had told me was dishevelled. I adjusted my hat and brushed my jacket, discovering as I did so a rent slashed through the jacket, lining and bodice. To my dismay I could see the gleam of my skin through the tear. I held my arm tightly across it, wondered what the cook-shop owner might have seen, and blushed.

I disembarked from the omnibus in a sober mood. I had not succeeded in tracking down either the writer of the letter or the deliverer of it. They might be the same person, and both might be Rotten Potatoes, whoever *he* was. I believed in Rotten Potatoes, even though I had not succeeded in meeting him. Rotten Potatoes had held the letter to me in his hand, had spilt his beer on it, and had delivered the missive to the house in Masham Square. He knew my name and where I was to be found. He might come calling again. I wasn't entirely sure I liked that thought.

I remembered then that, although I had not yet seen Rotten Potatoes, my aunt's maid, Emily Barlow, had received the letter from him, and would certainly know his face. I could talk to her. Full of this thought, I was walking briskly round the corner to Masham Square when I heard a rushing movement behind me and an excited bark.

The dog had caught up with me and followed me home. The omnibus had proceeded so slowly that it had been, I suppose, no trouble to him to trot behind. I looked down in dismay. I knew I could not find it in my heart to abandon him on the doorstep, and equally I flinched from taking him into the cool elegance of my aunt's house. The dog circled my feet, barking his pleasure at having found me. As I mounted the steps to the front door of Number Forty he leapt confidently beside me. He wagged his tail when I rang the bell. Behind us came the solemn clip-clop of a cab horse.

The door was opened by a very young, thin footman, the very one, I supposed, who had been crying in his bedroom at being forced to share his only luxury, his bed.

I picked up the dog and, clasping him in my arms, ran up the stairs. My poor aunt. Yesterday, Frank with an abandoned boy, today me with a lost dog. Nor could I hope to keep the immigrant secret, even if I persuaded him never to bark. The expression on the footman's face as we sped past convinced me that the arrival of another lost soul was not welcome to him, and that he would not hesitate to tell the appropriate authority.

My room was blessed with tall windows opening on to a tiny balcony. This balcony was a London garden in miniature, blooming with geraniums and lilies and roses, all in big pots. Except for the gardener who came once a day to water the pots, it was private and sheltered. I put the dog there, giving him a coat of mine to rest on, and held up a warning finger against barking. Thank heaven he was quick to learn, because no sooner had I closed the window behind him than there was a tap on the door.

I knew the knock. It had the little extra edge to it that only Emily Barlow's knuckles could achieve. It was the privileged servant's knock, with long years of training behind it. I knew, because I had never succeeded in training any of my country girls at the rectory to knock with quite that refined force.

Barlow was in the room at once. She never waited for a summons. (This was another of the assumptions behind her knock: that her employers were *never* in a state where she could not be let in. If she had found you standing on your head, naked, she would have acted, and so would *you*, that was the point, as if in Court dress.) She was carrying a large box. 'A dress for you to try on. M'Lady had it sent round from Madame Poitier just now. You're to try it on, and, if it fits you, to come down to her wearing it, straight away. She's waiting for you.'

'I've been out.' I was hurrying to get out of my jacket before she saw the knife cut.

'Yes, I know, miss,' she said briefly, kneeling down to help me with my skirt. 'But your aunt doesn't.'

'Oh, good.'

'Keep still, miss. Here, hold your arms up and let me slip this over ... You can't count on keeping your outings from her, though, Miss Errol.' She stood up and studied me. 'Well, you *do* look nice. You could be a beauty, miss, if you did yourself justice.'

There was a long pier-mirror between the windows, and I stared at my image. I saw a tall girl with smooth fair hair, wearing the prettiest dress she had ever worn in her life. In lavender and white, it kept within the colours of mourning, but it had a lightness of touch and a subtlety of cut that achieved distinction. I knew I had never looked so well in my life. Only my thick boots underneath spoilt the picture. Barlow saw me looking at these and smiled.

'Haven't you got anything lighter, Miss Errol? Wait a minute, I'll have a look.' She searched through my shoes and boots, with little cries of rejection, until she came to a pair of bronze kid slippers. 'These will do.'

'I'd forgotten those. Aunt Geraldine sent me them on my last birthday. They pinch rather.'

'Never mind. You can't stride around London as if it was the country, anyway, miss.' She fitted them on my feet and sat back on her heels. 'You aren't thinking of eloping, are you, miss?'

'No.' I'm sure my eyes were round with amazement, because she started to smile. 'Why do you say that?'

'Well, miss,' she was industriously tidying up, picking up the clothes I had taken off, and shaking them and hanging them up. 'There was that letter, then you keep going out. We've all noticed downstairs in the servants' hall, and it's a wonder they haven't noticed upstairs. I thought it must be a young man, for sure.'

So behind her stiff, black bosom beat a romantic heart. I felt touched and amused and, suddenly, much older and more worldly-wise than she, with all her London sophistication. 'No young man, no love affair.'

'I don't know whether to be disappointed or relieved, miss, to hear you say so. There's not been a bride in this house for such a long while. Not that all love affairs lead to weddings, no, indeed they don't, as you'll find out. Oh.' She had come across the slit in my jacket, and was staring at it in surprise. She held the garment out. 'This coat is past it for sure. You *have* cut it.'

'I had an accident,' I faltered. Through the balcony window I caught sight of a black nose and two bright

73

eyes. Another complication coming there, any minute, I thought.

'You had, indeed, and with something sharp, too.'

'Yes.' From where I stood I could see a tail beginning to wag. The dog was taking my mind off what I would say to Barlow. Suddenly I had too many problems. From being a girl without much to think about, I now had too much. I knew she wanted an answer. 'You saw the man who left the letter the day I arrived, didn't you? What did he look like?'

'Oh, he was a funny one. Dirty, dressed as if he slept in his clothes and with such a nasty, thin face on him. A man that'd come down in the world and would be going up again. Oh, I didn't like him at all.' She pursed her lips in a prim fashion. 'And the smell. It would have been quite frightening, but for the fact there is always a policeman in the square. I wonder the policeman did not arrest him. But I fancy that was how he came to give me the note. *Give* me, thrust it at me, I should say.'

'How came you to be the one to receive it, Barlow? For I take it the man did not come to the front door.'

'No, indeed. He would have got short shrift from Fletcher. Although I suppose Fletcher would have been obliged to take the note for you,' she conceded reluctantly. 'The way it was, I was just on my way out, when he pushed his hand out with the note and muttered your name. I suppose he was hanging about waiting for just such a chance to occur, not daring to try the door. I wonder the policeman did not take him.'

'Yes, you said that before.'

'Is it a lover, Miss Errol? I know young men use strange messengers.'

I shook my head. 'It's a family matter, Barlow.'

She flung up her hands. 'Say no more. For mysteries the

74

Maurices have all beat.' She was a privileged old servant, and said what she liked. 'But mind you, miss, if you are running a little mystery of your own, then your aunt will find out, and then we shall have a dance.' To herself she said, 'And she's got enough on her mind, my poor lady.' Still muttering, she smoothed my jacket and hung it up. 'Come along now, Miss Errol. They're waiting downstairs for you in the drawing room.'

'They? Who is there, then?' I questioned, as I prepared to follow her.

'You'll find out. That's another little mystery for you, then.'

She triumphed in her sally, and amusement carried her down the stairs and across the hall. She bore over her arm the skirt I had taken off, to sponge and brush it. 'For it's as dirty, miss, as if you'd rolled in it.'

I went into the drawing room, where Lady Geraldine awaited me. She was tapping her fingers gently on the table, which denoted impatience, but she had it under good control and no sign of it showed in the pleasant voice in which she conversed with her companion. I felt the censure, though, in the slight but perceptible delay before she agreed to notice me. 'Ah, Errol, my dear, there you are.' A little emphasis on the word 'there' underlined this displeasure.

Seated with her on the sofa was a small, dumpy, black-gowned lady. She had a plump, round face, a clear complexion and an air of energetic good health. When I knew her better (as I certainly came to do) I learnt that she had periods of diplomatic ill-health and that she gauged to a minute how to time them and what benefit to extract from them. When it suited her, however, she could be as tireless as a little pit pony.

Lady Geraldine introduced me with a pretty little show of formality. 'My niece, Errol Vesey.' I bowed, and held out a hand, which was taken and given a decisive press. 'Miss Craven.' Miss Craven, in her turn, nodded and smiled.

There was a distinct note of deference in my aunt's voice and so innocent was I of where real power lay in this new world I had entered that I expected to be introduced to a duchess, at least. Who was Miss Craven, I thought, to make Lady Geraldine so humble?

Miss Craven got about her business at once. 'And so, my dear, you speak and write French and German very nicely?'

'Italian too,' I said. 'Only not so well.'

'Italian will not be necessary.'

Lady Geraldine smiled benignly, as if she was delighted that Italian would not be necessary.

'I'm hoping to go to Italy next spring,' I said, although the thought of Italy had never entered my head until that moment. But who was Miss Craven to tell me whether my Italian (so painfully laboured at with my father's curate) was necessary or not?

Harriet Craven put her head on one side: she would have to think about that. She consulted a piece of paper in her hand. 'And you write beautifully, read music from sight, and sing a little.'

'My father thought every young woman should see Florence,' I said.

'Florence is a delightful city,' Miss Craven said politely. 'It has not so far come my way. My travels have, naturally, been almost entirely in Germany, and of course to Nice, we always go to Cimiez. I understand you are quite heart-whole, my dear? We have had some bad experiences, and it is necessary I should be quite sure. Lady Emily told us she was quite without attachments, and she married within three months.'

'How shocking,' I said. 'She was swept off her feet, I suppose.'

Harriet Craven looked at me in surprise, and my aunt coughed. 'The Queen would have had nothing against an engagement, provided she had not insisted on getting married,' said Miss Craven. 'Such a disturbance for the Queen, and as if a wait of two or three years could matter to a gal of twenty odd. We thought we were quite safe from nonsense of that sort.'

'The Queen ...?' I began and stopped. The Queen, I thought.

Miss Craven put her hands together, fingers pointed up as if in prayer; she smiled, seraphically. 'I am happy to tell you the Queen has chosen to appoint you a Maid of Honour.'

Silence fell on the room.

Miss Craven continued, still smiling. 'Her Majesty is convinced, from all she has heard, that you would suit her.'

The silence was prolonged.

'Dear Errol,' began Lady Geraldine, in a sort of flutter, so unlike her. 'Such an honour ...'

The words the cab driver had used this morning rose irresistibly to my lips. 'Good God Almighty,' I said.

Had I uttered these words aloud, as for a moment I supposed I had, then my career at Court might have ended before it properly began. But apparently I sat in dumb silence and the cry was in my own head. I know this, because presently my aunt said gently: 'Errol, say something.'

Then I spoke, and it came out in a pathetic little croak. 'I need time, I need time. Oh, please, I need time.' I thought of the future that had seemed to stretch in front of me, endlessly exciting because unguessable. I might

77

do anything or become anything. In a few words they had circumscribed me. 'I have so much to do, so much to become. I must have time to think.'

CHAPTER THREE

I was allowed three months. Three months in which to weigh up the magnificent offer and to say yes. It never seriously occurred to anyone that, in the end, I should say no. The Queen herself, it seemed, was unexpectedly sympathetic. She thought it a good idea that a young girl, straight from a retired country rectory (she little knew the wild intellectual doings we indulged in), should have a London season to get to know the world. Her comments were reported to me. 'We ourselves,' she is said to have remarked, wistfully, 'had no time of carefree girlhood at all, responsibilities descended upon us all *too* young. We know the evil of it. A girl should have a chance to enjoy the innocent pleasures and recreations of her sex, before she enters upon the sorrows and cares of matrimony.' A great sigh here. '*Then* all light-heartedness flies out of the door. Only after marriage do we know what real worry is.' Thus encouraged, I was to be sent out to enjoy a London season, before the shades of the prison house of life descended, a happy prospect. I got a most affectionate note saying that all was quite understood and that the Queen hoped to see me in the future. 'The Queen is really very reasonable,' said Lady Geraldine happily, 'when you can get at her directly. But this terrible practice of doing everything through a third person makes for trouble all the time. But I feel quite comfortable in my mind now.' The general opinion was that I was a very lucky young person. That was the phrase used, as I remember. Even my sex was denied me: a lucky young person I was called. So, carefully neutralised, I was to be let loose upon society on the tacit assumption that I was to attract no man and feel no attraction in my turn. I was in a nunnery, or as good as.

Lady Geraldine had recently started upon her four months out of waiting. If all went as she hoped, I would go into waiting at the end of that time under her wing. She had it all planned.

But although she proclaimed herself happy I could see she was not. She had a harassed, anxious air which sat upon her prosperous good looks uncomfortably. I remembered what Barlow had murmured about my aunt being changed.

A preliminary visit to Windsor to be introduced to the Queen before I took up waiting was decreed for me, in spite of my mutterings that I had not yet given my decision. I could not understand how the Queen had ever heard of me in the first place. Had I not been anonymous in my country home? What was Miss Errol Vesey to the Queen that she should have heard of her? I said as much to my aunt.

'Oh, our family have served the Court for generations,' she said quickly. 'And that weighs with the Queen. She likes to have people about her that she knows. And then, you see, she saw your photograph.' She stopped short.

I turned my head slowly and looked at her. 'Yes, she has taken an interest in me. I seem to be a much more interesting person than I had guessed.'

'Quite natural,' said Lady Geraldine uneasily. 'The Queen knew your grandmother when she was a girl. She drew a portrait of your mother. The Queen used to draw very nicely, you know, or at any rate, she enjoyed it. Of course, she wanted to see what you look like now you have grown up.'

'And what do I look like?'

'Charming,' said my aunt with a smile. 'Delightful. We all admire you very much.'

So I went away and looked in my mirror and was troubled. All girls want to be admired, but it seemed to me that my face was being studied for reasons I did not understand. I associated it with my mother, but yet I could not make my fears explicit. I thought if I listened and observed I might one day learn what it was all about. Meanwhile, I was girl enough to feel a little flattered that a Queen should interest herself in me, and that the élite of London society should want to stare at my face.

Because the quiet observation of me still went on, I was acute enough to notice it at the morning parties, the soirées, the receptions and the balls to which I was taken. After a bit I began to notice one other thing, too. The great ladies, although they were most friendly and gentle to me, welcoming even, were very careful to see that their sons did not dance with me too much, or even talk to me too long. At a ball I was invariably taken in to supper by some respectable elderly stick. Well, I was not rich, indeed, I had hardly a penny, but, still, their caution seemed excessive.

I gradually became convinced that, although I was an object of interest and possibly of admiration too, I was also a little feared.

And this, as you may suppose, made me ask exactly what my mother had been like. As I waltzed and walked and gossiped my way through the London season, I asked myself this question. I asked my aunt. I chose the occasion of the long-heralded drive to Windsor. Frank had been gone three weeks. 'What *was* my mother really like?'

'The greatest beauty imaginable,' she replied promptly, 'and the greatest dear. We all adored her.'

'But you were much younger. She was grown up when you were still in the schoolroom.'

'Not so much younger,' she said. 'Not so young I couldn't perceive her brilliance. She was made for the world, really, and that was why it seemed so sad when ...' She paused, and then said, 'When she shut herself up in a country rectory ... I mean no criticism of your father,' she apologised. 'He loved her always.'

I said: 'You don't think there might have been a reason?' I waited to see what she said.

Lady Geraldine looked out of the window. The towers of the castle were visible in the distance. 'There was,' she said. 'Love.' She turned to me with a smile. 'Love.'

And that was all I got out of her. Then.

We approached Windsor down a long lane of trees, heavy with summer leaves. I leaned back in my seat and enjoyed the prospect. There across the river was a vista of grey towers and battlements, unexpectedly solid, no touch of whimsy, not a fairy-tale castle at all, but unmistakably the home of sovereigns, a place where kings had lived for eight hundred years.

'We could have gone by train,' said my aunt. 'It takes longer this way, but the Queen is so fussy about the Household. Men may go by train, the ladies must, if possible, come from London in a carriage. Goodness knows why. I expect it was a rule laid down by the Prince Consort the year they were married.' She sneezed. 'Oh, dear me. The sneezing I've been afflicted with lately, you'd think we had a dog in the house. I'm so sensitive to that sort of thing. Fortunately I've got used to the Queen's dogs.'

I picked a rough, ginger hair off my skirt, and allowed

no expression to appear on my face.

I had solved my problem with the dog and solved it brilliantly, it seemed to me. Meeting with Frank's boy on the stairs, I decided that two strays could befriend each other. I gave the boy a half-crown and told him where the dog was. He was to feed, exercise and keep the animal safe. I suppose it meant the young footman now shared his bed with the two of them, but I would worry about that later. No doubt I had an enemy there.

But in the boy I had made a friend. I knew his name now and it was Harry. We had struck up a bargain. He was to look after the dog and I was to pay him. Not in money. He wanted payment in another form. He was a tidy figure by now, in a pair of neat trousers and a dark jacket. I had never seen him, of course, in his unregenerate days, when Frank had first brought him home. I suspect I might have seen a wilder figure. Now he seemed reasonably content. 'Plenty to eat and drink in the kitchen,' he told me with a confident little nod of his head. 'And they're pleasant enough to me, all except Alfred.' Alfred was the young footman. 'And I 'elps with the odd job or two, but they don't want me down there.' He was living in an interregnum, waiting for Frank to get back to decide his fate and dispose of him. But he had plans himself. He told me about them as we walked in the garden. This was where we met. Rules and protocol governed where we might meet in the house in Masham Square, so that it was by no means as straightforward as you might suppose. He could not go into the drawing room and I could not ascend to the attics. We were both free to walk in the garden, although it was as well for him not to show himself too obviously. The first rule of all people like Harry was to be invisible except when wanted. Even Fletcher and Barlow were meant to appear and disappear like puppets on a string. (Except that you

83

knew both those strong characters pulled the strings themselves.) In keeping with this impossible rule, housemaids must never be seen brushing the stairs, or polishing the brass, or laying the table or performing any of the tasks that were performed daily. If we, the privileged, did catch sight of them at any of these duties, and, really, it was impossible not to sometimes, then we had to pretend they were not there. That was our part of the game, the best part you might think. In the country, at the rectory, we had behaved more naturally and not kept to this fiction, but at Masham Square the old rules still held, imposed by servant and mistress alike.

So Harry and I walked a secluded path in the garden behind the house. On one side was the mews, on the other the coachman's cottage, and over all the strong smell of horse. One of the things I noticed most about London that summer was the smell of horses. Over the scent of flowers, the smell of the lime trees, the scents of humanity, was always and for ever the smell of horse, acrid and strong.

Harry and I met on equal terms, I'm not quite sure how, but he established that quite clearly from the start. Part of his secret was that he seemed to take everything very calmly. He had, of course, one way and another, seen a good deal of the world. And a pretty rum world it had been, too. He gave me illuminating little glimpses into it.

'Haven't had a beating since I got here,' he said happily. 'And they know about the dog, don't think they don't. But they're turning a blind eye. That's clever, that is, saves trouble and don't do no harm. That's what eddication does for you. I mean to get some myself.' He spoke as if it was a commodity you could parcel up and sell at so much a pound. He explained further: 'A bit of book learning never does no harm. I'll put it up to Mr

Maurice when he gets back. He's took me up, I reckon he won't let me down. He's a top, he is.'

'You seem to understand him.' I was amused. Short-lived amusement.

'Oh yes, I knows Mr Frank well. Decent he has been, many a time, to me. Not a regular, of course, he wasn't.'

'Oh no, of course not,' I breathed.

'No, he wasn't. Not one of your regulars, straight up-and-downers.' I stared. 'He couldn't be, Mum said.' The boy laughed jovially. 'He wasn't far adrift, mind, but one to be considered, oh yes, indeed. Yes, you had to consider his tack, Mum said.'

I realised that I was looking at all knowledge, all depravity, and yet combined with such innocence and good will that evil melted away. He knew and had seen everything, and yet was untouched. I wanted to cry.

Instead, I said: 'I'll teach you.'

His face became red with pleasure. 'You will? To read, to write and to add up? I must be their master, you know? Can you do it?'

I nodded. I had taught in the village school since I was sixteen years old, and knew all there was about getting the rudiments of elementary education into dull heads. Harry's head, I would guess, was far from dull.

The bargain struck, we got down to work straight away. I set up a regular routine, so much each day of reading, writing and arithmetic. I would teach him, making every lesson a new step forward, and then he would take away work to prepare. As I had thought, he had a quick mind, but what was new to him was regularity in anything. His way of life had been spontaneous and unregulated. The idea of discipline, of self-discipline even more, was novel and at first alien to him. This was where I could teach him. What any ordinary public-school boy had, he lacked. How I wished I could find him a place in a school like Rugby or Charterhouse. But it was not to be hoped that Frank's patronage would go so far. I dared not think that he would do much for the boy beyond what he had. An apprenticeship in a respectable trade to a good master was the utmost that could be hoped for. We met always in the garden, sitting to work on a rough bench contrived by Harry's clever hands. Fortunately the weather continued fine and hot. Had it rained we should have had to find another home. In the stables, possibly, with the horses. The dog already lived there, having been set up in a kennel by Harry with the help of a friendly stable boy.

'Have you ever heard of someone called Rotten Potatoes?' I asked, over one day's ration of *Easy Arithmetic, Book One*.

He shook his head. 'Plenty of people have nicknames,' he said. 'But they change 'em round. Might be Rotten Potatoes in one street and Strong Boots in another.'

His comment confirmed me in my belief that the London poor found anonymity convenient. After all, they did not live on the same terms of amity with the police as the rest of us.

'I'd like to find him. Or at least, learn where he could be found. He seems to be known in Jockey Fields Passage.'

He sat back from his task and studied my face. 'The Passage, eh? Want me to look? I'm good at finding people. Didn't I find my mum when she scarpered? Could have found her this time, only she had it fixed. Locked me in. Lucky for me Mr Frank had a key, weren't it?'

So Frank had a key. I could just see Frank adding the key to his ring with a little air of mystery, being careful not to distinguish it from the other keys, and yet always keeping the knowledge of it in a little, buttoned-up pocket of his mind. The information extended my picture of Frank, and made it a touch less comfortable.

'If you could help me get on the track of Rotten Potatoes, I would be grateful,' I said carefully. 'But it would
have to be done quietly, and kept a secret between you
and me.' I said it with some shame. I was conscious of
using the boy for my own ends, and in this found myself
a little bit too much like my cousin Frank for my own
comfort.

'Tell me.' His face was bright and keen. He *wanted* to
be used, that made it more shaming.

'I think he was given money to bring a letter to me.'
I left it at that. From the look in Harry's eyes I could see
a fanciful imagination was already at work. I did not
enquire during the next days what he was doing, but from
his manner I guessed he was at the search. He came and
went as he liked, no one seemed to exercise much control
over him. Once I saw him disappearing round the corner,
the dog at his heels.

Our conversations kept strictly to matters of learning,
he was discretion itself and never mentioned his mission
aloud. At the end of the first week, he asked one question.
'This Rotten Potatoes, was he once a schoolmaster?'

'Yes,' I said slowly. 'It is possible he may have been
once.'

'Then I think I'm on to him,' he answered, and said no
more that day.

But on the next day he brought the subject up again.

'I've found a cove that knows of Rotten Potatoes. If it's
the same feller.'

'There can't be two, I think.'

'So says I. Not hanging about Jockey Fields Passage. But
Rotten Potatoes hasn't been seen about the Passage lately.
Seems he's avoiding it. There was a murder done there,
y'see, and Rotten Potatoes doesn't like the place.'

'So we are really no nearer finding him?'

'I don't say that,' he said mysteriously.

'Perhaps we should give up the search.' There had been no further letters, no overt sign of a threat from my half-brother. If the letter had indeed been from him.

'We shall have him if you want him.' He sounded confident.

'I wonder if I really do.' Suddenly it seemed a dangerous and unwise quest. Why was I bothering with a man like Rotten Potatoes?

The next day the boy came in with a strange story. He had gone to the place where he was to meet his informant and found him not there. This in itself did not surprise him. His friends and acquaintances, not having expensive watches and clocks among their possessions, were bad time-keepers. He was used to waiting and never found it much trouble to sit there in dreamy contemplation of the world. 'You learns to hang around,' he said, terribly summing up his previous life.

On this occasion, having in his pocket an arithmetical table which I had set down on a piece of paper ready for him to learn, he found the time passed pleasantly fast. He heard a nearby church clock chime the hour. Then the half-hour. Still he was patient. But when he had the table thoroughly learnt, he did begin to think he had been there long enough.

There were plenty of people around in the busy open market where he and his crony had arranged to meet, but nowhere could he see Joseph, a boy of about fifteen, working as a porter in the big hospital not a hundred yards away. Harry was disappointed, but philosophical. Joseph had not been able to get away from his work. Or he had forgotten. Or he had decided not to bother. Harry was used to his world's caprices and changes of mind, and he knew where to find Joseph if he wanted him. He decided to come back to Masham Square, where he and I had an appointment to meet in any case. He had been sitting on a pile of vegetable boxes, not much noticed by anyone apparently. He made his way slowly through the market, passing a stall where the market workers were drinking tea and smoking, when he heard a soft whisper.

'Harry!' He turned to listen. There it was again. 'Harry!' He looked about but could see nobody who seemed to be talking to him. Then he realised that behind the stall was the mouth of a narrow alley. He walked over.

'Harry, old codger, I've been on the look out for you to pass. I've been watching you sit there, and waiting for you to get a move on.'

It was his friend Joseph. He drew Harry into the alley. 'I dursn't come out and meet you. Look at me.'

There was a livid bruise down one side of Joseph's face and the eye that same side was black and swollen.

'Who did that to you?'

Joseph shook his head. 'I dunno. I was set on on the way to work and hit something shocking.' He drew in a painful breath and coughed.

'You won't die of it, Joe?' asked Harry anxiously.

'No.' A shake of the head and a wince. 'The doctor at the Casualty patched me up. I told him a dray hit me. But it weren't true. I was deliberately set on. And I think it was about your business, young Harry.'

'How's that, then?'

'Because I've been living as quiet as a mouse, not doing nothing out of the way. There ain't nothing I've done that's out of my common run more than talk to you.'

The two boys eyed each other. They knew the strange violences of their world. It was easy to fall into trouble.

'Could have been by accident. Not meant for you,' suggested Harry.

'Don't believe it. I was hit with a stick about the face and he beat my ribs. He saw my face clear.'

Harry asked the crucial question. 'And did you see him?'

There was a pause. 'I can't say,' said Joseph evasively. 'But I come here to warn you to give over looking for Rotten Potatoes. It won't do.'

'It was kind of you to come and tell me,' said Harry. He recognised a well-meant act when he met one.

'You and I have always been friends, young Harry,' said Joseph awkwardly. 'You've gone out of my way now, I think. But I wish you well.'

'He knows where I am living at this moment,' Harry explained to me as he told the story. 'But he won't take advantage of it, Joe won't. He's a good sort, as has kept himself since he was ten years old.'

'How old are you, Harry?' I asked absently. It was a question which had puzzled me. He looked young and slight, but he had a mature way with him.

He shrugged. 'She was never sure. Sometimes she said one thing, sometimes another. I can remember back to the year the *Furious* sunk. I remember the newsboys crying it in the streets. I wasn't but a little nipper then.'

'I remember that too. It was ten years ago.' So he was probably about twelve. 'I'm sorry if I got your friend into trouble. We'd better drop the search for Rotten Potatoes. Now let's get back to work.'

The next day we did not meet. I was all day at the Chelsea Flower Show with my aunt, glorying in roses and azaleas and camellias.

On the day after he came to me, in tears, which he struggled to control, to tell me he had heard a story that his friend Joseph had been picked up out of the river, drowned, and now lay on a mortuary slab in the hospital where he had worked.

'If it's true,' he sobbed, 'then Joe didn't do it to himself and it was no accident either. He was drowned on purpose.'

'But that would be murder,' I said. A cold, horrified feeling was moving inside me. I told myself that people like Harry turned naturally to thoughts of murder and violence, inventing them even when they did not exist. But I knew I had found Harry reasonable and sensible, not at all given to flights of the imagination. He was rather inclined to see the world coolly and clearly. I could by no means discount his feeling.

What seemed to distress him as much as anything was that he had no way of checking on this story. He had tried at the hospital and no one would answer his questions.

I stood up and put my hand on his shoulder. 'We can do something about that at least.'

'You'll come with me? We'll go and look at him together?' Beneath my touch I could feel him tremble.

I hesitated. It had not been my intention to look at the body of the drowned boy, only to ask questions of the doctors, but I could not draw back now. 'I'll come with you. But first we will visit someone who may help us.'

I meant Jessie, Jessie Falconet, of course.

Jessie had the great gift of never letting you down and always being there when you wanted her. No virtue can be greater in a friend.

Because we were in a hurry we went by cab. I reflected that travelling about London was using up my small reserve of money rapidly. The sight of Coutts' Bank through the cab window as we hurried past reminded me that I had some money there, and that I had better find out exactly what was at my disposal. That one must cut one's coat according to one's cloth is an old truism, but one I meant to use. I would buy nothing on credit. I knew a girl in Suffolk who ran up such a bill at her dressmakers and milliners that by the time she married it was as long as her arm, and the dressmaker sent it to her rolled up in a wedding favour, so that it arrived on her wedding morning. She wept all the way to the altar as a consequence and the bill was the occasion of the very first quarrel between her and her husband. He was a stern young man and he would neither pay the bill himself nor send it to her father, but forced her to pay it herself out of her marriage settlements. She went on to have six sons. All in all, a dangerous example, and not one to be followed.

The boy's pleasure at the treat of a cab ride, politely repressed because of the seriousness of the occasion, but manifested in a brightness of eye and an alertness he could not hide, made the fare worth while.

Jessie was at the door talking to her landlady as we approached. She was wearing a dark cloak and carrying a bag. 'Right, Mrs Besant,' I heard her say. 'A-pamphleteering we will go. Together to prison if necessary.' She sounded quite jolly.

We hurried up. 'I've just caught you,' I said.

'Come and join me while I breakfast.' She moved forward briskly.

'Breakfast? At almost four o'clock in the afternoon!'

'When you have eaten nothing since seven yesterday evening, then it's breakfast. But we will call it tea or dinner, if you please.' She was in a grimly humorous mood. 'Saved a mother and twins last night. They are little mites, but healthy. Who's the boy?'

He went up to her politely to carry her bag. 'I'm Harry.'

She gently pushed him aside. 'No, no. I can manage. Harry, is it?' She turned to me. 'Nice manners your little friend has.' I nodded. Barlow, no lover of children, had already confided to me, albeit reluctantly, that Harry was, to use her phrase, 'one of Nature's gentlemen'.

The black kitten, now a little larger, darted across our path at this point, and while Harry fondled it and teased it, I took advantage of the distraction to explain to Jessie who he was.

Her eyebrows were raised and she shook her head slightly. 'Such children ought not to be born. A just society would not allow it.'

'He's here now, Jessie. Clever and ready to make a life for himself. He's a bit unhappy at the moment.' I hesitated for a moment, then said : 'Can we go upstairs and I will talk to you as you eat your breakfast, but be quick over it, will you?'

'You want your friend Jessie's advice, do you?' Her large, dark eyes were fixed on me with that strange, sad look which they had sometimes and which, to tell you the truth, worried me about Jessie, suggesting, as they did, a world and a sadness of which I knew nothing. At such times she was always sharpest against the human race and particularly men. 'You remember the drawing of the baby I showed you?' She nodded. Of course she remembered. Jessie always remembered everything. If she forgot, it was because she wished to. I had long observed this fact about her. 'I believe, yes, I believe that it was a picture of my brother.'

Her eyes opened wide. 'Now I understand.'

'What do you understand? Tell me, what is it you understand?'

'Why my father called yours a saint. But said the only woman who could have deserved him was your mother.'

There must indeed have been some strong cause to call such a comment out of that remarkably stiff old stick, her father. My aunt always spoke of him as if he had been a paragon of wit and learning, but by the time I saw

93

him he was a quiet, dryly spoken man with sharp black eyes. He had died suddenly while staring at Raphael's great fresco of the pagan philosophers in the Vatican, leaving Jessie very well off. She had stayed in Europe, assuring me, however, that she would go home at last. It seems she saw a more fruitful field for her work over here, the European working class and the European working woman in particular being more in need of Jessie's own particular brand of help than the women where she came from. I think she did, indeed, see herself as stretching out a hand to the labouring classes, and who am I to say that she did not? I knew that my father and my aunt did not take Jessie and her activities wholly seriously, believing, in their conservative way, that no woman brought up as she had been, and with her birth, could possibly be as revolutionary as she claimed, holding it, really, no more than an aristocratic whim, like the Duchess of Devonshire kissing the butcher. A whim persevered in, more to *épater le bourgeois* than from any deep-seated belief. But I, more nearly Jessie's contemporary, and much closer to her, believed absolutely in her serious intent. I remembered my father saying that Rousseau had been the solvent of what he called the 'old society'. I thought Jessie might be such a solvent for the nineteenth century. But it was no use expecting people like Frank and my father to see this: they would never believe that a woman might be a danger. Jessie could always gather about her people of like mind. How she found them, I don't know, but wherever she moved she always fell into a nest of them. I suppose one such contact led to another. If you are interested in growing roses you will always find another person who is interested in growing roses. Jessie was interested in changing society and so she kept a look out for others of like mind. Her landlady, Mrs Besant, was one. I saw that much.

All the time we were talking, Jessie was despatching a healthy breakfast of eggs and bread and butter and coffee. She had boiled the eggs and made the coffee herself.

'Mrs B can't cook, you know, no hand at it at all.' She was as brisk and masculine about it as Frank himself might have been. 'Butter the bread, Harry, and you shall have an egg. Coffee? With sugar? Oh, you proper little Englishman.'

'I have seen you take sugar yourself, Jessie,' I protested.

'Never mind,' she said with a radiant smile. 'Let him know what he is. You can do nothing more useful to him.'

'What are you then, miss?' asked Harry, sitting down to his egg.

'American.' She threw an egg in the air and caught it. 'As American as cranberries and turkey.'

'And tobacco,' I said slyly.

While she smoked and Harry ate, we talked, and I told her all I knew.

'So that's the story?' She nodded. 'I knew there was one. I could tell from your face and your manner.' She whistled when I told her about Jockey Fields Passage. 'You could soon be in trouble down there, my girl.'

'It's a strange place.'

'Strange?' She shrugged. 'A regular thieves' kitchen. Professionals, the lot of them. But from all I've heard, not always so quick to violence as you found them. You must have frightened them in some way.'

Jessie probed my motives. 'Errol, why do you want to find your brother? From all accounts he would be better left unfound.'

I hesitated and then honesty would have its voice. 'Curiosity: I must admit that is a factor.... And then, I want to help him. He is my brother.'

Jessie threw up her hands. 'I hardly know which motive is the more dangerous.' Then she smiled, that

95

smile which always won my heart. 'But, if you want help, I am your woman.'

Harry had finished his egg by the time I got to the story of Joseph, and was sitting looking at Jessie with a serious face. He seemed to regard her as a woman of power, which she was.

When I had done, Jessie stood up and reached for her old black cloak, which she draped with a swagger round her shoulders. 'You were right to come to me. I am known at that hospital and can help you.' She held out a hand. 'Come, I can show you a quick cut across what once were fields. We can walk it.'

She talked rapidly and cheerfully as we marched along. I suspected her of working to take our companion's mind off what lay ahead of him. All the same, he got quieter and quieter as we drew nearer the hospital and by the time it was in sight and we were walking up to the main door, he had fallen absolutely silent. So too had I.

Jessie left us at the entrance. 'Wait here for me.' We sat side by side on a wooden bench, not daring to move, not wishing to speak.

In a very short time she was back, and with her a short, tubby young man wearing a formal dark suit. From the shabby, battered appearance of the suit and the young man's youthful, anxious manner, I had no difficulty in identifying him as a medical student, now 'walking the wards'.

'Mr Jones,' said Jessie briefly. 'He will take us where we want to go.'

Mr Jones cast a harassed look at Harry and me. Quite clearly he was under Jessie's thrall, and equally clearly he would have been glad not to do her bidding. He turned to me for deliverance.

'Not the place for a lady,' he panted. (We were all

hurrying after Jessie.) 'Not the place for a lady or a child.'

I did not answer.

'Oh, very well,' he went on. 'But remember what I said. Do you have any smelling salts about you?'

'No, why?'

'Oh, you'll see.' And he subsided into silence. Our party strode through long corridors, past doors which swung open to show glimpses of beds ranged along the walls of narrow wards. We passed out of the main building and crossed a courtyard and then a small garden where a few sad roses tried to bloom. Ahead lay a low building with few windows.

Mr Jones unlocked the door. I soon understood what he meant about the smelling salts. There was a strong smell of carbolic, but underneath was another smell that went in at the nostrils and straight down to the stomach. I met Jessie's eyes. 'Oh, I deal in life and death,' she said, and did not change colour.

Nor, for that matter, did the boy, but his face was always London pale. He pressed sturdily forward. I lagged behind a little. But it was because of this that I observed what I did.

A shrouded table was unveiled. Yes, this was it. I heard Harry suck in his breath and make a little cry, at once muted. He hardly needed to say that he had recognised his friend. Jessie kept quiet, just studied the boy. I gave one quick glance, then let my eyes fall away. I was still standing a little to the rear.

In that one quick look I had seen a thin spare frame, a boy taller and bigger than Harry, but still lean and slight. Without being told, you knew he had not come to his full growth. Now, he never would.

As I stood there with head down, words were filtering through to me. Jessie's voice, clear and dominating. I had never noticed before how dominating, and how like

97

her father's. When you looked at her you were swept away by the enthusiasm and the sharp intelligence, but her voice, listened to alone, was full of cadences and subtleties that enriched. How much more there was in her than I could understand.

'Well, Mr Jones, how did the boy die? Tell us that.'

'He drowned.' A gentle Welsh voice. 'There are facial bruises, and bruises on the body. But done well before death.'

'Yes, but why did he drown?'

Mr Jones sighed. 'How can I say, ma'am? He jumped or fell. It goes in seasons with us on the Thames. Sometimes such bodies are ten a penny, ten a penny. One follows another and you never know why so quick.'

'Joseph could not swim,' said Harry in a low voice.

'And, therefore, you see, ma'am, if he fell in he could not have saved himself.'

'And therefore on that account he never went near water,' said Harry.

There was dead silence. My gaze took in the next table. A sheet covered the face, but one hand fell forward and could be seen. A man's hand, dirty and stained, but delicately made. It was a left hand, and on the middle finger of that hand was a 'writer's bump', the mark of someone who had often used a pen or pencil. A left-handed writer lay on this table.

'Where was Joe found, Mr Jones?' It was my own voice, speaking quietly.

'South. Towards Deptford. They both were, the two you see here. But the boatman brought them up here because he was coming this far. A strange journey he must have had of it, but there, they are used to it, these men. It's almost a trade with them.'

I could not repress a shudder.

'That shows then,' said Harry triumphantly, 'Joe never

98

went towards that district in his life. He had no call to go. Least of all near the river.'

'No accounting for it. Ten a penny, as I said. I declare, ma'am, the river is prodigal at times. And the bodies move with the river.' He cast round for evidence to support himself. 'Now, take for instance this man on the next table. He was brought in with the lad. The same waterman picked 'em both up. That's how strange a river and its currents are. To bring in two men who presumably never saw each other in their lives, but were so close together when they were found that their hands might have been bound together. Now, that's a strange thing, isn't it? And it proves that you can go in the river where you will and it brings you together and casts you up as it chooses.' The river seemed a living force in Mr Jones's life. No doubt it was. 'I see a lot of the drowned,' he said heavily.

There was dead silence. Perhaps he had seen too many. But I broke the silence, my voice rough and unsteady: 'May I see the face of this other man?' The drapery was drawn back to the chin of a sallow-skinned face, heavy and black of beard. The face was lined and marked with signs of hard living. In life he had not been a good man, or a friendly man, or an innocent man. But neither had he been a labourer. Behind the veil which the blurring fingers of dissolution had passed over it, the features still bore traces of refinement and breeding, even.

'He lived hard, ma'am,' said Mr Jones. 'He did, indeed. But the river knows its own.' He covered the face again with gentle hands. A disquieting man behind a placid exterior. Perhaps he feared he might be one of the river's own. I turned my thoughts away sharply.

'Is his name known?'

'It is possible it will be,' he said politely, 'for some things were found in his pocket. See, there is a list of them attached to the table. And among them was a notebook.

99

I believe there was an address in it.'

'Do you know what it was? Could you find out?'

'Do you think you know him, ma'am?'

'Yes,' I said. 'That is, I can guess, and if I am right, you have given us terrible proof that the boy was killed.'

Rotten Potatoes, I thought. Dead. Did I say these words aloud? I believe I did, because Jessie, Harry and Mr Jones were suddenly staring at me in deep surprise.

'The objects found in the pockets of both men are over here.' Mr Jones led the way to a table by a window. Spread out on a tray to dry were two carefully separated groups of objects. One set had come from Joseph's poverty-stricken pockets and comprised a little leather purse which looked empty, a piece of rag and a dirty handker-chief. From Rotten Potatoes' pockets had come a key, a few pennies, a spotted neckerchief and a book like a pocket diary.

'You can read the address on the flyleaf,' Mr Jones said. 'The police will already have been there,' he remarked as he handed it over. His jaw moved nervously. He thought me, I saw, a touch unnatural, as I did him. We both knew too much, and we knew it in the wrong kind of way. Where did it come from, this sudden knowledge of mine that this dead man was Rotten Potatoes? It was my first experience of a process outside the rational habits of thought my father had taught, far removed indeed from any ways of knowing he believed in. I shrank from it a little as from a malformation of the mind.

'Twelve Dryden Street,' I said aloud. On the flyleaf of the diary, beside the address, was written the name Tom Perry. And facing it, on the opposite page, was the word 'King'. As far as I could see, the rest of the book was blank.

The address meant nothing to me, and not much, either, to Harry. 'Dryden Street, where's that?' he asked.

'I understand it is near Seven Dials,' said Mr Jones.

'I know of it,' said Jessie. 'An ordinary enough little street.' By which she meant, I supposed, that it was not like Jockey Fields Passage. 'Poorish. A poor street.'

We had satisfied part of Harry's query about his friend, only to confirm the rest of his alarm. Joseph was indeed dead, but how he had drowned and in what circumstances was the sinister question which now pressed upon us.

The day was hot and sunny, a brilliant June day, but we stood close together as we emerged from the hospital, as if seeking warmth. Mr Jones parted from us with clear relief. One way and another, we had been more than he bargained for. Me particularly he was glad to see go, because between him and me there had been, willynilly, a horrid, mutual cry of communication and pain. Smelling salts, I thought; it was beyond being a matter smelling salts could remedy.

Dryden Street, when we came to it, was exactly as Jessie had described it. The house we had been directed to was a tidy lodging house. Jessie made the enquiries, Harry and I standing behind her, listening. She received the answer the police enquirer must have got earlier that day.

'No, no one was missing from this house, and no man like the man found drowned had ever been known there.'

We were not permitted to go into the house. The proprietor of the lodgings stood on the doorstep and barred the way. He had had enough, he let us know from his manner, from the police. Such enquiries did an honest man no good. Every hair on his beard was abristle with his honesty. Only his eyes blinked nervously. I thought him a liar.

'Do you have a Mr King living here?' I asked.

He was taken aback, and for a moment did not know what to answer. He shook his head. Then his reputation for honesty, reluctantly remembered by him, came to my rescue. 'No, but we've got a Mr Koenig. That's near enough for it, I suppose. Only he ain't drowned. I saw him myself, this morning.'

'Where is he now?'

'I don't ask my gentlemen where they're going. That's not the way to conduct my business.' He laughed jovially. 'I dessay as he's gone to get crowned. "Koenig" is German for "King", isn't it?' And he continued to rumble with laughter at his own wit, then straightened his face and said: 'He's servant to a foreign gentleman, and only lodges here in the season.'

We walked back through the crowded streets, and it seemed to me that the dark alleys had poured out all their inhabitants and that they were walking about with the rest of us. There were the maimed, the deformed, the poverty-stricken, the depraved, walking along with the shoppers, and it was their world too.

'A bleak world, is it not, my darling?' said Jessie. 'And infinitely more complicated than you suspected in your country parsonage.'

I came back to the present as the carriage swung down Eton High Street. Groups of College boys were strolling towards the bridge over the river. Others could be seen clustering around what looked like a remarkably well-stocked baker's and cooked meats shop. To my amusement I saw one boy, silk hat on head, carrying a large covered dish down the crowded street, gravy spilling as he ran.

I leaned back in the carriage with a smile. 'Boys and their appetites,' I thought. I remembered my father saying that he had been proud to serve his own fag-master, a 'real swell', who never counted the strawberries left in the tub, or the sausages on the platter. Forty years and more since, my father had been the black-clad figure hurrying down the street, carrying a dish of hot food from Webber's for Lord Ponsonby's supper. A little contraction of sorrow squeezed a muscle inside me, and then relaxed.

'We were invited to dine and sleep,' said my aunt, as Windsor Castle grew nearer. 'But I got the permission of the Queen to drive back to London tonight. We shall be very late, but I expect Frank back any minute. Just smooth out that bow on your dress, dear. That's better. Considering how plainly she dresses herself, the Queen has an eagle eye. Wear the same dress too often and you hear about it.'

'I shan't like that.'

'Oh, there's a good side to it. The Queen can be very generous. She has ways of giving little presents. And the Princesses, of course, can be kindness itself. I forgot to ask if you are good at acting? Well, it's really of no account, neither are they. But they do a good deal of it, all the same. Tableaux, mostly. You can't expect them to learn any lines. If there is anything like that needed, you will have to do it. In fact, in general, dear, all the boring bits are done by you.'

'How unattractive you make it sound,' I observed.

'One takes the rough with the smooth. And all in all there is much that is pleasant. And a good deal that is downright enjoyable. The Queen is the least of your worries, my dear. She is really very easy. Once you get to know her ways,' she added.

We had passed the soldiers on guard, and been saluted by the policeman, who appeared to know my companion well. She asked after his wife and the new baby and was given reassuring news of both.

As we drove through the gateway and towards the entrance the Household used, I saw a group of Eton boys strolling on the terrace. They were behaving in a quiet, polite way, but I was surprised to see them.

'Oh yes, they have the privilege,' said my aunt, as we alighted. 'Thank you, Brewster. We shall be leaving about eleven. Have the carriage round by that time. Oh yes, it is an old Etonian right that they delight in. Especially as it is out of school bounds and therefore presents certain difficulties, you know, which add to the spice of it.'

'You mean it is forbidden for them to walk here, but once here it is allowed?'

'Droll, is it not? But it is all arranged by a splendid Eton invention called shirking. Frank told me all about it. So simple. If you were caught out of bounds and saw a master approaching, then all you had to do was 'to shirk', which might be done by stepping aside into a shop or the gutter. The master was not supposed to see you, and so you were safe. Frank has shirked ever since. At every difficulty that has come his way he has simply stepped aside.' She gave a huge sigh, gathered up her skirts with one hand, waved me forward with the other and before I knew it I was inside the Castle.

It was very quiet, and it smelt of the centuries, as if the windows had been opened, but never quite far enough. There was a constant stale sweetness on the air, made up, I decided later, of beeswax scented with lavender and old pot pourri. Perhaps it was just my imagination, but I thought of it always afterwards as the 'Windsor smell'. We were led down a long corridor to a small drawing room. Or possibly it seemed small because there were a number of people in it. Miss Craven I already knew. The others I came to know. Lady Waterperry, Mrs Monk, a friend of my mother's, she told me, Sir James Henderson and Sir Alfred Large. A little alarming the latter two were at a first glance, but I came to know and appreciate their softer side. After a very few minutes' conversation we withdrew to the corridor by the Queen's private apartments to wait for her. There were other guests, an elderly

clergyman and his wife. He was of such a nervous dis-
position that he was shaking in every limb as we waited.
His wife remained steady.

Dinner was at a quarter to nine, and punctually on that
time the Queen walked in from her private sitting room.
She was what everyone says she is: small, plump, dressed
in sombre black silk, but with diamonds on her hand and
at her ears. Gentle of manner, immensely sure of herself,
and the centre of authority. More humour in the mouth
than I had expected and less austerity. In some ways a
soft old lady's face.

Before I knew what she was about, she had kissed
me gently on the cheek and pinned the Maid of Honour
badge, a miniature of herself when young, circled with
diamonds and mounted on a blue ribbon bow, on my left
shoulder.

It was done. I was appointed. I was a courtier.

But I was a Maid of Honour in Jessie's court too, and
I had only just begun to realise it. Unconsciously, and
without my knowing it, but influenced by the story of
Harry and Joseph, and yes, Rotten Potatoes too, I had
been recruited, and I could no more help myself than I
could help being my father's daughter. My mother's
inheritance had yet to be made manifest.

Although dinner began so late (even by London standards), it was soon over. An enormous amount of food was
provided, it always is, I believe, but very plain, as this is
what the Queen prefers. She eats very fast, and being
served first had finished before a slow eater like me had
taken more than a few mouthfuls. The minute she had
laid down her knife and fork, my plate was whisked away
by a flunkey stationed behind me for the very purpose. I
met Lady Geraldine's eye across the table. She was fond
of her food. The amused, aware gleam in her eye con-

vinced me that she knew exactly what my glance meant. I saw that she had neatly despatched all the food on her plate, while keeping up a cheerful conversation with her neighbour, a young naval officer. He had a thin face, but deep set, dark blue eyes. Real sailor's eyes, I thought. My neighbours were elderly members of the Household, with whom I made laboured conversation. After they had asked me one or two questions about my father and his work and his death, they ceased to take much interest in me and talked across me about neuralgia, an illness both seemed to share, I might almost say delight in. Orchids were on the table, a bunch before each lady's plate. This pleased me. I noticed an Indian servant in the room, standing as near to the Queen's chair as he could get. I also noticed that not *one* of the other servants spoke to him, or noticed him in any way. I thought that would bear watching, and might perhaps be my first lesson to have been learnt in Court ways. 'Munshi', the Queen called him. Well, the Munshi was not popular, as I came to realise.

After dinner we went to another room where we stood about for a while making conversation. Dick Monk, the sailor, came over and stood by me, and after a moment's shyness we fell into an easy conversation. I discovered that he had a dry sense of humour. He was, he told me, sailing under false colours. The Queen had taken the notion that she would like to have him serve on the Royal Yacht, the *Victoria and Albert*, and so he had come here to be inspected. Her Majesty naturally assumed he was eager to serve and etiquette demanded he *appear* so; while he, for his part, was determined not to be recruited. 'It would be death to my naval career,' he said. 'I am a serious sailor and what would this amount to? A cruise in the Scottish waters every autumn, and a crossing of the Channel in the spring. I should be miles in experience behind the rest of my year in the old *Britannia*. No, I shall stay with the Dover Patrol.'

'The *Britannia*?' I queried.

'I trained on her, Miss Errol, good old ship, at Dartmouth Creek. She was the successor to the *Illustrious* and *she*, you know, was the successor to the training college in the naval dockyard at Portsmouth. Nelson recruited his sea captains from there, that whipped Napoleon.'

'It might be difficult to disregard the Queen's wish.'

'I expect I shall manage somehow. I shall give a loud laugh at the wrong moment and the thing will be done,' he said gravely. 'They are entering upon a prolonged period of mourning and grief here. I can read the signs, and a cheerful laugh will automatically disqualify me.'

I burst out laughing, but checked myself before the Queen noticed.

'Good girl,' he said softly. 'I like to hear a girl laugh.' Then other people came up, and we were parted.

There was a good deal of gossip about the Courts of Europe. They were, of course, well informed, these people, and what facts they did not know they were able to guess. I heard the latest terrible mishaps to befall the house of Saxe-Lotharingia and the *real* facts behind the love story of Princess Victoria of Prussia (poor girl!). Censure was passed on the King and Queen of Saxe-Lotharingia for the heartless way they had treated their four daughters (hardly knew the girls' faces), having first neglected them, and now punishing them because one had married and another fallen in love (seduced by a groom of the Chamber, my dear).

I had no more talk with the Queen, and she withdrew quite early. Her face was a little flushed by this time, and as I had observed that she had eaten a huge amount of chocolate ice-cream, followed by a great quantity of apricots, I thought this natural enough. As for me, having had very little to eat, I was downright hungry.

Once the Queen had gone, we were free to go too. I waited. Then I saw something was about to happen. My aunt saw it as soon as I did and looked flustered. One of the other ladies stepped forward. She had something in her hand. I saw that everyone else was watching. I tried hastily to remember the lady's name. 'Mrs Monk, is it not?' I faltered. What she had in her hand I saw now, as she held it out, was a tiny picture. Set in an oval of gold filigree, most delicate old work, were the portraits, painted on ivory, of three girls. Two in profile, the one in the centre seen full-face. All were dressed in the style of a generation ago, long ringlets of hair on the shoulders, dresses cut low over the bosom, sleeves puffed. The girl in the centre had a pleasant, pug-nosed little face. Although I did not know her face I thought her ancestry was apparent. She bore a marked resemblance to Queen Charlotte, the consort of George III. In other words, she was 'old' royal family.

'That's the little princess, Princess Sophia,' said Mrs Monk eagerly. 'And I am on her left and your mother on the right.' The girl on the right hand had a soft, pale beauty that gleamed. She had an aristocratic nose and a young, eager tilt to her head. She looked the patrician, not the Princess.

'I wanted you to have this brooch. A little memory of your mother.'

I protested: 'But it must be very valuable.' I could tell that a masterly hand had painted the tiny portraits.

'Yes, it is by Giradouze,' she said fondly. 'He was Court painter to the old Duke. He had hands like an ox, my dear, but he painted like an archangel. Each touch as light as a feather.'

'Yes, it's beautiful. Too lovely for me to accept.'

'This portrait was made for the Princess, of course. We

three had been such companions. She wished it, you know
... It came into my hands in strange circumstances which
I will tell you some time. But I made up my mind when
it did so, that I would give it to you if that was possible.'

I took it in my hands tenderly and studied it. The girl
who was my mother had never seemed so far away. 'Keep
it for me,' I said. 'I should like to know all its history, but
let it remain your property.'

Nevertheless, as we drove away that night a small,
wrapped parcel was put into my hands and I knew it at
once for the miniature by Giradouze. I left Windsor with
it clasped in my hands, and from the slight shake of my
aunt's head I knew she deplored the whole episode. 'Yes,
yes, it is very kind of her. But she should either have kept
it or, more properly, returned it to the Saxe-Lotharingias.'

'Mrs Monk was a friend of my mother, then?' My
curiosity had naturally been aroused.

'The Princess came to England for a time, to finish her
English education. She always had had English governesses
and spoke English beautifully. Two young ladies of suitable family, Maria Grey, who became Mrs Monk, and
your mother, were provided as companions for her. I was
in the schoolroom at the time, and used to wish it had
been me.' She seemed to have talked herself out of her
ill-humour and into a gentle nostalgia.

It was a calm, marvellously still evening with a huge
silver moon hanging low in the sky. We drove through a
countryside which the moonlight had freed from all
physical properties. It melted away before us, weightless,
timeless and endless.

'All the same, I dare say she had her reasons for giving
away the portrait.' My aunt leaned forward confidentially.
'Just as the Saxe-Lotharingias had reason for losing possession of it in the first place. Giradouze's miniatures are
supposed to be unlucky.'

My poor young mother, I thought, all things about her seemed to bear bad luck. 'What happened to the Princess?'

'Dead. She was thrown from her horse and broke her neck. She had got pretty fat by that time.'

'Mrs Monk seems prosperous enough,' I ventured. 'I never saw such sapphires.'

'Oh yes, a wealthy marriage. But such a tragedy there.' She leaned forward again. 'Her husband was in the terrible collision between the *Tiger* and the *Black Prince* and was drowned when his ship sunk. That was her son I was talking to. A clever boy, he'll be an admiral in the end.'

'If he lives,' I almost said aloud. And then I thought, of course, that's why his mother wants to get rid of the Giradouze portraits, *she* believed in the bad luck too. And I wished I was not holding the picture in a tight grip.

The carriage slowed down while the horses negotiated a difficult bend. I saw a signpost. I could clearly read it: 'Charde,' it said.

'What an odd name,' I said idly. 'As if it was a place that had been burnt.'

'Can a name presage events?' said Lady Geraldine, leaning forward and holding up her lorgnettes to read the sign. 'How strange to come upon that name again. For twenty years I have not thought of it. And yet Charde haunted my childhood.' She put down her glasses. 'And you have never even heard of it? That's what time does.'

I shook my head. 'No, I never heard the name.'

'And yet that place has been the evil genius of our family. If houses can be said to have a spirit.'

'Oh, surely they can.'

Lady Geraldine called to the coachman. 'Brewster, take the turn towards Charde.'

Hunched over his horses, his face was invisible and his voice expressionless, 'Yes, M'Lady,' came the reply from the coachman.

'I believe he took us this way on purpose. The old wretch meant to go there all the time. He remembers it, you see.' She sighed. 'As it was, as it was, as it was.'

She said no more as we jogged along. The lane narrowed where we travelled along by a high stone wall. Presently we came to a pair of great iron gates with an heraldic lion prancing on each. They were wide open and thick with rust. Then the stone wall gave way to iron railings. Further along the road I could see more railings, and a second splendid gateway. A drive, running through the park, must join the two gates. We stopped.

'The house lies near the road. Such old, old places often do.'

Through the railings I saw a sward of silvered grass and beyond, nothing.

'There *is* no house,' I whispered.

'Look again.' She too was staring out of the carriage window.

Then I saw here a broken stretch of wall, there a pile of masonry near to a flight of steps that rose to nowhere.

'Charde Castle,' said Lady Geraldine. 'The ruined castle of the Maurices. Once it *was* a castle, but what it was more properly was the curse of the Maurices, their pride and their curse. We put our money into stones, and more stones.' She leaned back. 'Ah well, it's been a ruin as long as I remember. As a child I was terrified of it. Upon my word, I don't like it now.'

'What happened to it?'

'Burned down. As the name predicted.'

'And then just left a ruin?'

'What money have the Maurices ever had to rebuild? Oh, I believe that each generation made its plans, but they faded before the solid reality of the amount of money that would be needed. And now, the present generation has no interest.' The present Marquess was a clever professional soldier who never came to England if he could be with his regiment abroad. At the moment he was in Canada. As yet he had no heir. 'One day the land will be sold, and just as well. Once Charde could look across to Windsor itself on equal terms, and now ...' She shrugged. There was a touch of characteristic Maurice pride in the shrug, even though she was by far the most down-to-earth of the family. Except for me, of course; I meant to keep my feet firmly on the ground.

The horses whinnied and tossed their heads. 'Walk them about, Brewster,' she called.

'Wait a minute, if you will. Aunt, may I get out and walk and look at the house, and meet you at the further gate?'

'If you will,' said my aunt slowly. 'But walk carefully.'

The carriage moved on and I was alone in the moonlight. When I got closer to the ruins I saw they were covered with creepers and ivy. Here and there a stretch of brickwork or masonry reared itself erect but the woods were taking over. It had once been a huge house with many courtyards and inner quadrangles, traces of which could still be distinguished.

The turf was springy beneath my feet, but the surface as irregular as if the grass had grown over paving stones, and fallen bricks and broken walls. At some points the shadows were so thick and dark that they seemed painted on, but everywhere else stood bright in the moonlight.

I remained there looking around me for a minute or two, and thought I could almost trace out the outlines of the great house. Here had been the main entrance with a pillared portico, here the high hall, here a great courtyard. Separate and apart had been a tower. The tower still stood, a shell indeed, whose windows let on to emptiness, and whose staircase led only to the dazzling air.

I had to pass the tower to regain the path towards the

gate, where the carriage waited. A noble flight of stone steps led up to the entrance to the tower. At the top of those steps, still as if he had been a statue, a man was standing.

He looked down at me, then slowly came down the steps. He was wearing dark clothes with just a gleam of white linen at his neck and throat; I was in the white dress I had worn for the Queen, with a white silk shawl drawn round my shoulders. We were black and white. Both of us might have been figures conjured up by the night. But not for one moment did I think of him as a fantasy or a dream, nor was I frightened. He was as un-mistakably a warm, living being, as I was myself.

Besides, I knew his face, that elegant, beautiful counten-ance. Our eyes had met across a ballroom; and I had seen him approach down Jockey Fields Passage. I looked into his face, expecting recognition, and saw there only a blankness.

'Good evening.' I wondered how you spoke to a man you met in the ruins of a castle on a moonlit night. He did not answer. Then I remembered he was from abroad and possibly did not understand English. I tried in German. There was still no answer, but he smiled. The smile changed his face. The stiff dignity, the strength melted away and an almost childlike sweetness filled it instead. He bowed. Still, he did not speak.

I thought that, perhaps, where he came from servants did not speak easily or readily to well-born young women. 'The castle is very beautiful by moonlight,' I said. I spoke English again. It worked better this time. Perhaps my words reassured him by their ordinariness. In my flowing white gown I may have looked alarmingly wraith-like. At all events, he answered, slowly, softly.

'The landscape is most beautiful.' The English was pure, almost unaccented, but he used it as if it was strange to him. 'How sweet the moonlight sleeps upon this bank.'

The line from Shakespeare was familiar, hackneyed, anyone might have used it. Still, I was surprised to hear it now. And he said it so politely, too, not as if he was much interested, but as if he was practising saying it. In spite of my strange alarm, I found myself smiling back.

The smile seemed enough. He stopped quoting Shakespeare, which had perhaps only been out of a need to reassure me, and said nothing more. The moonlight fell now upon his smile, his brilliant beauty and solemn dignity. He bowed to me.

He walked down the few remaining steps. I saw he had a guide book in his hand (it looked like a Baedeker) and with it a riding whip.

I was young enough to think there were people whom you met in the moonlight, who rode away on a coal-black steed you never saw, and by whom you were then enthralled for ever. It was the other side of the Cinderella story.

'Come back,' I called. But the wind blew my voice away and a cloud over the moon at the same time, and there was only darkness.

My aunt said, 'I think you fainted.' She sounded anxious and alarmed. 'I came looking for you and found you leaning against a pillar with your eyes closed.'

'I was only dreaming a little,' I said. 'I didn't hear you come.'

'No, that's what I mean. I think it was a little faintness.' She had her arm round me, and led me back to the carriage. 'Oh, your shawl.' It was on the ground. She went back and got it and placed it on my shoulders. It smelt of grass and fresh air, which is how moonlight smells.

'There was someone here,' I said.

'No.' She looked alarmed.

'But there was. We spoke.' I looked about me. It was true there was no sign of anyone now, except that under one tree I could see where a horse had trampled the grass and left a pile of dung.

'Well, if there was anyone there, my love,' she said, looking at me tenderly, 'I noticed nothing.'

'It doesn't matter.'

Nor did it. We were away, the man in black and I, on some strange chase that nothing would stop. The news of it sang in my blood. We would meet again. Man or master, which was he?

CHAPTER FOUR

It was at this time I learnt, if I did not know it already, that life requires you to run in several races at once. But I didn't mind. I felt as if I had the strength for ten such competitions.

The house in Masham Square was empty when we returned, my aunt and I. The servants, except for Fletcher, who received us, were out of sight. In my aunt's bedroom I believe Barlow was waiting, for I heard her voice, but my room was empty except for moonlight and the wind blowing through it. I delighted in the silence and the night and went to the window and looked out. The square in the pale light was empty too, except for a dark cat figure flitting across the pavements from gutter to gutter. I sat there for a moment, watching: even the gutters seemed touched with magic that night. The meeting in the ruins of Charde, unbelievable, unforgettable, was part of my life now. I was the person this strange thing had happened to; it would have to be reckoned with. A door had opened in my life and I had walked through it.

As if to remind me that Jessie Falconet claimed my allegiance, too, I saw a letter from her propped against the dressing-table mirror. 'Dearest Errol', it began, 'I have found out something for you from one of my poor patients, whose husband is a policeman.'

The one with the broken nose, I thought, who had

waited outside Jessie's rooms that first day I had visited her and the day I had found the pistol in the cab. The thought of that pistol made me uneasy still. I knew it remained in the drawer where I had hidden it, because every day as I was dressing I put my hand in and felt the shape. As far as I knew, it was my secret, although in Masham Square secrets had a way of being no secrets at all.

I looked down again at Jessie's letter. 'Her husband has recently joined a new corps of detectives, a sort of élite, they are, and he is naturally anxious to be a success. He has been working on his own account, mingling with the criminal hordes in the rookeries and warrens of St Giles, the famous Holy Land, as they call it. Dangerous work, and his wife fears for him. And so would you, Errol, if you had four small children and another on the way. In the Holy Land he has heard tales of a man they call the King. He is feared but not much loved, I fancy, but who would look for affection among the denizens of the Holy Land, where you must pay them well to exact even safety? It is a terrible world there, Errol. Detective Anticknap has heard mutters about the King. It seems he is a foreign gentleman who comes and goes in the rookeries, paying well for whatever he wants. He wants 'servants', as he calls them, men and women who will do whatever he asks. More than this my friend does not know, nor whether the King is a regular criminal or not, but a corrupter he manifestly is. The policeman found the stories sufficiently remarkable to tell his wife, who told me. What I wonder is whether the King and Mr Koenig could be one and the same person?'

I put the letter down and went to the window and looked out. The magic was gone now and already the world outside looked grey. Dawn must be approaching. Dawn light would wash over the bridges, churches, towers, palaces and slums of this great city. More people lived here than had lived in Ancient Rome at the height of its imperial power, and every day it grew. Even now Jessie might be dragging into the world a screaming red-faced recruit, and calming with her words a tired mother. And here I sat, still in my Court dress. Crime and death and ugly birth, side by side with white satin and roses.

Although Jessie made it sound so easy, I guessed that she had extracted her information in the most clever manner possible, by shrewd questioning. I saw there was a footnote to the letter, hurriedly added by Jessie, in pencil. It said he had another name, used when they were in a more joking mood. Then he was called Kingsman. That was the slang name for the black neckerchief, much fancied among smart criminals.

I undid my bodice and for a moment felt the cool air touch my body, then I let my skirt slip to the floor and slid into bed. The down cushions received me softly and embraced me. I turned my cheek to the pillow and was asleep. I dreamt briefly and anxiously of the sailor, Dick Monk. It was the same dream over and over again, of a boat that tossed, and he and I were in it, and my body aching and arching, as if the waves and their motion had somehow got inside it and were rocking it.

I woke when Barlow drew my curtains with a rattle. Then she picked up my dress from the floor where, it seemed, I had left it, and clucked angrily. 'Not like you, Miss Vesey, to leave your clothes in such a mess. What got into you last night?'

'The moonlight, I think,' I said dreamily. I raised myself on one elbow. She was hanging my dress over a chair and straightening the slippers I had worn with it. Even from the bed I could see mud on the high, slender heels.

'It's got into her ladyship too, then. For she's taking her

breakfast in bed, which is a thing she never does. And drinking chocolate, too. She hasn't drunk chocolate since we came back from Paris together, the summer she married. What a lovely girl she was then, and how the smell of hot chocolate brings the look of her back.' Barlow was rambling on, as if the moonlight had got into her as well. 'I keep thinking of those days lately. Have you noticed, miss, how sometimes your mind will go back to a time in the past and dwell on it?' I shook my head. 'But there, you're too young.'

Not too young, I thought, but only of a different temperament. I knew already that I would always look to the future and never dwell on the past.

'I wonder if it means anything?' went on Barlow. Like all her class, she was intensely superstitious and always looking for signs and portents. She usually found them, too.

'What could it mean?'

'I don't know.' I met her eyes, pale blue and faded, and thought, suddenly, she was a woman too. What memories had she stored up behind those eyes? Not many of her own, I guessed. Most of her sorrows and her joys would be vicarious, lived through Lady Geraldine. I wondered if Lady Geraldine had had a lover in those long ago, chocolate-drinking days in Paris? But there was a quality about my aunt, not virginal exactly, but hard and clear-cut, that made me think there had been no confusion of that sort, no heartbreaks over the last waltz, no tears and despairs, only a marriage to a man much older than herself, but whom she had come to love. 'I do keep thinking about things past, though, miss,' went on Barlow, troubled. 'And I can't help thinking that we shall *see* something. There was a great big tealeaf shaped like a flower in my cup this morning. That must mean something.' She had finished her tidying up and was standing, hands pleating her apron. 'They were good, those days in Paris, Miss Errol. It was only a few weeks all in, but I sometimes feel we lived all our youth out in those weeks, me and her ladyship.'

I sat up in bed and clasped my hands round my knees. Sunlight flooded the room. On the floor still were my dead roses. A little glitter of diamonds came from the badge the Queen had pinned on my dress.

'When was it?'

'November, '64,' said Barlow. 'Such a cold sparkle in the air and crinolines were as big as big. Three times bigger than skirts are now. And we had a little velvet cloak trimmed with winter ermine, and a little matching cap. Oh, we did look ravishing.'

'Lady Geraldine, you mean?'

'Yes, of course. You didn't think I meant me? A fine sight I would look in velvet and ermine,' she said with scorn.

I studied her gaunt-boned, tired face and wondered how true that would have been almost thirty years ago. There must be some meaning behind her verbal identification of herself with her mistress.

'What was Lady Geraldine doing in Paris?' I was curious.

'There was some plan that she might be an English Maid of Honour to the French Empress, but it came to nothing, and just as well too, or she might have married a French gentleman, and we might have been mixed up in that dreadful siege of Paris and had to run for our lives.' She spoke with gusto.

'You'd have enjoyed it, Barlow,' I said from the depths of the bed. 'You know you would.'

'Perhaps a little bit. I knew a French soldier boy, teaching him English, I was. Lovely uniform he had, and beautiful whiskers, waxed so you could see your face in them.

The Prussians were the better soldiers when it came to it, though, and deserved to win, so the General said.'

'What was the General like?' I asked, seeing that Barlow seemed disposed to be talkative.

'You remember your uncle,' she said reprovingly.

'No, I don't. I hardly ever saw him. Once or twice, perhaps, then he died.'

'He was a good gentleman and a brave soldier,' said Barlow. 'And don't let anyone tell you different.'

'No, I won't,' I said. It paid to be childlike and nursery-innocent with Barlow in this mood. 'And he died in the ballroom?'

'Yes,' she said with a deep sigh. 'What a place to choose.'

'People can't choose where they will die.'

'Some can,' she said grimly.

There was a small, deep silence. I looked at her, waiting. She knew she had to go on.

'He shot himself,' she said, casting her eyes down. 'He'd been miserable, poor gentleman, ever since they took his army command away and retired him. He was nothing, the General wasn't, without his soldiers. And he'd been ever so miserable for months. We'd all noticed it. Her ladyship, she tried her best to cheer him up, but it weren't no good. Up he would go, but down down down, till he touched where he couldn't go no further.'

'Oh, how sad,' I whispered.

'Stretched out dead he was in the ballroom with the gun at his feet as if he'd thrown it away at the last minute.' She shook her head. 'Her ladyship shut the ballroom up from that day on and won't go near it. The Queen was very good to her. She loved the General, too. *She* didn't want him retired. Why, she'd pinned the V.C. on his breast herself. No, it was that Gladstone. Reforming the Army, they called it. I'd reform 'em,' she said fiercely.

'Poor Lady Geraldine left behind to face everything. The General might have thought of her. Don't have anything to do with a soldier or a sailor, there's no peace in the house with them, that's my advice to you, Miss Errol.'

'No, Barlow,' I said, thinking of a sailor I had met, called Dick Monk.

She straightened her apron and came back to the present. 'Shall I order you your breakfast in bed? Her ladyship won't mind for once. She doesn't really hold with it for young girls, and nor do I, but she knows you were late last night.'

I nodded. 'If you please.'

She had finished tidying up and was preparing to go. 'We shall have to get you a proper own maid, Miss Errol,' she said, 'or I shan't have no legs left. My knees are giving out already.'

'Oh, Barlow.'

'Ninety-eight stairs, miss, all told, from top to bottom.' At the door she said, 'There's a young person coming to-day for her ladyship to see.'

She was gone before I could answer, and I knew it was the real reason for her early morning visit. A lesser pair of hands could have tidied my room, but Barlow wanted to tell me about the new maid, whether from friendliness or plain zeal I was not sure.

In a short time she was back with my breakfast tray and arranged it in front of me. 'So you're following her ladyship to Court? Very right and proper. It's what her ladyship was hoping for. It shows what confidence the Queen has in you in spite of ...' She stopped short.

'In spite of what?'

'In spite of your being so young and inexperienced, miss,' said Barlow smoothly. But I thought she didn't mean it. I linked her words with that strange, quiet observation of me I had noticed in the ballrooms of

London. I was an object of interest; behind me was a question.

'In spite of my mother?' I wanted to shout at her. 'Is that what you all mean? Is that why you all watch me?'

How innocent of my father to think that no one knew. Everyone knew. Everyone, everyone, everyone.

I let her go out of the room without saying anything more to her. I understood it all now. The Queen, because she loved my aunt and had taken an interest in my dead mother, had appointed me to her service as a gesture of support. I was to be made respectable by attendance on her. But the great ladies of London society, all of whom thought me so romantic and interesting, and who loved Lady Geraldine too, were determined I should not make a match of it with one of their sons. All except, it seemed possible, poor feckless Mrs Monk, who was unlucky anyway, and knew it. But surely seamen were not like callow Guardsmen or stripling barristers or idle young landowners? Sailors know their own mind and how to use it. Dick Monk looked like a man who would be master in his own house.

Dick Monk was scarcely more than a face seen across the table, but I had seen interest in his eye as we talked, and a sort of devil inside me made me want to attract him. It would be simple, I thought. Sailors have notoriously easy hearts to conquer. They recover quickly, too, of course, and sail away to fresh victories. If I had reservations about Dick Monk, it was because I detected beneath his easy manner a steady, professional ambition that might make him, in the end, a hard man.

I got up and went to the window. The square was in daylight now, mundane and ordinary, the magic of the night fled away. But the effect of the meeting with the man at Charde had not left me. It had opened up something inside me I had kept shut. It might be difficult now for my aunt and the Queen to turn me into a modern-day vestal virgin.

Dick Monk had been just a face across the table. But I had to acknowledge him now a force to be reckoned with. I myself had given him the power. I thought that now I did begin to know what my mother had been like.

I met Harry with the dog on the stairs. He bowed as I went past, his face full of good-humoured intelligence. At once I thought how he had changed since that first meeting. Already and imperceptibly he was day by day losing his gutter manners and taking on the ways of a gentleman. I liked him so much. Of all the people in the house, I thought he was the one who promised most. Somehow a future had to be made for Harry. Why shouldn't he 'shirk', I thought, as well as anyone else. I bowed and smiled and passed on.

At the bottom of the stairs, in the hall, I saw a procession of servants carrying in a variety of boxes and valises, ranging from a great, leather-bound trunk to an elegant dressing-case.

Frank was back, and bringing more luggage with him than he had left with. I watched with amusement as a dark green leather bag was manhandled past me. So, Frank Maurice, M.P., had his bags marked with a crest in gold now, did he, the fine fellow? I thought of Lady Geraldine, wearing her gowns as long as she dared in front of the Queen, and was suddenly angry with him. Well, I had a task in store for Frank; he could begin to teach Harry Latin and then Greek. The mathematics would be my part. My father had trained me well in mathematics and the physical sciences. It would be a pity to let all my learning go to waste, I reflected, while I played simple duets with the Princesses and wrote polite letters in French and German.

The last bag had been carried through the hall and except for some pieces of straw from the cab floor no sign remained of the procession that had passed. Presently a little maid with a brush and pan knelt to remove these traces too.

But although the hall and staircase were empty, there still seemed to hang on the air the excitement of an arrival. Perhaps the baggage had left behind a smell of railway smoke and salt sea-water from the Channel packet-boat which one smelt without noticing. I had never crossed the Channel, but even I at that moment felt a dash of that mingled exhaustion and exhilaration which belong to the Continental traveller.

The little maid took a few happy skipping steps, saw me looking at her, stopped, and gave me a guilty smile as she departed.

But it was not only happiness that had inspired her dance. As I stood in the hall I could hear music. I listened, and then a smile came to my lips. I knew those tinkly, jerky strains; the music was coming from a hurdy-gurdy. In the street outside a hurdy-gurdy must be playing. I was delighted. As a country child a hurdy-gurdy man had represented to me the height of London sophistication and entertainment. Even now my feet were tapping. Gradually it came to me that the music was inside and not floating in from the street. I went across to where the stairs turned down to the kitchen. The hurdy-gurdy man was down there, in the servants' hall.

Picking up my skirts, I walked slowly down the stairs. The steps changed character at the bend, carpet gave place to dark linoleum. Decorous luxury gave way to austerity. I was not surprised, all houses were so, even the rectory, but it had shown less there because we were so very plain everywhere. In fact the two maids and the cook sitting by their cosy kitchen fire were better off than we had been in the stiffness of a drawing room whose fire never drew and always smoked.

I rounded the stair-well and ahead of me, doors open, was the kitchen.

Like a group by Luke Fildes or Frith, I saw the servants and their visitor. The maids were wearing their morning uniforms of lavender cotton dresses and starched white pinafores. The menservants—my eyes flicked over several of them, including the young lad whose face I knew well —wore striped shirts with sleeves rolled up and heavy black aprons. The cook, whom I had never seen before, I identified by her flaming red face and dark blue dress. What a lot of them there were, I thought, as I saw one or two faces peering through the scullery door, hinting at ever lower kitchen worlds I never guessed at.

Their visitor stood in the door by the basement yard, the sunlight falling upon his swarthy features, pulling vigorously at the handle of his music machine and tapping gaily with his foot.

He wore a red and yellow striped jacket and dark blue pantaloons. On his head was a jaunty red cap. A tiny monkey perched on his shoulder, a canary in a cage rested at his side.

The scene was full of colour and movement, some of the servants dancing and the cook waving her hand in time to the measure. Someone was singing.

I watched, fascinated. Then I was seen, the movement halted and the music quavered to a stop. Face after face stared at me, silently, coldly. I knew why. In coming down into the kitchen I had committed a breach of good manners. The gentry upstairs demanded loyalty and service, but in return they let the world downstairs swing to its own tune. The higher you were in the social scale, the less you interfered. In Buckingham Palace itself the

126

servants could hold a dance and dress up in their royal mistress's clothes with impunity.

In dead silence I descended the last stairs and was face to face with them. As soon as my foot touched the kitchen floor the picture broke up as if I had touched a spring. The cook went back to beating her pudding instead of the tune, the maids fled towards the neat piles of linen they were sorting, and the footmen melted into the darker recesses of the sculleries.

'I came to hear the music.' I kept my voice soft and polite; I felt the anger melt from the atmosphere.

'Oh, there, miss, I hope we didn't distress you,' said the cook comfortably.

'No, I liked it.'

'Just having a bit of fun, we were. No harm meant and none done, I hope.' She cast a sideways glance at the maids, who discreetly got on with their work, eyes down. Fletcher was nowhere to be seen, I noticed. Small doubt that the little gallivanting I had witnessed would not have taken place in his presence.

The hurdy-gurdy man neither spoke nor moved, but watched me with big black eyes. I noticed that monkey and bird remained immobile too, the monkey studying his master, the bird staring brightly at nothing. Then the man spoke hoarsely: 'Pretty music, lady.'

'Oh, yes. Do go on playing, please,' I said. And so he did for a little while, but the magic had gone, and when presently the music ceased it seemed right to let it rest.

'Tune too gay, eh, lady?' he said, and coughed. He looked thin and frail beneath his bright clothes.

One of the maids, she whom I had seen dancing in the hall, came forward and silently handed him a drink of water. She ran her hand gently over the monkey's head as she passed; the little animal looked up at her quietly.

127

'No, I enjoyed it,' I said, thinking that, after all, hurdy-gurdy music was best heard from a distance, that when you came upon it close at hand, the man and his predicament came through too strongly.

Fletcher's crisp tones sounded from the stairs. The hurdy-gurdy man heard them too and picked up his bundles as he prepared to move away. I went to him and pressed a silver coin in his hand. He put on his professional beck and smile, but mirth did not extend to his eyes.

'I should dance to the music while you can, miss,' he said. 'For we never know when it is going to change, do we?'

'It's always the same tune in the hurdy-gurdy,' I said sturdily.

He didn't answer, but turned to the door. I could hear Fletcher's voice raised in some command outside the room. I thought I heard him use the words 'the lady' and wondered if he referred to me. Although the musician appeared to be moving slowly, I noticed he was gone, invisible, as soon as Fletcher appeared in the kitchen.

Still, Fletcher knew the hurdy-gurdy man had been there. He stood on the threshold and proclaimed it. 'You will lose something one day. They are notoriously light-fingered, people of that sort. I have told you before. Good morning, Miss Vesey.' His tone was stiff, letting me know that I was out of bounds.

I own I thought wistfully of the Etonian device of shirking as I walked upstairs. I know now that the hurdy-gurdy man had taken nothing away, rather he had left something behind. There were a lot of things I missed in that scene, but I found out about them later.

When I returned to the hall a visitor was being ushered in. Dick Monk with his arms full of bunches and bunches of lavender.

I stared at him across the purple harvest and felt a

smile begin to form behind my lips. Even a well set up, beautifully uniformed naval officer looks a figure of fun when he is hung about with lavender.

'I felt sorry for the old girl, and I gave her half a sovereign and, by Jove, if she didn't thrust the basket load into my arms and scamper off,' he said helplessly.

'I expect she thought it was a mistake, half a sovereign *is* a lot of money, and she'd better seal the bargain and be off,' I said, gravely.

'It's hard on a chap.' Bundles of lavender were beginning to drop from his loosening grasp and fall all around him like autumnal leaves in Vallombrosa.

I bent to pick them up and so did the servant who had let him into the house, and so did Harry, at that moment appearing. He was more efficient than I was in relieving Dick Monk of his burden.

'I know what to do. I'll spread 'em out on a tray in the sun and dry them,' he said. He spoke politely in that neutral accent he had developed, yet the old street arab was not so far beneath the surface, for I noticed his hand come out and unobtrusively touch Dick Monk's sleeve. It was lucky, in his world, to touch a sailor.

I saw Dick Monk look at him thoughtfully.

'We used to live next to an old Mother Lavender-bags,' said Harry cheerfully, 'and I learnt to help her make her bags. Flash old girl, she was, when she was in funds, which wasn't hardly never, and could chaff down a peeler so uncommon severe when it suited her that a strong man would blush.' All this delivered in a voice which aped Frank. There was a lot of work still to be done on Harry.

'Who's the lad?' asked Dick Monk, as the boy departed.

'A friend of the family.' It was as good an explanation of Harry as any, and indeed was true in its way.

My visitor seemed to feel some explanation was necessary to explain his presence. 'My mamma told me to pay a call on Lady Geraldine. Or at least to leave my card. She wondered how you are?'

'Oh well, very well.' Did Mrs Monk feel that ill luck from the portrait would strike me so soon?

'She said morning calls were permissible among friends.'

'Yes, indeed.' I cocked an eye at the clock. Scarcely eleven.

'But?' He was clever enough to detect a surprised note in my voice. 'What have I done wrong? Come, now, tell me.'

'*Morning* calls mean anything after twelve, you know,' I admitted.

He struck his forehead. 'Fool that I am. I have been so long abroad, out of civilisation, that I have forgot its ways. I haven't lived ashore since I was a nipper. And little boys, you know, don't pay calls.'

Our eyes met in amusement. There was not much amiss with his manners, I thought.

'Come, now, you must tell me what to do next. I have another call to make and had better know the rules.'

'Well, you sit on the sofa, yes, that one will do. And you talk of nothing much, anything of consequence would never do.'

'I wonder if I can manage that.' His eyes met mine again. 'To you.'

'And then, after at least ten minutes, but no more than fifteen, you rise, shake my hand and say good-bye. Oh yes, and it is better to be trivial about that, too. In fact, it is better to be trivial about everything.'

'Ah!' He stroked his beard. 'Miss Vesey, I am afraid you are laughing at me.'

Nothing more intimate than this passed between us, and he was gone, walking briskly off, within a few minutes. But afterwards, I felt I owed it to him, and to myself, to track down my brother and to clear away, if I could, this cloud that hung over me.

Of the threat to myself, of which my father had spoken, I thought nothing.

CHAPTER FIVE

The sun had gone in and the day was hot but cloudy
when I set off. I like these heavy, grey days. London
shows a new face then. You can see the city as it really is,
without the drama of high sunlight, or the shadows of
the night.

It was a workaday world I walked through. Even in
Belgravia, which I thought of as so rich and feminine in
character, errand boys were tearing about on business
bound. This impression intensified as I trudged steadily
eastward, out of smart London towards the City. I saw
women carrying shopping, and men hurrying past with
important-looking papers in their hands or pushed inside
a breast pocket as if only their presence could be hinted
at to the world outside. How confident and prosperous
they all looked, planting their feet solidly down on the
pavement as if they owned both it and the sub-soil all
the way down to Australia. As they possibly did. I was
reminded that this was the commercial heart of the
Empire, and that all around me were men whose fortunes
were bound up with what happened in India, Africa and
the Americas.

For a moment I paused, absorbed in the drama of it all.
Straight in front of me was an office front, old-fashioned
but solid, with the name 'James Peck, Commercial Agent
to China and the Far East', printed in gold on the windows.

Clerks were passing in and out all the time. Next door was a plain-faced house which might have been a city merchant's dwelling, except for a small brass plate which said 'Frederick Bedower and Son'. Next door to that was a handsome house with immaculate paint and rich damask curtains, where a wealthy city man must certainly live. A fine carriage waited for him outside. I looked at it longingly before plodding on.

At this point I was, I admit, lost. I had set out to walk to Jessie and seemed to be walking instead into the heart of the City of London. Surely that could not be the dome of St Paul's Cathedral appearing over the roofs?

I was standing there, doubtful and worried, when the fine carriage, previously noticed, went past, slowed and then stopped. A lady put her head out and called: 'Miss Errol, Miss Vesey, my dear.' She held open the carriage door, still leaning out to look at me. She was quietly, but richly dressed in black silk.

'My dear, you don't recall me, but I remember you. I was always about the house in Masham Square while my father was there, even after I married. Anna Fletcher, I was, Mrs Bedower now.' She dimpled. 'Can I take you anywhere? I see you walking, and here is this carriage with nothing to do except transport me. And father is here, you see. A very old man now, but enjoying life with his daughter.'

I came to the carriage door and looked in. There was old Fletcher, bolt upright in the corner of the carriage, carefully not resting his head on the lavender silk, and smiling at me broadly.

'I *would* like a ride,' I admitted. 'Or at least to be set on my way, for I'm lost.'

'Step in, Miss Errol, step in,' he said. 'I remembered you at once. You've the family way with you.'

'So I'm told,' I said, seating myself.

133

'And we saw you driving one day in the park,' said Mrs Bedower, who seemed to feel that another reason for my swift recognition might be necessary. 'Where shall we set you down?'

'Would know the young lady anywhere,' said old Fletcher stoutly.

I told them the address, studying the two faces which were turned towards mine with the same open, friendly look which told their relationship even if I had not known it.

'What a beautiful carriage,' I said, as we moved off.

'Oh, it's my son's,' said Mrs Bedower easily, leaning back against the silk and speaking as if it was of no consequence at all.

I knew so much about them and they knew so much about me. Our families had had a relationship over the generations, they were my friends. I could see behind their eyes how much they must know about my mother, more, possibly, than my father had known, and yet, because they had been servants, I would not ask them. How stupid and wasteful this pride seems now. I paid for it, I believe, in the way one always does pay for false pride in the end, by suffering and humiliation beyond anything that a few questions would have inflicted on me then. They, for their part, although the international contacts of Mrs Bedower's son were alerting them to so much, were caught in the same convention, and could not warn me. Unless the soft grip of old Fletcher's hand as he bade me good-bye was meant as warning.

Jessie's landlady opened the door. She had ink stains on her fingers and a smear of ink across her brow. She looked at me absently, as if she had come from a deep abstraction to answer my knock.

'I am composing,' she said, in her low, beautiful voice.

I was surprised. 'Music?'

'No, a speech. A funeral oration, it will be, over a dead cause.' She sounded sad. 'Ah well, one cannot triumph all the time.'

'Oh.' I looked at her, abashed. I did not know what to make of a woman who made speeches. 'Where will you make your speech?'

'Hum, let me see, it will be in Manchester, in the Free Trade Hall,' she said in a matter-of-fact way.

My eyes shot open. I suppose I had expected her to say 'Oh, in somebody's drawing room'. But a lady who could take on a funeral oration in the huge spaces of Manchester's biggest hall was a woman indeed. I had underestimated her. 'Your subject?' I asked.

'Freedom,' she said. 'To my mind it is dead. It died on Bloody Sunday in Trafalgar Square. You have never heard of Bloody Sunday? Well, plenty have.' She moved her hand irritably. 'Come in, come in, Miss Falconet is out, but you may wait for her.'

'She is working, I suppose,' I said, more timidly than my wont. What a formidable woman this was.

'Working? Yes, she calls it working. To my mind she would be better employed doing other things. And what is work that you are not paid for and do not do for your bread and butter, but your pleasure?'

They don't see eye to eye, I recorded.

'But she can be very obstinate.'

The pot calling the kettle black, I thought. I could picture them together, both so earnest and intent, both pouring out a stream of opinions and enthusiasm, both seeking to convert. I wondered how they really got on.

'What cause is that, the dead cause you spoke of?'

'The Socialist Proletarian Movement.'

'I should think that has many aspects,' I observed.

This time the surprise was hers. She looked at me as

135

if I had unexpectedly revealed myself to be cleverer than she had expected.

'Many. Many indeed. If you are interested you too could be of use. To women particularly.' Her eyes shone. 'Who can help women but women?' I began to see what she and Jessie had in common. When it came down to reality, they were both convinced that the rest of their sex were victims, and only they were free. And who is to say that they were wrong? Still, I was mildly irritated. I thought I was well equipped to look after myself.

'I have so many causes. Do you know how women are exploited in so many industries? Have you heard how women work in the match industry? I could introduce you to some match girls and you could see for yourself. Oh, there is much to be done there, and soon, too.'

'Jessie seems taken up with other problems,' I said.

'She has the right approach, but it will be so slow and the work so difficult. Technically difficult, you know.' She sighed. 'With all the will in the world, in *that* sphere it is one step forward and two back. People are so shy, so stupidly reluctant to be frank.'

I nodded, not truly understanding.

'Generations of lies and false talk are behind such attitudes,' she said fiercely, 'As is the case with *all* issues touching women's lives.'

'I want to see Mrs Anticknap, whom Jessie has been helping,' I said, breaking in. I could see she would go on for ever. I no longer had any doubt about her being able to achieve an oration. I only doubted if she would ever stop. Ideas and images rose in an irresistible stream in her mind, demanding expression.

'And Miss Falconet is so rich,' she added, with a touch of wistfulness. 'And her money is entirely at her own disposal. With such wealth she could do so much. Do you know, I have supported myself and my daughter entirely by my own efforts since I left my husband?'

I suppose my enquiry was written on my face, for she answered it. 'A stupid, sanctimonious, mealy-mouthed parson,' she said bitterly.

How she hates him, I thought, and thought too of my father, who had been neither stupid nor sanctimonious nor mealy-mouthed either, and felt a flash of sympathy for that husband who had no doubt been sorely tried.

'Mrs Anticknap's address?' I reminded her.

'Twenty-seven Larson Street,' she said briefly, 'just round the corner.' Since I was obviously not going to be of use to her at the moment, she had dismissed me. But I caught a glance from a pair of extremely intelligent eyes as I left. Maddening she might be, supremely clever she was also.

It wasn't until I arrived at the doorstep of Twenty-seven Larson Street that I realised I did not know what I was going to ask. I pulled the door bell and wished I could walk away again. But as soon as I was face to face with Mrs Anticknap I found the words straightway on my lips.

'I am Errol Vesey. Please, Mrs Anticknap, *why* did you tell Miss Falconet the story about the man Koenig?'

Her tired, pretty face went white. She was a delicate-looking woman, still young, but with a strand of premature white hair across her forehead. A tiny girl gripped her skirts and peered at me from the protection of her mother's pinafore. A baby was wailing in the room behind. Mrs Anticknap cast a distracted glance behind her and made as if to close the door, but I put my foot in the way. 'Why, Mrs Anticknap? Jessie thinks she so cleverly got the story from you. But I believe you wanted her to know.'

'Come inside,' she said in a hurried whisper. 'Did anyone see you come here?'

'No.' I was surprised at the question, but sure of my

137

answer. There had been no one in the street.

'You are a watched woman, Miss Vesey. From what my Fred learned, this Koenig is interested in you and means you no good. Miss Falconet has been so good to me. I wanted to tell her, for I know she values you.' The poor woman wrung her hands. 'But I should not have done it. When Koenig learnt my Fred had been enquiring about him, he sent him messages to tell him if he went on he should be ruined.'

I stared in horror. 'How could that be?'

'Oh, he would have his ways, never fear, policemen have been done down before.'

I suppose I said something to her then, something reassuring and soothing, I don't remember. It would have been a lie, anyway, for I had no real comfort to offer her. From that moment I believed all the evil she had pictured of Mr Koenig.

I was drained of energy and felt ill. There was a small park not far from Larson Street, a little island of trees and grass amid the rows of brick houses. I sat there on a bench and let depression wash over me. What I saw of the world through Mrs Anticknap's eyes sickened me.

I took an omnibus back to Piccadilly, got off by Jermyn Street and walked the rest of the way to Masham Square. I had come to a decision: I would ask my aunt what she knew about my brother. The door was open to admit some more of Frank's luggage, a heavy trunk which had come separately and was being carried upstairs. I crept into the hall behind it, and quietly went to my room to tidy myself.

I had to pass the drawing room doors, which stood wide open. I glanced inside, thinking to see Frank or my aunt.

Someone was standing with her back to the door. A figure I did not recognise. Even as I watched she moved

138

out of sight. Mildly puzzled, I was walking away when I heard my aunt's voice.

'Errol, my dear. Errol come in.'

I walked slowly into the room.

CHAPTER SIX

My aunt came forward to meet me. I saw that faint flush
of red on her neck which with her was so telling of
emotion. Her voice was relaxed, her manner easy, but
she herself was not entirely happy. Obviously the euphoric
mood of the morning, with its breakfast of hot chocolate,
had gone. She looked her best this noon, however, beautifully groomed as ever and wearing a plain natural linen
dress and a choker of pearls.

Flowers were disposed all round the drawing room,
great bowls of roses and carnations, with here and there
an arrangement of lilies. The smell was almost too strong.
Nor was such extravagance like Lady Geraldine, who
had no greenhouses and no country-house garden to call
upon. 'The flowers are from Windsor,' she said briefly. 'A
gift from the Queen.' I must have looked unconvinced,
because she added. 'Count Gleichen sent them. But, of
course, it would be with the Queen's permission.' Edward
Gleichen was the grandson of the Queen's half-sister, and
the Queen treated him and his sister Feodora entirely as
royalty when they were at Windsor, as, it seemed, they
often were. Feodora, a talented sculptress, had been held
out to me as someone I would enjoy to know when 'in
waiting' at Court, but I wondered what would be the
chances of getting to know her.

Across the scent of flowers, forming an almost visible barrier between us, I looked at the third person in the room. She and the flowers fused, for ever after, into a double image in my mind. I think I came to the tacit belief then that the flowers had been sent for her.

Lady Geraldine put her hand on my elbow and led me to the newcomer.

'This is the Countess Telling.' I saw a pale-skinned, dark-haired girl, fashionably dressed, but now tired and faintly dishevelled with travelling. She held out her hand silently and I took it. Never had I felt a chillier, softer touch. And I was very, very slightly puzzled.

'She has come to stay for a while.'

The Countess's lips moved faintly in a smile. Then, as if she remembered she must say something, she said softly, 'How do you do?' She seemed totally at a loss how to go on after this, and stood there looking at me. It was hard to say that she was ill at ease, for she had her own aura of self-possession, but she seemed puzzled and shy.

I suppose that's it, I thought, the girl is shy. And a foreigner too, said my insular little heart. She spoke English beautifully, but all the same, it was not her native tongue. She was German, I guessed, from her name.

'It will be nice for you to have Errol,' said my aunt nervously, 'but she goes to Windsor soon, of course.'

I did not fail to notice the way she put it. It was going to be nice for the Countess Telling to have *me*, and not nice for Errol Vesey to have the Countess Telling. So the Countess was important to Lady Geraldine, more important, perhaps, than the little niece from the country. I did not resent this, I appreciated that there were loyalties and demands in my aunt's life that I knew nothing of. She was as much a professional woman as Jessie Falconet and Mrs Besant. All the same, I felt a little depressed by this silent, German aristocrat. If she and I were to be much in each other's company I hoped she would make a little more effort to entertain.

She seemed to feel this herself. 'I am tired now with the journey,' she said in her soft voice. 'Mr Maurice arranged the travel so beautifully, but still I am fatigued.'

So that's why Frank went off, I thought, to travel back home with the Countess Telling was his mission. Also, presumably to her belonged all the luggage I had seen arriving, including the beautiful, green morocco leather case stamped in gold. Well, she wasn't poor, I thought, and indeed, everything about her suggested wealth. She was about my own age, I judged, or perhaps a year or two older, it was hard to be sure.

'I haven't travelled very much myself, but it must be tiring,' I said, thinking of the energy and enthusiasm which I would have brought to any expedition had it been my luck to travel.

'Now you two have met I will take you upstairs, Countess. Your maid will have unpacked and you must rest,' said Lady Geraldine, still in that bright, and to my mind, slightly false tone.

'Is Frank tired too?' I suppose a note of wicked irony did creep into my voice, for my aunt's brow puckered.

'He has gone to his office.'

Strangely enough, my cousin Frank did have an office, but what he did there I had never discovered. It seemed a mystery to Frank too, sometimes. He himself always referred to the place as his 'chambers', implying that great legal matters were undertaken there, but I think this was not so. Years after, when I was a married woman, he gave me a luncheon there and I think this was the principal business of his chambers: to provide a comfortable, masculine setting for his entertaining. My aunt always preferred the more prosaic term 'office' and it was in accordance with her down-to-earth character that she should.

I hung about waiting while she went upstairs, wishing I was a man and could fill in the time smoking. Jessie smoked cigarettes and I had heard that the Princess of Wales did so as well. I poked about till I found the box of cigarettes that was provided for Frank. They were packed for him specially by Mr Sullivan of Jermyn Street and bore the words 'Mr Frank Maurice's Mixture' in elegant lettering on the label. I lit one and puffed away. They always smelt delicious when smoked by Frank, but I noticed that when you smoked yourself you did not smell the aroma. However, I continued smoking, standing by the window to let the smoke go out, until I heard my aunt on the stairs, and then I threw the cigarette out of the window.

'Is Frank back then?' she asked.

'No.' I shook my head.

'Funny, I thought he must be.' She looked about her, puzzled. I watched in amused silence to see how far her deductive powers would get her, but after a thoughtful shake of her head she gave it up.

'How long's she staying?' I said.

'Countess Telling? Some time.' My aunt gave me a ravishing smile, which made me think her still uneasy. 'I think she will stay until the autumn.'

'I hope she will enjoy London. Has she been here before?'

'Oh no, I think not.'

'She speaks beautiful English.'

'An English governess, my dear,' said Lady Geraldine absently.

I knew then that I would not ask my aunt any questions about my dead mother and the birth of my brother. There was something about this woman at the moment that made me want to leave her alone. Everyone has to carry their own burdens. I would carry mine.

I will not say that at this moment I grew up. How vain and ill-advised that would be, for my growing up proceeded, like everyone else's, by fits and starts. On some occasions I was a rash girl of nineteen, and on others a wise adult. But what I did perceive on this occasion was that one must solve one's own problems and live with the results. Perhaps I was prompted towards this by the realisation that it was what my cousin Frank did not do (although my aunt did), and that 'shirking' was built into his way of life by now.

The next few days passed quietly. I was busy getting my clothes ready for the new life ahead of me. Visits to dressmakers and sewing at home took up my time. For all that we were supposed to be such good company for each other, I did not see much of Countess Telling. She did not even appear at meals with great regularity. Even this seemed to be taken as a matter of course, and no comment was made. When she did appear, she only picked at her food. Silly girl, I thought, seeing her move a delicious salmon mousse round her plate without eating more than a forkful. I couldn't see what she was doing in London. As far as I knew, all she did was mope around her room and read books. Quantities of novels from Mudie's began to appear about the house and were absorbed by me with the same enthusiasm and despatch as the delicious food which seemed to date from the Countess's arrival. I realised now what a great gap there had been in my life hitherto. Eager-eyed, I read novels about handsome, well-born, but impoverished British officers who saved beautiful Balkan princesses from death, or worse, from revolutions, and later married them. Or sometimes, did not marry them, but watched with a noble breaking heart while they were crowned Queen, or married to a reigning sovereign. Sometimes, as variation on this story, the lovely princess ran away from the Court because she was unhappy with its stiffness and formality and tried to live a simple life, strictly incognito, as nurse or milkmaid or something similar. She wasn't very good at it and usually fell in love with a travelling artist or musician whom she met by chance. He turned out, as a rule, to be as well born as she was, but more reconciled to public life, because presently he went back to it and took her with him as his wife. Sometimes she didn't know till the final scene that she had really married a duke or a king, and sometimes he told her, sadly, fearing she would leave him just before their wedding. It was all great stuff, and I revelled in it. Another group of novels was about rich English aristocrats behaving in a very worldly and witty fashion. They, too, always made extremely happy marriages at the end. In fact, everyone did. It was all deliciously unlike life as I knew it in an English county, but that was the charm.

I think the Countess did a lot of embroidery and occasionally she played the piano, but that was about all. No visits to the opera and concert hall, no theatre parties, no balls, hardly even a morning drive.

One day she got into the carriage with my aunt and was driven off. They were gone all day and returned as evening came on, both looking tired. The Countess passed me on her way up the stairs and smiled in her usual gentle, remote, speechless way, but my aunt said by way of explanation that they 'had been on a visit to relations'.

'To the Countess's relations? Has she got any in this country?' I was surprised.

'Why, yes, my dear. Just a few.'

'Well, why isn't she staying with them?' I thought, and started to wonder what had brought the girl to England.

I began to feel sorry for her. In her room near mine I heard her having long muttered conversations with her maid. The maid spoke no English and was a hard-faced, tall woman with muscles like a man. Sometimes, idly speculating, possibly under the influence of the romantic literature I was reading, I thought she seemed as much a gaoler as a maid, and wondered if the Countess had committed some crime at home and been sent abroad to pay for it. 'Treason, maybe,' I remember saying aloud to myself, and then giggling.

I had a maid of my own too now, only mine was as simple and straightforward as the Scottish countryside from which she sprang. Mary Ross could sew beautifully and was skilful in arranging both dress and hair. These things must be considered by me now, because it was well known that the Queen, although apparently so dowdy herself, had an eagle eye for the turn-out of those around her. Mary Ross was so clever she deserved better wages than the modest ones I could pay. But beneath the hem of her skirt showed a boot with a thick sole, and when she walked she limped a little. As she said herself, with a sigh: 'Some ladies don't care to employ a cripple.'

The other activity that filled my days was teaching Harry. We had silently taken over the old schoolroom at the top of the house and there, amid old maps of the Crimean campaign and drawings of soldiers crayoned by Frank as a child, we did our lessons. Harry learnt incredibly fast. It was as if there were a well inside him that he must fill with information. He was not yet beyond me, indeed in Latin he was never to go beyond my skills, but his grasp of mathematics astounded and delighted me. It was not parrot work with him: he really understood the principles behind it.

Unknown to my aunt, I had talked to Frank. Several times he had appeared in the schoolroom to attend our lessons and sat there smoking and listening. But I did not let him go away unchallenged. I suppose he thought that I would not be so bold or so unmaidenly as to speak out. He little knew me. I waited, thinking he might speak first, then finally one afternoon when Harry and I had got on particularly well, shot on ahead on every subject we touched, and yet still Frank said nothing, I turned to him, when Harry had gone, as I gathered up my books.

'A clever boy, isn't he?'

'Very clever,' agreed Frank, puffing away.

'More than that, even,' I said. 'He seems to me remarkable. Not a boy to let slip back into the world he came from.' Frank fidgeted with his pipe without answering. 'So you thought, of course, or you would not have brought him here.'

'Fond of the little feller,' he muttered.

'No more than that, Frank? No closer, more binding relationship?' I probed.

'I've known Louisette a long while, of course, but Harry's about twelve years old, isn't he?' He fixed his gaze on the wall and went on. 'I would have been at Eton. I know that some of my friends at Eton did ... but, as a matter of fact, I didn't.' He turned round and looked at me. 'Forgive me, Errol, I shouldn't talk to you like this, but you're always so calm and reasonable, I forget what a girl you are. And I *can't* talk to Mamma.' He puffed furiously at his pipe. 'Always thought there was a look of me about the little fellow.'

'There might be as he grows older,' I said, reluctantly truthful, in spite of my desire to make as strong a case for Harry as I could. 'I don't see it now.'

'About the eyes, you know,' said Frank, not looking at me. 'Reminds me of the Guv'nor.'

'The General?' I was surprised again. 'Ah, I hardly know what he looked like.'

147

'Come along with me and I'll show you.' Frank got up. 'Show you a picture of the Guv'nor as a young lad.'

He led me into the small room beside his bedroom which he used as a dressing room. It was crowded with old-fashioned furniture, darkened by heavy red damask on the walls and at the windows. Everywhere were portraits and photographs.

'Haven't altered it,' said Frank huskily. 'Kept it much the same as when my father used it. Didn't like to clear things out. Felt as though I would be clearing *him* out. Used to come along here when I was a lad and say my little bit of Latin verse, and if I'd got it right he'd shake my hand and give me half a sovereign.'

'What, every day?' I exclaimed.

'Didn't see him every day. Usually saw him once just before I went back to college for a fresh half,' said Frank, lapsing into Eton lingo. 'He wasn't home much, you know.'

'No, he can't have been.'

'But we shouldn't have seen much of him if he had been. That wasn't the way the Guv'nor lived. He never saw much of his parents, and he didn't want to see much of us. Found us boring. Can't blame him. We *were* boring.' There had been a younger brother, now dead, and a sister who was married and lived in Ireland. 'And of course Mamma was always at Court.' For the first time I thought that if there were deficiencies in Frank's character, he was not entirely to blame. How much better children were educated and cared for now than they had been even a few years ago, I reflected.

'Here he is.' Frank was drawing my attention to a photograph in a silver frame. 'Here is Papa.'

I saw a whiskered face, a pair of direct eyes, and a mouth whose lines suggested both gentleness and sadness. Search as I might, any resemblance to Harry seemed non-existent.

148

'Of course, you can't judge from that, he was old then. But I who knew him see something, I can tell you. Here, take a look at this, done when he was a lad.' He thrust a picture done in pastel under my nose. 'What do you make of that, eh?'

I studied it. 'Perhaps there is something about the nose.'

'The nose, indeed.' He snatched it from me. 'It's the eyes, Errol, Papa's eyes again.'

To my eyes the young Ensign Edward Maurice looked no more like the young Harry than the old man, but I said: 'You may be right.' And then. 'Frank, if you think this of Harry, you will see to his education? Later on, I mean?'

He tugged at his moustache. 'The thing is, Errol, I haven't a penny to bless myself with.'

I looked at him, and thought about the seat in the House of Commons, the chambers in Gray's Inn, the little dinner parties, the very relationship with Louisette, and I thought such penury would suit me very well. I said nothing, though. It was never any use complaining to a Maurice about extravagance. And the reason was, that in their hearts they knew very well what they were about.

On the wall was a daguerreotype of a young man. He had an interesting face, with large, brooding eyes, with heavy lids.

'Who's that?'

'Oh, one of the crowned heads of Europe,' said Frank. 'Or at the very least he will have a coronet. There's hardly anyone here without a touch of the purple in his blood. It was one of Papa's little ways.' He had a closer quiz. 'Looks doomed, poor fellow, doesn't he? See a stare like that and it almost always means something bad. Most of Papa's friends died young, or went mad, or got shot. There wasn't much happiness going around then.' He laughed easily.

I swore he had already forgotten Harry. I smiled back. We'd see.

Dick Monk called again. He paced up and down the drawing room, talking. My aunt and Countess Telling were at the piano. Then he took my hand as he said goodbye.

'Off to sea for a spell, Miss Errol.'

'That's the sadness of knowing a sailor.' My voice was bright.

'Do you suppose, if a sailor, when he got back from sea, should speak of marriage to a young lady he knows, he would be taken seriously?'

'His request would certainly be considered seriously,' I said. 'Of course, I can't speak for the young lady.'

Poor Queen, I thought. I am only recruited to her service a matter of days and look what happens. I had the curious notion that Dick Monk was my workaday lover and the man at Charde my dark and secret lover who had put a spell on me. Poor Queen, indeed.

I had noticed one thing about myself just then. At the rectory, although people sometimes said that Miss Errol was in looks today, or my father, no great hand at praise, would comment 'that dress suits you, my child,' I was accounted no beauty, nor was any promise of it held out to me. No one ever took me by the hand and said: 'My dear, you *are* going to be a beauty.' But now, strangely, wonderfully, it was happening to me. I saw it reflected in my mirror and in people's eyes. Perhaps all girls, even the plainest, have their period of beauty, and this was my time. I believe now that my brother, who had eyes to see everything, and a heart full of something sharper than love and cleverer than hate, must have seen this change in me and grown angry.

One more day passed. The next day I had a message

from the policeman's wife. She made no bones this time about addressing me directly. It was a scrawled, pathetic message: Mrs Anticknap wants you to know, it ran, that she hasn't seen her husband for a week now, and no one will tell her where he is. The envelope had been addressed in another and neater hand. I knew that there was a practice with people like Mrs Anticknap, to whom writing did not come easy, to use professional 'letter-writers'. She had used one, I thought, to address her letter, but she had taken the trouble to write the message herself. Two things could be deduced from this, I decided. One, that she wanted the message to be kept private, and the other, that she wished to make sure the address was legible and I got the letter. She was anxious and afraid and she wanted me to do something about it. More, she clearly believed I *could* help her somehow. What was it she hoped I would do? My mind made a connection: go and see Mr Koenig, was the answer I arrived at instantaneously. I felt quite pleased with myself. I thought that I had used the power of deductive reasoning, that my father had trained me in, to some purpose. I wouldn't make a bad detective myself.

I dressed myself to go out. I must tell you what I was wearing, because it is important. It was summer, a hot day, and I wore dark blue muslin with a white spot. The low cut neck was filled in with a soft fichu, and a scarf covered my shoulders and arms. Because small hats placed well back were fashionable, I wore a small hat which didn't shield my face. My father had always said that he could not abide a hat or bonnet that did not shade a woman's face, but I was in London now and had learned not to look old-fashioned. My skirt had a large pocket on the right-hand side. I tell you so because the fact was important.

I studied the letter before I left Masham Square. Playing

the detective again, a note of caution sounded. Did I really know that this letter came from Mrs Anticknap? Amongst my burst of romantic reading lately, I had been reading the works of Mr Wilkie Collins, and he had taught me to be sceptical and wary. Fiction can teach us about life, I thought, as I turned my path towards Mrs Anticknap's house.

One mercy was that I now knew how to get there by omnibus. Another mercy was that Lady Geraldine was so absorbed in Countess Telling that she was giving me a free run. Today, she and the Countess had gone away for one of their somewhat mysterious visits. They would be gone some days. I suppose she thought she had solved my problems, I was safely launched in society and might be left to get on with it. In any case, she had troubles enough of her own, poor lady.

I got off the omnibus by Mr Truelove's bookshop and was standing absently staring in the window when I saw Jessie's face reflected in it beside me. I swung round.

'Jessie,' I exclaimed happily.

She was wearing a loose cloak. Underneath it I saw she was burdened with a big black bag, and a small carpet bag. A number of parcels appeared to be slung from her waist. Her left hand carried a small covered bucket. 'Off to work, as you see.'

'I am going to visit your friend Mrs Anticknap.'

'Oh yes. Helpful, was she?'

'She's very worried, Jessie.' I lowered my voice. 'About her husband, you know. He hasn't been home for a week.'

An ironic look crossed Jessie's face. 'Some wives I know would be truly grateful for the respite, but Mrs A is obstinately devoted, poor soul.'

'She loves him,' I said reproachfully.

Jessie shrugged. 'Oh, love, what is love?' She rummaged around her hangings and finally put her hand on what she wanted. 'You can carry this to Mrs A for me.'

'What is it?'

'Only a little book.'

I accepted a small packet folded up in brown paper and put it into the pocket of my dress. The policeman's wife had not looked much like a reader to me, but if Jessie said so I would deliver it.

'Into her own hands, mind.'

Then Jessie turned to the kerb. 'I have my faithful steed,' she said, pointing.

A large bicycle, hung about, as was its owner, with equipment, including, I swear, a kettle from whose spout came steam, was waiting.

'You can never ride that machine through this traffic.' I looked about me: the road was busy with carriages, drays and delivery vans.

'Certainly I can,' and she hitched up her skirt, bundled her cloak about her, tossed one end over her shoulder and was off, wobbling triumphantly away. She even dared a last look over her shoulder. 'So practical,' she panted, avoiding a carthorse only by a sudden swerve.

I almost envied her. What emancipation, I thought. I stored the idea for future use.

The door to the Anticknaps' house was opened slowly on my third pull at the bell. An eye peered through the crack.

'The lady of the 'ouse ain't 'ome.'

The door was about to shut, but I got my foot in it. Before me stood a wizened little figure, which might have been any age. Only the blueness of the eyes and the redness of the hair showed her real youth. A child, really, I thought, one of those elderly children whom the London streets create.

'It's Miss Vesey,' I said pacifically. 'I wish to speak to Mrs Anticknap.'

'She ain't 'ere. She and the children are gone away.'

The wailing of a baby from the passage behind gave her the lie.

'The baby is here,' I pointed out.

'I'm looking after it, then. It's a good baby, it is, and don't give much trouble. Excuse me, mum, if I go back to it.' And she banged the door hard in my face.

I felt sad as I plodded away. The signs of desperation in that little household were plain to see. And it was all somehow obscurely connected with me and my lost brother. I was sure of it. I put my hand in my pocket and touched the book I should have given to Mrs Anticknap. I could go back and slip it through the letter-box; but deliver it right into her own hands, Jessie had said.

The sky was growing darker and the air heavy, as if a storm approached. When we had a storm in the country it was enjoyable rather than otherwise, but a storm in London seemed against nature. The very air had gone yellow and smelt of dust and horses and people's breath. As I walked through the streets the crowds grew denser. I was pushed and buffeted from every side. Bodies seemed to block my passage and press against me whichever way I turned. As I came nearer the district where Mr Koenig lodged I had to pass through an open street market which seemed even more densely packed with people than the rest. I saw quantities of young men and women brightly dressed in gay, flash clothes. The men wore full-skirted velveteen jackets of an odd antique appearance, as if they had stepped out of an eighteenth-century picture by Morland or Stubbs. Cord trousers, tight at the knee, and heavy boots went with the jackets. Some of the lads carried beaver top hats and others wore them tilted back on the head at a rakish angle. The girls who matched them wore brightly coloured shawls and beribboned bonnets. They

154

seemed a race apart from the other people in the streets. Both sexes were smart, but the men were the smarter.

Hot and thirsty, I stopped to drink some lemonade at a stall by the kerbside selling ice-cream and cold drinks. I was served by a fat woman who looked as hot as I felt, and who fanned herself constantly with a branch of green leaves all the while she stood there, serving her wares, and indulging in repartee with her customers. I admired her skill. A couple of the brightly dressed people stopped by the stall to take a drink. I noticed that the man's jacket had long revers of plush and that the tops of his boots matched it with similar decoration. The girl wore a little muslin jacket. Her face underneath her spangled bonnet was thin, and out of it looked a pair of sharp, lawless eyes which took in me and everything about me. There was nothing rude or impertinent in it. She observed me as if she was an animal from one species and I was an animal from another. Her young man put his arm round her waist and chaffed her in a language I could not understand.

I finished my drink and put down the glass. 'Who are these people?' I asked. 'And why are there so many of them about today?'

'Oh, 'tis the costerboys' holiday,' said the stall woman tolerantly.

'Is it some special day, then?' I said, timidly I believe, for I was something in awe of my hostess.

'Some festival of their own, it will be.' She brandished a great arm like some primitive warrior. 'A law to themselves, these costerboys be.' As an established street-trader she rated herself a cut above them, I could see. Her eyes flicked over me. My cheeks were flushed, I could feel my bonnet was slightly awry, and I saw my skirt was dusty from my long, hot walk. I put up a hand to straighten my bonnet. For the first time in my life another woman was looking at me and assessing my respectability. I pulled myself together and walked on.

As I walked I thought about what I would do when I arrived where Mr Koenig lived. Would I accuse him to his face of being used by my brother to threaten and frighten me? Would I ask him about Rotten Potatoes? Dare I mention Detective Anticknap? Would I ask him what I most in the world wanted to know, where was my brother and what was his name?

I was out of the street market now and pushing through the crowds on my way to Dryden Street. I knew the direction in which I must go, but the streets were unfamiliar and I was suddenly at a loss. My confidence drained away, and I paused irresolute at a street corner. There was a policeman pacing slowly along a few yards ahead and for a moment I thought of asking him my way, but then, above all the other noises of the crowd, I heard the music of a hurdy-gurdy. I turned round and looked, and there down a side road was the hurdy-gurdy man. He was turning the handle of his machine and staring straight at me with his sad, sick eyes.

Hardly knowing what I did, blindly impelled by some strong impulse, I turned and walked in his direction.

'Did I see you not long ago in Masham Square?' Our eyes met and his expression never changed. But he did not answer, only went on turning the handle of his machine.

'I'm sure you are the same man.'

'This is my beat, lady,' he said, politely enough, but not admitting he knew me or Masham Square.

I stopped myself saying any more. I was sure it was the same man, but already people were beginning to stare. I moved away. The music from the hurdy-gurdy stopped. Behind me I heard the monkey give a little soft chatter and the man cough. I could not mistake that cough. It was he. I swung round and saw him hurrying in the opposite direction.

His appearance there, so apt and yet so surprising, frightened me. I do not believe over much in coincidences. I had the strange and unnerving feeling that a master hand was pulling the strings, and that both I and the hurdy-gurdy man were at its command.

I was now walking, although I did not notice it at once, into the famous Holy Land. I learned later that new building and the driving through of a road had cut into but not entirely destroyed its identity. It existed now in several pockets well known to the police. Detective Anticknap had been working in one of them, and Dryden Street fronted such an area.

I looked up at the façade of the house where Mr Koenig was said to lodge, and knew that I was frightened to face him. I did not even want to question the landlord now I had arrived on the spot. I stood outside in thought. Then I remembered Joseph and his death in the river Thames. I remembered the man who had rested on a table beside him. It was the entry in his book that had led us to the house in Dryden Street.

As I was standing there I saw a large woman sitting on a chair by an old pram. She had a wheel for sharpening knives on the pram and was at that moment engaged in putting an edge on a villainous-looking carver while the owner of the knife, a man in a leather apron, stood watching her. But instead of watching the knife as she laid it against the wheel, the woman was watching me.

'Here, mind that knife,' grumbled Leather Apron. 'Supposed to be putting an edge on it, you are, not taking it off. I've got to take that knife back to my master in good nick. You need a sharp knife in my trade, you do. You can't rip up a carcass and do justice to a nice side of beef without having confidence in your knife. It ain't fair to yourself to cut a beef up what is newly slaughtered, maybe, and the blood still hot, without having an edge on your knife.'

The woman took her eyes off me and got back to her job. 'Here's your knife then,' she said in a hoarse, deep voice. Her face was framed in a droopy old bonnet and, in spite of the heat of the day, she had a thick scarf wound round her neck. Her cheeks were brick red and I could see from her teeth that she probably smoked a pipe. I stared at her, fascinated. She resumed her unobtrusive interest in me.

'You look tired, mother,' I said. She did indeed. Her eyes lay sunken at the back of dark pits.

'Mayhap I am,' she said doggedly.

'Why not rest?'

'And you'll turn my wheel for me and sharpen the knives?' she asked.

'I believe I could do it as well as you, mother,' I was watching her closely. 'Let me sit down and try.'

'Get away with you.' She made a rough gesture.

'You don't do a good job, you know. Your last customer was quite right. You're not skilful.'

She looked at me from out of her great flapping bonnet like Red Riding Hood's grandmother. 'Go away,' she said, laying hold of the handle of her pram with a surprisingly solid and thick hand. 'Cease to bother me, missy.'

I heard the urgency, even the fear in the voice.

The air had got noticeably warmer and heavier as the day wore on. The sun was hidden behind a layer of cloud and the street was shadowless. I had never realised before how shadow gave solidity to the world.

The woman stood up, bulky and awkward in her heavy skirts. She picked up the chair as if she meant to move away.

158

'That chair is too small for you,' I said, 'and the pram too low for you to push easily.' I looked up at the figure. 'You are taller than you seemed sitting down.'

The chair came up as if she meant to aim it at me. But I knew that broken nose. I said softly: 'Detective Antic-knap, is it not?'

The redness faded from the face, so that the nose stood out more strikingly than ever. 'Hush.'

There were people passing on either side of us in Dryden Street, but we had been speaking quietly.

'Who are you?'

'Errol Vesey. Your wife knows me. I believe you have heard my name. And I have seen you before, on a street corner near Miss Falconet's.'

'Clear off. How do I know who you really are? Be off with you, I say. You don't look like a respectable young woman to me.' He began to grind another knife.

'I know you are here to watch Mr Koenig. Or Mr King, if that is his name,' I said deliberately.

The wheel ground to a stop: the blade of the knife shivered. It was true! He was a rotten knife-sharpener.

I pressed home my advantage. 'You told your wife. She told Miss Falconet.' That saint, I thought. 'And Miss Falconet told me.' I had his undivided attention now. 'I too am looking for Mr Koenig.'

'I must believe you, then,' he muttered. 'But for pity's sake go away. Leave it to me. What I am doing is good work and will one day be rewarded. Only I must hold steady.'

I wanted to talk to him more freely, but it seemed impossible. Then he said, still looking at his wheel and not at me. 'Go to the coffee-house across the way. I will come after you and sit by you as if by accident.'

The coffee-house was a decent enough place, crowded with young costers and their girls, all so noisy and exuberant that it was easy for me to sit overlooked in an alcove by the door. I sat there, drinking tea, or pretending to do so, and enduring the clamour about me with increasing irritation. I thought for a while he was not coming, but presently the strange figure waddled in and, taking a cup of coffee from the counter, sat down near me.

I waited.

'I fell into this business,' he said gruffly, 'on account of my "nose".'

I looked at him quickly and swallowed a laugh. In spite of the seriousness of the occasion I wanted to giggle.

'Not this organ,' he said, giving it a stroke. 'My "nose", that is my informer in the criminal fraternity. We call them "noses". All detectives have their "noses"—some several. My "nose" told me of two murders done. A boy called—well, no one of any consequence, nameless almost.'

'Joseph,' I said.

'He may have been called that,' said Anticknap. 'And another man, a fallen schoolmaster called Tom Perry, alias Rotten Potatoes. I knew Perry. He had a sort of trade in the neighbourhood writing letters and running errands. Perry had been used to carry messages, write them, too, I dare say, for this Koenig. Or at least, he boasted so. The boy Joseph heard him boast. They were both found drowned, miss. My "nose" tells me both were murdered by hands hired by this Koenig. There is many will murder for a few shillings, miss.'

'He is the dangerous criminal,' I said slowly. 'He who pays.'

'He is an elusive man. Hard to see face to face.'

'What about the landlord where he lives?'

Anticknap shook his head. 'Never sees him. Says he

comes and goes and is only a figure on the stairs.'

'I think he must be lying there.'

'If he is, he will never admit it. I know the man and he is obstinate to a fault. And then no doubt he is well paid. This is more than plain criminal business.' He lowered his voice even more. 'When I said Mr Koenig is hard to see, I did not mean this quite to the letter. No.'

'So I supposed,' I said drily.

'I believe I have seen him myself. And this is why I sit watching. To identify him positively.' He turned to me with a cunning look. 'There is one face I have seen twice. I saw a certain face once at the Austrian Embassy when I was on duty and then I sees that face once again, down here. Now that's strange, says I, and starts to think. Suppose that is the man Koenig, I ask myself. Or King as he sometimes calls himself, that would be a catch, that would be.'

'Is he so much sought by the police?' I asked. 'For what reason?'

'No, not so much sought as known, for nothing can be pinned on him. Devilish clever and quick he is, but behind all kinds of troubles. The last May Day Workers' March they said there was men paid by him going among the crowd inflaming violence. Then he paid for the men that tried to get the Army to mutiny at Woolwich in 1885. Some say he hates the British Government, and others say he's against the Queen herself.'

'And you believe you have seen him?'

'If he's who I think he is, then he is an Austrian nobleman, a duke or count or some such and a real bad lot. The bastard son of one of them archdukes, so I've heard, and angry that he should be on the wrong side of the blanket. For all that his relations have set him up nicely and with a title and all!'

'What is the name of this nobleman?'

'Ah, that I don't know, for I was on duty outside the Embassy and could only hear that he was a duke or it might be a count. But he got out of the carriage, very fine in his dark cloth suit with his fine white linen.' There spoke a man to whom a fine cloth suit made to measure would be the treasure of a lifetime. 'A great man for riding to hounds, they said, and comes here regularly for the hunting. I see the crest on the door and on one side it had fish that seemed to fly through the air. That's a way of tracking him down, miss,' he said triumphantly.

'I see why you think watching for him is dangerous,' I said. This was my brother, I thought, a man so full of hate that he wants to spread it all over the world in which he lives.

'And then, his position protects him, do you see? Naturally he keeps a good face turned to the world he meets in Embassies and fine houses. 'Tis only the likes of us that knows of this other side.'

More is guessed than you suppose, I thought, remembering my father's anxious voice and face. *He*, at least, had suspected something.

'But I don't understand why you must work alone?' It was a question that had been troubling me.

He hung his head, letting the folds of that terrible bonnet fall about his face. A mutter came out at me. 'Never told my Nellie. But I have had trouble. I'm suspended from the Police. She don't know. Must never know. Would break her heart.' It was breaking now, I thought, left alone, waiting for word from you. He went on: 'I shall get back, you see, if I do a good piece of work, and then all shall be set right.'

'What was your trouble?'

He was evasive. 'I'm a quick-tempered man and I spoke out of turn.'

And you drink a little, too, I thought, and are not without violence yourself. I was troubled by him. I sat there for a moment quietly thinking. He seemed to me more than a little crazed.

'Did Nellie send you?' he asked.

'No.' I suppose, in a way, she had, however.

'Does she know where I am?'

'Again, no.'

He finished his coffee, drinking as if it was the last drink he would ever have on this earth. 'And the baby, it thrives?'

I nodded.

'I have trusted you, miss. Trust me. My advice to you is to go away home and leave Koenig to us professionals.' He got up and then said, with a small attempt at jocularity, 'We are old hands at the game.'

I watched him walk away, a pitiful yet alarming figure. Some of the young people poked and jostled him at the door, but he got past safely and I saw him trundle off his borrowed equipment.

My thoughts had run through to their end and, forming a beautiful shape as completed, if unhappy, thoughts always do. I half-believed what he said. This mysterious nobleman with the dolphins that leapt in his crest could be my brother. It was a thought which was to grow inside me as the days went by and demand to be heard, and more and more believed in.

So there it was, I did not need any more to seek out Mr Koenig face to face. In my heart I acknowledged our relationship, and accepted all the pain and fear of connection with such a formidable figure. My father had been wise to warn me against this revengeful man. If he wanted to harm me he had the power to do it. So far he had used agents, such as the broken schoolmaster, Tom Perry. So far he had only been playing, I had felt nothing but the touch of sheathed claws.

Lady Geraldine and Countess Telling were off again the next day on another of their visits. The house was empty except for the servants and me and Harry, but we were happy enough together, working quietly in the same room. I was sewing some clothes for Windsor. To cheer myself through a task not pleasing to me, I told myself I was fitting myself out for my profession just as a soldier chose his uniform. Needless to say my spirits sagged the more surely.

On my desk was a letter from Dick Monk, handed for posting to the pilot who had seen his ship out of the Thames. Brief, laconic, it said little, but ended 'Your loving Dick'. Then, at the end, beneath the signature, scrawled as if the hand that penned it was unsteady, came these words: 'Errol, my love, I can't wait after all, I must speak. Will you be my wife? You can telegraph the *Tiger* at the Dockyard in October. Give me an answer, my girl, somehow. Will it be "Yes" or "No"?'

On a sudden impulse, I went across to my writing-desk, drew out a tablet of paper and wrote a short note to old Mr Dalrymple my solicitor, giving him the news that I might be considering marriage and that on my father's express advice I was telling him now. I blotted the letter and put it out to be posted.

That evening I saw the hurdy-gurdy man passing through the square. He looked up at the window and saw me looking down. I returned to my sewing and straightway pricked my finger so that blood stained my sewing. A drop fell on my dress, which was the blue and white muslin spot I liked so well. In the pocket, although I had forgotten it, was the book Jessie had given me for Mrs Anticknap.

In the cool of the evening I let myself out of the house and paced round the square. The sounds of the city were quietening and it was strangely peaceful. I had formed the habit of taking this lonely stroll. I liked to look up and see the lighted windows of the square around me and imagine the gay, busy life going on there.

I heard a carriage draw up behind me and the horses coming to a stop, I thought nothing of it. Everywhere I went I seemed to hear the constant sound of a horse following behind. I suppose that was what London was like.

I turned to look; it was a brougham. As it came level, a man jumped out, put a hand over my mouth, gripped me roughly round the waist and dragged me into the carriage. The door slammed and with a jerk and a rattle the carriage moved off. A bag smelling strongly of horse was pulled over my head and drawn close. A tight band was put round my wrists and another round my feet. In three minutes or less I had been swept up and trussed like a bundle.

The carriage rattled on, swinging round corners with abandon. There were two men in there with me and as I listened I came to realise that to them I was a parcel.

'Sure it's the right girl?'

'Certain sure.' A London voice. This was the man who had captured me.

Outside I could hear the rumble and jingle of the traffic, running beside us. We were on a busy road.

'You do a quick job when you've got to, I'll say that for you,' said the first speaker. 'Ever nabbed a haybag before?'

'Never you mind.' A pause, then the same voice said: 'I'll take a fag, if you please.'

For the moment there was silence except for the noise of the wheels on the cobbled road. We had turned off from the main road and were travelling through somewhere quieter. There was a lurch to the right, the sudden sense of being in an enclosed space, and the horses stopped.

'Stay put.' It was the cigarette smoker, issuing orders to the other man. His heavy hands rested on my shoulders, holding me down.

I heard the noise of the horses being uncoupled and led away; the carriage rolled forward, apparently down a slight slope. Doors slammed, and what light was filtering through to my hooded eyes now dimmed. We were inside a building.

I both heard and felt the two men get out of the carriage, which creaked and moved at their passage. They were solid men and heavy movers. My own bruises were already telling me how rough they could be.

'Leave her here. I'm not ready to do more yet.' It was the man who captured me speaking. 'I don't make a move till the moon is down.'

'It'll be low tide by that time,' came the warning.

'Never mind. We'll wait till it's on the turn.' In spite of the ominous words the speaker sounded nervous.

'I've never done a judy before.' No mistaking the unease in the second voice. 'And one of good class, too. There's bound to be an alarm raised. Why don't we just drop her near the river and let her make her way home?'

'No. And don't speak so loud.'

They must be standing close by me; I had no difficulty in hearing every word. It frightened me very much that they spoke so plainly in front of me. In spite of a show of nerves they must mean to kill me. They were just trying to get ready to do it.

'Why does *he* want her dead?'

'I'm not in his confidence,' said his companion with heavy irony. 'He gives the orders and he pays the money, and I take the money and I do what I'm paid for. That's an end to it. I don't ask why ... I *may* speculate.'

I was frightened, I was uncomfortable; it was my death

166

they were discussing, but I found myself thinking: 'Pompous ass.'

'She's an heiress, that's what she is. She stands between someone—we know him, don't we, but we won't name him—and a fortune. *That's* why he wants her dead. Must be money, if you ask me, with him it is and always has been money.'

I heard them pulling at a heavy door, dragging it across the cobbles. 'Leave the candle,' said one. 'It keeps the rats off.'

The voices died away and I was alone, still lying across the seat of this smelly old carriage, and shut inside what I judged to be a stable or carriage house. Everything smelt so strongly of old, damp leather and of horse that I thought I might be locked up in an old livery stables, a place where carriages and horses were let out on hire.

I lay still, silently assessing my chances. I was tied up, I was locked in, and I had at least three strong adversaries. I totted them up: two men had abducted me, a third had driven the horses and led them away. Something scrambled up my leg and ran down the other side of the seat. I heard the scratch and patter of its feet. I knew it was a mouse or a rat. It had felt heavy and big enough to be a rat.

There was a hole in the sacking wrapped round my face and I moved my head until I managed to get my eye level with it.

All I could see was the roof of the carriage, which was covered in stained green silk. Once, long ago, it had been a gentleman's equipage. But I remembered the silk. I had seen it before. This was the brougham I had travelled in on my first day in London. No wonder the driver had looked at me in surprise. He was not a genuine cabby, or, if he was, he was also in the pay of criminals. Perhaps he had been following me on that first day. I wondered why he had taken the risk of letting me hire his cab home to

Masham Square. Then I remembered a policeman, Tom Anticknap, had been watching him. I remembered too that *other* man who had stood near Jessie on the corner of the road. Had he just got out of the brougham and was it his pistol I found? I believed it was.

Once again the scrabble and slither of feet, but this time I heard, too, a strong miaou and the pounce of a powerful paw followed by a squeak and a crunch. 'An odious cat,' I thought, at once heartened and sickened by my agile companion.

My hands were tied behind me, but I swung my feet off the seat and found that I could make an effort at sitting, and from thence to standing. I half rolled, half stumbled my way out of the carriage and fell full length, face down on the floor.

As good luck would have it, my fall brought the hole in the sacking up to my eyes again, and I saw how near I was to the candle, standing on a small shelf and guttering away bravely.

I rolled over on one side, drew my legs up and tried to rise, but I couldn't do it. Then an old nursery trick came back to me. I managed to roll on to my knees in a sideways posture, then by rocking to the left and right with increasing vigour, I managed to swing my body over till I was kneeling. Then I pushed myself erect.

I edged over to the candle, turned my back, and, guided by the heat, lowered my wrists to the flame. When I felt the heat on my skin I knew I was in position. I could only hope that the frail flame would burn at the cord till I could wrench it apart.

I was in luck. The cord had been impregnated in some smelly oil and was willing to burn. I stood there, head in darkness, enduring the pain and the smell, till I heard a man's voice outside. 'This door ain't locked, Jem,' he called.

'Leave it be,' came an answer from further away. 'I'll be in there this minute.'

Only a minute. With a groan, I tried to wrench my wrists apart. I felt the rope give. Slowly, painfully, I dragged my hand free.

Not waiting to free the other hand but with the remaining tethers still clinging to it, I tugged and pulled the bag off my head. As it came off I saw that I was in a long, low building with rough whitewashed walls. The carriage I had left stood on my right. To my left stretched a row of shabby vehicles. On a shelf beyond I saw black plumes supported on a mount and by them a folded pall. My horrified eyes recognised a black and silver hearse. On a small metal plate at the side of the hearse was inscribed the legend: 'Jos. White'.

I was in the stables belonging to an undertaker's establishment. Whether the criminals who had kidnapped me owned it or were friends of Jos. White, I could not know and it hardly mattered. What mattered was to escape in the fraction of that one minute left to me.

I sat down to untie my legs. As I did so I met the cold-eyed stare of a huge tabby cat. Some cats look friendly and domestic, but this one looked the inhabitant of the London jungle it was, and uncommonly well-fed into the bargain. I felt no desire at all to pet it, only to leave its company rapidly.

I crept to the stable door and looked across the yard, which opened through an archway to the street. Lights were shining out of a room a few yards away, and its door was open. A man was standing in the door, but his back was to me. I picked up my skirts, and ran. As I ran I heard a shout.

Once through the arch, I turned right and then right again, running desperately according to no fixed plan through a warren of unknown small streets, one after the other dark and ill lit. There were figures in them, some of which lurched towards me and others which drew back with a curse.

I dared not look behind me to see if I was followed.

I hurried on without noticing my surroundings, fearing all the time to hear footsteps following. When I looked around again, the character of the street about me had changed. I paused to take it in. What I saw was a broad street, lined with shops and bars. Ahead I saw a theatre. It was crowded with people out to enjoy themselves.

I soon realised that I was emerging into one of the new roads that had cut into the old rookery of St Giles, the so-called Holy Land. People who had known the district years ago assured me that it had changed out of recognition, even the pockets of the Holy Land that remained were, so they said, but shadows of their former lawless selves. Jessie, however, told a different story. 'My dear,' she had said, 'get behind the new roads and it's as bad as ever. People who say different deceive themselves, and forget what they do not wish to remember.' Now I knew she was right. I looked behind. No one seemed to have followed me. I was away.

This street seemed prosperous and safe enough. All the shops had great windows of plate-glass, and behind them was displayed a wealth of luxury that seemed accessible to all. This was the difference from Piccadilly and Bond Street. In the older streets the shops were small, discreet and exclusive. Here, the world and its riches were wide open before you—India, Africa, the Americas had been dredged to bring up treasures for your pleasure. All you needed was the money and you could have them for the taking. I have to admit I was child enough and Maurice enough to find it exciting. I knew it was considered a mark of breeding and good taste to prefer shopping in the unostentatious establishments of Jermyn Street and St James's, and to leave these emporia to the new rich of commerce and industry, but I thought I would enjoy such intoxicating meccas. I slowed down, gradually becoming calmer, forcing myself to breathe more slowly, and deliberately pausing to look in shop windows. When I did so I took a discreet look around me to see if I was followed. But I seemed safe. I had left Oxford Street behind me and was now in High Holborn. I was steadier now. 'The Holborn Silk Market', I read above one shop. I stood gazing at a window of sumptuous silks that would have done justice to the Queen herself, if she could have forsaken her eternal blacks. Crimson, sea-green, purple and gold spilled themselves out in a profusion before me. 'Damascus silk', said a big printed card in front of the rolls. The price, also displayed, made my eyes open wide. They were princes here, too, I thought, princes with bigger purses than I'd guessed. I could dress for a year on the cost of two yards of this silk. No wonder the prosperous merchants' wives who thronged the pavements looked as though they would give ground to no one. I had already noticed in them a tendency to push anyone aside who stood in their way, I seemed to feel a distant, scornful look at me as I passed. I could see from my reflection in the plate-glass windows that I was bedraggled. Well, it was good for my pride to be humbled, I thought, or so my father (not himself noticeably a humble man) would have said. I held my head up and walked on.

There was an omnibus stage just about here, where passengers were set down and picked up under the genial eye of a tall policeman. Here the crowd was greatest of all, the numbers aggravated by the theatre, obviously an attractive rallying place, close at hand. I noticed a concourse of women strolling to and fro, studying the photographs displayed outside the theatre, and occasionally disappearing into the smart-looking eating place next door, from which floated appetising smells of grilled meat and coffee.

The citizens of London required the world to send them the best of its produce to eat as well as wear. I was hungry myself and moved, without thought, towards the restaurant.

Of course, I wasn't going in. I was just curious enough to look. I stood for a moment staring inside. The window was partly covered by a silk veil and edged with red plush curtains, but I could see through to the room behind. Small tables crammed the floor; sofas with long tables before them lined the walls; here and there stood a side table piled high with fruit and confections of cream and sugar. I thought it all looked delightful. My mouth distinctly watered.

How pretty, I breathed, aloud, I suppose, for a man beside me looked at me, then looked away again. A man and woman passed through the restaurant doors, the woman giggling.

I went back to where the omnibus was just drawing away from the kerb. I wanted to find out if it travelled a route that would put me on my way home. Just then a man put his arm round my waist. I pushed him away.

The crowd of people pressed around us. No one seemed to notice. I heard someone, a woman, laughing. The man, he was quite young and well dressed, reached out a strong hand and took me by the arm. 'Here with you, Betty,' he said. 'Don't be so stand-offish.' He was taller than me, thick-set, even burly, and he had a good grip on my arm, but I wrenched it away, turning my body so that his wrist twisted. He swore, and let go. I was glad I had hurt him. I tried to hurry away, but the crowd seemed to block my passage. Another omnibus was arriving and people were pressing forward to get on it. I became anxious to get on board myself and began to push forward. I found myself held from behind. Someone had a firm grip on my skirt. I heard the gathers at the waist rip as I tried to pull away.

I said something very unladylike under my breath and

turned to face the same burly man. I had my hands free now, however, and reached up to slap his face. By good chance or otherwise the claw of a small ring I was wearing scratched his face and blood appeared.

He said nothing, but his eyes were furious. I saw his mouth set in a peculiar and ugly way, with the corners slanting downwards showing his teeth. I knew him now, I knew him by his smell, his voice and the touch of his hands. It was the man who had dragged me into the carriage.

We were noticed now, and a small clearing opened in the crowd, in which we confronted each other. I looked around for help, but no one came to my aid, which I thought strange.

'Will no one help me?' I panted.

'Girls like you are a public nuisance and ought to be whipped,' said one thin-faced old woman in a sibilant whisper. 'I'd do it to you. Leave decent folk be.'

I stared in amazement. She hardly looked respectable herself. 'You old witch,' I said.

'You come along with me,' said my assailant, gripping my elbow and dragging me forward. 'I'll show you. I know what to do.'

'Leave the lassie be,' said a tired-faced old workman pushing past with his bag of tools. I think he would have helped me, but events moved too fast.

I saw a cab drawn up at the kerb, the driver drawing up his reins preparatory to departing. My hope was to leap into it and demand to be carried away. My hope gave me the strength to tear myself away.

But as I sped forward the cab began to move. It was occupied. I saw a negligent, elegant hand, a thin wrist, an edge of white linen, the fine black broadcloth of a sleeve. Then the cabby touched the horse with his whip and they were gone.

I stood feeling truly frightened for the first time, before a strong hand jerked me round to face a policeman.

He was stolid and thickset, as unlike poor mad Antic-knap as could be. His uniform was tight round his neck and my sharp eyes saw that it had worn a sore place in the skin. He looked like a man whose temper was naturally good, but now was as frayed as his collar.

'This young woman has been making a nuisance of herself to me, hanging on my arm and pushing herself against me, and telling me she'll give me pleasure of her company and other lewd things I wouldn't care to repeat, and I want you to take her in charge. She offends me.' The grip on my elbow did not lessen.

The policeman scratched his neck. 'Ah, well now, sir,' he said in a placatory tone. I could read his mind easily. Let's have no more trouble, he was saying, and let's all go away home.

I opened my mouth to speak. With a conscious effort I summoned up a memory of Lady Geraldine's voice. I knew that any echo of her tones commanded respect from men like policemen. They recognised behind it generations of the ruling class.

But when I tried to speak, whether from nerves or from some muscular fatigue following my struggle, nothing came out of my mouth except a little croak. Never let it be said that Errol Vesey was speechless, but although words were bubbling up angrily, voice was denied. Inside me I vowed fiercely that never again would I feel even the faintest amusement when a country girl come to be maid stood speechless before me. *Now*, I was the one to be tongue-tied.

But I expect my outraged eyes said something to the policeman.

'You're not making a charge, sir, are you?' asked the constable, gamely struggling to please all.

'I'm a respectable man,' said my enemy, 'and 'tis a disgrace that such creatures should be allowed to pester decent citizens.'

Now that the heat had faded from his face, I saw to my dismay that he did indeed look exactly what he said he was: a respectable citizen. He spoke up like an honest man. I remembered that arm round my waist, that hot anger, and found it hard to match with the man who now spoke so quietly. His voice, his very accent seemed different.

'She's injured me.' He dabbed his cheek where the blood was still fresh.

A drop of blood fell on the constable's hand. His expression hardened. 'There's too many o' you lot around here, and too bold you are becoming. Decent folk has no peace.' He had struck a sympathetic chord in his audience, and, like the natural actor he was, he sensed it. 'I'll have to ask you to step with me, sir,' he said to my accuser, who looked triumphant. On me he placed a tight grip.

Some people had gathered round us, sucking in the drama. Others were hurrying past, unwilling to be touched by the sordid scene. Still others lurked at a distance, wanting to see all but not be noticed. I took all this in almost unconsciously, but it was a picture imprinted on my mind that I never forgot.

A voice from the outer circle called, 'Let the judy go.' Another took up the call with a wailing cry of 'Let her go,' and then another. It was horrible.

And all the time I was being edged quietly through the crowd. I found I could neither free my arm nor impede the motion, there was something relentless about it all.

At the edge of the crowd, we paused. 'The station's just ahead, sir,' said the policeman.

Close to us, standing by the wall with his bag of tools at his feet, was the old workman who had spoken up for me. My voice had come back. 'Sir, sir,' I called. 'You can speak for me. Tell the constable that it was not my fault, it was not my fault. It was this man!'

He looked at me, and his old face was kind and sympathetic, but utterly resigned and hopeless. 'But who will believe you, you poor little drab?' he said.

I believe I shall hear those words till I die. They felt then, and they feel now, like a brand that had been put on my face and that I could never take off.

They shocked me for a moment into acceptance and I walked quietly beside the two men to the police station.

But I was coming to my senses. My voice had returned and with it my powers of self-command. For a minute or two I was quiet, as I have said, because I was shocked. But soon I was quiet because I was thinking. Of course, they cannot keep me here, I reasoned, or not for very long. I am a young woman of education and social position. I can soon prove it and then they must release me. Then this horrible fellow who has accosted me will know what it is to deal with a girl of spirit.

I glanced at the man. I did not fail to notice that he looked pleased with himself. And also shockingly respectable, damn him. I found I was able to say 'damn him' quite easily, although but yesterday my lips would have failed to form the words.

He was telling his story to a constable in uniform who sat at a desk. He was supplying name and address in glib, comfortable tones. He appeared to be called Bertram Biggins.

I thought it was ridiculous he should be allowed to go on any further and interrupted him. 'That's enough,' I said. 'There's no need to go on.'

No one stopped talking, no one listened to me. I might not have spoken. Frustration welled up inside me and I pummelled on the desk with both fists. 'Listen, I say.'

The man at the desk turned wearily round. 'Drunk, is she, then?'

His colleague shrugged. 'Like enough.'

'She'll calm down in the cell. Or the others in there'll calm her.'

The indifferent brutality of his remark enraged me. 'Let me tell you,' I cried, 'you will repent those words. And you will apologise to me. I am not what you take me to be.'

There was a guffaw.

'I am a woman of family and education.' By now I was beside myself with fury.

The man at the desk raised a cynical, worldly-wise eyebrow. 'So it's a governess come to the bad, is it? Or a dollymop that can act genteel?'

'I am not lying,' I said, with emphasis on each word.

There must have been something in my voice that carried conviction, because he stopped short and gave me an unsmiling look. Thank God, I thought, now we will come to the end of this nightmare.

'What's this, then?' he said, slowly.

'Yes,' I said, my breathing suddenly difficult to manage. I swallowed.

He got up and walked round, looking me up and down as he did so. I could see him appraising my clothes. They were not what he expected. Very slightly his expression altered. 'So, well, what's your name, then? And where do you come from?'

I paused, summoning up the courage to give my aunt's address. Errol Vesey, c/o Lady Geraldine Maurice, Masham Square. The pause went on too long. I remained silent.

'So. No name?' He flicked his eyes again over my gown. 'Steal the clothes, did you? Not your usual style, eh?'

'NO!'

'What's that in your pocket, then?'

I had a heart-shaped pocket on the front flounce of my skirt. We all wore them then, even the Queen herself. Such pockets were large enough to hold a purse for coins, a smelling bottle and a handkerchief. Mine held the packet Jessie had given me. He took this from my pocket, not heeding my protests.

'What's this? Your property, sir?' Mr Biggins shook his head. No one took any notice of me. A small book came out of the packet into curious hands. 'Is this *yours*, then, my girl? I might have known it. Pooh, you're all alike, your sort. Dirty stuff, this is.'

He handed the little book to the constable, whose kind country face grew long and solemn. He handed it back, shuffling with embarrassment.

'You can stop play-acting now, my girl, about you being this or being that. I know your sort. Here,' he called to an inner room. 'Here, take this one down to the lower room and put her in with the other pollies, and we'll get her particulars taken.'

'It's crowded.' A woman had appeared at the door, a tall woman with a face and figure more manly than many men's.

'Never mind that now. It'll do.'

By turns I had been frightened, frustrated, and finally, plain angry, but never once had it occurred to me that I would not be listened to in the end. I had believed that my explanations would be heard and believed. That no one would bother to listen to me at all was beyond what I had expected.

A door banged behind me and a key turned. I knew now what it was to be a woman, and a woman of the lower classes at that.

To be a woman, I thought bitterly, was to be ignored, someone whose voice was not heard, and whose person could be pushed and bullied by those of superior strength.

178

It was to be at the mercy of the stupid and the cruel and the blind. My social class had hitherto protected me, but as soon as that barrier was down, all my education and intelligence and courage seemed to avail me nothing.

I stood there before the iron door, without turning to face the room behind me. There were tears in my eyes and bitter thoughts in my head. Then I swung round.

The light was bad. What there was of daylight came from one small window high in the wall. I had a confused impression of the room being crowded with figures sitting on low benches, others sitting on the floor and leaning against the wall, and still others lying down. The air smelt ... but I will not tell you how the air smelt. The air of Jockey Fields Passage or the Holy Land was a scented paradise to it.

A steady, constant murmur like the buzz of numerous flies rose from the room. It was a sullen sound with no welcome in it. Not that I wanted a welcome. God forbid. I did not wish to feel at home here. I stood there, unmoving, determined not even to sit down. I stood near the door, clinging, I suppose, to the thought that it would soon open to let me out. I tried not to see the rest of the room too clearly, it was still a blur in which I saw no faces plain and caught no eye.

I don't know how long I stood there, long enough for my legs to ache. Then I felt a little tug at my skirt. I looked down. A young woman leaning against the wall pointed silently at a box pushed to the wall to make a rough bench. She said nothing, just pointed, then looked away. After a moment's reflection, I sank down.

I had plenty to think about. Images hung before my eyes. The face of the hurdy-gurdy man, seen near here and in Masham Square. I heard his dry cough. I saw a narrow aristocratic hand at the window of a dirty London cab. I heard poor Anticknap say: 'I saw him pass out, so lordly-

179

looking, in his white linen and black suit'. Poor Anticknap, did I say? Why pity him now? My predicament was, anyway for the moment, worse than his. And I began to believe it was not accident, but contrived.

I saw clearly now that the hurdy-gurdy man was a spy sent to observe and pass on what happened in Masham Square. He was well known in the household. The little servant had gone to get a glass of water without a word when she heard him cough. It was an action she must have performed many times before. I remembered the look that had passed between them. The girl knew him well and was in love with him, I was convinced of it. She would answer any questions he put to her and think no harm of it. Through her he could know all that the servants knew of what went on upstairs—and that was almost everything. My movements were probably as well known to my brother as they were to me. He must know about my appointment to the Queen, about Harry, about Countess Telling, everything.

The room seemed to grow darker with my thoughts as I sat there, slumped against the wall. I remembered the pistol I had hidden in the drawer at Masham Square. I had found that pistol in a cab the day I arrived in London. On the butt was the Imperial Austrian eagle. It was an old army pistol. Coincidence? I doubted it. On that day I had been followed by a man who had carried the pistol. On the pavement outside Jessie's there had been a number of casual loungers. The man who had lost the gun had been amongst them, rubbing shoulders with Anticknap. The one true coincidence had been that I had taken the very same cab. I shook my head. Even that could have been planned. Even the most ordinary details of my life seemed to be liable to manipulation.

I was gradually taking in the scene, willynilly. The girl who had motioned me to sit down was herself lying

languidly against the wall with her eyes closed. Two
women crouched on the ground seemed to be playing a
sort of gambling game with dice.

No, I thought, turning my eyes away. The pistol was
not left for me to find. It was a genuine accident, a
blunder. Remotely, at the back of my mind, stirred the
notion that the gun and the letter were solid evidence I
might one day find useful.

I kept going back in my thoughts to Mr Biggins, the
so-called Bertram Biggins, honest citizen of London. I
remembered how his accent and his manner and his very
expression had changed when he spoke to the policeman.
Natural enough, you will say, but I found myself wondering if my path through London had not been followed and
if my brother had sent Mr Biggins after me on purpose
to make the very accusation that had now been made.

'Perhaps he would like to humble me,' I thought. 'He
would choose to see me degraded if he could.'

I remembered the man in the cab, leaning back so that
his face could not be seen, only a shadowy presence, but
there watching to see what happened. A sour taste of
anger came into my throat : he must be well pleased.

I ground my teeth. When I got out of here my first act
would be to see Mr Biggins, if that *was* his name, was
tracked down and punished for his lying. And Jessie, too,
I am afraid I thought, for that book of hers had certainly
added to my trouble. What was in it?

The woman who had pulled at my skirt said : 'Best
make yourself comfortable. Far as you can.' She had a
soft, husky voice.

'I shan't be here long,' I said absently, 'I'll be out soon.'

'So we all say,' she said drearily. 'At first.'

I stared at her, the words were cold and hard to bear.
'It's true,' I said stoutly.

'It's natural to be impatient the first time, but you

181

comes to accept it wonderfully,' she went on, still in that terrible emotionless tone.

I couldn't bear it. 'No!'

You who have never been in prison will not know the emotion that rushes through the spirit the moment the lock turns in the door. However innocent, you feel guilty; however confident, the fear grows inside you that you will never get out. I knew both those feelings now and they flowered inside me like a sickness. I looked about me in fear that I might stay there for ever and never find my way out. Errol Vesey would be lost and another nameless, craven, cringing prisoner would take her place.

'Crying? Don't cry, dear.' She touched me with a tentative, tender hand. 'Lord, I remember how I cried the first time I saw this place. I was blubbering like a baby, but you see it was no use, no use at all. 'Tis better just to be quiet, like, and let time do what it will.'

'I'm not crying.'

'That's better, then.' She turned round to look at me and, seeing her for the first time full face, I saw she was about my own age, or younger. 'What did they bring you in for, my dear? They 'as various excuses when the mood takes them, I do know.' She was from the country, I thought. Her voice had an accent that reminded me of the villages at home.

'You're from Suffolk?' I said, leaning forward, eager in my turn.

She drew back quickly, her face hardening. 'Enough of that. Where I'm from is of no matter to you. What are you in for?'

'It was nothing to do with me. It was the man's fault.'

'We all say that,' she said, her tone dreary once again.

I stood up angrily, unable to bear her terrible passivity any longer. 'It's true,' I said. 'True, true, true.' Almost every word she said frightened me. It was as if I was inside a fantasy, common to all women, and that everything I did or said would find an echo in her mind.

A fight had started among the women gambling on the floor and they were rolling over and over, pummelling each other and screaming. I watched in horror, then I moved forward to try to separate them. My new friend stopped me with a tug at my skirt, as before.

'Leave them be. They enjoy it.'

'How can they?'

She gave a little laugh and relapsed into silence. Very soon I saw she was right. The fight stopped and the two women sat down side by side, having neither damaged each other nor torn their clothing beyond what was torn already. The game was resumed.

Seated behind them I now saw a figure huddled in a corner nursing a young baby. The child, which must have been aroused by the noise of the fight, began to wail. My companion deliberately turned, so that her back was to the mother and child.

One of the onlookers of the dice game moved away from the group and slumped herself full length on the bench near me. She rested her chin on her hand and stared boldly about her. Her dark brown eyes had a fierce gleam which gave a charm to the white face. She was wearing a skirt of orange flounces and a bodice of dark purple; the two articles must have come from different outfits, but so strong was her personality that she amalgamated the two and made them one. She checked me and the woman next to me with her eyes, visibly ticking off points about us one by one. It seemed to me they knew each other.

'I've been telling her not to fash herself. Why, you get quite to like it, don't you, Reba?'

'Like it? It's as good as Buckingham Palace, it is to me,'

said Reba, her tones full of savage irony. 'I tell you what: I like it better than the Grand Turkish Divans, I do, and that's saying something special, that is.'

'Ah yes, the Divans,' said my new friend, moving uneasily. 'I don't think that as a rule you meet any good gentlemen in the Divans.'

Reba yawned. 'Tedious, ain't it, waiting for the magistrate to appear.' She yawned again. 'I believe I'll make a dash at respectability.' And she looked at herself in a little broken bit of mirror and tidied her hair.

I caught sight of myself in the mirror, bonnet pushed back on my head, fichu torn, skirt ripped, and then looked from Reba to my image and thought we looked sisters beneath the skin. For the first time I thought Mr Biggins had not been without excuse. Because the incredible thing was that, battered and untidy as I was, I knew I had never looked better. My eyes were bright and my cheeks pink. Whether I liked it or not, I knew I *must* attract.

So unpredictable is human nature that the moment I took this in, my spirits underwent an unpremeditated change for the better; at once my courage came back and I felt full of resource.

I stood up.

'What's say I marry?' said Reba, having finished her toilet. She had a little bottle in one pocket, from which she refreshed herself.

'If you can, Reba,' said the other doubtfully.

'There's a sailor boy I've come across in Paddy's Goose that I dessay would make an offer for me if I gave him the encouragement,' said Reba. 'But then again, it'd be deuced dull married to a sailor. He'd never be home.' And with a loud laugh she slapped her friend on the back.

I am not a great baby fancier. Few girls my age are, I suppose, but my life in the country had meant visits to many cottages and had given me some experience of what sick and healthy babies sound like. There had been something in the wail of that child that sounded wrong. I could no more help going across to speak to his mother than I could help breathing. Generations of interfering rectory blood stirred in my veins.

They were two babies together, I thought, looking at the two little waifs huddled inside one old cloak. It was not cold in this room, rather the reverse, so the cloak must have been for shelter rather than warmth. I could understand and even share the impulse.

The girl stirred and finally looked up at me. Amazingly, she smiled. 'The baby looks ill,' I said bluntly. This was not the place for polite circumlocutions.

'He doesn't eat, you see.' I had to stoop to catch the words, they floated out like ghosts of a voice that had once been.

'Do you eat?' I asked. I thought I had never seen starvation so clearly written on a face, no, not in some of the starveling peasant cottages at home.

'I had something when I was brought in here. They have been very kind, really.' She hung her head.

'She was caught stealing two penny buns,' volunteered a stout woman by her side. 'What do you expect with a girl in her pickle? No need for you to pull such a long face, my dear. She'll go to her Maker soon enough, I dessay, and then they won't either of them be any trouble to anyone, leastways themselves.' There was a sort of hearty and unrelenting paganism in the voice that forbade any conventional sympathy I might have been about to offer.

'Something must be done,' I said.

The fat woman looked at me ironically. 'Ay, something will be done, sure enough. She'll be sent to clink, won't she? And then when she and the baby have been nicely improved by that, she can come out and start all over again. Or go to the workhouse. She'll have a nice choice, she will.'

'Or they might transport me,' whispered the girl.

'That's been over and done with for years,' I said.

She shook her head in weak obstinacy. 'When they choose, they can, I know. But what does it matter? I shouldn't survive, nor would baby.'

I could see she was not a girl of high intelligence, but she had a soft and gentle manner and her appearance, in health, would have been appealing. A year ago, she must have been a pretty, simple, shy girl.

Reba came sauntering over. I think I interested her, and like an animal caged with a strange beast, she wanted another look.

'Wish they'd get a move on,' she announced cheerfully. 'I want to be off. I shall pay me fine or my cash-carrier will, and I'll be out. Ta ta, the rest of you, in case you ain't so lucky.'

'You'll be back, Reba.' She was obviously well known to all. 'And one day they'll keep you here.' The fat woman nodded her head. 'You'll get the boat or something.'

'Not me.' Reba was fingering my skirt. 'Nice stuff. I can tell. I was a dressmaker before I took up with other ways. But, lord, you couldn't keep body and soul together on what they paid.' She studied my face with open interest. 'You're fresh, aren't you? Seems to me you rate yourself pretty superior. Where'd you come from, then?'

I cast around for something to keep her from going on. 'I am a clergyman's daughter,' I said stiffly.

The women roared with laughter, Reba loudest. 'So are we all,' she said.

'You'd better think of another tale. Why, I've been a clergyman's daughter, Bessie here is a clergyman's daughter regularly, aren't you, Bessie?' Bessie nodded. 'And even my old misery in the corner,' she nodded her head backwards to the woman who had first spoken to me, 'has been a clergyman's daughter at least once. No, my dear, you'll have to think of another story to tell.'

Having comfortably put me down, she and Bessie wandered off to make a nuisance of themselves to the dice players. The girl with the baby and I were left alone.

'You mustn't mind them,' she said timidly. 'It's only their way. They aren't so bad.'

'If they are, it's not their fault,' I said, thoughtfully.

'Oh, it's our fault,' she said. 'We're weak and sinful and so we has to be punished. I know that. I'm ready to be punished.'

'I don't think Reba's ready to be punished.' In spite of myself I smiled. 'She looks as though she might do some of the punishing.'

'Yes, there's a deal of spirit about Reba, there is,' sighed the girl, hushing the baby, which was making a pitiful attempt to cry. I thought she might have let it cry, poor little thing, it was its only sign of life.

While we were talking, I had been writing on a piece of paper. Now I wrapped some money in the paper and gave it to the girl. 'When you get out of here, go to the address I have written on the paper. They will look after you there.' I had given her Jessie Falconet's and Mrs Besant's address. I knew I could trust them. Where I might be myself by then I would not dwell on.

She took the packet in a grip at once limp yet tenacious.

I put out a finger and stroked the baby's head. He had a plain, pinched little face, very yellow in colour.

'He looks like his father,' she said. Then she sighed. 'As I remember him, that is.'

I waited. Slowly and clumsily she started to tell me her story. It was extremely simple. She had, she said, been a governess in the household of a London merchant, looking after his two daughters. The son of the house had come back from the West Indies where he had been visiting one of the family concerns, and found the young girl pretty and attractive. She too had liked him. They had been left alone except for the other servants one long hot Bank holiday. He had taken her to Hampstead Heath. She was not explicit. But the idyll had hardly lasted long. Her employers had discovered it, she had been turned from the house. When she went home her father (her mother was dead) had done the same thing. She had a little savings, she worked until it was impossible to work longer. A trickle of a tear ran down her face.

I believed it all except the bit about being a governess. I thought she had probably been a superior kind of nursery maid. But the story was nonetheless sad.

'And what about the child's father? What happened to him? Was he punished too?'

'Leonard? Oh, I don't know, I suppose not. It was different for him. A gentleman, you know.' She wiped away a tear.

Different for him, I thought, you poor little wretch. I patted her hand and stood up.

I will not moralise, let other pens than mine do that. I will be content to record my anger. Something my brother could not possibly have expected had happened. He had shown me one world, expecting me to flinch from it, and I had determined to change it. Hateful, detestable world in which men ruled. I vowed I would never bow my head to it again. I would love a man if I must, and I began to see I was the foolish sort that probably would, but I would master my own problems.

It was at that moment a fighter in woman's cause was born. I would help Jessie Falconet. The amused, detached observer of her world was gone and I was up in arms. How could I have guessed that beneath my quiet exterior lived such a tiger?

Time dragged on. I slept and woke to find greasy mugs of tea being handed round. I turned away from mine with a shudder. I was conscious of neither hunger nor thirst. I suppose a night had passed. It was hard to be sure. The timelessness of the imprisoned had bolted the door on me.

There was a jangling sound of keys, and the door opened. The police matron stood there, to be greeted with jeers and mocking calls from some of the prisoners, and ominous silence from others. She came over and tapped me on the shoulder. 'Here, you, you're wanted upstairs. Follow me.'

In silence, and watched by all, I followed her.

I walked down a corridor, up a winding narrow stair and emerged into a crowded courtroom. I looked across the room to a dais where a man sat alone. A tall man with a handsome, intellectual face. He stared straight at me and I saw surprised recognition come into his face. He leaned down and spoke to a clerk sitting at a table on a lower level.

I have confused memories of the next few minutes. I believe someone must have asked me my name, for I remember standing up very straight and saying, 'No name. No name, no name.' The words seemed to ring round the court till I was dizzy.

Then I was helped away, hands and voices were suddenly polite, and I was ushered into a small side room that was empty.

I was left there to wait alone. Presently the matron appeared, her voice courteous now, and asked if I would like some tea. This time I accepted, and when it came I drank thirstily, then sat back refreshed.

Finally the door opened and in came the magistrate. To my surprise, Fletcher was with him.

Fletcher said : 'I have come to take you back to Masham Square, Miss Vesey.' Then he motioned to the magistrate. 'This is my cousin, Sir Paul Bedower.'

Fletcher had a cloak of soft, dark wool on his arm, which he handed to me. It was nothing of mine and looked new, so it must have been bought for the occasion. I slipped it on gratefully, covering my crumpled and torn dress and drawing the hood over my hair.

Fletcher adjusted the cloak round my neck in a kindly, gentle gesture. He said nothing, neither did Sir Paul, but the action gave me courage to speak, which I knew I must do.

'Thank you for rescuing me.' Nothing could keep that telltale huskiness out of my voice.

'Hardly rescue, Miss Vesey.' Sir Paul's eyes and voice were kind, but his manner was grave. So this was the rich city banker, with his fine carriage, the man whom only the best would satisfy. Yes, I could believe it so.

'Well, I have been in a pickle,' I said, trying to make a joke out of it, but with poor material. The continued gravity of their faces convinced me I was not entirely out of it yet, either. 'But of course, it was all a terrible nonsense with that man Biggins. How could anyone give him countenance ?'

'Tell me about it, if you please, Miss Vesey,' said Sir Paul.

I told him of my odyssey through the streets of London, but I gave him an edited story, telling him nothing of my brother, and relating my behaviour more directly to a search for Mrs Anticknap's missing husband. No, I did not tell them everything, and I know now that he and Fletcher did not tell me all they knew, either.

He listened carefully to what I said. 'I don't think you understand exactly why you are here, Miss Vesey.' And then he produced Jessie's little book, and laid it on the table in front of me. 'How did you come to be carrying this?'

'It was given to me to deliver to ...' I hesitated to go on.

'You know what it is?'

I shook my head.

'The Knowlton Pamphlet.' I still looked blank. 'The Malthusian Principle, Miss Vesey, the limitation of population.'

I might have continued to look blank still, and many a girl would have done, but I was country-bred, when all was said and done, and I understood. Some of the country-women had their own ways of dealing with the problem, and dark hints about dosing with willow herb or visits to Mother Gamage, our local herbalist and witch woman, coupled with stories of babies that were 'overlaid' in the crowded box beds of the cottages, had been well assessed by me. Perhaps I would not have admitted it publicly, but I understood. Jessie might have told me more, trusted me more, I thought.

'Miss Vesey, I must tell you that by the Obscene Publications Act of 1857 you could be prosecuted for trading in this pamphlet.' He touched the book. 'That is the seriousness of your position.'

'I wasn't trading,' I said.

'You were passing it on, though, Miss Vesey. Who gave it to you? Come now, tell me, please.'

I kept silent.

He sighed. 'Well, I could make a good guess. It will be one of a small group of people. Tell me, do you know Mr Edward Truelove's bookshop?'

He saw recognition flash into my eyes, and nodded, satisfied. 'I see you do. Miss Vesey, my advice to you is to steer clear of its neighbourhood, unless ...' he paused.

'Unless?' I said.

191

'Unless you are in very earnest and it is your life's work.'

Meeting his steady, intelligent gaze, I saw that he was more in sympathy with Jessie's work than I had supposed. What a remarkable person he was. I sensed in him a steady, liberal humanism such as I had never met before. To me he was a new type, perhaps a new sort of man.

He stood up, his warning, or perhaps it was even his tribute, delivered. 'You may go now, Miss Vesey. Against *you*, there will be no charge brought. You were lucky I recognised you in court. Otherwise ...' he shrugged.

I could have told him and Fletcher then about my brother. But I stayed quiet; my vow, so recently taken, when in prison, to ask no man for help, was still fresh and hot in my mind.

On the way out, Fletcher at my elbow, I met Reba, sauntering out to the street.

She hailed me cheerfully. 'Hello, so you've been sprung, have you? Your ponce came, did he?' She gave an appraising look at Fletcher. To my amusement I saw him blush. 'He's a good-looking feller, he is. Good luck to you both.' And with a gusty laugh she sailed on her way.

By tacit consent, neither Fletcher nor I mentioned the incident again.

Except for Harry, who thought I was an angel from heaven and would raise no questions, the house was empty. Even Barlow had departed with my aunt and Countess Telling. I was in luck, there. Something must be said to Fletcher, of course.

He waited. I had not realised before how straight-faced and forbidding he could be. I had meant to say something friendly and grateful, but which re-established that I was the one who gave orders and he was the one who obeyed. How could I have been so obtuse? That command was gone for ever, destroyed as much by the straightforward simplicity with which he had brought me home as by his grand cousin, Sir Paul. He was a man and I was a young woman, and I held out my hand to take his and say a humble thank-you, before running up the stairs.

It was over. One stage in my life had ended, and another had begun.

Mary Ross was waiting in my room. She accepted my appearance without comment, some convincing story to account for my absence had evidently been told to her. She helped me undress, drew the curtains against the morning sun, and helped me into bed.

'I *am* sorry that your friend was taken ill,' she said with sympathy, 'but I'm sure you did your best. Lord, we *did* have a storm last night. I don't wonder your friend couldn't be left. Such rain and thunder, too. Now you sleep, miss, and I'll bring you some tea when you wake.'

'I never heard the storm, Mary,' I said. Then I yawned and fell into deep sleep.

Something of my adventure must have got through to Jessie Falconet, sufficient to make her pay an urgent call on Masham Square the next day, or perhaps she had other reasons.

'The girl, Alice Wilcox, with her child, came to see me,' she said, after a brief greeting. 'Not very strong in the head, is she? And perhaps a little bit of a liar? But no matter. I'll see she's looked after, of course. You were right to send her to me.' Then she said, 'I don't know what you were about, Errol, in your wanderings, but I advise you to watch your step. You were in dangerous waters. But in as much as I was partly to blame for your predicament in giving you that pamphlet to carry—yes, hush, I know about that incident, I have my spies, you know—I apologise heartily. I hope it was not too distressing.' She looked at me with concern.

I shook my head. Not even to Jessie would I tell everything. 'But it has made me want to help you. Let me do something active, Jessie.'

'In women's cause? You shall.' She paused, thoughtful. 'But not on my side of the work. You are too emotional, too, let us say it, too womanly, too attractive. It renders you vulnerable, oh it does indeed! No, you shall work with my landlady, Annie Besant. *She's* emotional too. Stay on the political, literary side with her. Only, Errol, you do not know what it may cost.'

'No matter,' I said. I thought of Dick Monk. Ambitious young naval officers don't like their wives to have a sense of sin, and I thought I now had a sense of sin.

'Anything about the policeman, Anticknap?' I asked, as she left.

'Yes.' She was gathering her goods about her, cloak, scarf, bag and small valise. 'We think he may be dead. Bad thing, very bad thing, shock to his wife.... His cap turned up on the doorstep. Blood-stained.'

'I met him the day of my wanderings, as you call it. He is no longer working for the police, Jessie.'

'Yes, we know that now,' said Jessie slowly. 'He was working on his own. We think he was more than a little crazed.' I nodded. 'He may have killed himself. In which case the cap will be the criminal world's way of letting his wife know. They may not wish to do it another way. Or, he may have been killed.' She frowned.

'In which case the cap is what, Jessie?'

She looked at me straight. 'A warning, Errol. Take care.'

CHAPTER SEVEN

You left me, a girl approaching twenty on the verge of
life. When you come back to me I am a woman, and a
thoughtful, wary one at that.

Yet very few weeks have passed. For one of those weeks
I remained in London. The short, brilliant summer season
was drawing to an end, and people were leaving town.
We went to no more balls, no more receptions. My wardrobe was almost complete. Madame Mangan, who was the
Court dressmaker in charge of my new clothes, had done
a prodigious feat of invention and skill for no great price.
But now I remembered Reba, and wondered how many
Rebas there were toiling away in the workrooms for a
pittance to produce this perfection of a flounce on a
black evening skirt and this miracle of tucking on a
white muslin day dress.

Harry's fate was all but decided. I had spoken to him
of my dreams of Eton but, little Londoner that he was,
he would have none of it.

'What should I do there among a lot of idle lords' sons?
No, can you not guess where I aim for?' His eyes gleamed
as he went on eagerly.

'As soon as I saw Lieutenant Monk I knew it was the
Navy for me.'

'You will need to be well up in mathematics,' I said
doubtfully.

'And I mean to be.'

So he was to go to Dartmouth, and where the money was to come from I did not know. Meanwhile we were working secretly at mathematics.

I was so full of Harry, of myself and the sorrows of womankind in general, that I hardly noticed the other girl in the house. She kept to her own room a good deal, sewing and reading, with only her formidable maid for company.

On my last day before going to Windsor I passed her room. The door stood wide open. She was lying back in a low armchair, wearing a loose white peignoir, for once relaxed and off her guard. Her face, seen in profile, looked young and sad. She turned, saw me and smiled.

'I have come to say good-bye.'

She stood up, stretching out a thin, delicate hand. 'To-morrow you go to Windsor?'

I took her hand and pressed it slightly. She seemed to expect it, but no returning pressure warmed my own.

On the dressing-table were laid out her toilet things of blonde tortoiseshell and silver. They had a fragile, old-fashioned air as if they had been used by some beauty who might have danced with Napoleon and made her curtsey to Tsar Alexander I on his visit to Vienna. On the silver-backed brushes was a crown picked out in brilliants, enclosing the entwined initials 'S L'. She saw me looking. 'I inherited them from my grandmother.'

'Very pretty,' I said. Well, well, I was thinking. *Of course*: Saxe-Lotharingia.

Windsor Castle was quiet, few guests were expected, the Queen was tired. But after all, a sovereign can never be entirely a private person, however hard she may try (and the Queen tried very hard, even having a little private cat-walk across the roofs of the castle so that she could enter her own chapel unobserved); and some formal entertaining was always necessary.

A few days after my arrival the Austrian Ambassador had to be entertained. Nothing was ever easy or simple at Windsor, this was one of the first truths I had to learn; the people there conspired against it. Something of this arose from the Queen herself and her strange character, but some stemmed from her entourage and the way they regarded her as a sacred object, which it was their duty to preserve from reality at all costs, although the Queen herself could sometimes be remarkably down-to-earth. The prime exponent of the protective attitude was Harriet Craven, who helped the Queen to live in quite a *false* world. Not *all* the suite were so bad. On this occasion I am told only the personal intervention of Lord Salisbury persuaded the Queen to receive the Ambassador. Tempers were frayed over this particular reception and on the morning of the Ambassador's arrival the Munshi, the Queen's Indian servant, was locked in his room by Fritz Ponsonby personally. Fritz was the son of Sir Henry Ponsonby, who had been Equerry to the Prince Consort and was therefore one of the inner circle at Windsor.

I stood by Harriet Craven watching the Ambassador and his suite arrive. His Excellency came first, Count Karolyi, a Hungarian. He had a charming wife, who spoke fluent English, which was a great let-off for us, and one at which Princess Beatrice rolled her eyes in relief; she was always deputed to talk to the Ambassador's wife, as the Queen never would.

I watched as the Ambassador, followed by his subordinates, came up the stairs. Amongst his suite, but walking on his own, was a tall, slender man in the uniform of one of the crack Austrian regiments, black and white. I had watched him arrive from a tower window and seen the heraldic dolphins on the crest of his carriage door. Was this, then, the man himself, my brother? Now we met face to face. He bowed, and stared at me.

'That's Victor, Count Hochberg. Handsome, isn't he?' breathed Fritz Ponsonby. 'But don't play cards with him.'

Count Victor was accompanied by his servants, and among them I recognised the man seen in the London ballroom, the man of Jockey Fields Passage, the man of Charde Castle. If he worked for Count Victor, he was my enemy's servant.

I looked across at Count Victor and wondered if in that decadent, handsome face I could really see an echo of my own features.

No one said anything to me on the subject. It was, after all, the sort of quiet knowledge that the Court abounded in. A secret that was never spoken of but all knew. I supposed that they thought me ignorant, too, and were enjoying with cynical sophistication, of which I knew them to be thoroughly capable, a situation in which I was both innocent and yet deeply involved.

One thing did puzzle me, however. My father had seemed to believe that all was a deep secret and that my brother's identity was known only to a handful of people. The Veseys were unworldly but they were clever and it was unlike him to be deceived. There was something to think about here, and so I did think about it, the while I turned a discreet face towards the world. I did, however, resolve to say something to Lady Geraldine when I got the chance. I would test her in some way and see how she reacted.

'Miss Vesey: Count Hochberg.'

A smile, a bow, we had met: it was over. I moved away towards the end of the room and then turned to survey the group that stood by the window. I saw a circle of people, including the Ambassador, and among them Count Victor.

I am sure the Court knew a good deal already about his character. I had heard murmurs about his gambling, his hard riding and his dissipations. None of which showed in his face, I may say, except for a certain dull look in the back of his eyes. But they were all enraptured with his black gleaming hair, his fine features, his uniform and his horses. Even the Queen seemed to admire him. I had already noticed she responded well to handsome young men, and although nothing was ever *said* on this subject, it appears she was not as remotely withdrawn in her widowhood as I had supposed. You might think that as I was her Maid of Honour, I saw her daily, but this was not the case. Sometimes days passed without my being in her presence, although I was fully occupied in her service, writing endless notes and running errands. I am told she thought me 'not as lovely as her mother, but a very nice girl, distinguished-looking, with a pretty figure.' The person who told me, Miss Craven, no doubt expected I would be delighted at the compliment. I am sure any notice from the Queen delighted her, but I find royal favours not so completely overwhelming.

Life at Windsor was proving dull and monotonous, mostly walking, talking and writing endless letters. My aunt had enrolled me as one of her correspondents and I was constantly required to write letters to her. Although away from Windsor, she desired to be informed of exactly what went on there, and every letter from her contained enquiries I must answer and information I must transmit. For like all good politicians, she knew that you have to give in order to receive.

Within a day I had a letter from Jessie. 'About the matter of the Anticknaps,' she wrote, 'you will be glad to know that things are better here. He has written to his wife. He told her that he thought men were after his blood and he was in hiding, but continuing with his work.

I think he is more than a little mad, but he is not dead. Mrs Anticknap seems more cheerful and I have contrived that she has a little money.' Dear Jessie, I knew where that money must have come from. The letter went on: 'I will keep in touch with her and what I learn you shall know. Mind you, we have come to a poor pass if we rely on lunatics for our information. Can we not do better than that?'

Yes, I thought, we can, Jessie, and we will.

Two days later I was visited by a policeman. He wore dark, sober clothes and was very polite, and sorry to bother me. He was particularly apologetic that he should have to follow me to Windsor to ask me questions. For that matter I was sorry too, especially as I saw the curious looks of the servants who ushered him to my little room in the North Tower (two servants, nothing was ever done at Windsor by one person if it could be done by two). I already knew how one was watched and noticed here.

The policeman observed that he had been to Masham Square, and had been referred to me here. I suppose he saw yet another look of enquiry in my face, because he added politely that Mr Fletcher had supplied the information.

I nodded to him to sit down, signifying that I was quite at my ease and ready to be questioned, which I was far from being, I may tell you. I supposed it was the affair of Jessie Falconet's pamphlets resurrected again.

To my surprise, it was Rotten Potatoes and Joseph who had stirred from the dead. The policeman, whose name was Ledger, led up to it circumspectly. There was this poor dead boy, he told me, his body picked up from the river Thames together with another man's, and for a while it was thought that both deaths were suicide or, more likely, accident. 'For that sort don't kill themselves as often as you might think,' observed Ledger. 'Having nothing left to them but life, they cling to it, as you might say.' But a series of rumours circulating in the criminal world had led to the suspicion that it was murder. My name and address had been found on a piece of paper in the leather purse in Joseph's pocket. So sodden and dirty was the paper that it had, at first, gone unnoticed. As it dried, my name stood out to be read.

He showed me the piece of paper, on which my name and address were indeed written in great staggering capitals, by the boy himself, I suppose. I looked at it, wondering what to say.

'There is a young boy called Harry, now living at Masham Square with Lady Geraldine Maurice, who was a friend of Joseph,' I said briefly. 'I expect Joseph got my name from Harry.' I was reluctant to say how I had used Harry and Joseph.

'Oh, yes.' He seemed unsurprised. 'Would that be Harry Eustace?'

'I suppose that is his name.' Eustace? So Harry had a surname. Had his mother chosen it because it closely resembled Maurice? Or was it her own real or assumed name? It sounded artificial to me. But it suited Harry. I could see quite a future for Harry with that name. Captain Harry Eustace, Admiral Harry Eustace, First Sea Lord Eustace. Yes, it was good.

'Take it from me, it is, Miss Vesey.' He smiled cheerfully. How unlike poor Anticknap this man was. 'There was a description of two ladies and a lad viewing the dead boy,' he said hopefully.

I bowed my head. 'I did go.'

'You had reason, no doubt, Miss Vesey?'

'Yes, Harry was anxious about his friend.' It was lame, very lame, as a reason, but he let it go.

Or perhaps only seemed to let it go. For then he said,

'Thank you for letting us trouble you, Miss Vesey. You must wonder at us taking all this bother over the death of a poor, nameless boy, but the Queen's peace must be kept, eh, Miss Vesey, and a poor boy may be as important in the end as a rich lord.' He lowered his voice confidentially. 'The fact is, Miss Vesey, it may be a bigger business than it looks. It seems to link up with a case of arson in a house in Dryden Street.' I raised my head and looked at him. 'Yes, a poor street but inoffensive, you will say. Yet this house, where it is thought that the man who was found in the river the same time as the boy, the broken-down school-teacher, Tom Perry, otherwise Rotten Potatoes, sometimes lodged when he was in funds, this house was burned down in the night. Someone went in and started a fire deliberately in one room, a room rented to a Mr King, and the whole house went up.' He shook his head. 'A bad business.'

'Was anyone killed?' I said breathlessly.

'Two bodies have been found. The landlord and one other, an old knife-grinder by trade.'

'Man or woman?' I asked. I was finding it hard to breathe.

He looked at me in a kindly, serious way. 'Woman, Miss Vesey,' he said. 'A woman of about fifty, well known for her trade as a knife-grinder in that district.'

'Poor woman,' I said, breathing more easily. So it was not my mad friend Anticknap.

'She was trapped in the attic where she was living, and could not get out. The door was locked.'

I wondered unhappily if the door had been locked deliberately on this old woman.

'Impossible to tell how or why,' he said, as if reading my mind. 'Or whether from the outside or inside, but the woman drank heavily, I fear, and if she had the key on her, might not have been in a state to use it.'

'And Mr King?' I asked.

'Mr King escaped. But the whole of the room he occupied has disappeared. Anyone who wanted to find out about Mr King or Koenig, for he was known by two names, will have his work cut out. Not a thing left. Not a trace. And the landlord gone too.'

'Are the police interested in Mr King?' I said, with dry lips.

'Well, he does have a bit of a name, you know, miss. Yes, he does have a name. And so, there is nothing you can tell us about the boy Joseph?' He gave me a keen look.

'No, nothing.' I shook my head.

As he stood up to go I saw from the window Count Victor's servant leading his horse across the courtyard. I could have turned to the policeman and said: 'Mr Koenig is here, staying at the Castle. I alone know who he is.'

I turned to see the policeman studying my face. I puzzled him. He was perplexed to find a girl like Errol Vesey on the fringe of London crime. But I was there all the same, and he was shrewd enough to sense what he could not prove.

What information had he really come there to seek? Not that I knew Rotten Potatoes, he knew that already. Nor what I knew of Rotten Potatoes. He must have questioned young Mr Jones at the mortuary where Jessie and I had gone, so he knew that too.

Then he told me himself. 'This boy, Joseph, and Perry, the schoolmaster, alias Rotten Potatoes, they were not, how can I put it, not getting money from you, not blackmailing you, Miss Vesey?'

'No.' My voice rang out in genuine surprise.

'No, I thought not, as soon as I laid eyes on you I knew there was nothing of that sort.'

'I'm not rich, you know,' I said. I had my voice under

control. 'Not rich at all. Even if I wished, I could not hand out bags of gold.'

Ledger held out a hand in departing. 'We live in strange times. When I was a lad you could fill yourself with sweetmeats to your heart's content at the price of half a penny. Now six times that would hardly do it. And yet I see many a child that hardly has a pair of sound boots to its name licking ice-cream which I never knew the taste of when I was a lad.'

An amazing man, he revealed yet another side of himself as he left. 'To tell you the truth, Miss Vesey,' he said at the door, 'I was glad to get a look inside Windsor Castle. Not the sort of chance that comes the way of a chap like me very often.'

'No.' I smiled at him, touched by the ingenuous confession. So *this* was his real, deepest reason for calling on me. Relaxing, I said, 'Do you know anything about Detective Anticknap? How he is?'

Satisfaction and triumph flooded into his eyes. He had got something from me now. 'I shouldn't trust to that one,' he said. 'He'll let you down. Can't believe a word he says.' He tapped his head. 'A little gone here, you know.' Then he said, 'Friend of yours, eh?'

'I have been trying to help his wife.' This was all right. Young ladies like me are allowed to help poor women like Nellie Anticknap—are even encouraged to do so, provided that help does not transcend acceptable bounds.

I was very close at this point to taking a first, tentative step to telling him about my brother. I trusted him, you see, and felt the urgent need for protection.

But at that moment he, too, saw Count Victor's horse in the courtyard. 'Fine bit of horseflesh,' he said, in a tone of deep admiration. The simple remark stopped me speaking and when he had moved back from the window, tearing his admiring gaze away, the moment had passed.

'I know a bit about horses, I do,' he said. 'My old dad was a farrier. The man who chose that chestnut knows what's what.'

'Yes, I think he does,' I said.

Shortly after this interview, walking in the park, I saw the chestnut being exercised. It was indeed a lovely horse. I stood by the shrubs which bounded this part of the park and watched. A groom was watching also, and with him a short, dark man in Count Victor's livery. I had already taken in his saturnine expression and the fact that he spoke no English.

The chestnut kept throwing up his head and every so often rearing in a spirited attempt to throw his rider. The man on his back hung on.

'Masters him finely, don't he?' said the groom, admiration in his voice. 'Takes some doing, that do. Needs a bit of bottom, that does.'

'Yes.' I knew enough about horses to know that the man controlling the spirited animal was doing so with consummate grace and skill. I watched as the horse and rider drew nearer. Now I could see that the rider was not Count Victor but his servant, the strange and fascinating man I had met already.

He dismounted and handed over the horse to the man in his master's livery. For the first time he saw me.

I stared at him longer than good manners allowed. I swear that he had begun to hold out his hand and move towards me. I would have welcomed him. Something inside me was willing to respond. Did I smile slightly in return? I don't know.

Count Victor came out of the stables near at hand and strolled towards the horse, whip under his arm, almost swaggering. I thought he had been drinking.

The groom helped him on to the horse while the other

men watched. I watched too. He sat well. I admitted it. He looked handsome enough sitting there on that beautiful animal. Then the horse threw up its head, with that characteristic gesture I had seen before, and its forequarters rose. Count Victor lashed at it with his whip. The chestnut whinnied in anger and reared again, pawing the air, and then letting his hooves swing back on the ground like hammers. The rider swore and flashed the whip down hard on the horse's neck. It was a cruel gesture which the horse repaid by jerking his head and charging forward in my direction.

I stepped back hastily, hoping its terrified passage would pass me by. But before I had time even for fear, the first rider jumped forward and interposed his own body between me and the flying horse. The horse stopped dead. Count Victor flew over his head and hit the ground.

None of us looking on said anything, except the English groom who gave a long, low whistle, then went forward and helped Count Victor to his feet. The Austrian groom stood motionless, his expression calm, only a faint curving of the lips suggesting a smile.

Then he went towards the horse's head and held it while his master remounted. The animal was quiet this time and Count Victor stayed on. As he moved away I heard his servant say in an undertone, 'That horse will kill you one day'.

I thought then that my presence there had gone unnoticed by Count Victor. He had been some days in the Castle now, and each evening we had dined at the same table and then stood politely around that seated royal figure in the cold drawing room, waiting for her to retire. Perhaps he had watched me, I had certainly observed him, but we had never spoken.

This was the last night of the Ambassador's visit. Tomorrow morning he would depart, but the Count was staying on in the neighbourhood for the racing. The evening found us facing each other across the table. Windsor manners were formal; you conversed with your neighbours on your left and on your right and did not talk across the mahogany. But I saw Count Victor watching me. When we were joined by the gentlemen in the drawing room, he came across to stand by the sofa where I was sitting.

'The Queen left early tonight.' He had a soft, attractive voice, and the German accent was not marked.

'I believe she was tired.' She wasn't tired, although she may have thought she was, but she was low-spirited and depressed, reluctant to meet people. This summer had seen the terrible death of her son-in-law, the Emperor Frederick of Germany. The Queen was still living in the shadow of his death. She had a taste, too, for enjoyable melancholy. A little mourning (or even a great deal) did not come amiss to her. I would not say that, at Windsor, when the cat was away the mice started to play, but there was no doubt that when the Queen was not present and the Household was on its own, things went more brightly. Now I was summoned to the piano. Harriet Craven came across and asked me to play for Sybil Keswick. 'She is going to give us a few songs.'

I took off my rings and sat myself down at the Broadwood, reconciled to an hour of the sentimental music that Sybil loved. Her singing was not very successful, because she was so short-sighted that she had to keep leaning right down to read the music.

Count Victor stood at my side and assisted by turning the pages, not much to my pleasure. Sybil carolled away; her voice was not *very* good.

'I trust you will not judge my riding by that episode this afternoon,' he said softly, so that only my ears could hear. Sybil did make rather a noise. 'I can put on a better performance than that.'

I concentrated on my playing and did not answer. 'I regret that you were frightened, Miss Vesey.'

I nodded slightly, but continued to play.

'I know English ladies admire a good horseman,' went on that insinuating, slightly plaintive voice.

'The page needs turning, if you please, Count Victor.'

He bowed, turned the page and continued. 'I hunt. You hunt also, Miss Vesey? It is dangerous, I think, this hunting.'

'It can be dangerous,' I said, my mouth dry. 'It depends on the rider.'

'Ah, you have spoken. I have made you speak.' He leaned against me, so close our limbs were touching and I could smell the scent he used on his hair. 'I would like you to talk a great deal with me, Miss Vesey.'

In a terrible kind of way he was trying to ingratiate himself with me.

'Jolly, isn't it?' said Fritz Ponsonby, bustling up. 'Go on, Sybil, sing us that swooning good song from *I Puritani*.'

'I can't manage the high notes,' said Sybil.

'Never mind, leave 'em out, but give us the tune,' said Fritz robustly.

'I don't know if I can find the music.' I spoke nervously, leaning forward to search; my hands were trembling.

'Let me help,' said Count Victor. He put his hand on my arm, a long white hand with perfect filbert nails. I saw that he had lost the last joint of his little finger.

I stared, trying to recall if the hand seen at the cab window that terrible day of my imprisonment had been similarly maimed. I could almost persuade myself that it had been.

Then he laughed.

I felt sick; I stood up. 'Forgive me, Sybil, I think I can't go on playing.'

I went into the corridor and walked down its length. At the end a figure was standing, face turned towards me, as if waiting. I recognised Count Victor's servant.

I was surprised to see him there. Rules were strict at Windsor about where servants might be seen or not be seen. We stared at each other. He stood, erect and disciplined. I guessed he had served as a soldier, once.

'If you are waiting for your master he may soon need you,' I said coldly. 'He is, without doubt, drunk.'

'I am not his body servant.' My anger was met with pride. 'But his major-domo. My name is Charles Louis Kyburg.'

I understood. I supposed someone like Count Victor *did* need what Frank would call a bear-leader. I knew, too, that the Emperor of Austria maintained a surveillance over his nobility. The man I was talking to might serve in that capacity also. Certainly he was no common servant.

In the semi-darkness of the corridor, it was easy to speak. 'Thank you for what you did this afternoon.'

'You were in no danger,' he said stiffly. 'In spite of what you saw, he is a good horseman. He would have brought the horse up. The horse is very fresh.'

'It seemed to me that I *was* in danger and you saved me.'

From the open window drifted in the smell of lime trees. I heard an owl hooting. A great summer moon hung in the sky. We had met once before by moonlight. Whether he was a servant and I a Maid of Honour seemed not to matter. We were equals here.

He had turned and the moonlight shone full on his face. Between him and his master there were certain resemblances; they walked and talked in the same sort of way, as men might who were brought up together, but there the resemblance ended. Count Victor was handsome, but in an ordinary way; this man was different. He had the most beautiful, the noblest, the most romantic visage I had ever seen. His eyes, his expression, were peculiarly his own, full of luminous comprehension. I thought then, and I think now, that in looks he was matchless. Years later when I saw the picture called 'The Polish Rider' by Rembrandt, I thought this was the nearest to *his* look I ever saw.

'How much do you know about how he lives?' I asked.

He paused. 'Over here, not as much as I should, no doubt.'

'Count Victor is either mad, or vicious, or both,' I said. 'Either way he will come to destruction and drag you down with him.'

'All that family are a little crazed.' He was cool. 'Off the rails. One accepts the hazard.'

'This is England,' I said. 'If you don't want to stay with him no one can make you.'

'I am not a serf. Austria is not like Russia.'

'No.' I was embarrassed. I could see I had angered him once more.

'Englishmen do not have the monopoly of freedom.'

'Of course not.' I was amazed at my own stupidity. I was constantly blundering into situations which any ordinary well brought-up girl would have avoided without effort. The truth was my intellectually bracing but socially sheltered upbringing at the rectory had left me ill prepared for the world. I knew a great deal too much of some things, and not nearly enough of others. Must the New Woman be inferior in guile to the rest of her sex?

What I could not control in myself, and what was operating now, was a flow of enthusiasm and sympathy which when called up *would* find expression. Whereas the laws of polite society told me it should freely be expressed within the same social class, and never summoned up outside it by an inferior one.

I stood there, momentarily baffled by the rules of the world and the rules of my own nature. Then I said shyly, 'We met, but I hardly suppose you remember, at the ruins of Charde Castle.' I had seen him other times before, in a London drawing room, in a slum alley, but on these occasions he had not spoken to me.

'I do remember.' He smiled. 'A tragic ruin, but interesting. Very interesting, I enjoyed it.' He added, 'Count Victor was hunting with the Queen's Buckhounds. He was staying at Bulstrode Park.'

'Yes, I thought it beautiful, but of course, in my case there was special interest. It was built by my ancestors. You know, it is strange, it all burnt in one single night.'

'But houses like that have no heart. Once they catch fire they go quickly. It is soon all over with them.'

I smiled, more at my ease now. 'You sound censorious, as if it was their own fault.'

'I don't like a world in which great castles straddle the landscape.'

'It's coming to an end, I think.'

'Yet here we both are. Both servants in a castle. I dream of a world in which there are no castles and we are all equal.'

'Oh, so do I,' I cried. 'If only you could meet my friend Jessie Falconet.'

From the other end of the corridor a door opened to let out a burst of song. Sybil was singing again. The door closed. I saw a figure approaching us. It was Count Victor.

'I will ask Miss Falconet to send you an invitation to one of her evenings,' I said. 'Where shall she address it?'

He hesitated. Count Victor got closer. 'We lodge in Mecklenburgh Gate,' he said. 'Address it there. Number

Five. But I do not know ...' The Count passed me then, silently angry, I thought, and after a pause, the other followed him.

I felt triumphant, as if I had scored a victory against Count Victor, against rules and against the enemies of my sex. I had proved I was no fine lady.

I was so pleased with myself that I went back to the drawing room, where the Household was still assembled and Sybil still singing.

'Better, dear?' she said, pausing between songs.

'Much better,' I answered. I felt sure of myself. I thought it a triumph for intellect against convention. I did not know then how much a part had been played by the same girlish passions and lightness of heart that had whirled my mother to her destiny.

'Want me to play again?'

'No, dear, I'm getting along splendidly with Fritz here to do it, as you see. Go and sit with Johnny Satchell and amuse him.'

I went and sat next to Johnny and later we played a game of cards, the noisy, sporting kind where you all shout eagerly and no one minds who wins. The Household liked such games when it was left to its own devices. Johnny was well known to be an expert on affairs of the heart.

'Can you fall in love with more than one person, Johnny?' I asked.

'Rather,' he said. 'With two or three, or even more. I'm always doing it myself. Repeatedly. Whenever I see a jolly girl I can't help myself.'

'Seriously, though, Johnny?'

'Very seriously, indeed,' he said pulling a long face. 'Let me tell you, it *is* serious when you're my age and so jolly susceptible and haven't got a bean.'

'And do they fall in love back?'

'Some of them do. The nice ones.'

'Do you think, Johnny, that it is possible as well to fall in love happily outside the set you were born in? You know what I mean.'

'With a servant or a stable boy?' he said lightly. The Johnnys of this world never really fell in love outside the charmed circle, and though their hearts broke they made good marriages.

'Something like that.'

'Well, there was the Lady Strachy. She did.'

'Oh, did she?' I'd never heard of Lady Strachy.

'Malvolio said so.' Seeing my blank look, he said: 'Malvolio, stupid girl, *Twelfth Night*.'

'Oh, Shakespeare, but that was long ago.'

'Well, we have an example nearer home,' he said naughtily. 'The Queen herself. She was devoted to John Brown.'

'Oh, devoted. Anyone can be devoted. It means nothing.'

He lowered his voice. 'What would you say if I said I know a man who swears he has seen the wedding certificate of the Queen and John Brown?'

I was thoughtful for the rest of the evening and glad when it ended.

The law moves slowly when it is personified by an elderly gentleman whose practice is among quiet, old-established families. I have no doubt that Sir Paul Bedower could command sharp city lawyers who moved speedily about his business, but the Maurices and the Veseys dealt with the dignified Mr Dalrymple and paid the price in slowness.

So some weeks had passed before he got in touch with me, and then, true old gentleman that he was, he had sent a letter asking if he might come to Windsor. He sent another announcing his arrival, and finally he came. It all took time.

I received him in my room. 'You will stay to luncheon, Mr Dalrymple?' One of the privileges of the Household was a little mild entertaining of our friends. Windsor food, although on the plain side, was plentiful and delicious. Nourishment was taken seriously and even a short train journey called forth hampers filled with cold meat, stuffed rolls, grouse, cake and biscuits, together with tea, cream, claret, champagne and seltzer water. So you may judge how we lunched at home. Of course, we never saw the Queen at this meal. She breakfasted, lunched and very often dined alone.

'Delighted to do so, Miss Vesey.' Mr Dalrymple rubbed his hands softly. He put his head on one side. 'Business first, Miss Vesey?'

I sat down, put my hands in my lap and waited.

'Marriage, Miss Vesey?' He tilted his head to one side. I remembered of old his bird-like trick of putting his head on one side and then asking a sharp little question.

I decided to be very businesslike. 'I am not yet settled in my mind, but I have received an offer. I am considering it.'

'*Good* offer, Miss Vesey?' Again the little settling of the head.

'Very good,' I said firmly. 'If I fancy it.'

He blinked a little at this, but took it in his stride with a nod. 'Fancy is fifty per cent of the matter, Miss Vesey, so I'm told.' I knew very well he was an old bachelor.

'My father advised me to get in touch with you the moment I considered marriage. Commanded it, almost.' I recognised now that there had been a mixture of command and entreaty in my father's voice.

Mr Dalrymple straightened his head and looked serious. 'Yes. I have a duty bounden on me as one of the executors of your ...' He paused. 'Your mother's will,' he finished.

'My mother's?'

'You are surprised it should be her will and not your father's?'

'I am.'

'And yet she left you something,' he said softly.

'She had nothing,' I said. 'I know she brought nothing to her marriage.'

He put his head on one side. 'There was something she wished you to have. She chose to leave it to you on your marriage, or on your twentieth birthday.'

'My next birthday?' I cried. 'In November?'

'Or if you die before you can inherit under either of those conditions, it goes to your natural brother.' He carefully did not meet my eyes.

'Did she know where to find him?' I said.

'She knew the name of the lawyers in Vienna who had charge of his affairs, yes.'

'Then I could trace him, if I wished?' I asked.

He peered at me round his spectacles; he had numerous little ways of looking at one, all indicative of some mood of his. This conveyed surprise and faint reproof. 'They have not been very ready to pass on information in the past,' he said shortly. 'You could try. But I assure you he knows about the will. He knows what he stands to inherit.' Then he corrected himself. 'That is, he knows what can be known, Miss Vesey; your mother handed to me to place in the vaults a small, but heavy, iron box.'

'Can I see it?'

'At the right time it shall be produced. But I must warn you.'

I looked and waited.

'It is locked and we have no key. We never *have* had a key. For all I know, no key exists.'

There was a sort of humour to it, I thought. A locked

215

box with no key was my inheritance. I wrote to my aunt, Lady Geraldine, and told her about the box. Her spies would have told her of Mr Dalrymple's visit, although his professional discretion was impeccable. I believe now that this letter to her was read by one of the maids and the news it contained passed on, either for love or money.

There was always some sickness about in the royal palaces. I suspected the drains. Now a housemaid fell ill. The housemaids of Windsor were multitudinous and anonymous, trained and bred to appear faceless. Indeed one never saw them. They knew how to disappear. But illness was a great diversion of the Queen, and this girl having come originally from the Balmoral estate, H.M. took a passionate interest in the sad decline. She was called a girl, but she was a senior housemaid, had worked in the Castle for twenty-five years, and was forty years of age. Every detail of her path downwards was transmitted to the Queen and hence to us as the Household. We heard it all, from the first feverish symptoms, to the diagnosis of typhoid ('that dread disease that killed my angel') to the final sinking.

I was deputed to represent the Queen at the funeral. The next day the remains of Katherine Gilchrist, formerly senior housemaid to the Queen, were interred in St Clement's Churchyard. The Dean of Windsor read the burial service and the deceased was followed to the grave by Sir John Cowell, Master of the Royal Household, and other members of the Queen's establishment. Her Majesty sent a wreath of immortelles bearing the inscription: 'A mark of regard from Queen Victoria'.

Do you know what immortelles are? They are species of flowers of papery texture which retain their colour after being dried. Everlastings, we call them. I never liked them and I do not like them now. The flowers of death should be ploughed back into the earth so that they can come back again as new life. It was the great fault of our Queen that she could not accept this.

CHAPTER EIGHT

Immortelles suited the image I was forming of the Queen. The dried simplicity, the call of nostalgia, seemed to match her character, but she was really a very complicated person and I did not pretend to understand her. My first period of waiting as a Maid of Honour was drawing to an end. We were one month on duty and then were two months at home. This was the arrangement, but I gathered from Harriet Craven that it would not do to rely on the free time entirely, because the Queen reserved the right to break into it as it suited her. 'And, of course, for *her* any of our little plans must go by the board,' she said simply. 'We go to Balmoral in the autumn,' she added. 'Next time you are in waiting I dare say it will be at Balmoral. It is not entertaining there,' she sighed, 'and very cold. I feel the cold, my rheumatism becomes acute. But there, one bears these little inconveniences. It is one's pleasure, one might say. Still, it is dull there, as well as chill, and one is thrown much on one's own resources. It is as well to know.'

Her delicate hint that Balmoral was not popular with the Household was an understatement. In fact, not to put too fine a point on it, they hated it and intrigued not to be in waiting there. I foresaw that, as a junior and unimportant member of the Household, I should do my full share, and more, unless I could devise my own system of evasion.

There had been no entertaining at the Castle after the departure of the Austrian Ambassador and his entourage. Count Victor was rumoured to have remained in the neighbourhood, staying at the King's Head in Windsor and driving over to a stables at Ascot to choose horses. Once, driving into the town myself on an errand to the apothecary, I saw his groom, he who had held the chestnut, strolling through the town with that insolent swagger that seemed natural to him, and perhaps meant nothing at all. I wondered how much he knew of his master's plans and whether or not he acted as his master's agent.

Various rumours about the Count came to my ears at this period. Did the people who passed them on know they were talking to me of my brother? Sometimes, I was sure they did. At other times, I questioned it. I could never be certain. Fritz Ponsonby let me know that Count Victor was spending with reckless extravagance. 'As if the devil was after him,' he said. 'A thousand guineas for one horse. That's going it, you know.' Johnny Satchell told me that the Count was gambling hard. 'He'll come a cropper, you mark my words. I've seen many men do it and he bears all the signs. Funny thing, the only extravagance he doesn't seem to have is women. One never hears anything of that, and I should if there was anything to hear.' I absorbed this news with interest and some quiet amusement. I had already noticed that my position as Maid of Honour seemed to have emancipated me from some of the restrictions of girlhood. In other words, people like Fritz Ponsonby and Johnny Satchell would talk to me as freely of certain matters as if I had been an old married woman. Or perhaps women of the highest class, of the aristocracy, had always been freer than the girls from the landed gentry, and I was now getting the benefit of it.

I had taken care, since my experience in prison, to watch what I did and where I went. I was careful not to be alone if I could help it, and I never walked by myself in the Castle gardens. It meant I saw a good deal of Harriet Craven, which, I dare say, she found natural enough. I learned to turn a deaf ear to her gentle, incessant conversation and to continue with my own thoughts. She seemed to demand very little of life except to breathe the pure air of royalty undefiled.

When my month of duty was up, I travelled to London with Harriet. Her time of waiting had come to an end too, and even she, in her quiet way, was ready for some liberty and a little jollity. The rest of the entourage were off to Balmoral. We were shut into one of the royal carriages which was to deposit me at Masham Square, and Harriet to stay with her brother, Lord Craven of Crawley, an elderly and impoverished bachelor whose only interest was in genealogy, his own in particular. There was a gap in his family tree between 1086 and 1120 which he had spent fifty years trying to bridge, so far without success.

'How well you have done,' said Harriet, patting my hand. 'I hear nothing but praise of you. I am so glad. No one knows better than I what an ordeal one's first time in waiting can be.'

'I have found it very interesting,' I said.

'So clever. You *are* clever. I hope you won't find it a nuisance to you, Errol. I have never found cleverness much of an asset in Court life,' she said reflectively. 'A little wholesome dullness suits better there.'

'I'll try not to be too clever,' I said apologetically.

'Yes, do, dear.' She drew into her corner and devoted some time to careful observation of the countryside, now sodden with rain, before addressing me again. 'We shall have a hard winter, I think. I have been studying the hedgerows, and the rose hips are particularly red and bright. That is always a bad sign.'

I parted from Windsor with some regrets for leaving its ancient beauty, but with the knowledge that I would go back and the feeling that I had been presented with a challenge there and had faced it. And I looked forward to being in Masham Square again. I had made up my mind to talk a good deal about politics to Frank and try and broaden his views. He could be a useful ally, I thought, for Jessie and me, besides being somewhat in my power because of Harry. You will see that I was not above a little womanly blackmail.

'Has your maid gone to London by train?' asked Miss Craven. 'Mine has, and the complaints...! The trains are perfectly comfortable, I told her, and this talk of not being safe is all a nonsense. And really she is better off, for she's inclined to be carriage-sick, and of course there's nothing of that in the train. So I had the guard lock her into a carriage to herself and he'll let her out when they arrive. How does your maid manage?'

'Very well, I believe. At least she never complains. And I'm sure she'd hate to be locked in a railway carriage.'

'They are so stupid, these gals,' said Miss Craven. 'As if harm could come to them. All hysterical imagination, in my opinion. No harm can come to a good gal in London these days.' She settled comfortably into her seat to enjoy the journey. She appreciated travelling to London in a well-sprung carriage, painted in the royal chocolate and with the royal arms on the door. Nothing bad had ever touched her and probably nothing ever would. She would go to her grave without a hand being laid on her in anger or in lust.

I turned to the window and looked out. It was difficult to believe that Reba and Harriet Craven existed in the same world. Neither would be able to describe their experiences in a way the other could recognise. Only I knew how to bridge the gap between the two.

As we drove into the busy city streets Harriet turned to me. 'I gave orders to take you to Masham Square first, and then I will drive on to Bruton Place. My brother expects me.' She looked around her with happy anticipation. One of the minor pleasures of her life was to drive up to her brother's front door and alight, beneath the interested gaze of the onlookers, from a royal equipage. With me to deliver at Lady Geraldine's she would have the pleasure of creating a small commotion twice.

Frank was standing in the hall at Masham Square when I arrived. He was wearing his great-coat, as if he too had just returned from somewhere.

'Hello, Errol.' He gave me a kiss on the cheek. 'Returned in glory from Windsor?'

'I was very happy there, Frank,' I said, giving him a sedate kiss back.

'And did you wear all those pretty dresses I saw being prepared for you?'

'Every one. And they were not nearly enough, I can tell you. The Queen eyes one quite sharply if the same dress appears too often, as mine were bound to do. "Have I not seen that dress before, Miss Vesey?" she said to me one evening. So I was obliged to get my maid to rig up an overskirt of lace to try to make it look different, and even then I think the Queen knew. And it is one of my prettiest dresses, too.'

'Errol,' said Frank, 'that is a very good imitation of Harriet Craven you are giving there, but it is not *you*. You don't talk like that.'

'There, and I thought you wouldn't notice.' I looked demure. 'I must model myself on Harriet Craven, must I not? Everyone says that she is the best model for a courtier there is.'

'Old Craven is a prize, isn't she? She used to be the bane of my infant life, always persuading my mother to dress me up in velvet and lace and trot me out in front of the Queen. Who didn't take to me, I may say. She and I used to stare at each other and say very little.'

'How is my aunt?'

'Missing the Court, really, I suspect. She hates to think of it all going on without her. However, she has one or two nice new horrors to trot out to the Queen when they meet, so she has not altogether wasted her time.'

'Horrors?'

'Yes, there has been a very nice murder in Whitechapel that is beginning to be noticed.' Frank pretended to be bored, but the truth was he was quite as interested in such horrors as the Queen and Lady Geraldine. 'A poor unfortunate woman (you know what I mean?) was cut to bits with a sharp knife and then the bits of her distributed nicely about a small area of the East End, parcelled in newspaper.'

'And how is Harry?'

'Oh, going on finely.' Frank sounded happy. 'I'm teaching him to ride. It's amazing how fond I am of him. I do wish he hadn't got this fever for the Navy. I blame you there, Errol. Ah yes, you may look innocent, but I know about Dick Monk, don't think I don't. Do you truly care for him? Monk, I mean.'

'I believe so,' I said thoughtfully.

'Well, I trust you may know your own mind. Not a man to play fast and loose with.'

I was silent. 'Nothing can be settled for some time. Does Aunt Geraldine know?'

'No, my dear innocent, she does not. I have my own means of knowing things, and I should advise you not to tell her. She will throw up her hands and say "What, marry, you ungrateful girl, just when I have set you up finely for life as a Maid of Honour?" '

I burst out laughing and gathered my skirts in one hand to ascend the stairs to my room. 'Frank, you monster,' I said, over my shoulder.

But as I mounted the stairs I was serious at heart at the thought of Dick Monk. October was approaching, and with it the time for me to answer him 'Yes' or 'No'. When I left for Windsor I believe I meant my answer to be 'Yes'. But now I hardly knew. I had realised it was possible to have stronger, stranger, wilder feelings than Dick Monk called up in me.

I sat down in my room, took off my bonnet and mantle and stared at my face in the mirror. I was beginning to know I was my mother's daughter. What a strange thing inheritance is, and how it catches one unawares. I had never really known my mother and yet now I felt I understood her and the way she acted better by far than my father had, who had loved her. I *was* her.

I unpacked my own clothes. I had given my maid Mary a short holiday. I knew that she had found the long corridors and the many stairs of Windsor hard on her lameness. I suspected, too, that she had found some of the other servants superior and critical. So I had sent her home to her mother for a short rest to set her up. Also, in truth, I preferred to be alone. So when I had unpacked and changed my dress for the comfortable sort of tea-gown suited to a quiet dinner with my aunt and Frank and Countess Telling, I went down the stairs.

No one was in the big drawing room, but in the little room beyond, which my aunt loved to keep filled with stands of fragrant roses, geraniums and ferns, a figure was standing. She turned and I recognised Countess Telling. She moved towards me with her usual air of lassitude.

'Welcome back, Miss Errol.' Her voice was as low and soft as ever, her tone as melancholy, but there was no mistaking the welcome. In her own queer way she was glad to see me.

She was wearing a long, loose robe, not unlike my own tea-gown, but whereas mine was cherry coloured, hers was white and trimmed with blue. It had a vaguely invalidish air which suited her subdued manner. As she stood there, longing, I thought, to be more friendly, but not knowing how to set about it, I began to take her in. Weeks had passed since we last met and they had made something clearer which perhaps I should have guessed before. 'Why, she's pregnant,' I thought.

Our eyes met, and although I said nothing to her then, no, not till very much later, from that moment her condition was accepted between us. She gave me a nervous smile.

'Lady Geraldine will be back soon.' She paused. 'She is very much interested in this new murder and she has gone to drive round to see the street for herself. I find it very strange, this interest English ladies have in murders.' She moved her head sadly.

'Not all ladies do.'

'She says she must see with her own eyes. After she has seen, she will collect some books for me from Mudie's and then return home.' It was the longest string of sentences she had ever addressed to me. She frowned slightly, as if there was something amiss in what she had said, some point social observances demanded which she had failed to provide. 'She looks forward to seeing you,' she said finally.

But when Lady Geraldine came in, flushed and handsome, all I could remember were the secrets I was keeping from her: about my brother, and about Dick Monk.

'My dear Errol, how delighted I am to see you. How pretty you look. The life at Windsor always does a girl good if she has anything in her at all. Now, tell us, what is the latest in the quarrel between Harriet Craven and Sybil Keswick? Did Sybil really accuse Harriet Craven of locking the piano and hiding the key?' She deposited an armful of books on the table in front of the Countess, put a bundle of newspapers on yet another table, and sat down on the sofa, prepared to receive and transmit gossip. 'Well, you can tell Harriet Craven from me when you see her next that I shall tease her about it.'

'Won't *you* see her first, aunt?'

'No, I don't go into waiting before the New Year,' she said. 'My doctor has prescribed a thorough rest.' She leaned back against a cushion and tried to look frail. Then the Maurice vitality burst through. 'My dear, the poor unfortunate that was killed in Whitechapel was chopped into ten pieces, and they are by no means sure they have *all* the parcels yet.' She looked wistful. 'I wish I could have got out of the carriage and had a good poke round myself, but alas, it would *not* have done. Still, I sent Barlow.'

The thought of that grim-faced, disapproving figure pursuing my aunt's investigations in East London made me smile. I imagine she had not enjoyed it.

'Wasted on her, of course,' said Lady Geraldine.

I shook my head. The Maurices were incurably frivolous. Nothing showed it more clearly, to my mind, than my aunt's light-hearted interest in a sordid and terrible crime. I knew now a little of that world from which the murder had sprung. How many Rebas ended terribly by violence? I would never forget Reba. Not for me any longer the wide-eyed, child-like interest of the Queen. I could guess at the reality behind the puzzle.

Lady Geraldine rose from the sofa. Her eyes looked into mine with that radiant, hypnotic Maurice stare. 'Errol, we must have a long talk tonight.'

She smiled, and I smiled back, but I was thoughtful. I

recognised the phrase. It was Maurice language for 'I am going to ask you some searching questions to which I shall require an answer'. So Frank was wrong when he said she knew nothing about Dick Monk.

At the door she paused and put a hand to her head, on which rested a hat of quilted satin with a curved brim and a fountain of feathers. 'Really, hats this year are too much.'

We met in her comfortable dressing room where she had her bookshelves filled with the memoirs she read so constantly, and the desk at which she penned her flowing, gossipy letters. The low chairs were soft and the fire there always seemed to burn better than anywhere else, bringing out the scent from the great Chinese bowl of pot-pourri.

Lady Geraldine was wrapped in a soft wool robe and her hair was on her shoulders. A Sèvres chocolate pot stood on the low table by her side.

'Some chocolate, my love?' She took a delicate sip from her own cup.

'No, thank-you.' I was too clever to impede myself with a cup of hot chocolate when I might need all my wits about me. I took my seat on a low stool by her feet.

'You'll burn your complexion at the fire,' observed my aunt.

I shook my head impatiently. 'It never worries me.'

She sipped some more chocolate. 'I've seen Alicia Monk once or twice lately. *She* has called on me. A compliment, I suppose, she rarely goes out these days.' She gave me a sharp look. 'A compliment to me or to *you*, Errol?' She took some more chocolate. 'She is devoted to her son. Thinks the world of him.' She put down the cup on the saucer with a decided ring. 'So, Errol; is there anything in it? You and Dick Monk? Alicia Monk thinks so.'

227

'She doesn't like me,' I said. 'Does not approve, any-way.'

'Oh, nothing to do with you. Nothing personal at all.'

I let a coal in the fire crumble and blaze while I watched. Then I said, 'When I first went out with you in London I noticed how everyone stared at me and watched. Why was that?'

'They wanted to see if you were like your mother,' said my aunt, finally.

'And am I?'

'You are, my dear, in many ways, but without her look of being *different* which made her irresistible. You ought to be glad. It's no help to a woman to look like that.' She gazed into the fire. '*Une âme bien née*,' she added softly.

'But that was not the only reason people stared at me, aunt,' I said. 'They looked in my face as if they were *waiting* for something from me.'

'It's a wicked, inquisitive world, my love. I suppose they were looking to see if you would cut a dash like your mother. There, I've said it. Dragged out what was meant to be a secret and what everyone knows. Except you, of course.'

'Oh, I know,' I assured her calmly. 'My father told me. He also told me that *you* were in ignorance.'

'Well, as a girl I used to pretend that I was, and I sup-pose your father preferred to believe the whole affair was totally buried, but of course it never could be. It was all so publicly conducted, so much in the world's eye.'

I wanted to know all she could tell me of the whole sad story, so I sat waiting, silently beseeching her to go on.

'I never saw him myself, but his portrait still hangs in the Austrian Embassy. He was the Archduke Salvator. He, too, is dead now. Killed by a fall from his horse. But they

were a fatal pair. I'm told you only had to see them together to guess how it would be. They eloped, lived together as man and wife. I believe there was even a
marriage ceremony. They fled to Scotland and then stood
up and declared they were man and wife. Then they tried
to hide in Italy, but it could not be done. The Emperor was
too powerful for that. He had the poor things separated.
A child was born.'

'My brother.'

'Your half-brother,' corrected Lady Geraldine. 'Well,
it's all over now. They are all of them dead.' She turned to
me. 'So you know now why they stared. She was the
talk of Europe for a few months, your poor mother. They
wanted to see if you too would have a tragic destiny.'

'I don't think I shall,' I said stoutly.

'No, you have your feet on the ground. There is a
Vesey look to your face as well, I'm glad to say.' She
laughed. 'Now it is so ridiculous, I can tell you, my dear,
but there *was* another reason they stared, all those curious
old quizzing cats.'

'I knew it.'

'You see, it was some years before your mother married
your father, and although the lovers were parted, rumour
had it that they still met secretly, that they went on
meeting till the Archduke was killed. They wanted to
see whose daughter you were, after all.'

I sat silently thinking about it all. I had wanted an
explanation and now I had certainly received one. Before
I could stop myself, I had picked up a hand mirror of
my aunt's and was studying my face. Then I put it down.
There was no Imperial Austrian blood in my veins. I was
the English Errol Vesey and I knew it. What Austrian
Archduke had ever been good at mathematics?

Still, I was not wholly satisfied. I remembered the
searching, interested, speculative look I had surprised in

some faces. Surely it was not only my origins they were fascinated by, but my future also?

'There is something *more*, Aunt Geraldine?' I pressed.

'Oh, it is all a nonsense,' she said uneasily.

'You'd better tell me, aunt.'

She turned her eyes away so that she did not look at my face. 'There is a tale going round that the Imperial Austrian family are interested in you.'

'In me?' I was sharply surprised.

'Oh, as I say, it's a nonsense.' She shifted uneasily. 'But the marriage of the Crown Prince Rudolf is a very unhappy one. It's known that the Crown Princess Stephanie can have no more children. There is a rumour she's a dying woman. And this same rumour says that if you *did* appear to have Imperial blood you would be, well, an interesting person to them as a possible successor to her.' She said vigorously, 'Oh, I dare say it is all a fine rubbish. But you must remember the Maurices have as many quarterings as the Habsburgs. We go back to the Plantagenets.' Her voice rang out. Never before had I seen the Maurice pride so manifest.

'It is utterly fantastic,' I declared.

'Oh certainly, certainly,' she agreed irritably. 'But it has been the *On dit*. So people looked and wondered.'

'Yes,' I said, standing up and moving about. 'I can imagine how they would speculate. What an amusement I have been to them! What stories they could weave, what fantasies they could embroider!'

'My dear, forget it.' She patted my hand. 'It all goes back to that old, old story. But they are all of them dead and so will the stories be soon.'

'They aren't all dead, though,' I reminded her. 'My brother is alive.'

Now it was my turn to surprise her. She stared. 'My dear, he died when he was a little boy of four. He caught scarlatina and died. Such a dear little fellow. I have seen his picture.'

'My father thought he was alive. Still alive and a grown man.'

'Errol: I have seen his grave.' She spoke solemnly. 'The General and I travelled with my sister to see it just before her marriage to your father. I suppose it was her farewell. We took her to it, she placed some flowers on it, and, as far as I know, she never went back.'

'My father thought my brother was alive,' I said obstinately.

My aunt threw her hands up: 'Errol, what do *we* know of what passed between your mother and father, what she thought right to tell him and what she did not? She told *me* nothing. But she asked the General and me to come with her on her journey and this was how we came to see the grave. A simple stone in a little churchyard near Florence. Remember the boy had been baptised into the Roman Catholic Church. And there it was on the stone. I saw it with my own eyes. "Salvator, son of the Archduke Salvator of Austria and Elizabeth Maurice, aged four years and ten months", and the date of his death. It was the same year as her marriage.'

'She did not tell my father,' I repeated. 'It was not what he knew.'

'If so, there will have been a good reason, for she loved him, as he loved her. One thing I do know: your father, so gentle, so upright, would never have probed. He would not have searched her heart. What she wanted to keep secret he would have let lie still. Who are we to say he was wrong?'

We sat together before the fire, quietly talking till the heart of the blaze had grown dim and the room chill. We did not mention my mother or her son again, but talked of Windsor and, a little, of Countess Telling.

'She expects to be confined in January,' said my aunt with a sigh. 'I'll tell you her sad little saga later, not tonight.'

Finally I rose to go. At the door my aunt took my hand. 'My dear, don't forget about Dick Monk. Don't break his heart. He's a good fellow.'

'So Frank says.'

'Oh, Frank! I wish someone would break his heart for him.'

So, half-laughing, half in earnest, half-candid, half-reticent with each other, we parted.

In my room I paced up and down, considering the information my aunt had given me. What she had told me about my brother's death seemed to make a nonsense of all that I had believed to be happening to me.

And then I remembered the message that blood was thicker than water, the deaths of Joseph and Rotten Potatoes, the effort to kidnap me in London, and I felt bewildered. Before, I had often felt frightened, but I had also believed I knew my enemy's face. Now I had to ask myself if Count Victor was quite innocent, if my brother was dead and all the things that had happened had nothing to do with him at all.

I covered my face with my hands and almost groaned aloud. Somehow or other I had been led into a terrible maze and must now find my own way out. But as I went at last to bed, drawing the blankets up to my ears and huddling into their warmth for comfort, I remembered Mr Dalyrymple. I thought he might be able to answer some questions, and there were certainly some pertinent ones I wished to put.

A London fog hung over Masham Square when I opened my eyes next day. I dressed carefully in the sort of clothes a lady of quality wears when about to transact business with her lawyer. Frank was eating some ham and drinking hot tea when I arrived in the breakfast room. Lady Geraldine and the Countess were, of course, breakfasting in their rooms. Frank had Harry by his·side and was hearing a passage of Greek from the scholar as he ate his ham.

'Not bad, all things considered, Harry,' I heard him say. 'I don't say it would exactly have got you the commendation of m'tutor, but it ought to do for the Navy.' He looked· at me as I sat down across the table. 'We will leave the mathematics to this lady here. Now, don't you think this fellow would make a Senior Wrangler?' He put his hand affectionately on the boy's shoulder.

'Yes, if he would go to Cambridge.' I buttered some hot toast.

'The Navy for me,' said Harry exultantly.

'Seriously, I think he has a genius for mathematics,' said Frank, when Harry was gone.

'The Navy will use it.'

'The Navy!' said Frank. 'What will he do there? We shall never have war and he will go on sailing round and round the oceans getting barnacles on his mind.'

'The Navy is not all hearts of oak and sailing ships now, Frank,' I said, thinking of Dick Monk. 'And a clever man will make his mark anywhere.'

He was prepared to gossip. 'So who did you have at Windsor besides the Karolyis?'

'No one special. Very quiet, really.'

'They had the French Ambassador at Marlborough House. Difficult to think of him as a Frenchman with a name like Waddington. I met the United States Minister there, General Lawton. He tells me that old Falconet's daughter is going mad. She's a friend of yours, isn't she? Setting herself up as one of the free women and agitating

233

for equality for women. She got up a strike among a group of girls, did you know that? She seems to have some wild friends. Lawton was congratulating himself she was doing it all over here and not in her home country.'

'I expect she'll go back and work there when it suits her,' I said.

'Well, one can go too far and your friend Jessie may do, take my word for it,' said my cousin, settling himself to his newspaper.

I ate my breakfast, thinking about Jessie and making up my mind to see her soon. She would provide a nice counterpoise to Windsor.

Frank raised his head from the newspaper. 'I see that the Empress of Austria and the Archduchess Marie Valère are leaving for Ireland tomorrow. I suppose all the swarm of people that hang about them will travel off too. We'll be able to get a decent ride in the Row in the morning and not be pushed out of the way by the crowd. They are all said to ride well, these Austrians, but to my mind they are pushing riders. And they punish their horses, too. No gentleman rides the way they do. They are either too good or too bad.'

'I suppose the Empress has a fair number of gentlemen in her suite?'

'Oh yes, de Reichel and Gorowski, not bad fellows. I know them both.'

'Will Victor Hochberg go away too?'

He raised his head. 'Victor Hochberg? What do you know of him?'

'He was at Windsor.'

'Oh yes, come to think of it, he would be.' He turned back to his newspaper.

'Is it true that he is the bastard son of one of the Austrian Archdukes?'

'Not he. Does he say he is? I dare say he wishes he was. No, his father was one of the great sugar barons of Austria. You've heard of them? They were a group of rich merchants and manufacturers who managed to get a monopoly of all the sugar coming into Austria. Rich as kings, they made themselves, and one or two managed to creep into the fringes of the nobility. Victor's father was the most successful, because he was the richest. Society is really very simple. I'm told Victor's going it strong these days and spending money at a prodigious rate. He's got no Imperial blood in him, though, he's nothing but a sugar-almond prince.'

'And he's not wicked?' I asked. 'You wouldn't call him corrupt and evil?'

'What, Victor? Not he. Why he thinks too much of his looks and his tailoring to do anything very desperate.' He gave me a curious look. 'What strange story have you been cooking up?'

'It was all a mistake,' I said. 'What a pity.'

'Oh, you women are all alike,' said Frank, folding *The Times* and getting up. 'You like a bit of romance and if you can't get it, you make it up. But take my word for it, there is nothing in the least romantic about Victor Hochberg. And I've known him, on and off, almost all my life.'

So there it was, the fact had to be faced, despite what my father had said. Count Victor was not my half-brother. And, if I believed Lady Geraldine, I no longer had a brother. I had listened to Detective Anticknap, poor mad fellow, and let myself become as mad as he was.

I found Mr Dalrymple, my lawyer, in his offices near the Law Courts, in rooms which looked as though they had been old when his grandfather had been young in the business. His clerks still stood at high, old-fashioned desks, or perched, comfortless, on stools. I was not expected, but I was at once shown into his room, where a bright coal fire burned and a decanter of sherry stood on a silver tray. I had wondered already if Mr Dalrymple was not a little too fond of his glass.

He held out his hand, bowed, and led me to a chair. 'Sit down, Miss Vesey, and take your time. You are a little breathless with hurrying up the stairs.'

His offices were at the top of a narrow wooden staircase, with uneven treads. 'Every time I come up them I swear we must move, but you know, Miss Vesey, we have been in these offices two hundred years, and one does not lightly pull up such roots.' He sat there smiling, waiting for me to speak. Lawyers do not get rich by doing all the talking themselves.

'About my mother's will, Mr Dalrymple.' I too knew how not to waste words. 'You drew it up for her yourself?'

He nodded and gave me a bright, keen glance. 'Myself, indeed.'

'Was it long before she died?'

He rang a little silver bell on his table and at the tinkle, tinkle, tinkle a clerk appeared. 'Jenkins, get me Mrs Vesey's box, if you please.'

Presently a box was brought, black-painted and with the name 'Mrs Edward Vesey' printed on it in white. 'Is there a box for me?' I asked, suddenly, like a child at a party.

He smiled. 'No, my dear, not yet. You still repose in your father's box and in your mother's, you are split, we might say, between the two. When you marry or become of age you will have a box of your own.' He put on a pince-nez and regarded some papers he had withdrawn from the box. But I believe this was only window-dressing and that he knew very well all that he now told me, without having to refresh his memory. 'She came to me just before her marriage to your father. She was staying with her married sister, Lady Geraldine, preparing for her wedding. The will was drawn up, naming the eldest child, whether son or daughter, resulting from her marriage as her heir or heiress, to inherit either on marrying or on attaining the age of twenty. If she had no children by this marriage, then what she had to leave went to her illegitimate son. And indeed it was some years before you appeared.' Again he smiled. 'Marriage, as you know, cancels all wills, so the will, although drawn up before the wedding, was not signed by her until after the ceremony. It was thus perfectly legal and effective and has remained so from that day till this. No trouble, Miss Vesey, no trouble in the world.'

'I wasn't thinking about legality,' I said, 'but whether my brother is dead or alive.'

'Dead, Miss Vesey?' He put his hands together and looked inquiringly at me.

'I have been told he is dead,' I said. 'That he died as a child. That all these years I was growing up he has been in his grave.'

'Hm,' said Mr Dalrymple. He put his head on one side. 'There was no reason why your mother should tell me, of course, no reason in the world.'

'Confusing. She knew when she signed it that she had lost her son and might not have another child. Strange, was it not?'

'I know she hoped very much for a daughter. I remember her telling me that as we sat in this room. I got the impression that she had thought very carefully about her will. Yes, she wished to leave you what she did, even although you were not yet born to inherit it. And as for the signing ... I remember now, she came in briefly, before setting off on her honeymoon, did a little other

237

business with me connected with a family trust and signed the will ... Your father was with her. Yes, she might not have wished to speak much in front of him.'

'He knew everything ... And yet he thought my brother was still alive. He said so.'

'You must weigh your evidence, Miss Vesey. Your evidence for the survival of your brother is your father's word to you. What is your evidence that he is dead?'

'My aunt, Lady Geraldine, saw his grave,' I said.

'Confirmation, Miss Vesey? What we call corroborative evidence. Does she have a witness to what she saw? Was anyone with her?'

'Her husband, the General.' And then I added, 'And my mother was with them.'

He put his hands up and straightened his head. 'The General and your mother are both dead, Miss Vesey, but you convince me. I think we must accept that Lady Geraldine saw your brother's grave.'

I felt light-headed as I walked away. For weeks now I had had an overpowering preoccupation, obsession even, with my brother. And now he had been moved from the stage. He was dead.

At the same time, the figure of Count Victor had undergone a transformation. He was no longer a corrupt and evil man, but a rich and extravagant Austrian gentleman of only recent nobility. He was not the mysterious Mr Koenig, he had played no part in the strange violence that had surrounded me. Had I let poor Anticknap mislead me?

An invitation from Jessie awaited me when I got back to Masham Square, and with it a short note.

'I see from *The Times* that you have gone out of waiting,' I raised my head from the letter. Of course, I had forgotten how the Court Circular would henceforth proclaim my comings and goings to the world. Anyone who wanted to read *The Times* and the *Morning Post* might know where I was. 'As you are home in London, will you come to this little thing of mine? Card enclosed.'

I picked up the card. It invited me to an assembly at the London School of Medicine for Women. There was to be a ceremony at which Miss Louisa Stevenson would distribute prizes and certificates.

I smiled. Jessie had got her diploma and no doubt a prize, she was clever enough. As well as organising strikes among the girl workers of London, she had been about her other business. There was something admirable about such driving force. But it frightened me a little. Still, I had taken a vow and I must march with her, even if I was always two paces behind.

Jessie had written a postscript which said, 'Please bring a friend if you wish. We need a large audience.'

I wrote my acceptance to Jessie's invitation. Then on an impulse I sent a note to Charles Louis Kyburg, inviting him to join me there. We had corresponded. He had sent formal, civil little notes in German, and I replied in the same language. It was, I told myself, good practice for me, for my duties at Court, but the truth was I enjoyed it.

Once we had gone together to a concert, held for working people in one of the great London parks. Relaxing in the atmosphere induced by the free and easy good manners of the audience, we strolled on the turf, talking of poetry and music. In consorting with Charles Louis what I was doing was odd in one of my social class. I felt bold, almost revolutionary. One link there was with my other life; he admired (as so many foreigners did, I noticed) the poetry of Robert Burns, and things Scottish were greatly in fashion at the Court at Windsor. 'Burns is the poet of human equality,' he said, eyes ablaze. What the Queen admired, of course, was a full-hearted rendering of 'My

Faithful Johnnie'. I addressed the letter to Mecklenburgh Gate and posted it myself in the post box in Masham Square. But I did so in broad daylight when plenty of people were about. Moreover, the Foreign Secretary being at home, we had a policeman in the square.

As I stood there watching, a funeral came round the corner from Masham Street, crossed the end of Masham Square, and began to make its way towards Piccadilly. Two men dressed in deep mourning with crepe streamers floating from their hats walked in front: the mutes, as they were called, for during the whole ceremony they maintained a complete silence. They were only professional mutes and, I dare say, prattled away enough at home. Behind the mutes came the hearse, a great affair of black with four silver columns supporting a black and silver canopy. The horses which drew the hearse were black, crowned with nodding black plumes. They moved with solemn, slow pace, specially trained to lift each foot from the ground so far and no further. Behind the hearse, two more mutes, then carriage after carriage, with blinds drawn. I knew that behind the first three or four carriages in which the family travelled, the rest were empty, sent as a mark of respect by friends.

I walked slowly forward, not wanting to look, but unable to resist doing so. Funerals were common enough in London. Even in this rich area of the city, where pleasure was the aim, death took in as many as elsewhere. We were not immune. But there was something about the slow solemnity of this procession that stamped itself on my mind. Then, as I looked, for the first time I comprehended the significance of the coffin. It lay there covered by a white pall with a single lily on it: a young girl's coffin.

I was moved. Impossible not to feel sad that this girl, who might be younger than me, was dead. A small crowd had gathered along the kerb to watch.

They were silent as the hearse passed. Then a murmur began, a susurration passing up and down the crowd.

'Poor thing,' said a respectable-looking woman in front of me. She spoke to no one in particular, to the air, but her neighbour took her up.

'Poor girl, indeed. Such a pretty thing. Rich, too, an heiress, I've heard. They say she was slipping out to meet her betrothed, secretly, when it happened, and that's why she didn't look right nor left.'

A man standing near the two women spoke out in an angry voice. ' 'Twouldn't have done any good if she had looked. The carriage came rushing down the road at a rate of knots, and the horses bore down upon her before she could save herself.'

'You aren't safe on the roads these days for the traffic, and that's true enough,' said the woman who had spoken first. 'You saw it all, then, did you, sir?'

He nodded vigorously. 'She came running down the road with her cloak wrapped round her and rushed out into the road. "Watch what you are doing, missy," I wanted to say, but before I could speak the carriage came thundering up. I believe it had been waiting down the road and had just drawn out, but it was of no use, it was almost as if the carriage could not or would not stop. And then it was upon her and over her.' He dabbed his eyes. 'Poor girl, poor girl.'

'It was murder, I say,' said the woman. 'Common or garden murder.'

'Not much different,' he agreed sadly. 'And the driver whipped the horses on. That was the monstrous thing. He drove on, not caring to stop. I ran out into the road, chasing after him and waving my umbrella (for it was a wet night), but it was no use, no use at all.' He tipped his hat to the woman and walked away.

241

'Who was the dead girl?' I asked the woman nearest to me.

'A Miss Jeffreys. She lived round the corner from Masham Square. A pretty slip of a thing.' The woman looked at me. 'Like you, miss, as young and pretty and much of a height.' She shook her head. 'There, girls shouldn't have lovers and go chasing after them, but oh, what a punishment, poor girl!'

The plumes worn by the horses must have been old for they began to disintegrate in the damp wind. Little bits of them began to blow off, and a kind of black confetti sprinkled the streets. A tiny speck of black landed on my hand and settled there softly, till with a shiver I brushed it away.

I walked away, back to the house. I tried to put the story aside; it could have no connection with me. It was true, as the woman had said, the streets of London were very dangerous.

Jessie's 'little thing', as she called it, took place a few days later, before which time Countess Telling and I had talked.

I was watering the geraniums in the little sunny room off the drawing room, bruising the fragrant leaves between my fingers and sniffing them happily, when she came up behind and stood watching me. I was in that happy, wordless, mindless bliss that the sweet scent of living things can bring sometimes. I only became aware she was there when I turned round.

'Harry has gone out with his dog,' she said. It was strange how she had slipped into the ways of the house. She talked of Harry as casually as Frank might have done. 'What a funny way of speaking he has, that boy.' She smiled. 'Sometimes like an old gentleman and at others ...' She shrugged. 'He said: "Tell Miss Errol I'm off on my tod." ' I nodded. It was cockney slang for a walk on his own. 'And you know, the little dog can limp on three legs when it likes, holding up a front paw so pathetically, and then running off as gay as you please a minute later.'

'Oh yes, he's a professional begging dog, no doubt of it,' I said. 'Retired now, of course.'

Her pretty face looked blank. Not strong on humour, I thought. She tried to join in, though. 'I too am retired,' she said. 'At least, I live in retirement.' She sighed.

'Not for ever,' I said, sympathy aroused.

'You know how unfortunately I am placed?'

I nodded. 'Yes.'

'Who can help? And yet, I did not know. How stupid, how ignorant I was.' She stood there, hands held in front of her like a good child.

'Hardly your fault.' I put down my watering-can, and brushed my hands clean. Inside, I was passing indignant censure on her parents. But plenty of girls were as ill-informed, as I very well knew.

'I wish I was *you*, Miss Vesey.' I looked up at her in surprise. She went on: 'You seem so much in command, so wise.'

'Not so much as you suppose,' I said, and then added, 'But between your upbringing and mine there must be a difference, your Serene Highness.'

She jerked. 'Then you know?'

'I guessed.'

'Oh, of course, I am an object about the Courts of Europe to be studied and laughed about.' She looked at me angrily. 'But how could you understand?'

More than she thought, was the answer. I saw that it was just as hard to be a Serene Highness as to be a Reba, once you had lost your way. 'No,' I said. 'Please believe

243

me. I have never heard you mentioned except with sympathy.'

'Oh, at Windsor perhaps, but you should listen to them at home. Lock her up, marry her off, beat her, send her away. Oh, yes, they said all those things. Not know what it all meant? Frightened to speak? Bullied, intimidated, ignored, neglected? What rubbish, they replied, she's a little liar, let's have nothing to do with her, send her to England and let's forget she existed.' Her voice was rising. 'A hundred years ago they would have walled me up in a castle. I expect they wish they could do the same now.'

Her stalwart maid appeared at this moment, with a bottle of medicine and a spoon, and being, as she undoubtedly was, a sort of gaoler, her charge allowed herself to be taken away. At the door, still hysterical, she almost shouted at me: 'You know how it was with me? One evening I was dancing at a Court ball and the next morning ... the next morning ...' she burst into tears, and her guardian, who perhaps, after all, did care for her, had an arm round her shoulder in an instant and led her away.

I was left to pity, and not to judge. And I was also, I feel shame to admit, alive with curiosity. What a pity, I thought, that the Countess (I stuck to her incognito) had been dragged away before her story descended to detail.

The London School of Medicine for Women was having its annual prize giving and assembly. The day had turned warm and the sun was shining. The gathering in the quaint garden behind the building of the school took on the air of a garden party. A marquee sheltered a platform at which the notables would presently gather to hear Miss Louisa Stevenson deliver an address and hand out the prizes and certificates. Then, in another tent, we would take tea. Meanwhile, we strolled in the sun and looked at each other.

As Jessie and I walked on the grass and talked, I observed a tall figure that I recognised. To my surprise Jessie was the first to acknowledge him and bow.

'You know Sir Paul Bedower?'

'One of our principal benefactors,' she said. 'Rich, liberal and well disposed to our cause.' She gave me an appraising look. 'I am glad to see that Windsor and contact with the great has not spoilt you.'

'Did you think it would?'

'Oh yes,' she said bluntly. 'I always expect the worst. I may be calling upon you for help soon. Will you give it?'

'What sort of help?'

'It's a bad autumn,' she said abruptly. 'Already it begins to be cold. Think of winter coming on if you are poor and ill-housed. Yes, and without employment. Again and again I hear the monotonous tale: there is a reduction of wages at such and such a place, or, so many men have been discharged owing to the slackness of trade. Everywhere I see petty injustices and meanness. All the workers suffer, but the women, being the weakest and most easily turned aside, suffer most. Imagine: a finisher of boots paid two shillings and sixpence a dozen pairs and find your own polish and thread. Women working ten and eleven hours a day making shirts, "fancy best", God knows what that means—not my fancy and no one's best, I'm sure—and earning about two shillings a dozen shirts and finding their own cotton and needles.'

I looked down at my own beautifully shod feet, and saw the flounces of my skirt created at Madame Mangan's. My aunt Geraldine had praised Madame Mangan for her moderate prices and the despatch with which she completed the dresses. I had to ask myself now, at what cost to other women had this been achieved?

245

'I tell you it is going to be a savage winter, and if the women, yes and the men too, can't help themselves, then we must show them how. It must be war, Errol, not brotherly co-operation.'

'Strikes and so on, you mean, Jessie?' I said. 'But I know so little about economic affairs, I wonder ...' Jessie's views, always forceful, had now taken on a sharper, more precise shape. 'This is your landlady's doing,' I said.

'Trust her, then,' said Jessie. 'A woman who has thought herself out of Christianity and Whiggism and into Free Thought and Radicalism. Let her be your guide.' She looked at me defiantly.

'I won't trust any woman's judgement but my own,' I said. 'But that doesn't mean I don't agree with a lot of what you say. I see people are going up on to the platform. The speech-making is going to begin.'

Miss Louisa Stevenson delivered an address referring to the fight she and others had fought at Edinburgh under the guidance of Dr Sophie Jex-Blake. She had something to say about the excellent work done by the Countess of Dufferin in India. She mentioned the Kama Hospital under Dr Edith Pechey.

She seemed a cheerful, active, optimistic woman, but Jessie's intensity diminished her.

Along the row from me I saw Jessie's landlady sitting beside a thin, lanky, red-haired young man. Then someone moved into the seat beside me and touched my arm. I turned quickly. It was Charles Louis.

The words I uttered welled up spontaneously from a deep source inside me. 'My dear friend,' I said.

He bowed, the steady, sweet gravity of his face never changed. 'Of course, I was happy to come.'

'How kind.'

'I wished it. I am interested.' He was looking around with alert interest.

'Oh, I'm glad.'

He was surveying the platform. Almost all the women seated there were middle-aged, what my aunt would have called 'dowdy, my dear' as to dress, but piercingly intelligent as to countenance, and formidably resolute as to expression. Miss Stevenson was standing expectantly by a pile of prize books and certificates, hand poised ready to present them.

'But surprised I should come? A servant, *here*.'

'Of course, you are not that.' I was embarrassed.

'You are unusual, Miss Vesey. Most people would say I was.'

I turned to study his face. There had not been much expression in his voice, perhaps I could read some in his face. But it was calm and gentle.

'I don't forget that some people say a barber helped to start the French Revolution,' I said in a light voice.

He raised his eyebrows.

'Figaro,' I said. 'The hero of Beaumarchais's famous play, *The Barber of Seville*. Wasn't it thought an incitement to revolution to have the servant triumph over the master?'

'Ah, now I understand you better, Miss Vesey. You are that serious thing, an English romantic.'

Was he mocking me? 'Yes, I believe I am,' I answered. 'I won't be bullied, though.'

He gave a sudden burst of laughter. 'Do I bully, then?'

'In your own way, yes.' I turned my attention back to the platform, where events were moving forward with a comfortable, gentle bustle. Another speech, and yet another, polite hand-claps. A piano piece. Prizes were handed out.

The afternoon wore on.

Practical Chemistry :	Miss Porter
Organic Chemistry :	Miss Farrers
Physiology :	Miss Wood
Materia Medica :	Miss Ward
Midwifery and Gynaecology	
Prize :	Miss Falconet
Certificate :	Miss Sorky, Miss Hill, Miss Hunt

Jessie mounted the platform, took her prize, faced the audience and bowed. Then she raised her right hand, clenched her fist, and shook it. It was an abrupt, energetic, defiant gesture. It was as if she had said, I am here, and on behalf of all of you I declare war.

I heard my companion draw in his breath, and indeed there was a sort of *frisson* among the audience.

'I hope she knows what she is doing,' I heard him murmur. I didn't myself, but I could see that to those who knew, Jessie had indeed done something spectacular and shocking. 'So that is Miss Falconet? I admire her.'

'You will meet her. She is coming this way.' The audience was breaking up and we stood there, waiting for Jessie to force her way through the crowd.

To fill in the time I said: 'Where is Count Victor?'

'Gone to Ireland to buy horses. Leaving me in charge of the establishment. I am my own master.'

'How do you come to be in his service?' I asked curiously.

'I was born to it.'

'Oh yes, like Fletcher,' I said.

'Who is Fletcher?'

Suddenly I did not want to say: Fletcher is my aunt's butler, and his grandfather was the same before him. Instead I said, 'He is Sir Paul Bedower's cousin.'

'Sir Paul? Oh yes, the elegant gentleman on the platform.'

I saw Jessie making her way towards us. Her face was flushed.

'Well, that was a brave deed you did, comrade,' said Charles Louis.

I introduced them: Charles Louis, Jessie Falconet. By the introduction two streams in my life had come together.

'I wanted to shock them.' She had succeeded, I thought. She went on, 'But it was stupid. One should never show anger.' This was not like Jessie. She usually showed anger readily. I had even thought she was proud of it.

'I congratulate you on your prize, Jessie.' She still clutched it in her hand.

'A means to an end,' she said impatiently. Still, I knew she was glad to be good at what she did. I hoped so, otherwise I was sorry for those poor women. 'One uses any means that comes to hand. Besides, I do good. One must do what one can do for one's fellow-women.'

The audience was dispersing rapidly. It seemed to me that as people passed they gave us a pretty wide berth. Only Jessie's landlady and her red-haired friend stood around us, smiling approval.

Mrs Besant came up and shook Jessie by the hand. 'Now you are absolutely one of us, sister and comrade.'

Jessie gave me a defiant look.

Our party left together, falling naturally into two groups. I walked with Charles Louis, the others followed behind. The three of them were talking; we were silent. The streets seemed crowded, with the wind becoming cold as evening drew on. I was tired. I told myself that this was all my silence meant.

I began to walk faster and faster, till Jessie ran from behind and caught my arm. She walked on one side,

Charles Louis on the other, so that I was between them like a prisoner.

'Jessie,' I said, impelled to ask the question, because of the undiagnosed unease growing inside me. 'How is Anticknap? Have you heard?'

'Well, it is strange you should ask, because I have lately come to believe that he is secretly back at home and in hiding there. Certain things I have noticed and something about his wife have made me think it.' She shook her head. 'But I may be wrong.'

Our roads divided then; Jessie and her friends to catch an omnibus to Holborn, and Charles Louis and I to walk home. Once again we fell into silence. He spoke first.

'Miss Vesey,' he said, 'have you any reason to think you might be followed?'

'Why do you say that?'

'Because all the time there has been a man walking along the other side of the road who has been watching you. He is there now.'

I stood still and looked across the road. It was poor Anticknap, loping along, his puffed swollen face turned towards me, his gaze never moving.

'It's a sad, mad fellow,' I said, with a shudder. 'He led me into a mad world once before. I do not want to go there again. Let us hurry on.'

Charles Louis caught me up. 'Please tell me what you mean? What you say sounds so strange.'

I walked more slowly and as we turned into the quiet square I said: 'Let us go into the garden here, and I will tell you.' The garden in the middle of Masham Square was railed in and lined with small trees. The gate was always locked, but was opened for known inhabitants of the square in the hours of daylight by an aged custodian who sat for this purpose in a small hut just inside the gate. At dusk he shut up his box and went home. It was taken for granted that no one would want to walk there after dark.

'Thank you,' I said, as he opened the gate now and let us in. The sun was going down and I thought he looked at us impatiently. 'We won't keep you,' I said gently, 'I will see the gate is locked behind me as we go out.'

'It's my duty to see all's square and shipshape before I go,' he said obstinately.

'I give you my word,' and I smiled and drew Charles Louis along. Behind us I could hear the old man grumble, but he began to depart.

'How gently, yes, and kindly, too, you spoke to the old devil,' he said.

'But I'm sorry for him.' I was surprised. 'It's a dull, cold day for him. Naturally he wants to be off.' In this little pool of greenery at the heart of the city it was easy to talk. 'The man you pointed out *may* have been following me. I think he was. He is a policeman, or was once. Yes, don't look so surprised. I tell you I know him. He is, alas, more than a little mad.' I tried to laugh. 'And for a little while I was mad myself. For various reasons, and they seemed good to me at the time, I was convinced someone was trying to harm or even kill me. You look surprised. My cousin Frank says I have read too many novels.' Without realising it, I had once again been walking faster and I saw now that Charles Louis was having to hurry to keep up. I stopped short. 'Nevertheless, imagination or not, there were two episodes that seemed dangerous.' I thought about them for a second: my attempted kidnapping, and the night in prison. 'I won't describe them.' A faint flush rose on my cheek at the memory of the prison. 'But it is possible I may have been mistaken for another girl. She died last week. Killed. For her death there may have been some reason. I must not let my mind dwell on it ... About her death I may be wrong. Perhaps Frank is right. I do imagine things. It is possible she too died by accident. But I believe she was knocked down and killed deliberately. And that the first attempt on me was meant for her. Now, you smile and look sceptical.'

'No.' He shook his head. But at the back of those grave eyes was something like a smile.

He took me to the door of the house in Masham Square where Fletcher with a forbidding countenance admitted me, so that I knew he had been watching from a window and had seen me come out of the garden with Charles Louis.

He didn't warn me, he ought to have done, but perhaps he thought I deserved what I got.

So I walked into the drawing room, straight into the arms of Dick Monk, newly returned from Malta and promoted in rank to Lieutenant-Commander Monk.

Dick was sunburnt and cheerful and he hugged me hard to his breast and then released me, and looked at me. 'Thin, my girl, and a little pale, but otherwise a pleasure to the eye. I am here just for the rest of the day. Then I must report back to Pompey, that's Portsmouth to you civilians, and then perhaps back again, perhaps not. The Sea Lords in their wisdom have directed me back to England for a spell, and who is Dick Monk to say them no?' And when I remained still, seeking for words: 'Here, what's this, no answer for me?'

'You've seen your mother and she has seen my aunt and you've fixed it all up between you,' I answered.

'It's still for you to say "Yes" or "No". Wait.' He held up a hand. 'Nothing is to be decided now. You are to be left in peace till you are ready.'

But looking at his merry face, I knew he was sure of his answer. He put his arm round my waist and drew me to sit down on the sofa. 'The aunt is keeping out of the way. I am licensed to talk to you.' Then his face went serious. 'You see, this promotion means I may be away for two years. Out to the China Station. I couldn't take you there.' He looked at me hopefully. I said nothing. 'No, of course not. I know better than to ask. My mamma tells me no lady could be taken out there.' He nearly got a firm answer then, born out of irritation with his mother, who certainly did not wish me well. 'I shall be gone two years.' His face was serious. 'I ask for nothing from you, I dare ask for nothing, but anything you could freely give ...' He stopped. I still sat silent. 'Errol, speak.'

I got up and walked to the window. Masham Square was darkening. The street-lighter was going from lamp to lamp, raising his long pole to pull down the chain that made the gas jet flame. I watched. Up they came, one after the other, like flowers. I was very tired.

Dick came up behind me, put his hand on my shoulder and turned me towards him. Slowly he said: 'I can see in your face, there is no answer.' The merriment had left his face. He squared his shoulders. 'Well, I have a day or two still. See here, I want to take the boy Harry to Portsmouth. I have fixed for him to take the exam there to give him entrance to the old *Britannia* in Dartmouth Creek. He is fully old enough. You need to take to the sea young.'

'The fees still have to be found.'

'Leave that to me. Let that be my part. No, no protests. I am not a poor man. Indeed, I could be fairly said to be a rich one.'

'You are very generous,' I said huskily.

'Generous nothing. The boy's a good one.'

'Give me a month more of work with him at those mathematics.' I found my voice still difficult to control. 'And then we'll come to Portsmouth.'

He took my hand, held it tightly, then was gone.

*   *   *

I expected some raking questions from Lady Geraldine that evening, but I was protected by the arrival of my cousin Frank in company with a lively, talkative group of fellow-members of the House of Commons. The early evening was dominated by their chatter.

They talked about the topics I had already noticed politicians always talked about: money and Ireland.

'We shall never solve Ireland,' said one, a tall fellow with a monocle. 'It's beyond solving. Give them Home Rule, you say? That is the same as not solving it.'

And then, money. 'You can have social reforms and no Navy. Or a strong Navy and no reforms. You can't have both,' said another.

They were a world away from Jessie's frantic cries. These men had never heard of Jessie, perhaps they never would, but it seemed to me that the world for which she spoke would make itself felt.

I looked at them, gathered round Lady Geraldine's sofa, wearing their beautifully tailored clothes so casually, spilling cigar ash down their silk lapels, a far cry from Jessie's cloth-capped crew of politicians with their scream of pain.

'Good-bye, Errol. Good-bye, Mamma. I leave for Scotland tomorrow for a little stalking. Hartington is giving me a month's sport.' Hartington bowed. 'Come along, Harty, Joe, are you ready?'

And they all swept out.

The room seemed quiet after they had gone, piling out of the house into cabs and carriages, still talking loudly.

Lady Geraldine yawned. 'How different things are now from when I was a girl. Then hardly anyone remained in London once the season was over in June; now London is full of life in the winter.' She put her hand to her head. 'My dear, they've inflicted a headache on me with those cigars.'

I got up to put a cushion behind her head. She relaxed

254

her head, but not her spirit. 'Nor is that the only change, you know. The laws of etiquette, now so lax, were severe in the extreme. Now I can recall when it would have been considered a dreadful thing for a lady of birth to go out walking without a manservant behind her.' She gave me a very sharp look indeed. 'I·remember,' she went on, 'that the old Duchess of Cleveland (Lady William Poulett that was) was the last lady who, when she went out, was always followed by a footman bearing a cane. Cabs were not considered at all proper, while omnibuses were absolutely tabooed, which today is by no means the case.' No mistaking the sharpness of the look now.

I threw up my hands. 'I admit it, aunt, I am a hard case and frequently go about in omnibuses and cabs.'

'And so Dick Monk has asked for you?'

'In the teeth of his mother's opposition.'

'Ten thousand a year,' she said thoughtfully. 'A snug fortune, sufficient to have a little shooting, some hunting, a modest house in the country, a small *pied-à-terre* in town, but it is not riches.'

I admired the aristocratic spirit; I knew she managed everything on a tithe of what she named.

She leaned back against the cushion and closed her eyes. 'My dear, do you know, I believe I really *am* tired.'

But in the morning it was clear that her lassitude was not fatigue, but illness, and as the day wore on, that illness had to be reckoned serious. The fever mounted and her restlessness increased. I stayed with her most of the day, and left her only at night.

The next day she was, if anything, worse. A long illness began to be talked of.

The house in Masham Square was not a house to be ill in. The four floors were joined by numerous stairs and every drop of water and fuel for heating had to be carried up. Nor was my aunt an easy invalid. Ill she might be, but the Maurice blood was strong and she required constant conversation and attention. The doctors (naturally there were two, no Maurice could be safely ill or confined or dying, except in the hands of at least two doctors, one a royal physician) withdrew, conferred, and returned with the decision: removal to Lady Barnaby's Nursing Home.

'Never! Death first,' cried Lady Geraldine. 'Rachel Barnaby is a lunatic.'

But she went, or was taken, and her maid went with her, arms overflowing with all the cushions, books, sewing and letters that must accompany Lady Geraldine wherever she went, in sickness or in health. As she was carried out, swathed in cashmere shawls, she continued to issue a stream of directions as to the management of the house.

'And remember to order your fish from Craven's in Bond Street,' floated back to me as she was borne away.

I was in charge of the house in Masham Square.

At first it was an idyll. A spell of pleasant, autumn weather set in and Countess Telling, Harry and I settled down to a happy routine. In the mornings I worked with the boy, in the afternoons I wrote letters or walked with the Countess. Several times Charles Louis came and was accepted without comment by her as my German tutor. Even worry about Lady Geraldine receded. For a little while a dream-like placidity prevailed, with blue skies and tranquil days. All my faculties, critical and perceptive, seemed to sleep, and I was content simply to live.

But one by one the black themes crept in.

The weather broke first. It began to be cold. The skies remained blue, but the colours hardened and became more intense; the wind blew cold. People began to look pinched and nipped in the streets. The leaves fell from the trees and littered the pavements and were tossed in the wind. The summer birds were long since gone, only the sparrows and pigeons remained in the square gardens. One day there was a seagull, lone herald of storms in the English Channel, which presently arrived and howled over London.

Jessie, who called, reported evident signs of unemployment and distress in the poor areas where she worked. She looked tired and depressed and brought in the first report I heard of a terrible murder in the East End of London. It was the murder of a woman, committed with great ferocity. It was thought at first that there might be a connection with the earlier killing which had so interested Lady Geraldine, but soon came news of a second murder of an even more savage kind. The two murders had taken place in a small area of London, but alarm spread out all over the city, so that even in Masham Square it was noticed, and people hurried through the streets after dark.

'You have no idea,' said Jessie, sipping tea with us, 'of the effect in the slums and alleys where I work. After dark people run even from me. It would be laughable if it were not so terrible. Well, they have not caught the murderer and there seems no sign that they will. How is your aunt?'

'Not better. The illness drags on.'

'It's a bad season. I hear of nothing but strikes and sickness on every side. And now these murders ...' Jessie stood up to go. She yawned. 'I think your friend Anticknap is back in his own house but on the quiet, just as I told you before. His wife more or less admitted it to me. Well, I'm off. They will catch the Whitechapel murderer in the end, I dare say.'

But there was another killer loose in London then, who was soon to make his presence felt.

The next day a message came from Dick Monk and the

visit to Portsmouth was arranged. Harry and I were to set out together early the next morning, travelling by train. We would meet Dick, lunch in Portsmouth, Harry would be examined, and we would return late that same night. The boy was all delight. I was less eager.

The day we met was one of cobalt sky and windless air, a lull in that ferocious autumn. To this I attribute something of the events of the day. I believe our minds and our bodies, which had been at stretch, were as responsive to the currents of that day as was the Aeolian harp to the winds.

'The sun. It's a good omen,' said Harry cheerfully at Waterloo. He was so changed from the waif I had first seen that I marvelled. He was wonderfully resilient and practical, never looked back, lived entirely in the present and the future. He would make a splendid sailor. His true home would always be his ship, his happiest dream one of the next day's action. I had noticed he never mentioned his mother. Would he forget me as quickly?

'How do we travel?'

'In a first-class carriage,' I answered.

The expenses of the day were being borne by a five-pound note unexpectedly sent down from Scotland by Frank.

'First-class, eh?' Harry said gleefully. 'Like a gentleman. I shan't be able to travel in such style when I am a naval monkey.' This was the name given to a midshipman, the lowest rank above deck.

When the train came in, he walked up and down, a trim figure in his dark serge suit, inspecting the carriages and selecting the best one for me. Then he offered me his arm and led me to it. I kept my face grave and allowed myself to be conducted thither.

'Of course, I am the gentleman on this trip and it is my duty to see you are comfortable, and well looked after, and all that,' he said seriously. 'And I mean to do it. I try to keep my eyes open and watch what's what so that I know how to behave. Seeing that I'm to be a naval officer, I model myself on Mr Monk.'

'You can't do better.'

'And well I know it.' He sat down beside me. 'Just as if I ever have a wife or a daughter, I shall want her to be like you, Miss Errol.'

'Oh, I'm no one to follow,' I said lightly.

'Now, there you're wrong. Joseph and me,' he swallowed at the thought of his friend, 'we talked of you, and decided you were the greatest lady there was.' He looked out of the window and I saw a hint of tears. 'I don't forget Joseph, you know. He was true as oak, he was. Never mind if he could hardly read and write. Shall I ever have a friend like him again?'

'Perhaps not. But if you are ever to find one, then the Navy will be the place to do it.'

He brightened. 'Yes, I fancy they are all good chaps there. And seriously, Miss Errol, for a boy without anything behind him, it is a fine chance to make a name. I mean to do it.'

'Yes, you're right.'

'And my fortune, too,' he said vigorously. 'Think of Lord Nelson.'

'But seriously, you may not be so lucky as to find a Napoleon to conquer.'

He laughed, bouncing up and down on his seat. 'There's always the German Emperor. My, what wouldn't I give for a whack at him.'

'I pray you never get it.'

The train hurried through the green countryside.

'Pompey, Pompey,' shouted the porters at the end of our journey.

Dick Monk met us on the station platform and hurried

259

us to a waiting cab. As we jolted across the cobbles I looked out of the window at the town.

I could imagine the young officers of Nelson's day hurrying through the streets of old and handsome houses. Going down towards the dockyard the rows of houses became older and smaller. But everywhere was trim and shipshape, as Dick would have said.

He engaged himself in cheerful conversation with the boy and did not talk much to me. I was happy to be silent and to observe. I saw groups of sailors moving jauntily through the streets, with here and there an officer or two walking along, hands behind the back, with that rolling gait that men of the sea so often seem to have.

'We lunch at the Royal George,' said Dick briefly. 'I have engaged a room for you. I thought you would not wish to lunch in a public room.'

Harry looked disappointed, and I could see that the noise and bustle of a luncheon in the coffee room of a busy hotel would have pleased him. 'Quite right,' I said to Dick. 'We can be on our own and Harry can draw his thoughts together for the ordeal this afternoon.'

'A strange day, isn't it?' asked Dick, as he alighted. 'The air almost vibrates and yet is very still. Do you notice it?'

'I noticed how crystalline clear the colours of the landscape were as we came along in the train.'

'That, too. We shall see a storm before nightfall.'

'I was calculating,' said Harry eagerly, 'that I could see with my naked eye what must be ten miles or more away.'

'You must calculate better than that, my lad, or their lordships will have nothing of you. Now, to begin : onion and mussel soup to start, that will suit you?'

'Please.' Harry tucked a starched napkin in his collar and sat down ready. In such flashes he showed that the street arab was not so far away. Nor did his appetite falter all through lunch, from the soup, through the Porterhouse steak to the chocolate pudding and the Stilton cheese, which he characterised as a 'right good one'.

When the time came to deliver him to his examination chamber I shook him gravely by the hand to wish him luck. Dick Monk put his hand on the boy's shoulder and turned his face towards him and studied it. 'You'll do,' he said, and with affection.

Together Dick and I walked down to the sea. It was a deep blue and the waves had a crisp, finished look, as if they might be brittle.

'Good old Pompey,' he said. 'It's a town you get fond of.'

In the bright sunlight every building seemed to have a hard outline that looked unnatural. Then I looked out across the water in the direction of the Isle of Wight. It was resting there across the water like a miniature toy, perfect in every detail, with roofs, steeples, clearly articulated. I turned to the sea and even miles out saw vessels with perfect clarity.

'Harry was right,' I said to Dick. 'There is some strange quality in the air today.' Later I learned that all along the Channel coast other observers were noticing the same phenomenon. The air had become so rarefied that objects could be discerned with remarkable distinction. From Dover and Folkestone could be seen the lighthouse at Cap Gris Nez in Calais, and Napoleon's column in Boulogne. I did not know that then, of course, but I knew it was a remarkable day. An unnatural day.

Slowly Dick and I strolled along, looking at the sea. If I had feared that he would once again press me to marry him, then I was wrong, he didn't. Instead he walked beside me, looking young and tense. The clarity of the day did not extend to personal relationships and I, who had laughed and flirted with and teased Dick Monk, now felt a million miles removed. As if I was across the Channel and in another country. We talked, of course. That is, I talked and Dick listened and said very little.

'If they take Harry, when will he be expected to join his ship or the college or whatever they call it?' I asked eventually.

'They do keep naval discipline there,' he said absently. 'Soon, I suppose.'

'Yes, soon, I know, but when?'

He seemed to come to the surface from some depth of memory. 'In the New Year, I would imagine. He will join his year late. It is a special concession.' He looked into the past and smiled. 'I did it myself. It worked well enough. I was lonely at first.' He smiled again, as if remembering interesting and absorbing events which no woman could understand.

Far out at sea I saw a small ship and it seemed to me I could even make out the figures moving on her deck. I wondered how long this preternatural clarity of the air would last and what would bring it to an end. 'Don't you find this day rather fearful?' I asked. My own head was beginning to ache.

'Not so much as if I was at sea. At sea the weather is a constant preoccupation. Here, unless it obliges me to, I hardly notice it.' He cast a professional eye at the sky. 'There will be a storm, though.'

'Thunder and lightning, you mean?'

'No, more likely a high wind that blows everything to bits.' He pointed to the horizon. 'See that pale yellow colour that is appearing in the sky? That's the sign.'

There was a kind of held-back energy in his voice that I could not help noticing, as if some strong emotion was there but must be kept in check. It was the first time I had detected this force in him, and I thought that if I had felt it before I might not have found it so easy to return my bland answer, 'No'.

'You mustn't worry about the boy.'

'No, I don't,' I said. If ever anyone was blessed with the power of rising to the surface under any condition it was Harry, I thought. 'Although I suppose the Navy is a hard life?'

'Not near so hard as it was. No, times have changed. You need have no fear in sending him in. He's a good lad. It's amazing how one gets to like him.'

'Oh yes, he has all the Maurice charm,' I said thoughtlessly.

'Good God,' he turned to me in surprise. 'Is he?'

'No, not Frank's.' I shrugged, halfway between amusement and embarrassment. 'We think . . . the General.'

'I *did* wonder,' he said honestly.

'Everyone must, I should think. It only amazes me that my aunt never sees anything.'

But even as I spoke I wondered how I could be so naïve. Of course she knew, or guessed. Probably Fletcher and the servants knew, too, everyone knew. It was an open secret, just like me and my brother. I laughed aloud and Dick looked at me with a question in his eyes, then turned away. We were neither of us at ease with the other.

A group of two or three young sailors came past us then, and, seeing Dick, saluted and smiled. They seemed hardly older than Harry himself but already looked as if they knew how to give an account of themselves in the world of men. I supposed the Navy would give Harry this look too, and, when he had it, he would be formidable indeed.

'Time to get Harry,' I said, as the church clock struck the hour. Besides, I was beginning to be tired and my head throbbed. 'Where is he to be collected?'

'I told a seaman to wait for him and bring him back to the Royal George.' He noted the time and nodded. 'He should be waiting there for us now.'

Harry was standing there, alertly watching for us in the hallway by the stairs as we came in, and turned a radiant face towards us with a smile which he tried to hide, but could not. 'Well, we need not ask if we should congratulate you,' said Dick.

'I was in rare luck,' said Harry. 'They chose all easy problems and in the Latin and Greek, which I was fearful of, they chanced upon some nice easy pieces that I had read with Mr Frank.'

'That sort of luck often attends people who have worked hard,' said Dick drily.

'And they said I was so up in mathematics for my age that they could hardly believe I had been taught by a woman.'

I supposed I had to be grateful for what compliment there was to be extracted from that grudging thought. 'Another time don't mention you were taught by a woman,' I said sharply. 'It may lose you credit.'

Dick moved forward quickly. 'Let me order you some tea.'

'Thank you, no. I should rather return. It'll be late enough when we get back.' And dark, I thought, there was an uneasy feeling about the dark. Even the house in Masham Square no longer seemed so safe and protected, but seemed to whisper and creak in the dark. After the first two floors there was no gas light, but candles and oil lamps must be used. I looked about me. 'Oh, Harry, I came with a book I was reading in the train, I believe I must have left it in the room upstairs where we had luncheon.'

'Let me go.' He was already running up the stairs. He was out of sight when I recalled what I had been reading.

'Oh, Dick, it was a novel by Zola, I had rather Harry did not see it. Would you go?'

'With pleasure.' He hurried up the stairs, round the bend and was gone.

I strolled around, observing the throng sitting about the hall of the hotel, mildly interested and amused by the bustle and activity. There was a large family party clustered around a fat, flushed mother in shiny black satin, a prim lady in spectacles and a dull bonnet sitting in the window, and an elderly man drinking wine and smoking. I amused myself by imagining who they were and what they were doing here. The fat lady in black was, I feared, a widow, but a prosperous one whose only worry was the flightiness of her daughters (they *were* very pretty, and excessively fashionable) and the unsteadiness of her sons (one could see at a glance that they raced and gambled). The bespectacled lady was a governess changing posts. She was now waiting to be collected by her new employers, having just said a sad farewell to her former pupils. No doubt she was what people called 'a treasure'. As for the wine-drinking gentleman, he was a banker, perhaps a nefarious swindling one, who was now on his way to the Continent with his ill-gotten gains. He raised his eyes to me at that point and I saw that, in fact, they were honest and kind!

Dick and Harry were taking their time. I walked up the stairs to look for them. I looked along the corridor just as they appeared at the end. The corridor was painted dark green so that it produced the illusion of looking at them down a green tunnel. I stood there watching.

Harry was talking away nineteen to the dozen; he raised his face towards Dick. And then, as I watched, I saw Dick bend down and kiss Harry full on the lips.

Down the green tunnel I saw the two figures, small but clear. Harry took his handkerchief out of his pocket and slowly wiped his lips, and then deliberately threw the handkerchief away.

I turned round and walked slowly down the stairs. When they appeared at my side, they were silent.

On the train journey back I was not talkative either, but I studied Harry and marvelled at his self-command, his capacity to hold his tongue; he gave no sign that anything had discomposed him. Any other boy would have been bound to let me know, somehow, that something untoward had happened, but from him, nothing.

'Harry,' I said, and then stopped.

'Miss Errol?' He had taught himself a sort of formal politeness, which I had found touching, but now I felt saddened and oppressed by it. He was too old for his years, by far. Older than me in some essential experiences.

'You're happy, are you, at the way things have turned out?'

He looked at me gravely, a long, serious, adult stare. 'I'm lucky beyond anything, Miss Errol. I fell into your hands at the right time, and what I've become now is something I could never have become a year later, or even six months later.' How well he put it, how clearly he saw the situation; and it was true. He had come into Masham Square just when he was ready for explosive growth.

'Are you crying, Miss Errol?'

'Oh no, Harry, of course not.'

'I thought I saw ... a tear, you know,' he said delicately.

'Oh, no.' I leaned back against the cushioned wall and closed my eyes. 'My head aches a little, that's all.'

The storm broke on the journey home. We arrived at Waterloo Station to a screaming wind and heavy rain.

'Beastly cold,' said Harry, with a shiver.

'Yes.' The carriage was laid up now my aunt was ill and Frank away, and we had to take a cab. I had come to be selective about choosing a cab these days and inspected

driver and vehicle before I stepped in. It would be a
long time before I lost that habit. My brother was dead.
What had I to fear? But uneasiness remained. There were
questions I longed to put to my aunt.

Fletcher opened the door. He was wearing, unexpectedly, a dark overcoat and carrying a hat. Plainly,
he had been out of the house and had just returned. I could
see the damp on his hair. For the first time I saw how like
he was to his cousin, Sir Paul Bedower.

'Something's wrong,' I said at once. 'Is it my aunt?'

'Yes, Miss Vesey. The doctors have come to a decision.'
He looked at me. 'Typhoid.'

Typhoid, the disease that had killed the Prince Consort,
the very name made me chill and apprehensive. I looked
at Fletcher, unable to answer him.

'She has good nursing. And, you know, Miss Vesey,
there is a lot in how you confront an illness of this sort.
Her ladyship keeps a great deal of her liveliness and good
humour.'

'You've seen her?' I asked.

He shook his head. 'No. Only spoken to the nurses. And
indeed, they say she is doing very well.'

I gathered my mantle around me and prepared to go out
again. 'Call me a cab if you please, Fletcher. I am going
to see my aunt.'

He stood quite still, without movement.

'Fletcher,' I said, my tone peremptory, 'A cab, please.'

'Lady Geraldine expressly forbids you to visit her.'

'On that matter I am old enough to make up my own
mind.' I moved to take hold of the door. 'I shall walk, if I
must.'

I moved towards the door, hand outstretched to take
the door handle. Fletcher stepped decisively between me
and my departure. All the misery and frustration which
had been building themselves up inside me that afternoon

exploded. Before I could stop myself my hand came up and struck his face. With a movement equally instinctive he gripped my wrists hard and held them together. We stared at each other.

I don't know what he saw in my eyes, the baffled fury of a child, I should think, but in his I saw, not anger, but understanding, and yes, a faint hint of humour.

'I beg your pardon,' said Fletcher seriously. He released my hands.

'No, no, the apology must be mine.' I was shaken by the wave of anger that had risen up inside me and vented itself on him. God knows whether he or Dick Monk was its true object, they seemed to share it equally.

Tom Fletcher bowed; I suppose he accepted my apology, he never said so.

'I will not go tonight, but first thing in the morning, I insist.'

Before I could say anything more the door bell was given a short, sharp tug.

We were all standing in the hall, so when Fletcher opened the door to Harriet Craven I was fairly at her mercy.

'My dear, you will forgive me coming upon you unawares and so late.' Her eyes were going rapidly round the hall, taking in all the details. 'But we are old friends, are we not, and need not stand on ceremony.'

'No, indeed.'

'And you are just come in, I see.' Indeed her sharp eyes had observed my travelling clothes and Harry standing there, and no doubt the signs of recent emotion in my face. 'Well, I am here to tell you that I am summoned back to Court.' There was satisfaction in her voice as if glad that the Queen could not get on without her.

'And am I to come too?' Aside, I said, 'Harry, go and ring for some tea.' I prayed there might be a servant there to obey him. 'Come into my aunt's sitting room, Miss Craven, we always keep a fire there, though she is not here.' Another prayer was added that this might be the case. The housekeeping at Masham Square, always a little ragged was now erratic.

'No, you are *not* required.' She bustled after me. 'A special messenger was sent for me. It seems Sybil Keswick has lost her voice with all that singing, as I told her she would. No, I am coming at the Queen's express command,' and she drew herself up quite strikingly for so small a lady, 'to offer her sympathy for Lady Geraldine, and to enquire after her. I was *expressly* told to enquire in person.'

I told her : typhoid, but not a bad case.

'Ah, typhoid,' she nodded sagely. 'As the Queen feared. She knew it.'

'We did not know it ourselves till just now.' The door opened to admit Fletcher, Harry and a tray.

'But the Queen has a *special* perception about illness ... Yes, I will take some tea. Thank you, my dear.'

I drank thirstily. She talked on for a while. I did not listen carefully. To my horror I yawned, hurriedly covering my mouth with my hand, but she saw. Our disorganisation and my fatigue would all go back, suitably enbellished, to the Queen. The Court was about to return from its autumn holiday in Scotland and to stay in Windsor until it was time to remove to Osborne for Christmas.

Soon she rose to go. At the door, lowering her voice, she said : 'And how is the young lady you have with you? How does she go on?' And she screwed up her face into a knowledgeable expression.

I looked blankly at her.

'Oh come, I know, we all do, although it's supposed to be a secret.'

'She's well enough, I believe.' I answered reluctantly.

'The story was, you know, that she was brought over here to be married to Count Victor. You look surprised? An ox of course, but immensely rich. Still nothing seems to have come of it and we cannot leave such matters *too* long.' She gave a little cackle. 'And, after all, it would not have done, because I seem to remember there was something odd about *his* birth, and two wrongs do not make a right.'

My heart beating, I said, 'Do you mean he was not Count Hochberg's own son?'

She frowned. 'I'm not sure I ever heard the rights of it, but Countess Hochberg was a model wife and as plain as a pike-staff into the bargain.'

Bother the model wife, I thought.

'I suppose he may have been adopted,' I said, pretending to sound indifferent.

'He looks the image of the old Count,' she said. 'Besides, I remember her confinement. The worst in Europe I heard, and lasted seven days. So unlike me to forget. I shall be forgetting my own name next, but it can't signify, for you see, he is not to marry your little visitor or he would be here now and it would be all over and done with.' She smiled and shook her head. 'Old gossip, old gossip.'

Very soon after this she was gone, and I was left alone to think over my day.

Dick Monk, Tom Fletcher, and now an insinuation from Harriet Craven about Count Victor's birth. I could not dismiss it as lightly as she did. I was interested in that old piece of gossip.

The next day I went to see my aunt at Lady Barnaby's Nursing Home. She was said to be much better, mending in fact.

Sickness had not changed her. She lay back on heaped

pillows, her long hair, in which a pleasing streak of white
had appeared at the temple, fell behind and about her.
A soft white dressing-jacket with blue bows was wrapped
round her. Altogether Lady Geraldine was a charming
invalid, who understood the value of freshness. Only her
hands, white and thin, showed traces of her ordeal.

'Errol, my love.' She was fragrant with Mrs Taylor's
Rosewater Essence as usual. Not for Lady Geraldine the
smell of the sick room. 'Prettier than ever, but a little
fatigued. You have had too much to do. How do things
go? Be frank.'

I meditated how much to tell her, but she was enough
of a Maurice not to be deeply disturbed when her own
present comfort was not threatened, so I told her a little.
We talked of Sophie Telling too.

She was full of sympathy. 'Poor child, poor child. But
really it will be best if the baby dies. What else is it but a
little encumbrance?'

I nodded.

'But of course, her parents will have to know. I am
ill and cannot manage for them. And someone must get
a message to the Queen.' She began to look flustered.
'Arrangements must be made.'

'I shall do that.' I had promised Sophie.

'If you can get Princess May on the quiet, *that* will
be the thing. She is always so practical.'

'I'll do my best,' I promised.

Lady Geraldine relaxed. 'And then you will be safe with
the Bedowers. Old Fletcher is a good sort and his daughter
the same.'

'And his grandson? Tom Fletcher.'

She stared a little at the mention of his christian name.
'He is very efficient. I have no fault to find. I depend on
him. An ambitious man, but I don't mind that.' She seemed
perfectly content with her summing up, as if to serve

her must satisfy even the most ambitious man. I marvelled. The Maurices truly were of the breed that laughed and gambled on the way to the guillotine.

For a little while we talked of small things. I could see her eyes on my old brown mantle and knew she was thinking that a visit to Madame Mangan must be set in train. Then she said, 'I have a letter here from Frank.' She fumbled in a satin purse to produce it. 'You will wonder he has not been home, with me so ill.' No, I thought I did not wonder that Frank should keep well away from trouble. 'But you see, there has been a reason for it,' and she gave me a contented smile. 'He has met with a charming young woman, Scotch, an ancestry as long as your arm and not a great fortune, but it will *do*. Let me read you what he says: "Dearest Mamma, I am so glad you are feeling better and quite out of the wood. The weather here has been atrocious and the stalking worse ..."' She turned over the paper. 'No, here we come to it: "Dearest Mamma, I look forward to showing Catriona to you. She is a thoroughly nice girl, with just the sort of soft, plain manners I like, and will hold her own anywhere, given a bit of time and some of the right sort of clothes." There now,' and my aunt leaned back with a pleasant smile.

'He sounds passionately in love,' I said dryly.

'Now, Errol, you know how Frank is, one couldn't look for, nor indeed want abandon with him. And this Catriona sounds as if she has the right style. I tell you I am thoroughly thankful to have him off my hands. I only hope she does not have red hair. The Queen does not like it.'

'I'll do my best about Sophie,' I said, rising. 'Shall I tell them Frank's news?'

'You can hint at it. Yes, a good idea, you know how to do it; just a word or two. And find out if you can if

General Newbury *has* been obliged to resign. I'm terribly out of things here.'

She held my hand. 'I shall not be with you to celebrate your birthday, which grieves me. Postpone the celebration, my love, and you shall have a festivity when I am on my feet again. But you will go to collect your box from Mr Dalrymple? You have not forgotten? I long to know what it contains.' Her eyes sparkled.

'I shall go, I promise, and then you shall find out. But, Aunt Geraldine, one more question before I go. About my brother, my little half-brother that died.' She stirred uneasily. 'I know you told me all you knew, but really you were only a remote onlooker. By all accounts my mother told you very little.'

'She was silent, but that was her way.'

'Are you sure there is not something more? Some detail, some fragment of any story you remember told about my brother's death—his birth and his death?'

She lay for a long while silent, then sighed. 'If you really want someone you can ask, you had better go to Charde.'

'Charde? But it is all ruin.'

'The South Lodge is inhabited. My sister's old maid, Mrs Teviot, who was with her all that time, lives there. She was our old nurse once. Go to her.'

The Court had returned earlier than usual from its autumn holiday, because one of the royal ladies, long married and long childless, had 'expectations' at last. A journey later in the month was thought to be a risk for her. So they were at Windsor again before repairing to Osborne for Christmas. The Queen hated her children to marry and once married lamented the arrival of children, but none the less was unfailingly kind and good to them when they needed help. An intense loyalty to those she loved was the hallmark of her character. Thus, although she liked things to go on as usual, without deviation, she had returned early from her beloved Scotland. I decided to fulfil my promise to Lady Geraldine and Sophie, and then to visit Mrs Teviot at Charde. Unlike Miss Craven I looked forward to the freedom of a journey on my own by train.

Nerves were frayed among the entourage after their gruelling little holiday. This year's quarrels had been bitter and prolonged. A truce must be declared in the war before the exodus to Osborne and they all knew it. Life at Court was exhausting enough, without feuds raging on.

So my arrival, unexpected and unannounced, made a nice interruption for them. Word that I was there went by the usual chain of messengers to the Queen, who sent back a message that I was to come to her. She received me sitting at her tea-table, on which every single object except her cup of tea was made of gold. Everyone else was exhausted by the long journey south. She seemed spry.

I told my story, explained our problem with Sophie now that my aunt was ill, was heard out in silence, then dismissed. I was not offered tea or any word of counsel.

'You must not mind,' said Harriet Craven. 'The Queen is made uncomfortable by talk of babies, and really she has had a lot of it lately. She had to be told, of course, and you did quite right to come, but the best thing the poor little creature can do is to die.'

'So my aunt says.'

'Exactly; she always knows what the tactful thing is. Still, little as you may believe it now, the Queen will be helpful. She always is in the long run. Now, let me give you some tea before you return. Your little hint about dear Frank is *most* interesting.'

Before tea was over a message from the Queen arrived,

saying that the royal horses and carriage were to transport me to London. 'What a mark of approval,' smiled Harriet Craven. 'It shows how highly the dear Queen thinks of you.'

But all I could think of was that it would make easy my journey to Charde.

A thin river mist had spread its fingers over Charde; it was dusk on this November evening, and lights were springing up in the cottage windows as we passed.

The South Lodge, with its pointed gothic windows and its little turrets, was like a gingerbread house, or a house in a fairy-tale. Smoke was coming from the chimney, and I could see a cheerful fire in the sitting room with a kettle boiling on it.

On the only door was a brass knocker with a lion's face. I banged it.

Immediately it was opened by a tiny little woman who only came up to my shoulder. She had a plump, cheerful face, with white hair drawn back in a tidy bun. A pair of spectacles perched on her nose, but her grey eyes looked above them straight at me.

'I am Errol Vesey.'

She took off her spectacles and put them in a pocket. 'Ay, I know you. I'd know you anywhere from your likeness to *her*. But you are taller than her by an inch or two. Come away in.' She had a very slight, but pleasant Scots accent. She led me to a crowded living room where a cat lay asleep by the blazing fire and a canary swung in a cage by the window. Photographs and pictures covered walls and furniture. Unobtrusively my eyes sought a picture of my mother. 'I saw you once in Hyde Park with your papa. Just a baby you were then, but with feature enough for me to say, yes, that's my lady all over again.' She made me sit down by the fire and took up a

275

seat near me. 'But you've a stronger look in your face. You'll never be beat. She was beaten in the end, my poor girl. They wore her down and fretted her, so that what she came to be was just a shadow of what she had been, so gay and pretty, that it made your heart bleed to see her.' She got up to give the fire a vigorous poke and blew her nose. 'You mustn't mind me. I'm just old Nanny Teviot that can say anything.'

She picked up the picture of my mother and held it out to me. 'There she is, my lady, look at her, as she was.' I studied the picture in the firelight. My mother seemed young and lovely in her ball gown. My fingers felt something stuck to the back of the picture. I turned it over to look. It was a toy key, cut out of thick paper and painted gold. Prettily patterned, it was the sort of thing you saw on Valentine cards with the words 'The key to my heart', written near. Mrs Teviot saw me examining it. 'That was my dear lady's last little present to me. She said, in her joking way, to keep it near me and that I have done. I believe she may have had it from the Queen for it has the letters "V" and "A" and "O" as the pattern in the shank. I keep it for her sake. For shortly afterwards the Archduke died and we all parted.' She took the picture from me and replaced it carefully where it had been. She was crying a little, and so was I.

It was comfortable by her fire, *gemütlich*, as they were fond of saying in Court circles. My body relaxed. 'You're tired, girl,' said the old lady. 'And you've come a long way just to see me.' She popped her spectacles back on her nose and looked through them, eyes like big, grey, glass marbles now.

'I came to ask you about my brother, my little half-brother. Did he really die as a child?'

Silence fell and continued, a silence in which I could hear the hiss of the fire and the cheerful bubble of the kettle. She tapped with her finger on the arm of her chair. 'He did die.'

The kettle boiled over with a spurt of water through the spout that fell into the coals and made them sing. She leaned over and took the kettle from the trivet.

'Are you sure?'

'Quite, quite sure. He took scarlet fever or diphtheria or one of those new diseases and was gone within the week. I nursed him myself.'

'I have a right to know what there is to know,' I said steadily. 'Perhaps, after all, he did not die.'

'He did, poor wee bairn.' She hesitated, then seemed to make her decision. 'But there were two boys. Two days separated their birth, as can happen. Twins. One, the elder, was taken off by the father's family, the second she kept. They were parted as babies, but already were as different as chalk and cheese.'

'Twins,' I said. Was that what Jessie had seen in the troubled picture of the baby my mother had drawn? Had Jessie seen the ghost of a double image on that infant face?

'The younger was all love, the elder ...' She looked into the fire. 'A strong baby that must always be first, must always win. "You must always be the victor," I said once to him, "young as you are." But the truth was harder, there was a streak of wildness in him. When his mother knew he was to leave her, she drew his portrait, and, babe as he was, he seemed to stare at her in anger.' She shook her head. 'Thrawn he was born, and thrawn he always will be.'

Thrawn, that old Scots word, meaning damaged, torn, tormented. How well my mother had drawn his character in his face and how perceptively Jessie had read it.

'What happened to him?' I asked.

'He was taken away by his father's family. I heard that he was to be educated and that they were going to set him up as befitted his birth and station. In some good family near enough to the nobility to suit, maybe, or some good bourgeois family a little lower down the scale, willing to take on a little boy. But whether this is so or not, I don't know.'

'I believe they did, they did,' I said, and according to their lights, they had done so.

So, I thought, I had had two brothers; one was dead and one surviving. Might not the survivor after all be Count Victor? It fitted in. My brother and enemy, once thought dead, had come back to life.

'Mrs Teviot,' I asked, 'do you remember anything about a heavy metal box that my mother had?'

She frowned, casting her thoughts back through the years. At last she said, 'I mind a box the Archduke had made, but I don't call to mind what became of it. I do know it had two keys and he kept one key and she had another. Then later, when her life there was ended she sent off one key to some lawyers in Vienna. It might be she meant it for the other boy.'

'I believe she did,' I said. 'The box is my inheritance now, as things stand.'

If my brother does not get it first, I thought.

And then chance, unconscious thought, call it what you will, put surprising words into my mouth. I heard myself say them aloud. 'And I have the key, her key. I know where it is; it is in my mother's work-box, which she left to me. I always knew the key in its lock did not turn and was not in its right home.'

The girl who came back from Windsor was perplexed and tired; more in need of comfort and wise advice than she wanted to admit. I let myself into the house quietly.

First Fletcher and then Harry appeared quickly, as if they had been waiting for me.

'You're tired,' said Harry. 'Fagged out.'

'I am a little tired,' I admitted. I began to unfasten my cloak. My fingers were trembling.

Fletcher took my cloak, and Harry was sent downstairs for some hot tea.

'She's waiting for you in the drawing room,' he said over his shoulder. 'Wants to know how you got on at Windsor.'

I went into the drawing room, peaceful in the firelight; to my distress the trembling would not cease, and I was obliged to steady myself by clinging to a chair.

'Goodness,' Countess Telling gave an anxious little cluck. Only Fletcher looked calm.

'No, not hysterical,' I said wiping my eyes. 'The tea has quite restored me. Sophie, all was well at Windsor and I have many kind messages for you.' But, in effect she was left on my hands still and knew it. 'Harry, you may dine with us tonight,' and I stood up.

'Oh, hurrah,' he said.

'A chop or something simple, please, Fletcher.' He nodded and followed me to the door.

Outside I said simply, 'It was monstrous what I did yesterday. Forgive me, please. I cannot forgive myself.'

'No need for that, Miss Vesey.'

'It was bad, especially as you couldn't say anything.'

'But of course I could,' he said in a matter-of-fact way. 'And held your wrists a good deal harder if I'd wished to hurt,' he said, a little less steadily.

'I had been hurt lately,' I said. 'That was the trouble. I took Harry to Portsmouth. He was successful. I believe he always will be. But there were other circumstances ... In short, it was not entirely agreeable. That is, the visit was agreeable, but I learned ...' I stumbled over the words and to my horror tears began to well up. I brushed them aside, and went on. 'It's no excuse for what I did to you.'

279

'We all get one or two painful lessons, Miss Vesey, and I fancy you have had too many lately.'

'It's the fault of what people call a sheltered upbringing. It's so much better to know the worst from the beginning instead of learning it by degrees.'

There was a coal bucket, together with a small broom, left outside the drawing room door by the disorganisation of the household and Fletcher bent to pick them up. He did so with an unself-conscious dignity nothing could diminish.

'That is not the job for you,' I said.

He smiled. 'I think no job beneath me, Miss Vesey. Nor much above.'

Harry appeared through the door just then, and heard us. 'Do you not know that his cousin Sir Paul has made plans for him to become a great merchant? He is to go to Canada. Only he holds back. Why do you not go, Tom, eh?'

'Why not indeed?' I said.

'I can't leave her ladyship at this moment.'

'No, perhaps not at this very moment, but later.'

'I am thinking about it, Miss Vesey. There *are* home ties.'

'Your sister, Mrs Bedower, you mean?' I said uncertainly.

'Hopes and fears eh, Tom?' joked Harry. 'You know what we would say where I come from when some young chap does not look to his main chance? We say some pretty girl has him tied to her apron strings. But that's not the case with you, eh, Tom?'

To my surprise the impeccable Fletcher had flushed. I looked away so that I should not seem to study his embarrassment. 'That's enough, Harry,' I said. 'Now you go too far. I'll see you at dinner.'

So even Tom Fletcher had a 'someone', I thought.

I went up to my room and as I changed and put my things away in the drawers, I came across the note I had received that first May day in London when I had been so blissfully gay, and close by it was the gun found in the cab. I hadn't forgotten them, but I had put them away in the back of my mind, and if I let myself think of them at all, had tried to reason them away.

But now their witness would not be denied. I had not been indulging in fantasies. What had seemed to be a real attack on me, had been a real attack on me. I had always been the destined victim. If the other poor girl had died in a vicious running down and had been deliberately murdered (and I had to remember that this was only speculation), then she had died in mistake for me. I had never been mistaken for her. It had been me, me, me all the time.

The idyll was over, the black, black time was about to begin.

In the next few days the servants left us. One by one, offering various pretexts or none at all, they melted away. They were all of them, except for Fletcher, Barlow and the old coachman who lived above the stable, temporary and hired for the season. Fletcher said he thought that they dreaded infection, and it was true that typhoid was greatly feared.

Yet I thought he was holding something back. And then Harry told me.

'It's a rum go, isn't it?' he said. 'One and all have hopped it. Scarpered. It's empty down there, except for the beetles and the mice.'

'Beetles,' I exclaimed in horror. The rectory kitchen, stone-flagged and ancient as it was, had been clear of beetles.

'Lord, yes, by the bucket,' he said cheerfully. 'I stamp

on them and they crunch.' His eyes shone. He would be able to tackle the nastier side of Navy life, I reflected.

'Fletcher thinks they've been bribed. Paid. Had their hands greased to take themselves away.'

'Bribed? Who has been bribed?'

'The lot below stairs. He suspects that someone paid them good money. He can't think of any other reason for them all to go like that.'

'He was joking,' I said.

'Not he,' said Harry confidently. 'Serious as a judge.'

'But who would do such a thing? And why?'

Harry shook his head. 'Doesn't know. Thinks someone's up to no good. Perhaps we're all going to get murdered in our beds.' He sounded quite happy about the prospect.

I was not. I had more reason than he to think he might be quite right.

'We must hire some new servants, then,' I said. 'And I shall tell Fletcher so. It should be easy enough. There is much unemployment.'

'They haven't caught the Whitechapel murderer yet,' said Harry.

'That has nothing to do with it.'

And of course, it had not. But the killings added to the rumour and tensions abroad in the city that autumn. The evil weather and increasing unemployment all added to it. The summer, which had begun so brightly, was ending in a wicked autumn.

Of course people like us in Masham Square were relatively little affected. Life went on as before in the other houses with carriages coming and going, dinner parties and lighted windows. Only the Maurice household in Number Forty kept darkened windows and locked doors.

No more servants appeared. None, it seemed, could be hired. If one came round to be interviewed from Pratt's

Agency for Domestic Servants in Knightsbridge, where Lady Geraldine had been known for years, she never came to take up the job. Something always intervened, an illness or death in her family, an accident to herself, or even in one case just an accident to her luggage. Ill-spelt, ill-written, the little missives always contained the same message: not coming.

Fletcher removed himself to the stables, where he lived with the old coachman, leaving Harry in the house with us as the only male presence to guard us. Of course, we had Countess Telling's huge maid, whose sex was, to my mind, doubtful. Presently she began to make growling noises about removing the Countess and her unborn child to a better conducted household. I could hardly blame her. To my surprise the Countess exerted herself.

'We do not go,' she said, eyes commanding. When her servant began to mutter something in a German dialect unknown to me, she simply said: 'You forget to whom you are speaking. Be silent.' And this apparently was enough. For the time being.

Fletcher attended to the cooking, some of it being done by an aged crone, related, I believe to the coachman. I had been used at home in the rectory to a few household tasks. No one but I ever dusted my father's books and desk. So it was not hard for me to keep my aunt's drawing room in a reasonable state. Furthermore, it amused me. It did not escape my notice that Fletcher watched my work as carefully as he had ever done that of any parlour-maid, and, although he did not exactly ask me to repair any omissions, it somehow happened that I did.

Every day I called at the nursing home where my aunt was laid up, and spoke to her nurses. I was not now allowed to see her, because of the infection. One terrible day, listening through an open door, I heard a high, rambling voice that I scarcely knew to be hers, but on the next day she was said to be better, with her fever decreasing. It was an anxious time.

I continued my almost daily German lessons with Charles Louis. We worked together in the drawing room, chaperoned by Harry, and, sometimes, the Countess.

He disliked the Countess. I saw that straightaway. I thought at first he was abashed by her condition, about which she began now to make very little pretence of concealment. Every day she relaxed more openly into what I can only call a luxuriance of pregnancy. With experience I know it is common to many women and is quite unconscious. But certainly when you came across it in this hitherto shy girl, it was a surprise.

Charles Louis did not ask me any more about the vision of poor Anticknap we had had that day on the way home from Jessie's prize giving, but I think he must have been puzzled about the quiet of the house in Masham Square. Emptiness cannot be hidden. Nor did he speak of Jessie Falconet, although I believe they met. Count Victor was still in Ireland. But since I had concluded that he was innocent of any evil intent towards me, and was indeed, just as the Prince of Wales had said, nothing more than 'an idle donkey', it did not matter to me where he was.

I considered writing to ask the policeman, Inspector Ledger, who had called on me at Windsor, to ask if he had any more information about the mysterious Mr Koenig, but a peremptory summons from the man himself reminded me that the law had teeth as well as a protective arm.

He was not so kindly and polite as he had been before at Windsor. 'Miss Vesey, I think you were not quite open with me the last time we met.'

I said nothing. It was borne in upon me that lately I was not quite open with anyone. Errol Vesey was becoming *deep*. Perhaps she always had been so, really, and only circumstances had allowed her to act the part of a simple, cheerful girl with no secrets.

'I find that you took a more continuous interest in Mr King, or Koenig, than you explained.' He held up a hand. 'I have my ways of finding things out, Miss Vesey. Never ask how I know. Accept that I do. May I ask why it was so?'

'I thought he might have been responsible for hiring the man Tom Perry to write and deliver to me an anonymous letter. Later, I thought he might have been responsible for the death of the boy Joseph, which led me to Tom Perry's body.'

'And why did you suppose Mr Koenig should do these things?' He looked sharp and unkind. Gone was the gentleman who liked horses, whom I had seen at Windsor.

'I thought he might have been hired by my brother to harm me. I had some reason for thinking this.'

'And have you other enemies, Miss Vesey? Is there any other person who would like to harm you?'

I shook my head silently, meaning I did not know, I did not know, I did not know.

He took a deep breath and looked kinder. 'Well, we come a little into the open, Miss Vesey. Now I will tell you some things. We know now that the house in Dryden Street was burnt down deliberately. That is arson, Miss Vesey. And we know that Mr Koenig, whatever his connection with the house and with you, escaped the fire.' He stood up and came from behind his desk. 'We have arrested two men on the charge of burning down the house. They have confessed, under some pressure from us, Miss Vesey, to being concerned with the drowning of the boy Joseph and the man Tom Perry. But there is blood on the wheels of a cab they used, so I believe there are other crimes I must question them about. I want to show you something.'

He led me down a long corridor. At the end was a plain, wooden door with a shutter set high in it. He drew the shutter. 'Look through there, Miss Vesey, and tell me if you recognise anyone.'

My mouth felt dry, but obediently I went up to the door and stared through the aperture.

Inside, seated on a bench, were two men. One face I did not know, but the other I recognised as the man who had dragged me into the cab, and who had later pursued me through the streets. He had called himself Bertram Biggins in the police station. Then, he had looked almost comfortable and prosperous, now he looked dirty and hang-dog and beaten.

I drew back. 'Yes,' I whispered. 'I have seen one of them before.' I began to tremble.

'Come, my dear,' said Ledger, kindness itself again. 'Come back to my room and tell me all about it.'

And so I poured out to him an account of all that had happened to me, both in London and Windsor, which was, I suppose, exactly what he had intended all the time. But I did not tell him how I had identified Count Victor both with my brother and with Mr Koenig, because I now thought this to be false. Nor did I say very much about Detective Anticknap. And, of course, I told him nothing about my mother, or what might be my inheritance, or anything else private to the Maurice-Vesey connection.

And at the end he did not call me foolish or rash, but said I had been wise to tell him, that these men were now under lock and key and would certainly not escape.

I only noticed as I walked home that he had not been precisely reassuring, though.

Soon we had an unexpected recruit. Jessie arrived on the doorstep one dark morning when our strange way of life had been going on for about ten days.

She looked thin and worn, but was as jaunty as ever.

Hung about her were more than usual of her possessions. At the kerb stood her bicycle, likewise festooned with odds and ends of her equipment. My fascinated gaze took in a small green trunk, attached to a rack at the back, a basket containing two geraniums in the front, a bird cage and an umbrella. Jessie herself carried a bag like a sack.

'May I come in?' She stepped inside the door. 'Wait, I will get my cycle. It won't do to leave it there.'

'I believe it will be safe enough in Masham Square.' I forbore to say that to my mind no one in this genteel purlieu would want any of Jessie's abused and abandoned-looking objects. But it was true one could never know what valuable trifles she might have hidden away among the rubbish.

'May I stay here?' she asked. 'Not for ever, of course, just temporarily, till I find suitable lodgings. I've left Mrs B. Had a row.'

I was not surprised. No one could have been who knew them both. Fierce intelligence, noble ideals and not much sense of humour make difficult living companions. Jessie could make plenty of jokes, but they were of her own peculiar, sharp sort. I don't believe her landlady could laugh at anything.

'You're always welcome,' as indeed she was, particularly so at the moment.

'Thanks. Knew you'd say that.' She was energetically heaving her possessions into the hall. 'Nothing really against Mrs B. Admire her. She'll be remembered. But she's taken up with theosophy. I can't go along with that.'

'Oh, no.'

'I'm an agnostic myself. It suits me. Still, it wasn't just that.'

'No?'

'No. And then there's this red-haired Irishman. No, he isn't her lover, but he and I don't agree. I'm too much for

287

him in some respects,' she said with grim pleasure.

'I remember him from the afternoon when you took your prize.'

'And he remembered you,' said Jessie, with a laugh. She finally had her travelling equipment around her in the hall. It made a fair pile. 'He observed you with interest. Do you know what he called you? *Venus toute entière à sa proie attachée.* He sees what he calls the Life Force in you, Errol.'

'Does he, indeed?'

'Yes, he thinks you a very model of what the New Woman is, or rather *will* be. You are a forerunner. But don't worry. He won't persecute you with attentions. To begin with, he is more timid than he looks. And moreover, I told him you were more interested in your beautiful Austrian. He calls him your "chocolate soldier".'

I flushed. 'How malicious,' I said.

'Well, it means something, you know. I think it means he finds Charles Louis very romantic but a little improbable.'

The weather began to be even more inclement for the time of year. Jessie went out every day and returned looking more and more exhausted. After a few days of this I began going out with her, not to assist in her work, I could hardly do that, but to carry her bags and walk with her down the shabby streets she must travel. I went on no night trips, Jessie would not allow this, but set off alone on her cycle.

'But Jessie, supposing you were attacked?' The city was full of alarms about the Whitechapel murderer.

'In the first place, nurses are *not* attacked. Everyone knows us for what we are and we go through where others dare not. And in the second place I carry a police rattle.' Here she swung it above her head and rattled hard, so that Harry, the knowledgeable, came belting into the room in alarm. 'Any policeman within hearing distance will hurry to me. But it's not necessary, I assure you. I don't wish you to come. And you cannot leave the Countess alone; I tell you frankly I don't like the look of her. If I was her doctor I should be on my guard. Who is he? Sir John, eh? Very old-fashioned, they say.'

I suppose I had done two or three of these journeys of support when I returned to Masham Square one mid-morning to see a tall figure pacing up and down outside the house.

'They told me you were out, but would return soon,' said Dick Monk, coming forward to greet me.

'You should have waited inside.' It was a windy, damp day; his normally ruddy face was pale with cold.

'I would have suffocated inside,' he said with feeling. 'I have spent these past two weeks trying to get up courage to see you. You saw, that day, of course you did, I knew the moment I saw your frozen little smile.'

'I saw,' I acknowledged.

'Will you walk with me round the square?'

We went into the garden and I saw the attendant, the same who had greeted me and Charles Louis, purse his lips as if to say: '*Two* lovers'. You little know, I thought.

Once round the garden, and once again before he spoke.

'At first I thought I might carry on as if nothing had happened, hoping against hope you had seen nothing. Then, I thought, even if you had not, the boy Harry would have spoken.'

'No. There you underrate Harry's loyalty.'

He went on as if he had not heard what I said, speaking out from some vision of his own. 'You don't know, Errol, how can you, the world from which such behaviour springs; you, who have had such a sheltered life.'

'Oh yes, very sheltered,' I said, thinking of Reba and

289

my experiences in prison. 'Except that no woman is ever as sheltered as you think.' But I could see in his eyes that he would never believe me. It is one of the illusions of men of his class that women *can* be sheltered, never guessing that the workings of their own bodies force all women out into the real world. What is this shelter, but pretending not to know the real name for something you understand very well?

'We were all crowded together on the old *Britannia*,' he went on. 'Conditions were very harsh, the food poor, naval discipline. I don't complain much, but remember I went there straight from home. My mother would never let me out of her sight till I became a naval cadet.' He smiled gently. 'A proper namby-pamby I was, yet dead set on being an admiral. I had to stick it out and live with my fellows. Boys under such conditions form their own associations, yes, and loves too. Yes, I can use that word, for it was true love. And, in some cases, free from ...' he hesitated, 'its grosser manifestations.'

I looked at him steadily, but said nothing.

'What there was to me of softness or tenderness in my life then came from my friends. It seemed as natural to express one's feelings as for two young puppies to play together. Repeated floggings (for the authorities tried) did nothing to stop it. Added spice, I dare say.' He shook his head. 'Have I made you understand how it was?'

'Yes, you have made me understand. But you have also made me understand that you could never have loved me,' I said, with sympathy. 'You have made me understand you should never have tried.'

'No.' He put his hand on my arm and gripped it hard. 'When I first saw you, Errol, it was as if a new sun had come out to shine. Do you not know your own power and force? How could I resist it? But you, Errol, have I not learned something about you? If you had had any urgent

290

love for me, any real attraction, even a spark, you would have stormed at me, raged, had hysterics, anything. You have been understanding, reasonable, kind, but cool, always cool.'

'Very well,' I said. 'We agree not to have broken each other's hearts.'

'That's exactly what I mean,' he said, with sudden passion.

We looked at each other angrily. I *was* angry now.

'Yes, we'd better part as enemies,' I said. 'It would be better.'

'I haven't decided yet if we do part.'

'I have dismissed you,' I said icily.

But the British Navy is not so easily dismissed. 'Errol, when I came here today, I swear it was to kiss your hand and beg your pardon and to say good-bye. But now I know I could no more bear to let you go out of my life for ever than I could give up my high hopes for the future. You seem to be that future.'

I held out my hand. 'Good-bye.'

He took and held it for a moment and then let it go. 'Good-bye. But remember, I do not say good-bye for ever. You have not heard the last of me, Errol Vesey.' He bowed, and walked away, dogged determination expressed, I know not how, in his very back. All sailors are natural actors, I believe.

I was walking away when I heard him hurrying after me. I turned.

'Errol,' he panted. 'I meant to ask you, are you planning a ball or a big reception? No, I thought you could not be. As I stood waiting for you I saw a face at the ballroom window. A man, I believe, he stood there for several minutes staring out, then moved away and then came back again. I thought I should tell you.'

'It was Fletcher, I expect.'

'No, he was not near so big or broad as Fletcher. Fletcher is a big man. I hope I should know Fletcher.'

I was looking at him without really seeing him. Instead I was seeing, once again, the desolate ballroom. Who could possibly be in there? Dick Monk recalled me to him: 'Shall I come in with you?' He hesitated. 'I know how you are placed there. My mamma told me the servants are gone.'

'No. Fletcher is there. And Harry. I am not alone.'

I walked up the steps to the house and let myself in, leaving him watching me. I know now that he stood there watching until I disappeared and then went back home to his mother and said: 'Mother, I believe I may have lost Errol Vesey, but win or lose, I will never hear a word against her. Remember that.'

Harry was in the hall, and I spoke to him at once. 'Have you been in the ballroom?'

He shook his head in surprise. 'Couldn't if I wanted. The door is locked.' He had his dog by his side.

'Have you been in the hall for long?'

'No.' He sounded reproachful. 'I've been doing all the problems you set me, Miss Errol. And that little bit of Latin prose I'm to take over for Canon Ackerly to check. Now I'm off for a walk.'

I started up the stairs. 'Come with me, please. I believe there may be an intruder in the ballroom.'

But when we got there the door was locked. I rattled the handle. 'Where is the key? I suppose Fletcher has it. Run and get him.'

While he was gone I knelt down and peered through the keyhole. It was a large, antique keyhole and gave me a good view of one end of the ballroom. It looked undisturbed. Even the dust lay still and tranquil. When Fletcher appeared with the key, the door opened easily. He frowned. 'Goes easily, but I recall I had it oiled.' He stepped into the room and looked about. 'No sign that anyone's been here, Miss Vesey. All the same,' he studied the room, 'I wouldn't like to be sure.' He sounded uneasy. 'Could be someone is here.'

'Dick Monk says so.'

'Yes.' He ushered us out and locked the door on the deserted room. He sounded non-committal.

'But how *could* any person enter the house without a key?'

Harry spoke up at once. 'They *had* a key, of course. One of the servants must have sold one. It's a well-known thing that dishonest servants sell keys of big houses that they've left and where the pickings are good. They think it fair game.'

I looked at Fletcher. 'Is this true?'

'I believe it is,' he conceded. He never liked to admit that Harry was right, but in an understanding of the criminal world he had to give Harry best. 'But I don't take it for granted it's what happened.'

'Go on. Bet your life,' said Harry. 'They've all cleared out and left us. Something funny's afoot.' He sounded happy at the thought.

'I shall keep watch,' said Fletcher soberly. 'And if I see anything wrong, then I shall tell the police.'

As evening came on I saw him making his preparations. He had dragged from its alcove the huge padded leather chair in which, in happier times, the footman who opened the front door had been used to sit, night and day. On a table by it he had an oil lamp, and a pipe and tobacco. Quite unconsciously I am sure, and by degrees so that one hardly noticed each change, he had shed the discreet airs of a servant and adopted a more positive stance. He was now, effectively, master of the house.

It gave me a strange feeling.

That evening I stood looking out of my window on

Masham Square. How changed everything was from the evening of my arrival. Then it had been high summer, with the prospect of a brilliant social season ahead and on every side gaiety and life; now it was autumn, the darkness setting in, the house deserted and quiet. Then I had been part of a rich circle of friends, now my friends seemed diminished in numbers and status. Even my weeks in Windsor now seemed distant. The Court would soon be moving to Osborne. When I went into waiting again I should be there. It might be a long while before I saw Windsor Castle again. Life had taken one of those imperceptible shifts it does take sometimes, and, it seemed, for the worse.

I went over to the drawer where I kept the gun and the letter—if you could call it a letter, when all it said was that blood was thicker than water. I was used to putting my hand underneath my corset covers and embroidered camisoles and feeling the two objects. Now I felt and found nothing. I turned the drawer over, but the objects were gone.

I ran downstairs to the small drawing room where the Countess was lying on a sofa in front of a fire while her servant knitted. She was getting lazier and lazier or sicker and sicker, I couldn't decide which. Jessie said the latter. I knew that soon I would have to take matters into my own hands and talk to her doctor. Lady Geraldine was too ill to be bothered and the Countess had refused, absolutely refused to give me the names of any of her kin in England. I knew there must be some because of the visits she and my aunt had made. Not all of them had been to visit the doctor and interview nurses for her confinement.

'Sophie,' (she had asked me to call her Sophie) 'have you noticed any signs that anyone has entered your room and searched it? Have you lost anything?'

294

She shook her head.

'To be sure, pray ask your maid.'

She passed on the message in that North German dialect I could not understand. The maid stood up and started to shake her head angrily.

'Tell her I do not accuse her of stealing things,' I said wearily, understanding the dumb show.

'She says nothing has gone from my room, neither has anyone entered it, because she is always there. But she says, all the same, on several occasions she has heard someone moving about the house quietly at night. She has splendid hearing. She is strong in every faculty,' went on the Countess. 'It is one of the reasons my parents engaged her. I only relate what she tells me, of course,' she said with a sort of lazy sarcasm. 'If you were to ask me I should say that in one faculty she was weak. I find her a little stupid, don't you?'

'I think she understands you.' I saw the anger in the little dark eyes.

'It is a matter of indifference. I detest her. My gaoler.' She shrugged. 'I would kill her if I could.'

'So you certainly would not. Don't be a silly girl.' But I was alarmed at her desperate air of abandonment and her pale transparent skin. Jessie was right. She *was* ill. 'Ask your maid what she has heard.'

A short exchange took place between them. 'She says that once during the day and twice during the night (only you will please remember that as she chooses to go to bed before nine o'clock, night could mean anything) she heard someone walking about in your room and on the stairs. Each time she looked, but saw no one. Still, she says she does not think the house is haunted. She does not believe in haunted houses.'

'Neither do I. Thank you, Sophie.'

So Harry was right. A key to this house had been sold

by one of the servants to an enemy. I had to use that word. Intruder, robber, thief were words too impersonal and weak.

The Countess's maid muttered something from the back of the sofa. The Countess gave an irritable wave of her hand. To me she said, 'She wishes us to leave. She says without Lady Geraldine the house is not as it should be. But I refuse to go.'

'I think she may be right,' I said seriously. 'I believe you should leave. It is not fit for you here now. But where would you go?'

The maid muttered something again, and I looked for the Countess to interpret it.

'She said the Queen herself is the person to ask. That the arrangements were made with her and the Duchess of York in the first place and that her advice ought to be sought now.'

I nodded. 'It shall be done.'

The Countess made a little moue of distaste but otherwise said nothing. I think she was not reluctant to have the Queen of England herself and the sympathetic young Duchess of York interest themselves in her little matter.

'You still continue your German lessons?' she observed.

'Every day.'

'He really has an atrocious Austrian accent.'

'I like it.'

'And yet, you know,' she said in a wondering voice, 'he speaks English most beautifully. Better than me, even, and I was the best in all our family.'

'He has less accent. But you have very little.' Or I hardly noticed it, I thought. The truth was, almost everyone at Windsor, all the royals anyway, had German accents. I sometimes wondered if I was developing one myself.

Up the stairs and through the door floated the sound of

a drum, banged rhythmically, a flute, and voices singing. I looked at the Countess and we both listened. Then the music stopped. Now came a sharp ring at the front door. I went to answer it myself.

Outside stood a small group of women, shabby but tidy, with shawls and jackets hugged tight against the biting wind, a hat on every head. The three or four performers who made up the band stood in the road. A banner, red and blue, was propped against the railings.

'Please, ma'am,' said the foremost woman, 'we're the match girls.'

I stared at them silently for a moment.

'You make matches?' I said.

'That's right, ma'am,' she said impatiently. 'We're matchmakers. We've come for Miss Falconet.'

'She's not here.' I looked at the darkening sky. Night was not far off and although they stood there bravely and were still flushed with their walk, the wind must be cutting through their thin clothes.

'Can you tell me where she might be found, then?' said the leader.

I pondered. I could take them to where I had left Jessie, but it was a long stretch and I had no real certainty she would still be there. I knew she had several other calls to make. I could see a policeman approaching slowly round the other side of the square. So could the match girls. 'Get a move on, Edith,' one of them called out. 'We're perishing here.'

'You had a strike, didn't you?' I said. 'I remember hearing about it.'

'Yes, and we won,' said the girl called Edith stoutly. 'And we won't never be beat again, take my word for it. And now we've made up a Matchmakers' Union, and we're the Executive Committee,' she said proudly.

I nodded my head to show pleasure and congratulation.

'And we didn't get no help from the men,' she said fiercely. 'So don't think we did, and now we need a few words from a sympathetic magistrate to prove that we're what we say we are or the men will stop us in our advancement.' She managed to put the word 'men' in fiery letters. I guessed she was a soul after Jessie's heart. 'So that's why we want Miss Falconet to intercede for us. She has friends in high places.'

'What about Mrs Besant? Can't she help?'

'Yes, she *was* our patron, and still is, for all I know, but when we asked her to help us now, she told us to call upon a higher force and trust to Love. We don't think this will be enough, and we prefer a magistrate,' she added firmly. 'A magistrate to sign a deposition accepting that we are operatives and not women, which the men say we are not. More fool they.' She saw me looking at the banner and the band. 'I know what you are thinking: you are thinking if these are serious women with a sensible purpose why do they come with a flag and banging on a tin drum. I'll tell you why: when you have to walk, ma'am, and walk a fair way in the cold, then a banner to wave and a drum to march to are great comforts. If you cannot lead me to Miss Falconet, then I'll say good-bye.' She started to turn her back on me.

'Stop,' I said suddenly. 'I'll take you to a magistrate.'

Her face lit up. 'You will? Good girl.' She took my hand and shook it warmly. 'Who?'

'Sir Paul Bedower.'

'The City baronet?' She slapped her side. 'He'll do. Girls, hear that? We're off to Sir Paul Bedower.'

A little ragged cheer went up. I heard it as I rushed to get a cloak and bonnet.

When I came back I gave them a quick look: too many for a cab, alas, so there was nothing for it but to walk. 'Come,' I said. The leader, Edith, strode beside me. 'Fall in, girls,' she said, and with another cheer they did.

So, at the head of a small column of marching women, with a banner flying, and a drum banging, I, Errol Vesey, led the way out of Masham Square.

An omnibus, headed for the City, had drawn up in the busy road to which our march had brought us. I gave it a quick look.

'Hop on,' I called. 'Upstairs. It's empty.' I patted my pocket. Yes, I had enough money.

'Up aloft, girls,' called Edith.

'Why do you wish to be certified "operatives", then?' I asked, when I'd got my breath back.

'It's necessary to us in order to be acknowledged a proper trades union.' she said, voice determined. 'And why shouldn't we be, eh? We honestly earn our bread. But it's the men who block it, short-sighted noodles, thinking themselves the only ones entitled. But they'll come to it, never fear. Only we have to have a shot in our locker, see? Sir Paul Bedower shall be our shot.'

She had it all worked out, hard-headed little person. She was small, fine-boned, with thick dark brown hair drawn low on her forehead. Her face was intelligent, but not beautiful; her eyes were small but clear, her teeth very bad.

'There's to be an International Trades Union Conference in London in November,' she said, 'and I intend to represent my girls there.'

Sir Paul was at home and received us calmly. Mrs Bedower was, to my relief, out visiting a friend, and her father, old Mr Fletcher, was in the country. Edith and I were shown into the library while the rest of the band crowded into the hall. He listened quietly, took Edith's problem seriously, but declined to do anything himself.

'There is no need, Miss Simcox. You will be much better

off with this person whose name and address I am giving you.' He was scribbling rapidly as he spoke.

'Go and see him, or better still, write a letter.' It was the only comment he allowed himself about the band and the drum and the banner. 'Put yourself in his hands.'

'And he'll see us right?'

'Right as a trivet, Miss Simcox,' he said gravely, holding out his hand. 'He's a solicitor who takes an interest in your sort of work.'

'But he'll charge. We've no cash for a bill, I tell you straight.'

'He will do it for love.' And the account will go to Sir Paul, I thought, watching that fine, noble, unimpassioned face. He was like a Roman senator cast in bronze and done larger than life.

He had worries, however, which were not Roman ones. As we left, I to go back to Masham Square, the girls to south London, he took me aside.

'Miss Vesey, I have large interests, as you may know, in many places. This allows me, obliges I may almost say, to pick up various bits of information. I have agents. From them I know that the London police have talked to you about the deaths of two men. From my agent in Vienna I know that the secret police take an interest in you.' He sounded concerned. 'I know too that Count Victor Hochberg is hurrying back from Ireland.'

It was the first intimation I had that he and Fletcher knew and had always known a good deal more about my life than I had guessed. Sir Paul Bedower with his network of correspondents and agents all over Europe was very well informed about many matters. It was his business to be. I suppose he knew as much of what went on, both secret and public, as that other circle of gossips, the Court at Windsor. Indeed, in some respects, clearly he knew a good deal more.

'If you should need help, Miss Vesey,' he said gently, 'you have only to ask.'

'I will,' I promised, my smile stiff.

'And you will say nothing of this? I tell you in confidence.'

'Nothing,' I promised again.

He touched a bell. 'I will call for the carriage. You must go home in that.'

Mrs Bedower bustled into the room. 'My dear Miss Vesey, how sorry I am I was not at home. You will take some refreshment? Some Madeira?' She touched the bell. 'A little old Madeira always sits well at night.'

'Mother, Miss Vesey is leaving.'

She looked so disappointed, and because I wanted to show the gratitude I truly felt, I said: 'Mrs Bedower, your family looks after me only too well. Your nephew, that is, your nephew and I ...' I stopped. I had blundered into an awkward way of speech and paused to rephrase my sentence. But I was too late.

She turned to me, a radiant blush spreading over her face, her eyes sparkling with pleasure. 'Is it so? Has he spoken? Have you settled it between you?'

'Oh, Mrs Bedower,' I began, 'it is not that, not what you suppose.'

The pretty flush faded. 'I see I have said what I should not, and betrayed a confidence. You will forgive me,' she said with dignity.

'Mother, you make too much of it. Miss Vesey is leaving.' Coolly Sir Paul separated us and bore me to the door. 'My carriage is waiting.'

The match girls had gone when the carriage rolled through the street with me inside, but I caught a distant roll from the drum and a last defiant peep from the flute round a bend in the street. Tired but undaunted, they were fighting on. They were braver than me, I thought, but they had the advantage of knowing what enemy they were facing. Whereas my enemy seemed protean and able to assume a different face whichever way I turned.

I had feared my half-brother, but my aunt had assured me he was long dead. Only, was he dead? I had feared Mr Koenig, but the policeman had told me that the house where he had lodged was burned down, and all trace of him gone. I was told that the Austrian secret police took an interest in me. Now another perplexing thought was offered to me. I had felt courage and support in Tom Fletcher, leaned upon his strength. It had seemed a natural part of our relationship. Now I had to ask myself if I had not unconsciously given encouragement where I should not. A social gulf divided us, but had I not prided myself on ignoring social classes? In my country world I had left behind, when one of the village lads was attracted to a girl, we said he 'fancied' her. Why should not Tom Fletcher fancy me? Or I him, if it came to that?

I leaned back in the carriage and watched the scenes of London go past me. On the corner of the street a newsboy was shouting 'Murder' as he offered his papers for sale. Sudden death and murder were on every side of me in this great city. I felt sad and lonely. How could I now ask too much of Tom Fletcher when I had so little to offer in return? Cold I was, Dick Monk had said, and hard of heart. By her innocent revelations Mrs Bedower had made it impossible for me to lean any more on Tom.

Charles Louis was just walking away from the house when I arrived. 'I came to give you a German lesson, but no one answered the door.' He looked cold and tired, huddled in his greatcoat. 'Eventually Harry appeared and gave me news of you: he said you had marched off with a brass band.'

'Hardly that. No brass, but plenty of drum.' I told him what had happened and where I had gone. I had expected enthusiasm from him, but got nothing but a shake of the head. 'They have nothing to worry about. Time is on their side, do they not know it?'

I thought of those shabby, persevering women and knew that no diurnal clock could run fast enough for them. I had seen the patched shoes and the thin faces. 'No, you're wrong,' I said. I could tell by Charles Louis' skin and hair, his air of physical well-being, that he had never known real poverty. Something had marked his life, I read it at the back of his eyes, but semi-starvation had not distorted his bones and ridged his nails and darkened his teeth.

'Time is short for *me*, though. Count Victor is about to return from Ireland. I prefer my master's absence to his presence, as you will have gathered.' I had never heard him so openly contemptuous before. 'Oh, he sends a stream of orders, but at least I have the use of his carriage.' He was bitter, his face sombre.

'Yes, I know he is coming back,' I said; my promise to Sir Paul not to be indiscreet being clearly unnecessary with Charles Louis. 'The police want to speak to him. Or *have* spoken to him in Ireland for all I know.'

'What's this?'

'I should have told you before this, but so much seemed fantasy and speculation.' I stopped. If I was to embark on the story of my brother, my inheritance, puzzles over Count Victor and whether he was my half-brother, it would need a patient listener. And Charles Louis did not look patient. 'To be brief, my mother had twin sons before her marriage to my father. Oh, it is no secret. I dare say you have heard yourself.' He bowed his head and did not deny it. 'For a long time, it was a secret from me. I have now learnt the details; one child died, one, it seems, survived and was reared by a noble family. Perhaps, I cannot be sure, my own conviction of it ebbs and flows, it is Count Victor. At all events, my brother, wherever he is, and whoever he is, is no friend to me.'

He stared.

'You may well look,' I swept on, pouring out the whole tale, beginning with the letter and taking it up to the present. 'And I believe he hates me and would like me killed. And all for a relationship I do not claim with him and an inheritance that is a mere nothing. A box— empty for all I know.'

'Count Victor has a dark side to him, and strange friends. I should keep your box from him if I were you,' said Charles Louis. 'I shall leave his service soon. The time has come for it. So that is why you have let me be your friend. It was not just a desire to learn to speak German well at your Court. No, you wished through me to watch Count Victor.'

'Not only that,' I protested. 'I *like* you, Charles Louis. I like you very much.'

He studied my face for a moment. I think he saw something there that satisfied him, for he said : 'At least you have learnt to speak German, even if it *is* with an Austrian accent. Oh yes, I know what the Countess says, stupid girl.'

'No, she's not stupid, but very ignorant and lost, poor soul.'

'You must get her to tell you her history one day. There is one. All the world knows it.'

'Some of it, I suppose. Only she can know it all.'

'You defend her ?' He gave me a keen look. 'Yes, I suppose you must. She has her story, no doubt. But they are a loose lot, that family.' He shook his head and the beautiful mouth set in a firm line, hardening the face.

'I like her,' I said mildly.

Suddenly as if a decision had been reached, he swung round. 'Miss Vesey, on what terms would you assent to come to Austria ?'

'On no terms at all. I could not.'

He put his hand on my arm. 'I have spoken too quickly. I have taken you by surprise.'

'No,' I breathed, meaning, 'Yes, indeed I am surprised'. I felt like a swimmer in a rough sea.

'We cannot part. You must wonder that I say that. But do you not feel it?'

'I might come to Austria on a visit. I have always wanted to travel. I dare say my aunt ... or Frank ...' I did not go on.

'When?' he broke in. 'How soon?'

'The spring, perhaps,' I faltered.

'Too late, too late.' He was gazing forward vigorously, not looking at me, eyes fixed in the distance. 'I cannot wait.'

'Herr Louis,' I said, 'you *must* wait.'

A church bell tolled the hour. A yellow fog was beginning to creep towards us from the river. Soon London would be beneath its blanket.

'I suppose Vienna is a most beautiful city,' I said. 'More beautiful than London, but I think I shall never see it.'

The old custodian of the garden toddled past us on his way home. He looked at me and Charles Louis and offered a knowing wink. I was the girl with the lovers. He followed the wink with a smile and a pull at his battered old hat.

'You subjugate too many people,' said Charles Louis. 'But remember you have not subjugated me.'

We had come to the door of the house in Masham Square. I glanced up at the windows, which were dark except for the Countess's windows and one small window behind which Harry and the dog sat together. Peace, of a sort, dwelt there.

'How can I come?' I said, giving Charles Louis my hand. 'Sir Paul Bedower has told me the secret police take an interest in me. I would be unwise to set my foot on their territory, don't you think? As an unmarried girl, that is. I believe I might come when I have made a suitable marriage to an English gentleman.'

'Miss Vesey, you know how to tease.'

Dick Monk's accusation, differently put. I was stung. 'I do it in self-protection.'

He was wearing a full dark cloak, cut in a military way with square shoulders. I remember it swung about him as he moved impatiently. I doubt if he had heard what I said, although my words were true enough. My beautiful Charles Louis.

As I watched for a long deliberate moment, I knew my mother's inheritance to the full, it stirred in my blood. The Maurices were ever susceptible to physical beauty, you saw it in their eye; the very way they faced the world. But I was a Vesey too and that detached, cool-headed observer inside me stood and watched even though it could not check me.

'Yes, I will come,' I said slowly. 'I will.'

There was a moment during which I could hear the traffic moving about the city, and feel my heart beating in its cage of bone. I suppose I expected he would touch me, embrace me roughly, as Dick Monk might have done.

'Remember, it is not marriage or anything of that sort I am offering you.'

'I know.' But my heart was beating madly.

'We go as free and equal partners. I know of a circle of like-minded friends we might join in Vienna.' He spoke briskly. 'Can you be ready the day after next?'

'Tomorrow I go to Mr Dalrymple to open the mysterious box,' I said. 'The day after, I will be ready, box and all.'

'Do not travel as if you were going to Court,' he advised. 'Nor as if you were your poor lame maid. She is still away and will not pack for you.'

'Charles Louis,' I said lightly. 'If I have used you to spy on Count Victor, I think you have a spy set on me. How else could you know so much about me?'

'I know it from the heart,' he said, and then was gone.

CHAPTER NINE

On the next day, the fog began to collect around the tree tops and chimneys and to lurk at the end of alleys. It was the beginning of the great fog of that autumn. So opened the strangest of birthdays, about which I still find it difficult to speak because of what came after. It started with a bunch of flowers from Harry and a book delivered from Harriet Craven. A small jewelled bracelet was sent round from Mappin and Webb's jeweller's shop. There was no card. I guessed the donor was Dick Monk. From my aunt, Lady Geraldine, came a brooch of a circle of seed pearls enclosing a strand of her own hair. With it the anxious message: 'Pray let me know what your box contains, fondest love, your devoted aunt, Geraldine Maurice.'

Then, putting aside the offer of his company from Harry, I set off to Mr Dalrymple. Harry watched me depart with a severe expression. He was man enough to think no woman should go upon a serious business call such as a visit to a lawyer without a man to support her.

'Wait for Tom Fletcher,' he suggested. 'He won't like it else.'

I was buttoning my gloves. 'I cannot and will not accept more help from Tom Fletcher. There are circumstances . . .' Harry's face lengthened. He knows, I thought. Only *I* have not seen that which I should have seen.

I shook Harry off, and evaded Fletcher, but I had the greatest difficulty in eluding the dog, who for some reason was hanging about the square, growling at the old garden-keeper.

The traffic was crawling along the busy main road. A few carriage lamps were already lit. A cabby told me it was growing worse towards the City and advised me either to go on foot or turn back. Mr Dalrymple's offices were near Gray's Inn, I knew my way well, so I decided to walk.

I walked fast, wrapped in my own thoughts. I was well on my way before I noticed the dog was with me, trotting at my heels, keeping a wary eye on my movements. Half-exasperated, half-amused, I patted his rough head. He was by no means the companion I would have chosen to visit an elderly, conservative lawyer. I suppose we made an odd couple as we entered his outer office.

'Is the dog to come in, Miss Vesey?' asked the clerk. He was keeping his distance from the animal.

'Try to keep him out,' I said.

'Mr Dalrymple expects you,' he said, accepting the unacceptable. 'Down, sit,' he said in a quavering command to the dog, who continued to look at him with indifferent, bored eyes.

The lamps and the fire were alight in my lawyer's comfortable room. A little light fog had already penetrated the room and was lurking in the corners.

'Ah, a happy birthday, Miss Vesey,' he beamed cheerfully. 'Allow me to congratulate you.' He shook my hand, up and down, several times. 'And your marriage?'

I prevaricated. 'Nothing is yet decided.'

'Marry in haste, repent at leisure is a true saying,' he said. 'I see a great deal of it, you may take my word for that.'

We had to wait for several minutes, then a young clerk

appeared, bearing my box. It was still dusty from the cellars where I judged it had been stored.

He set it down on the table before me, and with a wave of his hand Mr Dalrymple offered it to me. I examined it with interest. I saw a box of plain, solid appearance. I picked it up, it was heavy but not impossibly so. I judged I could carry it.

'As you see, it is locked.'

'There is a key I want to try.' Hesitantly I withdrew from my glove, where I had hidden it, the key, from the work-box. I put the key in the lock. Mr Dalrymple and the clerk watched. 'It turns,' I said, 'only it is stiff.'

'Allow me, Miss Vesey.'

'No, I will do it myself. There!' The key was turned. I prised the lid open. I was eager to see.

Inside the box was yet another lid. Set in the centre was a round knob and a small lozenge-shaped metal piece with a row of letters A. B. C. D. showing.

'A combination lock,' breathed Mr Dalrymple. 'Upon my word, how very interesting.' He pointed to a piece of paper with some writing on. 'And here must be the key. Read it, my dear.'

I picked it up and read. But all it said was: 'Take this box to the key. If you can do this, dear child, you will understand and treasure what it contains.'

So there it was. I had my inheritance and it was a locked box inside a locked box. It was the sort of thing that could only happen to a Maurice. A touch of mystery and drama never came amiss to them.

I said good-bye to Mr Dalrymple and allowed him to put me into a cab with my box and the dog. Cross and disappointed, I felt all Vesey then, I assure you, as I jogged back to Masham Square.

Inside the house I saw Countess Telling walking down

the stairs, and beside her, looking grave and interested, was Harry, and, prancing beside him, the dog.

'Our numbers are again decreased,' announced the Countess; she was in an exalted state.

'Not Fletcher?' I was horrified.

'No. Fletcher, indeed!' cried Harry. 'Not he. Do you not know a good man when you have one?'

'No, not Fletcher,' said the Countess. 'Although it is true, he is nowhere to be found. No, it is my maid, faithful Brigitte,' she said in a nasty tone. 'She has left us.'

'Went off in a huff and a hansom cab,' Harry's voice was gleeful.

'I dismissed her.' The Countess raised her head proudly, then spoilt things by adding, 'But I never thought she would go.' I saw a frightened look cross her face and then pass away again. 'You see, I am a Serene Highness, she *had* to obey when I said so.' The frightened look came back and settled down more permanently this time. 'But how will I dress? And how will I find my clothes?' She looked around her as though she might see her bodices and petticoats lying on the stairs.

'I'll help you,' I said hastily. I didn't like the almost wild light in her eyes, or the small pink patch underneath the cheek bones. 'In fact, I'll take you up to your room and help you undress now. Would you not like to rest in bed?' I put my arm round her thickened waist and led her back up the stairs. Somewhere under my arm I could feel a great pulse beating.

'Yes, I think I *will* rest.' She sounded breathless. 'It is very tiring being independent.'

I unhooked her elaborate dress and got her into a loose dressing-gown. Her wrists and arms were very thin, but there was an unhealthy puffiness about her hands. Soon she was lying back against the pillows, still bright-eyed

311

and restless, and unwilling to be left alone, even while I went to take off my hat and mantle.

'How did it happen that she dismissed the maid?' I asked Harry, who was on the prowl outside her door.

He shook his head doubtfully. 'They had a fine old shouting match, but it was all in German. Then the Countess threw a bottle at the old girl. I *heard* that and smelt it—lavender water, it was; and then the maid came stamping out, and after a while came down the stairs, lugging her bag, and was off. She ain't gone far, though, and I reckon she'll be back when it suits her.'

'Oh, I hope so,' I said; the responsibility of the Countess resting heavy on me.

'Don't be down-hearted, Miss Errol.' And he put an arm round my shoulders.

'How you've grown, Harry,' I said, absently. 'You're nearly as tall as me now.'

'Another half-inch to go yet, Miss Errol. Fletcher's downstairs, and would like to speak with you.'

I tidied myself quickly and ran downstairs. At the curve of the great staircase I paused and looked. A double branched candelabrum stood on a table and made a feeble attempt at lighting the hall. Fog had crept into the house and dulled the candle flame. Fletcher stood at the bottom of the staircase; he wore a thick dark ulster and held his hat in his hand. He did not smile when he saw me, instead his black brows drew together in a frown. But his voice was polite.

'I am sorry to have left you alone so long. I had difficulty in getting back from my cousin's house—the fog, and not a cab to be had.' He sounded tired. 'Just the hint of another murder in Whitechapel, and it draws them all down there like flies. We shall have her ladyship asking for the newspapers soon. The doctors say she is on the mend.'

312

'Thank God.'

'Today I was able to talk to her. She agrees it is not suitable for you and the Countess to be here now. My cousin, Sir Paul, will be glad to give you hospitality. I have been to see him and it is all arranged.'

'I'm not sure ...' I began.

'Lady Geraldine agrees. It is a large house, plenty of room, extremely comfortable. And after all, if it does not suit, Sir Paul has a house in the country where you might do very well. My aunt, Mrs Bedower, will be happy to keep you company.' The words were polite, the tone implacable. I was meant to obey.

'I think you take too much on yourself, Fletcher. I do not choose to be told where I must live.'

'This house is no place for you now. My aunt will be glad to receive you.'

'From her and from you, of all people, I can accept no more help,' I burst out.

He went white; he knew at once what I meant. The truth was out now and the old relationship between us was gone for ever.

I was driven recklessly on: 'I have made my own arrangements. I am going abroad. No, you need not bother. I shall tell my aunt.'

'Miss Vesey, you shall not go. You *must* not go.' He tried to hold my arm.

'It is all settled. I am off to pack my bags.' I pushed past him and ran up the stairs, my box in my arms.

I began my packing. I meant to take very little, so my main problem was to eliminate what I meant to leave behind. I must write to my aunt, to be delivered when I had gone.

My simpler dresses and shawls that I had brought from the rectory were soon assembled. My heaviest boots and sturdiest stockings were folded and ready. My days as a fine lady were over. My books, my few jewels, I packed in a big leather bag with two handles. The locked box was squeezed into this too.

I heard Harry calling for me. I hurried down.

'What is it?'

'It's Sophie. She's taken bad. Will you come?'

Sophie, lying back upon the pillows, opened her eyes when the two of us came in. She smiled. 'Hello.' Her tones, always gentle, seemed now to me more breath than voice. No doubt about it, a new quality had entered into her appearance. I wished Jessie was home to take a look and pass judgement on her.

Harry said awkwardly. 'I'll be off, then.'

'Thank you, Harry.'

He went out, closing the door behind him with a dexterous kick.

'What a boy,' said Sophie. Serene Highness she might be, but somewhere buried deep inside her was a simple, friendly girl, and this girl was coming always nearer the surface. 'And his mother, she never bothers about him?'

'So it seems.'

'Nor Harry about her?' She sighed. 'My child, if I have one, will it care for me so little?'

I was disconcerted. 'Of course you will have a child, and a dear one too.'

'No, I think it will be a monster, like its father.' Her manner was calm and unmoved. 'One might love a monster, I suppose. God might give me that blessing.'

'Oh Sophie, Sophie.' I went and sat beside her and took her hands. We were almost the same age; usually I felt the older of the two, but not now. She closed her eyes. We sat quietly together for a moment, then she said, 'I will tell you, I will tell you what happened to me.' I made a demurring noise. 'No, I wish to tell you, Errol. But you must not interrupt and you must ask no questions.'

I nodded. 'As you wish.'

She looked at me, then, and afterwards turned her head away so that she did not look at me as she spoke. I studied her delicate profile, it gave away no emotion, but looked remote and aloof.

'You who are so free,' here she pressed my hand harder, 'can have no idea how we lived at my father's court. You cannot dream of the rules and strictness by which we must live. I took it all without question, but since I have been in this house, with you and Lady Geraldine, I have understood how stupidly we lived there. My sisters are living like it still.... It was the task of one manservant to go round the castle at night and see that every window was fastened and all the shutters locked. For over a hundred years such a tour had been made, ever since one of my ancestors found a drunken soldier had climbed through a window and gone to sleep on his bed. It was something that happened as a matter of course. No one questioned it. My bedroom was high on the third floor and had two windows. They were looked at each night with the others. When I was a little girl it disturbed my sleep not at all. I took no notice, it was part of the ritual of my life. As I grew older I found it more disturbing. As long as I remembered the search had been performed by old Franz. Then he died, and his son, a boy whom no one knew, took over.... It was customary for these jobs to be handed down from father to son.... I was so frightened the first day he came in. No one had told me of the change. I did not even know the old man was dead.... I think he saw that I was frightened. From then on he set himself to terrify me more, and to make me do what he wanted. He told me not to call out, or tell anyone, but just to lie very still.... If I ever spoke he would say I had enticed him and no one would ever believe me. He was right. No one has ever believed me.' She stopped for a moment, then went on. 'And I was so stupid, so ignorant, I had no idea what was happening to me.'

There was silence. I waited; but she had done. At last she turned her head and looked in my face. 'It was not so bad, after all, was it, talking to me?' I said.

She took a deep breath and visibly relaxed. 'You believed me,' she said. 'You really believed me. Once before, to Princess Mary I said a little, but although she was so kind, I could see on her face ... But with you, no, there is not that *look*.'

'No,' I shook my head. 'It is quite beyond me, that look,' and I squeezed her hand. She gave a giggle of pure merriment, showing me for a fleeting moment the girl she must have been.

Down below I heard the front door close. I knew it must be Jessie. No one else banged the door with such force. I turned round to tell Sophie, when I saw she had risen in the bed and was pushing herself upright with the palms of her hands as if she suddenly found breathing difficult. Then she fell back against the pillows, giving as she did so a groan that seemed pushed out of her.

I rushed towards her. 'Sophie, what is it?' She was very pale, but the bright patch of colour on her cheek seemed to grow as I watched.

'A great pain. It's gone now.' She was breathing more calmly, but I was anxious. 'Don't leave me.' She took my hand.

'No, I won't go,' and I sat there, with her hanging on to my hand, wondering what to do.

Then I heard the unmistakable bang, jingle, clatter of Jessie and her equipment come up the stairs. I called to her and, after a pause, she appeared at the door, still weighed down with a black handbag and umbrella, but without the bath and the kettle.

'Yes, what is it?' But immediately she saw Sophie's

face and came straight over to the bed. 'Bad?' she asked.

'Yes,' said Sophie. She gave that strange groan again. It was as if a hand took her and squeezed the sound out of her. I saw her anguished eyes above her opening mouth.

'Who is her doctor?' asked Jessie.

'Sir James Mason, I believe.'

'Such a stupid old fellow, but at least he lives close by. He must be sent for. Send Harry.'

'In this fog? No, I must go myself.'

'The fog is lifting,' said Jessie, her attention on Sophie.

'Please don't go, Errol,' said Sophie.

'Very well, I'll send Harry. But you must let go of my hand, so I can go to him now.'

Harry got his dog and sped off as good as gold, declaring he knew the house and would be back in a minute. But when he came back it was to say that Sir James had been sent for urgently by a lady that lived in Hampshire and he would not be back till morning.

Jessie shook her head. 'Useless as usual. But he always is.'

Sophie moaned and Harry, who was standing, cap in hand, just inside the door, said: 'I could run to Dr Barker round the square.'

'No.' Jessie was decisive. 'Call a cab. Get some blankets and shawls, Errol. We will get her to hospital.'

'Oh, no.' I was horrified, and it was out before I could stop myself. Hospitals were for poor people, not people like Sophie.

'She will be better off there, God knows, than in that old idiot's hands.' Jessie looked down at her patient, whose eyes were closed. She took me aside and said in a low voice, 'I tell you, I am alarmed at her looks. There is something seriously wrong. Beyond my powers. And she is not up to it. A finely bred little creature like that, with no constitution, how can she fight?'

317

Harry returned with a cab, leaping from it as soon as he saw me at the door. 'Fog's all but gone. There's a moon coming up. Not a bad night now.'

Together Jessie and I helped Sophie down the stairs. She leaned against me heavily and seemed to have sunk into an alarming passivity, not far from unconsciousness. Jessie shook her head and gave the directions to the cab driver with crisp efficiency.

As I stepped into the cab after them, Harry said in a low voice 'Do you see that man across the square, standing under the tree? He's been there hours.'

I looked, and there was Detective Anticknap. I knew him at once. He was standing stiff and erect, wearing a wretched old coat and a cloth hat, but I could see his stare. He looked as mad as ever.

I ought to have guessed then, I ought to have guessed what he was waiting for.

'I suppose we should have told Tom Fletcher we are leaving the house all but empty,' said Jessie as we drew away.

'No need. He is only a servant.'

'Errol, I see that though you are charming and sweet, you are nasty as well. You have taken an unreasonable dislike to the man and therefore behave badly to him.' She added deliberately, 'But I think he is a good man and I am going to put it in his way to emigrate. My family have interests in the west; let him go there and we'll make a millionaire of him.'

'Jessie,' I said urgently over Sophie's head, 'I saw Anticknap outside the house.'

'Really? I know he is about again. His wife told me. But it is still intended as a secret.'

'He is mad, quite mad.'

'He won't kill you, Errol, he is harmless.'

'I wish I thought so. Why does he stare so?' I was sure he was there for a purpose, and when a man seems as mad as Anticknap, who knows what harm he may do?

The hospital, the one at which Jessie had received part of her training, was a plain building, painted a deep green inside and lit by flaring gas jets under white shades. The combination of dazzle and dark was unpleasing, but not uncomfortable. I felt a surprising peace.

Jessie knew what to do and who to ask for help. I was content to stand aside and let the wheels turn.

I stayed with Sophie as long as I could, but as I helped her into the bed I saw a great blotch of blood across the front of her white gown. She was bleeding badly, and I saw by the frantic look in her eyes that she knew it. I held her hand till Jessie detached me and pushed me out of the room.

'Dr Margery is our best doctor. And I shall stay. You go home.'

I looked towards Sophie, but she was past caring whether Errol Vesey stayed or went. I knew I ought to go back to Masham Square, but the thought of the house standing there, dark and untenanted, scared me. Harry was there, I knew I should go back to him, but a terrible tiredness settled over me.

There was a wooden bench further down the corridor and I sank on to it, leaned back and closed my eyes. It was a busy corridor, at the junction of two wings of the hospital, and I was aware of constant comings and goings. Voices filtered through to me, but I made no sense of them.

When I opened my eyes next it was with the sense that time had passed. I sat up, smoothed my hair, and looked around.

At the end of the bench on which I sat, half-leaning against the bench and half-sagging to the floor, was a woman; she was supported by a younger one. Even as I watched, the sick woman rolled limply forward and slid on to the floor.

Her companion put an arm under her shoulders and struggled to raise her. 'Oh, come along now, old lady.' The sick woman's arm swung round heavily, knocking the other's bonnet right over her face. 'Oh bless you, my old girl, you aren't trying, now that you aren't. Here, give us a hand,' she called to me over her shoulder. 'She's a dead weight, she is.' She was dragging at her friend as she spoke, raising her by slow degrees. 'She ain't dead, though, praise be, or I've wasted my labours.'

I came forward and between us we laid her on the bench. Stretched out, she was middle-aged, with dyed red hair and sagging cheeks. I put out my hand and gently straightened the younger woman's bonnet. 'Hello, Reba,' I said.

She stared, coming up close and looking hard at me. 'Well, I never,' she said.

'You remember me, then?'

'That I do. I remember the night, too. My luck changed that night, and I haven't had a good day since.'

She did, indeed, look pinched and ailing. There was the old spirit in her eyes, but she was bedraggled and spent.

'Had you before, Reba?' I asked.

'Ups and downs, my dear, like the most of us, but lately all down and getting worse. I've pawned all I can, even me joollery, and without a bit of glitter I can't seem to take up with a right class feller. And then I've been sick. But not so sick as this poor old love, here,' and she rested her hand softly on the other's forehead. 'She's been good to me, has old Flo.' She shook her head. 'Couldn't get no help from the doctors down our way, pushed us off, so I say, right, you're getting to hospital,

Flo, you are. And I got her here.' She looked about her. 'But even here they're slowish.'

'You *carried* her here, Reba?'

'No, she could walk a bit to start with, and we did it between us, didn't we, Flo?' She was stroking Flo's hair with a roughened hand. 'What one couldn't do on her own, we two could do together.'

'Reba, you're a Trojan.'

For the first time she was disconcerted, even alarmed. 'No, miss, no, I'm not what you name. I was born in Stepney.'

In spite of the tragic figure on the bench, I laughed, then checked myself. 'Stay here, Reba. I'll see you get help.'

Reba slapped her side. 'I *said* you were a lady.'

I drew myself up, summoning all the Maurice command of manner, and all the Vesey tact. I had learnt a lot while in waiting at Windsor, in particular how to assume that royal voice that took happy obedience for granted.

I approached a nurse, a senior one, judging by the elaboration of her cap, and said : 'Sister, I am Miss Vesey, help is needed here.' There it was, I had it, the right combination of charm and impersonal command. She could no more resist it than that moth approaching the gas lamp could resist its pull; she wanted to, I read a struggle in her face. 'Why should I obey this girl?' I could feel her ask herself; but she did obey. I had learnt my lesson well.

She hurried over to Flo and Reba, but when she saw Flo every emotion except professional concern emptied away. 'This is a bad case,' she said. 'She's in the tertiary stage of typhoid. She should have been treated before.'

'Those who want can't always get,' growled Reba. But she swayed as she stood there, and I could see that, now her self-appointed mission was done, she was done. She

321

shook off help, though. 'I ain't ill.' She bent her head and confided in me. 'If I was, you wouldn't get me inside one of these places. It was all right for Flo, 'cause I think she's going to die anyway and she'll die more decent here, but I'm not come to that yet, not by a long chalk.'

At that moment I saw Jessie approaching down the corridor. She hurried up, unsurprised to see me still there. 'She will do. It was touch and go, but she came through better than I would have thought. There is spirit in her, after all.'

'I am so glad, so very glad.'

'But would you believe me, the baby is alive. A little girl. I am afraid she cannot live, perhaps not into the morning. The mother is urgent for a baptism. Can you come?' She looked about her, seeming to see Reba for the first time. 'In such an emergency it is allowed for the doctor to perform the baptism, but we need some sponsors. Will you both come?'

Reba's mouth opened wide in astonishment, but she said nothing, only tried to straighten her clothes.

'It ought to be according to the old Catholic ritual,' I said to Jessie, who was hurrying us along.

'My dear, as long as something is done to quieten her, what can it signify? She just simply cannot bear that the child will go into limbo, as she calls it.'

So, not a monster, after all, I thought, and not unloved. Poor Sophie.

'It is the smallest scrap of humanity imaginable,' said Jessie. 'But here we are at the chapel.'

I said no more, there was a sensitivity wanting in Jessie that nothing could fill.

The hospital chapel was bleak and cold, its walls dark. The air was so cold that I shivered and looked apprehensively at the tiny creature swathed in shawls and blankets. Jessie shook her head.

322

The christening was performed by Dr Margery according to some simple ritual she seemed to have by heart. I held the child and named it for its mother, adding at the last moment a second name. Sophia Theodora, the child was baptised. Theodora means a gift from God. It seemed all I could offer my godchild as a gift.

Dr Margery murmured a prayer. Reba sank to her knees, I followed, and at last Jessie. So we knelt in prayer, Errol the churchwoman, Jessie the agnostic, and Reba, the outcast.

'Jessie,' I said softly, 'if I should go away, you will keep an eye on Harry?'

'What does that mean?' she asked sharply. 'Where are you about to go?'

'You shall have my address when I know it.' I laughed, 'You may wish me happy.'

'Wait—it is not the same with you as it was with Sophie Telling?'

'No.' I was indignant. 'It is to be a platonic elopement.'

'Oh you baby, you,' she groaned. 'Can you not see you are your mother all over again?'

'Good-bye, Jessie,' I said. 'Let us at least part as friends.' I kissed her cheek. It was hard and dry. Jessie had dried herself out without love. There was only Reba left to say good-bye to. Jessie remained behind in the hospital. I had in my hand a piece of paper, on which I had contrived to write Jessie's name and address.

'Reba, take this. Go and see this lady soon. I believe she could help you. Not with money. I have none of that myself. But supposing I should be able to help you later to emigrate, would you like that?' Not to Canada, I thought, it was settled by so many respectable Scots, but Australia perhaps? Surely Australia had a wilder, gayer society, which could learn to appreciate Reba, and where she could prosper?

She looked doubtful. 'I don't know about that. I've got an idea that if I could only get myself settled somewhere, I might take up with a better way of living.'

'It would not be easy where everyone knows you, Reba.'

'No. Miss, what you said about having no money ...'

'Only too true, alas.'

She hesitated, then said. 'Then miss, I must speak, because I know something you do not. After we met in the clink, I fell in with a cove that knew something of you, least ways I suspicioned it was you and now I'm sure of it. He said he'd been with the chap that tried to get you put away in prison, that was how I came to recognise who he was talking about, you see. You were to be killed, that was the first ploy.'

'I am not so easy to kill.'

'You knew it, then? But that's not all. You were to be killed on account of some great wealth you had or were sure to inherit.'

'So I have heard.'

'How hard you sound. Your voice sounds like flint.'

'The threat of death hardens the mind.'

'Yes.' She looked at me nervously. 'How strange you talk, miss.'

'Tell me what your friend said.'

'He was no friend of mine,' she said hastily. 'It was just for a while our ways ran together. He's gone to sea now, and may die there for all I know. It was always his trade. He tried other things, but he always went back to the sea. His first love, he called it.' I could see she knew him better than she wanted to admit. 'He told me he had tried to work a job for the man who wished you dead, but had fallen down on it and now was feared for his life. A real killer, his boss was, he said, who took up a false name when it suited him and knew the criminal world through

and through, and yet seemed to know the *police*, too. A
sort of policeman he was himself, my sailor thought. And
it was for his good you were to die. He said he was your
closest kin, but you would never know it, because he was
one of the great undead.' She looked at me fearfully; I'm
not sure if she did not cross herself. 'That means someone
who lives by drinking another's blood.'

'So it does,' I answered, slow, bitter thoughts revolving
in my mind, 'if you believe in that sort of rubbish.'

'I have wondered,' she dropped her voice, 'if it might
not be he that was responsible for the killings in Whitechapel. Very bloody, they were.'

'Oh, that is nonsense. Dismiss the thought, Reba,' I said
impatiently.

'He might get me, miss, aye, and you too. My luck
turned from the day we met, that I will swear to.'

'It has turned again.' She looked at me wide-eyed, hope-
ful, but still apprehensive. 'Yes, believe me, Reba, from
now on you will prosper. I shall help you. I will *make*
it happen.'

I left her still looking incredulous, but with a smile
beginning.

I like to think of her looking like that, as if a door had
opened.

It was a foggy dark morning as I hurried into Masham
Square. Time seemed suspended, whether it was late or
early I had no idea. It was a day on which the very sun
itself seemed slow to rise.

When I turned into the square, I saw a carriage standing outside the Maurice house. A coachman stood by the
horse's head and I recognised his surly face from Windsor.
I saw the dolphins emblazoned on the carriage door. The
dolphins carriage had come to Masham Square. Count
Victor must be inside.

325

I let myself into the house. The interior was very dark, lit only by a lamp at the distant end of the staircase.

'Harry? Fletcher?' I called. No answer. A silence that was a deadness hung in the air. I called again, my voice shaking. I feared to see Count Victor swagger down the stairs.

But there was nothing. Only a silence. Slowly I walked up the stairs. At the top where the great staircase branched I stood listening. I knew he must be here somewhere, my enemy, my brother, but I could not call his name. I feared to summon him.

The ballroom door was open. Drawn against my will, I went towards it. I remembered that General Maurice had died here by his own hand.

A candle burned, a lovely pure torch of light, on one of the gilt console tables.

And there, lying face upward, eyes open as he stared at the ceiling, was Count Victor.

I stared at him, unable to grasp the reality of what I was seeing. I saw, but did not understand. 'Count Victor,' I said. I tried to make my voice loud and commanding, but it would only come out a whisper. His face was grey and his waxed moustache stood out stiffly. There was blood on the floor beside him. He was quite dead. I had never seen death by violence before, but I saw it now. He had been shot through the heart. The pistol lay on the ground by his side. It looked very like the pistol that had been in my possession. I knelt and touched his body. Blood came away and stained my hand. I rubbed my hand clean on my skirt with a shudder.

I recall swaying as I tried to regain the door. But I got there and stood there, trying to steady myself, when I saw Charles Louis hurrying towards me.

'I saw the door open and came in.'

'I don't believe I left it open,' I murmured. 'No, perhaps I did.' I was incoherent, past knowing what I said. I swayed towards him.

'Why, there is *blood* on your face.'

'Count Victor ...' I said.

But he had already seen, taken in the gun, the blood on me, the body on the floor.

'You have killed him. My God, Errol, you have shot him.'

I had had a night without sleep, not much food and now the shock of finding a dead man. I think I must have fainted then, because I seemed to recede into a dark cold pit in which I was aware of Charles Louis first supporting me, and then forcing a drink between my lips. 'Here take this,' he said. 'It will steady you.' The spirit was harsh and fierce and burned me as it went down. I remember choking, and Charles Louis urging me to drink more; then there was darkness. But it seemed to me that in this darkness, I heard Tom Fletcher's voice. 'Lift her up. Quite unconscious, is she? To the carriage with her.'

Carriage, carriage, carriage; my body seemed to roll to the motion of the word. I was moving, travelling, and that was all I knew.

I have a memory of the motion of the carriage, and then it seemed to give way to another, gentler motion which rocked and soothed. Distantly I had the sensation of being on a larger vessel which was moving through a sea. In my fantasy I heard noises and shouts, none of which in this dream I could comprehend. Strangely, one memory came back months later. At one point I had opened my eyes and seen the night sky above me, moonless but star-studded. Then the veil drops again.

When I came to myself at last, I was aware I was in bed. But not my own bed in Masham Square; without opening my eyes, I moved my limbs, obscurely aware of something wrong. I raised myself on one elbow and looked around.

I was in a small room with a deep red flock wall-paper. On one wall was a large window hung with dingy muslin and red velvet. A dressing-table and a chair completed the furniture. I leaned back on my pillows, head throbbing, aware that I was lying in an old-fashioned four-poster. There was something inexpressibly scruffy and seedy about the room.

It was daylight, but which day and where, I did not know. I was wearing a nightdress, my own nightdress so someone had undressed me. My gaze, wandering round the room, saw my own bags, standing in one corner. The day dress which had been taken off me was flung across the end of my bed.

I had but just taken all this in when the door opened and Charles Louis came in.

'Oh, how glad I am to see you.' I held out both hands. 'I feel so lost and strange. And my head aches.'

'A natural consequence of a strong draught of brandy on top of powerful emotion,' he said calmly.

I remembered the body of Count Victor then. How could I have forgotten? 'I did not kill him,' I said quickly. 'I found him dead. You don't believe me? But it's true.' My voice was rising.

'Please, no more hysterics.' He held up his hand.

'But you must believe me. I want to be believed. And where am I? How did I come here?'

For answer, he went to the door and called a summons I did not hear, but presently a stout woman with a flushed red face and untidy fair hair came in, bearing a tray with coffee and food which she set on the table beside me. She smiled and nodded at Charles Louis, but avoided my eyes.

'Eat,' he said. 'Take some hot coffee. It will restore you.'

I drank some coffee, sipping it slowly. Then I took some of a buttered roll and ate what I could.

'You became quite unconscious,' said Charles Louis, 'and while you were in that state, it seemed better to get you out of the country and away from the consequences of your action.'

'But you can't believe I killed him.' I sat up, my energy beginning to return.

'I acted only to protect you.'

'And where am I?'

After a pause he said, 'Ostend. There can be no harm in your knowing that.'

I lay back on my pillows, shocked for a moment into silence. I had crossed the Channel, while unconscious I had been taken by carriage and ship to Belgium. Memories of noises heard in my dream in that strange sleep came back to confirm it.

'We came over on the Dover ferry. The sailors thought you were ill.'

There was a worry, a question at the back of my mind, struggling to form itself, but I felt stupid and dizzy. I put my hand to my head.

'Come now,' he said, more gently and affectionately than before. 'I did the right thing. You had your bags packed to depart, remember?' My eyes went to them and then I looked at my own night-gowned figure. 'You need not worry,' he said, 'the landlady, a good enough woman, put you to bed.'

She didn't look clean to me, and I disliked the thought of her touching me. I gave a little shudder, which I suppose irritated Charles Louis, because he frowned. 'You are too fastidious, Errol.'

'Yesterday was my birthday.' I numbered off in my mind the experiences of that day; the locked box handed over to me by Mr Dalrymple, the birth of Sophie's child, and the death of Count Victor. It had been a strange and savage day. It seemed necessary to explain this to Charles Louis.

'Before I found the body, I had been at the hospital with Sophie, who had her child. And before that I went to Mr Dalrymple to collect my box,' I said carefully.

'I know,' he said. 'I know it all. Now go to sleep again.'

For some reason his simple statement satisfied me and I closed my eyes. And, I suppose, slept.

After a while I opened my eyes. The room was perceptibly darker, as if dusk was coming on. I felt drowsy, but my head no longer ached.

Charles Louis was still in the room, kneeling in one corner by my travelling valise. Opened on the floor beside him was the box. My box. My inheritance.

I lay there for a second looking, still half-asleep. Perhaps I made a noise, because he raised his head. 'So you are awake.' He sounded surprised. Why should I not be awake, I thought. 'What are you doing?'

'Looking at your famous box, as you see.'

'It does not unlock beyond a certain point,' I said dreamily. 'I suppose you found my key to the first lock?'

He did not answer but came across to the bed and laid his hand on one of the bed curtains and stared at me. My own hands lay before me on the counterpane.

They were strangely alike, our hands, long, slender and filbert-nailed. I looked from his hand to my own hand, and then I put into speech the idea that had formed and grown in my mind: 'You are my brother.'

I said it without emotion; I felt no emotion. The fates, my own character, my inheritance, call it what you will, had finally isolated me in a foreign country, cut off from all my natural helpers, with the man I had most cause to fear.

'*You. You* were Mr Koenig, *you* were the man in the dolphin carriage that the policeman Anticknap watched. It was you he stood waiting for that last day in Masham Square.'

He laid his hand on the bedcover and measured it by mine. 'Yes, they are alike, our hands, are they not? Maurice hands, would you call them? And what would Lady Geraldine say to that?'

'If she had not fallen ill, if she had seen you face to face ...' I began.

'Do you suppose I would have been in and out of Masham Square like a tame cat or one of your lame dogs, if she had been there? No, give me credit, sister.' He smiled. 'As it was, I waited until your father died before trying for what I wanted.'

'And what did you want?' But I knew the answer.

'The box. I had my key as you had yours.' He took it from his pocket and laid it before me. 'Here it is. Now tell me how to open the second lid.'

'I don't know.'

'I have known of this box all my life, yes, and of what it contains, it *shall* be opened.'

There was a hard, fanatical note in his voice which I had never heard before. I suppose he had never let me hear it.

'Then everything that happened, the threat I felt hanging over me came because you wanted the box?'

'I had as much right to the inheritance of it as you, and I meant to have it. But once I had seen you, sister, I recalled the old fable about the sun and the rain and I saw I could coax the box out of your hands if I behaved prettily. But I liked you a little bit. There, is that a comfort to you?'

'I don't think it behaving prettily to tell me I killed Count Victor when you must have killed him yourself,' I answered. When he remained silent, I said, 'You *did* kill him?'

'Yes, but not willingly. He could be alive now, leaping fences too high for him in Ireland, and breaking the limbs of good horses if he had not come raging back from Ireland to pick a quarrel with me because the police had been to him. I told him that they would prove nothing against me, but what must he do but stalk round to see Lady Geraldine, ready to say this cousin of mine is a terrible fellow.'

'Cousin?' I cried. 'You are cousins?'

'His mother stood in much the same relation to the old Archduke as I do to Salvator; which was why it was deemed right she should marry into the new wealth and that I should be farmed out on them.'

I could forgive him his bitterness.

'He found me there and threatened me. So I was obliged to kill him. It was all or nothing at that moment, and I knew it.'

And then I had come back and cut off escape. Otherwise, I suppose he would have taken the box, my mysterious box, and fled. Much good would it have done him.

'I suppose you have a key to the house?'

'I have had one for some time, yes.'

'And a spy in the house?'

He did not answer but walked to the window to stare out. 'Yes, someone close to you,' he said with his back to me. 'Who saw everything.'

Into my mind swam the memory of Tom Fletcher's voice: 'Quite unconscious is she? To the carriage with her.' I pushed the memory away incredulously. Accomplices? Friends acting together, they?

But one thing I did say: 'You drugged me with the drink in Masham Square.'

With a shrug he admitted as much. 'You are all right now, at all events.' He went over to the box and lifted it on to the bed. The lid was back and underneath I saw the second, interior lock. 'Now tell me how to open it.'

'You must blow it off with explosives,' I said. 'And you may do so for all I care. Take it. I give it you freely. Only let me go back to England.'

'Tell me how to open the lock.'

'I do not know.'

'Our mother gave you some clue.'

'Just as she did you,' I said, pointing. ' "Take the lock to the key," that was her advice. And goodness knows what that means.'

'It means use your wits, search your mind.' He was impatient. 'Think Errol, think.'

I shook my head. 'I don't care if it is never opened. Now let me get dressed and go back to England.'

He struck me across the face then, one light stinging blow so that I gasped with pain. 'I want the answer. And when we leave here, we leave together.'

At the door he said: 'And don't try to come to terms with the woman here. In the first place she thinks you are my wife, and secondly she believes you to be sick in the mind. She is sorry for me for having a mad wife.'

He went out, banging the door; I heard him lock it behind him.

I lay back on the pillows, willing to relieve my feelings with tears, but too furiously angry to be able to do so.

I had never been to Ostend. My foreign travels with my father had consisted of one trip to the Swiss Alps and another to Florence. Ostend with its fashionable and raffish population, drawn from all over Europe, was not the place to attract him. Lady Geraldine had come to the watering place once or twice and Frank, as I very well knew, used to pop over to the Kursaal to gamble as often as the mood took him. Indeed he might well be here now. He was supposed to be in Scotland, courting his Scottish heiress, but he had ways of slipping the traces and seeking his own pleasures.

Much good it would do to me if he was here, seeing that I was a prisoner. I got out of bed and tried the door. Locked.

Then I went to the window and looked out. I found myself looking down on a busy street from a good height. I must be on the top floor of this tall, narrow house. I counted the windows beneath me: one, two, three, four and then the street. There was plenty of traffic passing up and down, including a horse-drawn tram. It looked like a working-class area, and from the appearance of one or two of the pedestrians I guessed I was not far from the harbour and docks.

After so much sleep, I certainly was not tired, and although my head still ached, I felt fresh and alert. I dressed myself, choosing clean clothes from my baggage, and took up my station by the window again.

I tried to open the window, but it was firmly fixed and not to be budged. I stood there, looking, as the daylight dwindled and the lamp-lighter came round and pulled on the street lamps one by one with his long pole. Down below was an everyday, humdrum world. I saw a donkey-cart go past with an old woman driving it. A crocodile of schoolgirls in charge of two nuns passed below. A Sister of Mercy pushing an invalid in a chair crossed the road. A fine rain began to fall.

Down there, I saw a dog chase a cat. I amused myself with making out a likeness to the dog of Masham Square, Harry's dog. This animal had much the same trick of cocking its head as it considered the situation before strolling on. But one rough-coated mongrel looks much like another.

I don't know how long I stood there, a long time, I believe. Then I heard voices behind the locked door. Two voices talking quietly away to each other, too low and controlled for me to hear much. Only occasionally a tone came through clearly, a tone I recognised.

Surely that was Tom Fletcher's voice? I listened again and was sure of it. So, after all, it had been Tom who had helped Charles Louis. It was only then, when I was quite sure he had betrayed me, that I understood how much I had trusted him and I had rested on his strength. I had come very close to loving him, because of all the men I had met he had seemed the truest and the best.

Then I did cry. I threw myself on my unmade bed and let the flood of angry tears pour out. Finally, exhausted, I slept. And after that it was morning.

My second day as a prisoner. It started with the arrival of the landlady and her tray of breakfast. She also brought me hot water and towels to wash.

As I sipped my coffee I tried her out both with French and German, but I soon realised that she understood neither. I guessed she was a Fleming, and neither could nor wished to understand French.

She smiled at me nervously as she backed away, revealing clearly that she thought me dangerous as well as mad. She pointed to the towels and soap and hot water and made gestures indicating they were for washing, as if she thought I was simple-minded as well as mad.

Outside it was still raining; I fancy it rains a good deal in Ostend. The room was cold and when I dressed I wrapped a shawl round me and went to stand at the window again. I had plenty to think about as I stood there. Across the road was a *Crémerie*, a dairy, where housewives constantly arrived with jugs and pitchers and departed holding them carefully. Presently a cow with a halter round its neck appeared at a side gate and was led out into the busy road. Next door to the dairy was a shop whose front was hung with pots and pans and all types of cooking utensils. I watched idly. The effects of the drug had finally departed and I was able to think. For the first time I began to assess my chances. My prospects seemed bleak.

What Charles Louis wanted from me was the solution to the combination lock. 'Take the lock to the key' my mother had advised, by which she meant, I believed, search your own heart and mind and you will have the answer. My mind seemed empty. Once my half-brother understood this I believed he would kill me. Otherwise, I was just a danger to his safety.

Equally, if I found myself able to provide an answer, he would surely dispose of me as soon as he had what he wanted. Escape seemed the only solution.

Behind me the door opened. 'I have been expecting you,' I said without turning round.

'Ah, you're yourself again.' He spoke with genuine satisfaction. 'I never wanted to hurt you yesterday but you were about to become hysterical.'

'Rubbish.' I swung round to face him.

'And now that clever mind of yours is working, we shall have the box open in no time at all.' He lifted it from the foot of my bed where it still was and placed it on a table by the window. It looked harmless to be the key to so much unhappiness.

'I cannot help you,' I said as steadily as I could. I turned back to stare out of the window. It was meant as a gesture of defiance, but as I looked I saw again the dog of yesterday, strolling along with that casual, jaunty air I could not mistake. I had to control myself not to make a noise.

If the dog was here, why not Harry? With Jessie perhaps or even my cousin Frank?

'Won't or can't, Errol? Won't, I think.' He pulled me round to face him. 'I did not enjoy hurting you, but if I must I will.'

I pulled my arm away. He let it go. 'Once more, Errol, *think*. I give you this chance. Give me the answer. My mother loved you best, of course, she left you the answer.'

'She never knew me,' I said.

'But she let me go, me she sent away.' All the outrage of the rejected child was in these words.

'Yes, she was selfish,' I whispered, admitting the heresy at last. Wilful, charming, beautiful, all these things my mother had been, but heedless in pursuit of what she wanted. The Archduke, my father, Charles Louis, me; she had brought us all down.

Charles Louis and I, co-heirs, equal in the burden put upon us, stared at each other. Then, in the strange way the mind works, mine produced the answer to the puzzle. I knew how the lock must be worked. I suppose he read the knowledge in my eyes, for he said: 'So you *do* know.'

I said nothing. I was thinking how close he had come to the answer once himself. I had found him amid the ruins of Charde. The answer lay there.

'Very well, Errol, you are silent, but I shall make you speak. I know you are brave, but is there nothing you fear? No, don't move away. I shan't strike you again. There are other threats. You are out of your safe little island now, Errol, and on a continent where I have friends who will gladly take charge of you and enter you in the lists of any stew or brothel I choose for you. Who would know you there? Who would find Errol Vesey again?' He shut the box with a bang. 'And don't watch by the window. No help will come that way. Tonight we leave Ostend.' He looked at his watch. 'I give you three hours, Errol.'

I watched him go. He drew the door quietly behind him. This time I did not hear the key turn. I stood there, heart thumping. To be dragged away from Ostend when the sight of the dog had raised my hopes was not to be borne. I went to the door and turned the handle. It opened.

The door opened into a sitting room. The air was heavy with cigar smoke. Seated at a table was a man I recognised as Count Victor's groom at Windsor. He stood up as soon as he saw me and motioned me back into the bedroom.

He was my gaoler and a nasty one too. He was a short fellow with bow legs and a swarthy face. I stayed where I was, determined not to show fear, but I felt sick. My little moment of hope was so soon gone. There was a glass on the table and I saw he had been drinking. I smelt the brandy. More to prolong my freedom than anything else, I pointed to it and asked for some. To my surprise he got up and poured some into a glass and handed it to me.

I was holding it when the door opened and Tom Fletcher came in. At once a broad smile spread across his face.

'Thank God to see you,' he said. 'They told me you were still unconscious.'

'Don't try to brazen it out, Tom Fletcher. I know you are Charles Louis' accomplice, and that you helped bring me here. If there is a special fate reserved for traitors, I hope you suffer it very soon.'

'Errol, this is madness.'

I glared at him. The groom, who was drunker than I had supposed, looked from my face to Tom Fletcher's with a puzzled stare.

'He understands no English,' said Tom. 'I gave him the brandy. Errol, I came here to protect you. I saw you with blood on your dress and with every appearance of having killed a man. You seemed stupid with shock.'

'I was drugged,' I put in.

'So I now think, *then* I could only guess. I had a choice of alerting the police and bringing ruin on you or helping the man you call Charles Louis to get you out of the country.'

'A good story.' I could not so easily forget my feelings of shock and pain when I heard his voice.

'Errol, whether I believed you innocent or guilty of murder I *knew* what Charles Louis was capable of.'

'I am innocent,' I said slowly.

'Then believe I dared not leave you alone with him, even while I tried to summon the police. Once you were gone with him you might be lost in Europe for ever. Dead or worse.'

'*So* he has threatened.'

'I had been with my cousin; I knew what he knew. When I saw that the crisis had come, what we feared, I *had* to stay with you. Luckily I made my way with him. He was glad to think me venal. But *you*, you might have trusted me, Errol.'

'I had decided you must be the spy I know there was in Masham Square,' I said, ashamed.

'There was one, indeed. One of the maids who was in love with an itinerant street musician, dying, poor fellow, of consumption. *She* was paid to watch. So was he.'

My gaoler had become uneasy. He comprehended not a word, but he was shrewd, he grasped that an understanding was being reached between us.

'We must get out of here. Come now, Errol. Don't alarm this fellow but move quietly forward.'

But it was too late, the groom had pushed between and now stood with one hand on his knife and the other ready to grab me.

The next movement seemed to come instinctively from me. I raised the glass of brandy and pitched it in his face and ran straight to Tom Fletcher who, acting as fast, grabbed me round the waist, dragged me through the door and then stood with his back to the door holding it firm.

'Down the stairs and out,' he ordered.

As I ran I had time to think of my box. Let it stay, I thought, what does it matter if it is lost to me and I never know what it contained? Behind me I heard the groom shouting and banging on the door. Then Tom's voice, 'Damn you,' the sound of a blow and a thud. Then Tom's triumphant footsteps behind me.

We were almost at the bottom of the stairs when the landlady, aroused by the noise, came out into the hall. Seeing me, she began to scream. At once Charles Louis appeared.

He was between us and the door. Tom moved in front of me, shielding me with his body, and edging me forward.

'No further,' said Charles Louis; he had a pistol in his hand.

'Run, Errol,' said Tom, pushing me towards the door, and throwing himself directly at Charles Louis.

I fumbled at the door handle and had it open. The smoky, damp air of Ostend in winter was pricking my nose; behind me I heard a shot and a scream from the landlady. I gave one frantic backward look to see Tom on the floor, face bleeding and then I was in the street, running.

After a few yards, I stopped for breath. No one was taking much notice of me. I had to decide which way to go, where to seek help, and I had not much time.

I looked down the street ahead, and then turned back to look at the house from which I had escaped. In almost the same moment I saw the dog I had watched before bolt out of a butcher's shop with the butcher's boot behind him, and Charles Louis emerge from the house. He saw me and moved towards me.

The dog ran down the street, dodging nimbly between the crowd. I followed the dog. Charles Louis followed me. I was neater on my feet than Charles Louis; Tom had hurt him in that quick attack and he seemed to stumble, but all the same he gained on me.

We came to a place where four roads ran into each other. Unhesitatingly the dog turned sharp left, and I ran after him. I was convinced now that he was Harry's dog and my old friend. The road was short, sloped sharply, and led straight to the water front. On either side of the harbour stretched two long wooden piers like arms. Straight ahead was the great basin filled with shipping of all kinds. Floating a few hundred yards out I saw a naval ship flying the white ensign, with the Union Jack at the jackstaff.

The dog had disappeared. I came to a stop. I was so near to safety and yet not safe. Charles Louis rounded the corner and stood looking for me.

I moved closer to the harbour, searching the crowd for an English sailor. I was not going to be caught without making a fight of it. Charles Louis had seen me and was pushing through the crowd towards me.

Then I heard an excited barking from below me. I had come to the point where a flight of steps led down to the water. The dog was jumping up and down barking wildly at a rowing boat approaching fast. Six sailors, three aside, were rowing, the white ensign fluttered, and seated in the boat, facing me, was Dick Monk.

I called to him and waved. He saw me at once and made ready to leap from the boat as it drew near the steps.

The steps, wet and slippery slowed me down. I had to keep my eyes on my feet. I heard the dog bark and Dick calling. I looked behind me.

At the head of the stairs was Charles Louis. He had his pistol in his hand. 'Wait, Errol,' he called, moving down the steps towards me.

Dick Monk too had a gun; he raised it. He says he never shot to kill, only to lame, but that at the last minute the dog leapt up and spoiled his aim.

I shall never know the rights of it. I remember Dick's shout, the dog leaping forward, and then the shot. I remember seeing Charles Louis jump and spin as the shot entered his body, then fall forward, rolling down the steps till he came to rest at my feet.

I went on my knees in the wet and the mud to raise his head. He stared at me and his lips moved. Dick Monk came forward and together we lifted him so that he rested against me. I was half-conscious of a crowd gathering about us, but their noise seemed far away. 'Charles Louis?' I said.

Once again he tried to speak.

'What does he say?' asked Dick.

I leaned forward, and Charles Louis said, in a soft whisper: 'Don't let the awkward squad fire over *my* grave.' Then his eyes closed and his features relaxed. I knew he was dead.

'What did he say?' said Dick.

I repeated it: 'Don't let the awkward squad fire over my grave.'

Dick took my half-brother's body from me and laid it gently on the stones. 'He cannot have realised he was dying,' he said. 'God forgive me, I didn't mean to kill him.'

'Oh yes, he knew,' I said. 'They were the last words of someone he admired very much. He used them on purpose to say something to me. Oh yes, he knew. I think he always expected to die in such a way.'

All my fear and anger had melted away. As I looked at

342

Charles Louis' face it was so much like the portrait of my mother as a young girl that I wondered I could ever have failed to see the likeness. Then this, too, faded away and he was someone else again, someone I had never seen, but who had moved in strange worlds and seen strange things and had terrible ambitions.

I stood up and walked away. The cool air blew on my face, drying the tears. I could smell the tarry, murky, salty air from the harbour waters, and mingled with it the smell of smoke and wine from this wild, brilliant city. I thought I could never bear to come to Ostend again, nor smell that smell.

It was not the end of the day for me. The Belgian police did not like a British naval officer shooting a strange Austrian in Ostend, even if the man did prove to have a gun in his own hand. The British Consul arrived and many explanations had to be entered into before either of us could leave. And even then, Dick Monk said he stood in danger of an imminent court martial for having brought his sloop into Ostend at all. But he laughed as he said it.

'How did you come to know where I was?'

'A mad policeman called Anticknap was watching the house. He told Harry, who got word to me and Tom Fletcher. Anticknap had heard the word "Ostend" mentioned. Ostend is one of the ports my sloop puts into on the Dover patrol. I was not so far off course, after all.'

'I am thankful enough,' I said soberly. 'And for the dog too.'

'I had Harry with me and what must he do, but go ashore with the dog, and then the dog slipped the hook and was off. I thought I had lost the lot of you. Where is Harry now?'

'With Tom Fletcher. The Sisters of Mercy have dressed his wound. He can travel.'

343

'Yes, there is the man that saved you.' Dick did not look at me then, but stared out of the window hard. 'It's lucky the Sisters were at hand. Never had much use for them before, but 'jove they served their purpose then. Real Trojans going into that house to succour him.' He added, still in the same voice, 'So it's Tom, eh? Well, I wish you well.'

We travelled back together in his sloop to Dover. Tom, Harry and his dog, and me. Tom was white with loss of blood, his head a turban of bandages. Harry talked nineteen to the dozen with excitement, explaining how he had walked the streets of Ostend looking for me, how he had lost the dog too, and what a rare state he had been in. I was silent, glad to let Harry talk. I let my hand rest on Tom Fletcher's. I was at peace.

Dick Monk tactfully stayed with his sailors and the Navy gave us an easy journey and made us welcome. But it was a strange home-coming, and a weary, travel-stained little group that finally found its way home to Masham Square.

To my surprise my baggage, together with my box of mystery, was rescued from the house in Ostend and delivered to me in Masham Square. My first impulse was to take the box and drop it in the Thames. But the powers that be, Mr Dalrymple and Tom Fletcher, would not allow it. So I decided to be womanly, yield to them and open it in the presence of my aunt, Tom and the lawyer.

We went together to the lawyer's office, taking the box to open. My approaching marriage, subject to so much scandalised comment, made a visit, in any case, necessary. Mrs Bedower had said: 'But what will Lady Geraldine say?' Lady Geraldine had said nervously: 'I wonder what the Queen will say?' The Queen had said she should be very glad to meet Mr Fletcher; she understood he was a

344

most worthy person. From the eminence of the throne how great was the difference between Thomas Fletcher and Errol Vesey?

I looked at the combination lock, and put out my hand. On my breast was pinned my brooch, left me by my mother. *Amor Vincit Omnia*, it proclaimed. Love had, indeed, conquered all things for her. At Charde she had left a paper key with Mrs Teviot. The key was decorated with the same legend, the initial letters of each word being writ large. Take the lock to the key, she advised. The key was Love. I spelt 'LOVE' carefully in my lock, and the lid yielded.

I raised the lid. Underneath was a pile of letters in pale, faded ink. Gently I removed them and put them aside. Beneath the letters was a handkerchief, neatly folded as if it was a treasure. Some sentimental association must be remembered here. And the same with a long silk scarf that came next. Then I found a wreath of faded flowers, a faint ghost of the pretty adornment my mother had once worn on her head. Beneath the wreath was a bed of tissue paper.

'She left me the things she loved,' I said. 'But their only value is a romantic one.'

'Look again in your box,' said Mr Dalrymple gravely. He was leaning forward, staring into its depths.

I followed his gaze and saw the gleam of pearls, and a bright wink of green, and a note of dull red. Carefully I extracted a long, triple row of pearls, an emerald brooch came next, then a parure of dark rubies, and a glittering diamond bracelet.

'These are valuable enough for anyone,' said Mr Dalrymple.

'Priceless,' said my aunt. 'What a sum they would fetch. A fortune.'

'Wait.' Tom was feeling beneath the tissue paper. 'Here

is something more.' He drew out an object and gave it to me.

I held in my hands a circlet of gold. It was plainly made, but of a rich, yellow gold such as one rarely sees. At intervals it was studded with diamonds cut in the old way, so that they gleamed pale like water.

'My God,' Lady Geraldine took it from me. 'I recognise it from a picture. It is the old crown of Bohemia. How *could* he give it to her? What power it would give, placed in the right hands.'

Antique, yet robust, my treasure lay on the table before us. I understood now what Charles Louis had desired to possess.

'The Bohemian treasures are never shown,' said Lady Geraldine; she picked up the crown and was studying it closely. 'But this must have been missed. No doubt whatever, the Imperial family knew who had taken it, or guessed, but could never lay their hands on it. Well, my dear, what a thing to have. I hardly know whether to congratulate you, or not.'

'It must be returned,' I said. 'I am sure my mother never meant me to keep it. At all events, I shall not.' I turned to Tom Fletcher. 'Tom, I come to you with a dowry, but without a crown.' For answer he took my hand and smiled.

My aunt still held the diadem in her hands and turned it, so that the diamonds caught the light. 'How mad he was to give it to her, how mad they both were. He always swore he would make her a princess, and, you see, he tried.' She laid it down reverently. 'Poor thing, poor thing.'

I will be happy with Tom Fletcher. He is one of the new men who will rise fast in the world. What the Bedowers have started, Tom and I will carry on. A new

346

aristocracy has to come from somewhere and it is fitting that a girl from one of the oldest English families (and the Veseys are that) should be part of it. This is the way society changes. Harry will be our charge, but already the Navy absorbs him. He, too, is on the way up. Detective Anticknap is restored to health and has been assisted by the Bedower connection to emigrate to Canada and make a new life there. He is better away from London, where there is too much to remind him of his days of madness. But I can never forget that he did me a great service at the last. I should have known that it was Charles Louis he watched for in Masham Square.

One last strand must be woven into my story. Dick Monk is to marry Sophie. Her child, my little god-daughter Theodora, survived and will live with them. Sophie has great wealth, and now she is in health is a pretty, lively girl. A future had to be made for her. The Queen and Lady Geraldine exerted themselves. Dick was amenable. He will found a family and have an illustrious career. With such a wife anything is possible. Let but a great war come at the right time and I will see him a duke yet. We shall both be happy. I was not the wife for him, our paths must lie apart. But I shall not forget. And I know that one day we shall look at each other across a crowded ballroom and think of what once was between us, what might have been, and what never could be.